THE TIME CAPSULE MURDERS

A Cambridge Mystery

ALEX CROCKFORD

ISBN (Paperback): 978-1-0684018-0-0

ISBN (eBook): 978-1-0684018-1-7

PROLOGUE

It was a cold, wet, blustery morning in Cambridge, and Albert Ross, the Deputy Head Porter at St Crispian's College, Cambridge, was worried.

Such days were common in this particular part of East Anglia throughout the long winter months, which stretched out languidly from early October to the end of the misleadingly labelled Spring Term (or Lent, for the initiated) in mid-March. This particular morning fell on an especially drizzly day in the middle of February. Sheets of sleet were blowing in relentlessly from the Urals thousands of miles to the East, and were now descending on the city and pummelling anyone foolhardy enough to venture outdoors.

The chilling damp was seeping its way into the very marrow of Old Albert's bones, but it was not the cold that was troubling him today. He was hardened to such things, having, in his former life, been stationed in West Berlin for three years in the mid-sixties. He had been as cold as Dr Zhivago's knackers for most of it, but that hyperborean climate had done him no long-term harm. Then, as now, his trusty long johns had seen him through.

Hardened or not, the scrawny Porter took a few moments to breathe some warmth into his shaking fingers before unlocking his bike as he prepared for his daily cycle down Castle Hill to the college's main campus. He was wearing a pair of fingerless gloves, which were doing absolutely nothing to dispel his garden-gnome-in-a-suit image.

The ride would do him good, he decided, as he stiffly saddled up. Even as a younger man, Albert had had a regrettable tendency towards shuffling, and now he was in his dotage even his "old man smell" seemed to move faster than he did when he was on foot. But when he had a pair of wheels underneath him, it was a different story altogether. It did not take the octogenarian speed demon long to build up a fair head of steam as he prepared for the descent. The hard, awkwardly shaped saddle was playing havoc with his haemorrhoids, as usual, but for all that, there was a broad grin on the old man's face as he felt the ground beneath him start to slope downwards.

His gap-toothed Cheshire Cat expression faded, however, as an unusually prescient thought struck him. This daily routine, which had kept him on the straight and narrow for the better part of the last half-century, was likely to be coming to an end, and soon. Eighty-three years of age, and looking older, Albert had never even contemplated retirement until a few days ago. Until he had let his guard down.

Last night, he had let the Master know of his intentions. One of the hardest things he had ever had to do. That had been a low point, he reflected. Now, in the cold, dull light of a rainy morning, the prospect of stepping aside was one he was able to greet sadly but stoically. What was that old saying he had picked up in Germany? Ah yes, that was it. *Alles hat ein Ende, nur die Wurst hat zwei.* Everything has an end, only the sausage has two. It was just a shame he had blotted his copybook at the eleventh hour.

The rational part of the old man's brain kept telling him that no harm could possibly come of it. Harmless japes, that was all it was. But rules were rules. College rules, doubly so. Albert was no saint, but he carried a saint's guilty conscience. He'd strayed from the path before, and he'd sworn he'd never do it again, but recently Albert had let his fondness for one of his favourite St Crispian's alumni get the better of him once more, and he had been coaxed into spilling college secrets. He was losing his touch. However trifling the spillage may have been, the college deserved better than that.

Albert was not possessed of a powerful memory for names or faces. Nevertheless, there had been something about the alumni from that particular intake that had rendered them unusually memorable, despite the fact that there had been almost twenty sets of new faces to displace them since. When was it that they had been up? Must have been some time in the early noughties. They had to be pushing forty by now. Old enough to know better. Very strange that so many of them had been popping up again recently.

It was a conundrum that Albert was never able to get to the bottom of, for his moderately distinguished career as one of Cambridge's longest-serving Porters was about to come to a more abrupt end than the old boy could possibly have anticipated. In the end, Albert went out not with a bang, but with a twang.

The noise barely registered with the old man. He was becoming increasingly deaf, and he was used to his bicycle making strange clanking noises every time he changed gears. It was a rusty old contraption, as befitted its rusty old owner. Only when he was halfway down the hill, and his rheumatic, knobbly fingers closed themselves around the brake lever, did he realise that something was amiss.

He continued to accelerate, squeezing the lever again and again with increasing desperation, to no avail, as he approached the junction with Chesterton Lane, just past the Museum of Cambridge. The Highway Code was Albert's Bible. This was the first time in his life that he had run a red light. It turned out that once was enough. He ran into an emerging delivery van with a sickening splat, and was killed instantly.

And that is the gruesome note on which our tale begins.

CHAPTER 1

*In which your humble narrator enters the narrative, makes his
way to Cambridge, and various old acquaintances make their
appearances, including a criminologist, a scruffy ex-war criminal,
a Baron, a couple of (live) Porters and various old friends, one of
whom doesn't stick around for long.*

I

My name is Roger Whiteley, and I'm going to tell you about a couple of murders I got embroiled in recently.

I will admit to having indulged in a spot of creative license when it comes to my description of the first of the aforementioned murders. I am no omniscient narrator (the very opposite, in fact—if there is such a thing as a nomniscient narrator, I would certainly qualify). In truth, I was not present when poor Albert Ross met his maker, and even if I had been, I have absolutely no way of knowing what was going through his brain just before it was pulped by a passing Aldi van.

But from here on in, everything I am about to recount of the remarkable events of early 2023, which have become known in the more salacious tabloids as The Time Capsule Murders, is an eye-witness account.

More intimate details of the weird and wonderful world of Roger Whiteley, Esquire (my backstory, vital statistics and so forth), will emerge, seamlessly and organically, as we steam through the narrative. For now, I will limit myself to a couple of the more salient biographical details.

Firstly, that I was thirty-nine years of age at the time these events unfolded. My comparative youth may come as a surprise given that my name is Roger and I am prone to using words like "embroiled," but if you haven't yet realised that it's possible to be both a millennial and deeply, deeply weird, then I hope that the rock you are currently living under has an adequate array of home comforts.

Secondly, that I am an alumnus of St Crispian's College, Cambridge, at which I spent what turned out to be the best three years of my life. I would normally add the words "so far" to the end of that statement, but I would like to put a bit more distance between me and those murders I mentioned before venturing such a ludicrously optimistic caveat.

I suppose I should also mention that I am a solicitor. But before you give up and hurl your book or other reading device of your choice against the wall in disgust, let me reassure you that we can remain blissfully free of that aspect of my existence for the remainder of the narrative, given that I was on a sabbatical when the events of this tale occurred.

The timing was impeccable, for the very first week of my little break coincided delightfully with a long-expected appointment at my alma mater. An appointment that had been almost twenty years in the planning but which I had, naturally, completely forgotten about until a couple of weeks earlier. My memory had only been jolted when Ed Dickinson (an old friend of mine with a very amiable manner, to whom you might not want to get too attached) texted me out of the blue to check I was still on board.

So without further ado, let's get stuck into the thick of the action by heading over to Kings Cross station, early one Friday afternoon. Good Friday, in fact. Had you been there at the time, you would have found me loitering in the middle of the main atrium, brandishing a large, misshapen travel bag. I was intent on taking advantage of my temporary status as a gentleman of leisure by getting back up to my old stomping ground early and fitting a couple of cheeky pints in before the festivities really got started.

As a South London man, with a small flat at the less salubrious end of Herne Hill, I had very rarely had occasion to go to Kings Cross for well over a decade. The new(ish) layout of the station was taking a bit of getting used to. In particular, the existence of a Platform 0. I can only assume that when they put this one in, they couldn't simply have rechristened it Platform 1 and bumped the other platforms up one, on the basis that it would have resulted in all the Hogwarts students getting confused and ramming their trollies into an extremely solid, non-magical brick wall, thereby causing unspeakable damage to their poor unfortunate owls.

I am also getting increasingly shortsighted in my middle age, and I was having to squint up at the departure boards to work out which platform I needed to be heading for. I found myself wandering backwards in an effort to perfect my squint, and that was when I found myself colliding with a stray tuba—and my destiny!

II

Naturally, I immediately lost balance on making contact with the aforementioned instrument and collapsed in an ungainly heap (has anyone ever collapsed in any other kind of heap?). Before I had a chance to rise to my feet and salvage whatever remnants of my dignity remained, the situation deteriorated further, as I found myself on the receiving end of an aggressively pointy finger. The finger was accompanied by a posh, plummy Scottish accent, which seemed vaguely familiar.

"You, sir! If you have damaged my tuba, I warn you I shall have no choice but to litigate!" said the little balding fellow who seemed to be attached to the finger.

This was a bit much, I felt. After all, the tuba, unlike its unwitting and bruised assailant, was thoroughly protected by its very sturdy case, which had not even had the decency to give the impression of a fair fight by falling over onto its side! No, the great big oblong bastard was just sitting there, wobbling smugly at me.

"Oh, do your worst! I happen to be a lawyer!" I snapped back peevishly. Non-legally trained folk often labour under a couple of misapprehensions about lawyers. Firstly that we know what we're talking about most of the time, and secondly, that we are possessed of a magical ability to mould the letter of the law to our advantage (and the disadvantage of those who dare to cross us) in any given situation. Wordy wizards, if you will. As such, I was expecting a hasty retreat from my adversary in light of my ominous declaration. What I was not expecting was a jovial chuckle.

"A bold assertion, young Roger Whiteley, to make to a man who once had the dubious pleasure of marking three of your essays! I believe, incidentally, that I am still owed a fourth, and after seventeen years, I am expecting a veritable humdinger!"

The penny dropped.

"Mr Sinclair?" I stammered. My tremulous words had barely escaped from the relative security of my lips before they were aggressively seized upon.

"Mr Sinclair, is it now? Not content with subjecting my tuba to unspeakable acts of violence, you now see fit to strip me of my professorship! Are there any further insults you would care to pile upon these injuries? Perhaps you would like to take the opportunity to cast aspersions on the attractiveness of my wife while you're at it?"

My mouth opened and shut like a blowfish, but no sound emerged. It was only then that I clocked the twinkle in the old fellow's eye and dared to venture a grin.

What can one say about Professor Gerald Ulysses Sinclair—criminologist, dabbling amateur detective, Sudoku fiend, obscure vexillologist and general clever clogs—that has not already been said? Well, probably quite a lot, if I'm honest.

I call him an "old fellow," but in fact, that's only half right. Gerald Sinclair is indeed a Fellow at my old college, St Crispian's, where he has taught Criminology, Criminal Justice and variants thereof for a couple of decades now. "St Crisps," as those of us in the know colloquially refer to it, is one of the smaller and lesser-known colleges sandwiched tightly between Kings and Trinity, like little farts squeezed between a pair of gargantuan buttocks. I won't regale you with a rundown of our alumni, as it is not a particularly impressive list. The rumour going around college when I was an undergraduate—that Timmy Mallett had once graced our hallowed halls with his illustrious presence (studying Classics, naturally)—had sadly proven to be a hoax.

As to the "old" part, however, it struck me as I looked at him that I must now be older than he had been when he had taught me more or less everything I had since forgotten about "Sentencing and the Penal System" back in dim and distant 2004. As he was already balding at that point, we youngsters had assumed that he was about fifty. Then, however, we stumbled upon his Wikipedia entry, which I am told has since disappeared and reappeared several times on the grounds that the "powers that be" at Wikipedia can't quite make up their minds as to whether he is important enough to justify an entry. At that point, the entry had run to a pithy three lines but had crucially revealed that our scholarly, myopic, almost aggressively middle-aged supervisor was, in fact, exactly five years younger than Keanu Reeves.

Twenty years of having to mark half-arsed undergraduate essays and supping second-rate port at formal halls, whilst making tedious chit-chat with wealthy donors, clearly ages a person a great deal more than clinging to the bottom of a speeding bus, firing a gun in the air and shouting "aaargh!", or taking multicoloured suppositories from strange men who wear sunglasses indoors. Sinclair was wearing every one of his fifty-whatever-it-is years and looked as though he had borrowed a few from someone else while he was at it. His round glasses were noticeably thicker than the ones he had worn in his thirties. And poor posture, or perhaps my faulty memory, seemed to have caused the professor to shrink slightly over the intervening years.

I vaguely recollected that Sinclair had been an enthusiastic dabbler in the dark art of amateur dramatics, always hearkening back to his years in the Tunbridge Wells Amateur Theatrical Society. Looking at him now, it struck me that if he had not yet bagged the role of Moley in a production of *The Wind in the Willows*, it was surely only a matter of time.

"Where are you headed?" Sinclair asked.

"As it happens, I'm off to Cambridge!" I declared breezily before my brain caught up with my big mouth and I realised that, as Sinclair would inevitably be heading in the same direction, I had almost certainly condemned myself to an hour of awkward chit-chat. Sure enough, he was beaming with delight.

"Excellent, so am I! Platform 9, I believe," he announced, scuttling off briskly in that direction without so much as pausing the conversation, wielding his tuba before him in a show of strength that belied his frail appearance. "What brings you back to your old haunts, then?"

"A bit of a reunion," I replied. Sinclair grimaced.

"You'd better let me know which pubs to avoid, then, my boy!"

I smiled. Once a student, always a student, at least in Sinclair's mind.

Truth be told, though, I suspected that he was not far

wrong and that the old gang, myself included, would find ourselves regressing back to our youthful ways pretty quickly once we were back in our old surroundings. At least, I hoped so. I needed a break from feeling middle-aged. I had even had a crack at Dry January earlier in the year, may God have mercy on my shrivelled puritanical soul. It had been a somewhat half-hearted attempt, with the first signs of moisture being detected on the 3rd of the month.

We boarded the train. It was well before rush hour, so we had the pick of the seats. Professor Sinclair treated his tuba to a window seat and plopped himself next to it. He was clearly expecting me to take the spot across the aisle and, as such, had left me with no socially acceptable choice but to do so. I found myself fervently hoping that the professor had brought a book to read. He had never struck me as a particularly sociable chap.

Clearly, however, he had grown more gregarious with age. He did have a book with him. His sort always does. It was a large and grisly-looking volume entitled *Sausages, Sex and Shootings: The True Story of the Butcher of Babraham*, which he perched on the little table in front of his seat. However, it quickly became clear that he had absolutely no intention of reading it and that he was just leaving it there as an insurance policy, in case it transpired that I had turned into a complete weirdo.

"So, Young Master Whiteley," he said as the train moved off, "what's the news with you? A dirt lawyer now, aren't you?"

"I practice in the field of real estate, yes!" I replied a little pompously.

"Yes, I saw your five inches in the *Estates Gazette* last year! Reserved rights of entry in leasehold property, no less! Riveting stuff—I couldn't put it down!" It would have been six inches, as it happens, if the killjoy editors had not cut out all the innuendos I had tried to surreptitiously slip in. But we dropped that topic as abruptly as we had picked it up, as Sinclair shifted the focus of his interrogation elsewhere.

"Married yet?" he demanded briskly.

"No," I admitted, reflecting glumly that this was unlikely to be the last time this topic arose over the course of the weekend. The vast majority of my friends were now married with kids, and now I was more than halfway through my allotted three-score years and ten, I was starting to feel as though that particular boat, although not yet missed, was definitely thinking about weighing anchor.

Probably the greatest Whiteley of all time, the former Countdown presenter Richard Whiteley (sadly no relation) had been known during his own time at Cambridge as "Twice Nightly Whiteley." In his later years, he had admitted that "Once Yearly, Nearly" was actually closer to the truth. But unfortunately, I lack my illustrious namesake's rugged charisma and raw sexual magnetism. My love life at Cambridge had been a very short catalogue of disasters. Things had not markedly improved since.

"Ah, well, you're still a boy!" Sinclair beamed at me reassuringly. "I was well past forty when I tied the knot, and now I've got a nine-year-old running me ragged!" His rolling of his "r"s was extremely, and I thought probably deliberately, Gandalfesque.

"And what does your wife do?" I asked, happy to move the conversation on to focus on his domestic bliss rather than my marked lack of it. The professor laughed.

"My dear Whiteley, you HAVE done a good job of dodging the grasping talons of our alumni relations department! My wife is someone with whom you are already very well acquainted! She has, in fact, mentioned your name in glowing terms on no fewer than three occasions during our eleven-and-a-bit-years of marital bliss!"

"Oh really?" I asked, my curiosity now genuinely aroused. "Who is she?"

"None other than Emily Morwyn, the Master of your old college! Which, I suppose, makes me a mistress!" he added dryly.

Well, talking of aroused...

I had been aware that The Reverend Dr Morwyn had recently assumed the mantle of Master of St Crispian's College, but back in my day, she had just been the Dean. And we had all fancied the pants off her. Fancying one's College Dean is not something most university students are prepared to admit to. But Emily Morwyn had been no ordinary Dean. A few years younger and a good couple of inches taller than the man who I was still struggling to believe was her husband, she loitered in my memory as a dynamic, stimulating and witty woman with a shock of lustrous but unruly black hair. Even thinking about her again was cheering me up. In choosing her, St Crispian's College had done well. Gerald Sinclair, even more so.

We returned briefly to the subject of my career, but that turgid topic did not even keep us going until Finsbury Park. I think it was a relief to both of us when we moved on to discussing his life's work and what was new in the world of criminology. I had forgotten how scintillating a speaker Sinclair could be when he got going, and the journey flew by with a bare minimum of awkward British pauses. Our discussion was peppered with anecdotes about the various criminals Sinclair had encountered in his time along our route, from the Stevenage strangler to the Letchworth lecher and the Royston arsonist. He seemed to have a particular penchant for alliterative criminals, albeit that last one was a bit of a stretch—there's never a good honest robber around when you need one.

"So what's keeping you occupied at the moment?" I eventually managed to ask, when we were already approaching the outskirts of Cambridge itself. A slightly cagey expression crept over Sinclair's face for the first time in our conversation, and when he spoke again, it was in a much quieter voice than he had been using previously.

"Well, truth be told, it's been a tricky few weeks for the college. I've been trying to support Emily in any way I can. Do you remember Albert Ross, the Porter?"

"I do," I replied, recalling a kindly, if absent-minded, old soul who had been greatly loved but who had seemed pretty doddery even in the early noughties.

"He was killed about six weeks ago," Sinclair said grimly.

"Killed?" I spluttered stupidly. "You mean…"

"Hit by a delivery van, knocked off his bicycle. All very unpleasant. The van was going too fast, but in fairness to the driver, Albert had apparently run a red light."

"Well, I'm sorry to hear that! What rotten luck. Although I must admit, when you said he'd been killed, in light of what we've just been talking about, I thought for a moment that you meant that there had been foul play involved." I chuckled a little nervously. Sinclair did not smile, falling disturbingly silent.

"Albert was one of life's Cautious Cuthberts," he said at last. "He did not run red lights."

"Well maybe his brakes failed?"

"That was the police's view," Sinclair replied sceptically. "There wasn't enough of either owner or bicycle left for them to reach a firm conclusion. But there was no reason for them to suspect anything more sinister. But as for me, well, a tiny seed of doubt has burrowed its way into my old cerebellum, and it's still an open question as to whether anything will sprout from it. He had been behaving very oddly, you see. The night before he died, he had telephoned my wife and offered his resignation!"

"You're joking!" I exclaimed. "He always told us he'd never retire, and that they'd have to carry him out in a box!"

"Well, he was right, as it turned out, but it wasn't for want of trying on his part. Emily tells me he sounded dreadful. He was so distressed he could barely get his words out. Said he had done something that meant he was no longer fit for his post. Naturally, she told him she wouldn't hear of it and tried to get to the root cause of what was troubling him. But he told her he wanted to 'come clean' in person. Alas, he died before he had the chance to seek absolution."

"Poor bloke," I said ruefully, feeling genuinely gutted for the lovable old worrywart. "I guess we'll never know what was gnawing away at him."

"That," Sinclair murmured, "remains to be seen. I have a feeling that we're tickling the tip of a rather ominous iceberg."

I shifted uneasily in my seat.

"You graduated in 2006, didn't you?" he asked, apparently apropos of nothing.

"That's right."

"Hmmmm. I would hate to put a dampener on your debauchery, Whiteley, but my advice to you is to keep your wits about you this weekend. Not all is well in our hallowed bosom!"

III

Before I had the chance to get distracted by the thought of bosoms of the hallowed or indeed the unhallowed variety, the train pulled into Cambridge station.

"How are you getting into town?" Sinclair asked as we strolled along the platform. "There'll be more Panther taxis than you can shake a stick at when we get to the exit, even at this time of day."

"Those guys were already operating in my time," I declared, sounding more like Rod Taylor in *The Time Machine* than I had intended to.

"Oh yes, but they've got a small army of cabbies these days. The Panther Brothers must be two of the most powerful businessmen in the whole of South Cambridgeshire now! I know them slightly. I have a rather tense relationship with the younger one, but the older boy, Hamish, is a likable enough cove, so if he is as intent on world domination as the growth rate of his business suggests, we could do a whole lot worse, I'd say!"

Fortunately, my old chum Britta had agreed to meet me at the station, and sure enough, there she was at the barriers, waving vigorously at me. I grinned, returned the wave, and, with all the glib recklessness of the second victim in a John Carpenter film, shrugged off all thoughts of Sinclair's portentous gloom. Now, the real fun was about to begin.

Britta had studied English and was one of the few members of our crowd who had settled locally. Her husband's career had been successful enough to justify the purchase of a second home in one of the surrounding villages, and Britta now spent most of her time up here helping to run one of the local theatres. Never having delved into Sinclair's murky world of murder and mayhem, she and the professor knew each other by sight but not to speak to. He nodded to her politely before gesturing vaguely in the direction of a new hotel, which seemed to have sprung up while I was away.

"I have an appointment at the Clayton," he declared grandly as we belatedly took the opportunity to exchange business cards before he started tottering off with his tuba.

"Perhaps we'll bump into each other over the course of the weekend," he called back over his shoulder, "but if not, don't do anything I wouldn't do!"

I grinned at him but pointedly avoided making any such rash pledge. For all I knew, the old boy might have turned into some sort of radical vegan mineral water drinker. Sinclair's tone was now jocular, and the twinkle had returned to his eyes. It was as if the prophetic doom-mongering of a couple of minutes ago had been delivered by someone else entirely.

He must have been having me on, I concluded. The insinuation that I was possessed of sufficient wits in the first place that "keeping them about me" would make a discernible difference was ample demonstration that he could not possibly have been serious. Besides, how could Albert's death, suspicious or otherwise, possibly have an impact on a bunch of people who had almost two decades' distance from their university days?

Britta gave me a warm hug, and then we wandered into the car park in search of her Mini Cooper, a typically idiosyncratic choice of vehicle. Short and sturdy, but a force of nature, Britta had always been a surprisingly fast walker for one her size. She bustled through the car park so quickly that despite being a full ten inches taller than her and presumably having at least six inches of extra leg, I struggled to keep up.

Born to a Danish mother and an English father (a diplomat), Britta had been bounced around all over the place as a girl, attending various international schools in Europe and the US. Her parents had later divorced fairly ignominiously. She once told me that Cambridge was the first place where she had ever felt truly settled.

Our crowd was a close-knit one, although there had initially been a bit of a divide into sub-groups between the "lads," who tended to spend most of our spare time mooching around in pubs, and the "girls," whose tastes were a bit more wide-ranging. This unspoken divide had inevitably diminished over time, as we gradually grew to regard such a division as just a little bit arbitrary and childish. Britta, however, gloriously profane and impressively uninhibited, had always behaved like one of the boys anyway. As I had remarked in Fresher's Week, using a line that at the time I had doubtless thought would cause Oscar Wilde and George Bernard Shaw to rest just a little more uneasily in their graves, "Britta has no filter." Boom, and indeed, tish.

"How long has it been?" she asked me as I squeezed myself into her car, having first cleared my seat of several heartily chewed pet toys.

"Um..." I paused for thought. Compared to others in my social circle, I had done a reasonable job of keeping up with Britta, who had maintained a relatively constant social media presence. She may have even been on Twitter, although that was one forum I myself had given up on long ago. If you have a family history of high blood pressure, twittering and lawyering is just about the worst combo imaginable.

"Well, let's narrow it down," she suggested helpfully, turning on the ignition. "Was Aaron taller than me?"

"Just about." Aaron, Britta's son, had made an appearance a little earlier than either of his parents had planned, just after we left university, and as such was now on the cusp of leaving school and venturing into that arena himself. "Let me guess, he's taller than me now?"

"Not quite," Britta said and laughed shortly. "He didn't inherit his father's height genes. He still towers over his tiny old mum, though! But that's quite enough about the younger generation. This weekend's supposed to be about us! Let's burn rubber—there's drinking to be done!"

She was pulling away before I had even started scrambling around for the seatbelt. Moments later, she narrowly avoided causing the second recorded velocipedal death in this story as a cyclist whizzed through the nerve-rackingly narrow gap between her car and the pavement.

"Shitting cyclists", she hissed terrifyingly as I clutched tightly to the edge of my seat. The one positive thing about hitching a ride with Britta was that at least the ride was likely to be safer for me, on the inside of her car, than for the poor sods on the outside.

Fortunately, on this occasion, the journey was entirely casualty-free. It was only a matter of minutes before she found a parking spot in one of the little residential roads leading off Huntingdon Road, beyond Castle Hill, which was where St Crispian's College's new accommodation had been built. Yes, we really were turning the nostalgia dial up to eleven, for our good friend Ed Dickinson, the self-designated organiser of this proud reunion, had booked us into college accommodation. Albeit it was not accommodation we had ever stayed in before.

Back in my day (if you'll forgive such an expression from someone who isn't eighty years old and a lifelong tobacco chewer), they hadn't even had enough rooms for all the undergraduates, and we'd had to go private in our third year. Now they were even able to cater for the postgrads, and, during the holidays, paying guests like ourselves as well, via their newly built site up the hill.

This even had its own Porter's Lodge, with the Porters dividing their time between this one and its larger sibling down towards the town centre. It was a cheaper option than most of the hotels in town, albeit from my previous experience of college accommodation, I was expecting something rather more spartan. In the event, the quality of the rooms (most of which, including mine, were even en suite) turned out to be a pleasant surprise. The quality of our welcome at the reception desk, decidedly less so.

"Hello, Gavin," I said as jovially as I was able to, as my old nemesis, Gavin the Porter, emerged from the back room of the brand spanking new Porter's Lodge to greet Britta and grunt at me, after the statutory three-second stare as he pretended he had no idea who I was. This was something that might have been forgivable after so many years, had he not insisted on going through the same rigmarole when he was seeing me practically every day in the 2003-2006 era. Mind you, his feigned ignorance wasn't entirely a one-way street—I had never discovered Gavin's surname and had never been entirely convinced that he'd had one.

Britta, in contrast, had always had an enviable ability to sweet talk every one of St Crispian's motley crew of Porters into an affectionate paternalism. She had even stayed in touch with some of them after graduating. A couple of them were actually on Facebook, which to me was tantamount to discovering that Mr Bumble from *Oliver Twist* has an Instagram account and is regularly taking cheeky selfies with his favourite workhouse boys.

Now in his mid to late fifties, Gavin was a short, stocky man with a perennially sour expression on his agate-hard face. His slicked-back hair was now thinner and greying, but I noted that he was still applying more grease to what remained of it than you would find on the floor of Cambridge's finest late-night chip vans. For all I know, that might have been where he was sourcing it from—certainly the smell was suggestive. Otherwise, he appeared to me to be virtually unchanged.

The Porter gave Britta a hug and a very continental four kisses on the cheek. This was something he had probably picked up from the "incredibly hot French wife" he had taken such pride in showing us inappropriate photos of when we were undergraduates. Or at least some of us. I had never got a look in and had had no particular desire to. I think it was safe to assume that this marriage had not been a love match, and I suspected that he had probably traded her in for a younger model by now. How chaps like him get away with it, I will never understand. If Gavin was a silver fox, he was one of the scruffy, mangy, bin-raiding variety, rather than the George Clooney breed.

"That bearded prick's been in already," Gavin muttered. "Had the audacity to ask me to pass on a message! He's down the Baron!"

I raised an eyebrow. Neither of us had any difficulty unravelling the mystery of which bearded prick he was referring to. In Gavin the Porter's universe, Dan Finn was "the" bearded prick. But as far as I was aware, none of the rest of us had set eyes on him for almost fifteen years.

Dan (Finn, a wastrel) and The Baron (of Beef, a pub) had, between them, played a worryingly prominent role in my undergraduate experience. It was not until long after I had left Cambridge that I discovered that, far from being a member of the nobility with a rather peculiar fiefdom, The Baron of Beef was, in fact, a technical term for a joint of beef comprising the two sirloins joined at the backbone.

In case that cut of deliciously pointless trivia is not enough for you, I had also discovered that that terrific goggle-eyed boozehound Tom Baker had rented the room above that very same establishment when filming the Douglas Adams-penned *Doctor Who* story "Shada" back in the 1970s. Tom's subsequent departure to other galaxies must have left a gaping hole in the landlord's bank balance, but Dan and I had done our best to belatedly make up the shortfall.

Britta and I wasted no time in dumping our weekend bags and heading down there to join him. Dan, never a man to hang about dry-lipped when there was drinking to be done, had clearly already been there for a while when we arrived, having "staked" out our old regular table (pardon the pun, but I'm afraid I can't help myself—Shakespeare has his knob gags, I have my puns). This was by the window, at the front, which had given us the perfect vantage point to watch the world go by and pass judgement on it.

Dan, who had studied History of Art as an undergraduate, had left with the rest of us in 2006. He had then wasted no time in making a small fortune by inventing an app of some kind just a couple of years later, the precise function of which still baffles me. Whatever the hell it does, it enabled him to effectively retire in his mid-twenties. I am unlikely to ever forgive the lucky bastard for this. Nevertheless, I was looking forward to further stoking the embers of my own insecurity by finding out what he had been getting up to since.

Dan had always had a certain effortlessly cool vibe about him. His interests ranged well beyond his chosen field of study, and he had a particular interest in economics, geopolitics and philosophy. He had regularly taken pleasure in lobbing a grenade into a conversation by throwing in an obscure reference to some Kant or other, then sitting back and gleefully watching the rest of us pretend we had the vaguest idea of what he was on about. Although there was no question in my mind that the philosopher whose teachings Dan had chosen to live his life by was not Nietzsche or Socrates but one Baloo the Bear. Disney's version, obviously— not the slightly grumpier, punchier Kipling original.

Two activities that had never featured heavily in Dan's Bare Necessities of Life were shaving and haircuts. Shoes had also been very much optional. He might, if pushed, have been prepared to dust off his second-best pair of sandals for a Formal Hall, but that was the extent of his tolerance for footwear. This look was one he had effortlessly carried off as an undergraduate. Now, however, the ravages of early middle age had set in, so as Britta and I trundled into The Baron, I was rather surprised to be greeted by a Goth Falstaff.

I had been in Cambridge less than an hour, but I had already seen enough of its inhabitants to know that this was not an uncommon sartorial choice in this neck of the woods these days. It was a little troubling to associate such a look with someone approximately my own age, though. We're not kids anymore, I thought. The world is taking its toll.

Ed Dickinson and Steve Taylor were already present and correct but were less than a third of the way through their respective pints. Dan, however, was already empty.

"All right, guys?" Dan beamed at us, making a movement that suggested that he was getting up to greet us, but without actually going to the trouble of doing so. "Rog, get them in?"

A familiar refrain. Dutifully, I navigated my way to the bar.

It may have already become apparent to the more eagle-eyed readers that I am a clumsy and ungainly fellow whose spatial awareness is not always all that it could be. The Baron of Beef, although colourfully characterful and boasting one of the longest bars in the city, is not one of Cambridge's larger pubs, and it was perhaps inevitable that I managed to jostle someone on my way over.

"Hey! Watch yourself, big feller!" snapped a familiar Glaswegian voice.

IV

I turned to find myself staring at Finlay "Mad Dog" McFadden, formerly Head Porter at St Crisps. Like most of our Porters, he was ex-army. I wasn't sure what Gavin's background had been, as people tended to struggle to steer any conversation with him away from the topic of his wife's boobs, but some sort of renegade gun-running to one of the nastier African warlords had probably featured.

Few of our bowler-hatted band of brothers had had as tough a time of it as Falklands vet McFadden, though. He had come from a long line of war heroes. I am told that it was McFadden Senior who, when Hitler's invasion of France in 1940 proved successful, is reported to have said that "if the English surrender as well, we could have a real fight on our hands!"

I had been saddened, if not particularly surprised, to learn that he had been hustled off into very early "retirement" a few years after I had left college. It had not officially been treated as a sacking, but it had come just weeks after he had assaulted a particularly obnoxious postgraduate, who we had nicknamed "The Worm." Mad Dog McFadden loved his college, his country and the children he barely ever got to see. He had tried hard to reintegrate himself into civilian society after his return from the horrors of war. But ultimately, he lacked the self-control to rein in the anger, depression, and self-loathing that had come to govern his life like the three heads of Cerberus. McFadden had had plenty of warnings. The Worm, despicable fellow though he was, had just been the wafer-thin mint that had caused the explosion. I remember hearing that he had found a job in security somewhere. God help anyone stupid enough to try and burgle it, wherever it was.

Now about sixty and bright red in the face, McFadden had clearly been drinking heavily for some hours. I greeted him as "Mr McFadden," and he squinted suspiciously at me for a few seconds without a glimmer of recognition. Well, it had been almost twenty years since he had clapped eyes on me, and even if he had remembered me, any historic affection he might have had for me was unlikely to make up for the fact that I had just spilled his pint. I took the only decent (safe) option open to me and offered to buy him another.

"Aye, I'll have a double vodka and cranberry juice, if ye're offerin'!" I was pretty sure he was daring me to snigger at this point. I managed to limit myself to a nervous squeak disguised as a sneeze. "And another pint for my pal here!"

He gestured over to a corner, where I was astonished to see Saddam Hussein nursing a pint of Guinness.

Before you start to worry that this tale is going off at a tangent you weren't expecting when you picked it out of the shelves, equivalent to Mussolini turning up at St Mary's Mead and taking tea with Miss Marple, I will admit that it was not actually the former Iraqi dictator sitting there, staring at me suspiciously with Guinness foam on his moustache. I was, of course, perfectly capable of telling the difference. Everyone knows that the real Saddam was more of a Murphy's man. I should also clarify that the incarnation of Saddam that this fellow bore the closest resemblance to was not the lusciously moustached psychopath in his prime, but the scruffy bearded fellow that they pulled out of the hole after it had all gone a bit Pete Tong for him.

None of us knew what "Saddam's" real name was, but his face was familiar to us. He had been a regular frequenter of The Baron and its neighbour, The Mitre, during our student days, usually sitting alone clutching a beer in one hand and the plastic bag containing his dinner in the other, or occasionally fraternising with some similarly dishevelled characters. Given the state he had been in back then, I was somewhat surprised to see that he was still alive, let alone virtually unchanged, and equally surprised to see that he was a chum of the Mad Dog. This was a tragic testament to just how far the illustrious former Head Porter had fallen since his unfortunate defenestration.

I brought the drinks for this unlikely pair of drinking comrades over to their table and was rewarded with a moderately appreciative grunt from McFadden and a scowl from Mr Hussein. Taking the hint with some degree of relief, I scampered back over to my friends with my tray of drinks.

"Was that Mad Dog McFadden and Saddam over there?" Ed Dickinson asked, somewhat incredulously. Ed was dressed in the trademark scruffy T-shirt, jeans and trainers combo that had served him well ever since he had been a teenager, and despite the fact that he had only arrived a few minutes before we did, he already looked like part of the furniture, laid back and confident. Short and balding, Ed was not a traditionally good-looking guy, but he had been one of the most effective and unscrupulous womanisers in college back in the day. I knew he and his wife had divorced a couple of years back, so I couldn't help wondering whether he had "plans" for the weekend. There were a couple of distinct possibilities on the guest list, although I hoped that they were now old enough to know better than to fall for his undoubted charms.

"It certainly was. And I had the pleasure of Gerald the Mole's company on the way up!"

"Amazing!" Dan, who had always been the unlikeliest of Sinclair fans, clapped his hands joyfully. "Do you remember that night we got him on our quiz team?"

I did indeed. Sinclair had seemed in equal parts bemused and delighted to have received the invitation. Needless to say, he had been worth his weight in gold in that context. The fact that he had even managed to come up with "Addicted to Bass" as the correct answer to the question "What single was No 2 in the UK Charts on 12 January 2002" was all the more remarkable, given that the way he had pronounced "bass" (like the fish) suggested that he had believed it to be an ode to the art of angling. He had furthermore saved us from acute embarrassment by knowing that the correct answer to the question "Which popular film from the 1970s contains the line 'What's that got to do with my knob?' was, of course, *Bedknobs and Broomsticks*. Dan had been way off-piste on that one.

"It's like going back in time, being here," I commented, looking around nostalgically. "Not much changes round here, by the look of it. Except that the students are getting younger," I added, nodding somewhat enviously in the direction of a group of four students at the table nearest to us. These fresh-faced specimens were looking over at us occasionally with what appeared to be amused expressions and were drinking what appeared to be some heathen, non-calorific variant of Coca-Cola.

"They don't drink as much as we used to," Dan—who had had the most recent student experiences—explained, a note of slight disdain in his voice. "Work harder too."

"How do you know?" I asked.

"Oh, didn't you know? I've been back up here doing a PhD. I remembered I quite enjoyed being a student and decided to come home."

"If you finish it, you'll have more letters after your name than in your name," Steve Taylor pointed out with a smirk. Dan scowled.

Dark-haired, saturnine and, if you're into that sort of thing, devilishly good-looking, Steve Taylor had been one of the most brilliant law students in our year. He had managed to secure a much-coveted internship with Mr Justice Reinhold in between his second and third years at uni and was now knocking it out of the park as a family law barrister. If he had gone down the route of selling his soul to "the man," he could have been raking it in by now in one of the more lucrative branches of the law. He had always been a little polished for Dan's tastes, although the two had generally managed to tolerate each other in the interests of group harmony.

"The undergraduates think I'm a bloody dinosaur," Dan moaned. "You'd never see any of those wet wankstains going up the bell tower after a few too many. Wouldn't even occur to them, not under the new Senior Tutor. South African git called Richard Du Toit. Word has it, he's a pissing teetotaller. College has been redeveloped too. Not sure where they got all the money from, but I keep losing my bearings every time I go in there now."

"Blame Forsyte Markby," Ed said.

"Who the hell's he?" Dan demanded.

"The firm I've been working for for the last five years, you muppet!" Ed chuckled, entirely unruffled by his old mate's evident lack of interest in his career. "Our construction team negotiated the building contract for the job!"

"So they're trying to drag St Crisps into the cutting edge of the twenty-first century," I concluded. "No more merrily sloshing around in the bottom five of the Tomkins Table for our successors then. Probably for the best, all things considered."

"We've got to curb THAT attitude, mate!" Ed declared disappointedly. "We're here to relive our youth! I'm not having you behaving like a fucking young person!" He took a sizeable gulp of lager before doing his bit to set the tone of the forthcoming festivities by belching boisterously.

"ORDEEER!" I roared, giving the room my best impression of former Speaker John Bercow.

"Mature, Ed," Britta muttered, rolling her eyes. She was right—the atmosphere in the Baron now had the pungency of a particularly elderly and overripe Limburger cheese.

"You can talk, Little Miss Cheesecutter," Ed scoffed. "I've heard more from your arse over the years than I have from your husband, the poor long-suffering bastard!"

We were now getting some extremely dubious looks from the smug teetotal vegan studenty types at the next table, but Ed's point was not an entirely unreasonable one. I had been next door neighbour to Britta and her jet-propelled derriere in our first year, and at times it had been like living next door to someone who deflated accordions for a living.

A familiar figure darkened the doorway. Another of our motley party had arrived.

"We're just talking about bowel movements," I cheerfully explained to the Right Honourable MP for Cambridge. "Pull up a pew!"

V

If Keir Hardie, that hoary, hairy, pioneering old socialist of yesteryear, had been asked at the founding of the Labour Party to describe what he would expect a Labour MP of the 2020s to look like, it is unlikely that the character he would have described would have borne much of a resemblance to the Right Honourable James Thaddeus ("Jammy") Jeffers MP.

Originally a land economy student, old Jammy had always

been lurking in a slightly creepy and sinister manner around the periphery of our social circle, primarily because he had spent far too much time trying to get ahead at the Cambridge Union (with all the scandal and skulduggery that traditionally entails, which he had embraced with an almost psychotic degree of gusto) to really get to know us.

He had subsequently managed to oil his way into the nomination for a safe Labour seat just in time for the 2010 election. Which he then proceeded to lose. I'm not sure that it was entirely his unvarnished and barely concealed contempt for the great unwashed masses that sunk his campaign, but most wannabe politicians would have taken the rather leaden hint that the electorate had pointedly dropped on his toes, and gone off to do something else with their lives. But what Jammy lacked in people skills, he made up for with a ferocious single-mindedness when it came to the pursuit of power. And if he had to change to get it, he would give them a different Jammy.

Traditionally, the Cambridge Union has always been the delivery address where the stork drops off baby Tory cabinet ministers to be reared, nurtured, and trained in the dark Machiavellian arts of political intrigue before emerging three years later as fully-fledged Alan Maks. But back in 2003, it had very much looked like the best way for a conservative politician to get ahead for the foreseeable future was to join the Labour Party.

It hadn't quite turned out like that, of course, and over the next ten years, it had been rather amusing to watch, from a safe distance, Jammy's absurd and painful political contortions as he attempted to convince his allies (Cambridge Union rats of his nature didn't have friends) that he was, in turn, a die-hard Blairite, a born-again Brownite, a nimble Millipede (switched brothers just in time to avoid making too much of a tit of himself), a fanatical Corbynista, who regarded "nuance" as something you acquire when your uncles get married, and then a fully paid up member of the Starmy Army.

I had been as astounded as anyone to see him selected as the candidate for Cambridge in 2015, and doubly dumbfounded to watch the awful little greaser actually win this classic swing seat. Worse still, he had managed to hold onto it, despite exuding all the charm of a secondary villain in a film where the main villain is a zombie apocalypse.

I had not for a moment imagined that he would be deigning to descend from his ivory tower to join us mere mortals this evening. Yet here he was, listening to us talking an entirely different variety of guff to the sort he was used to. He did make a point of continually checking his phone every few minutes after sitting down, and tried his best to look shocked and appalled whenever one of us told a rude joke, but his efforts were half-hearted. I guess you can't turn the politician off completely.

As it happens, he wasn't really given much of an opportunity to do so. It was only a few minutes before Mad Dog McFadden spotted him and made a beeline for our table, with the Butcher of Baghdad trailing grubbily in his wake.

"Well, if it isn't the local dignitary!" McFadden leered. "You've not been answering your mail, Mr Jeffers."

Jeffers silently mouthed something which looked to my untrained eyes like "Oh shit, a constituent!" But he had been in the game a few years now, so he knew how to mask his panic. He turned to the old bruiser with a smile.

"If this is a constituency matter, I would be happy to discuss it during my surgery hours, which you can find on my website. This really isn't the best time, as I'm having a drink with some" (short, revealing pause) "friends of mine. But I take everyone's concerns seriously and..."

He stopped, looking down at the gnarled finger that McFadden was pointing aggressively at his chest. The ex-Porter was now right in his face and breathing heavily.

"Now you listen to me, you jumped up little bastard!" he snarled. "I've been trying to get hold of you for weeks, but your bloody PA hasn't let me near you! Keeps accusing me of making a fuss. Well damn bloody right I'm making a fuss. Albert Ross may have been a small man in your eyes, but to us, he was family!"

"As I understand it," Jammy drawled carefully, "the police did carry out an investigation, and..."

"An' then they dropped it like a hot potato!" McFadden scowled.

"I get that you're upset, Mr McFadden," Ed interjected. Ed was usually on first-name terms with everyone but had clearly concluded that a modicum of deference to the resident nutter was called for here. "But Old Albert was pretty shaky when I last saw him, and that clapped-out old bike was creakier than he was. It can't have been that much of a shock to you, at his age, surely?"

"Besides, I'm not exactly sure what you expect me to do," Jammy commented rather limply. "I'm not responsible for what the police may or may not decide is worthy of investigation. Their resources are very limited thanks to over a decade of brutal Tory austerity and..."

"Don't you dare turn this into a party-political broadcast, you slippery wee shite!" McFadden roared. "You're a bloody MP. Do what bloody MPs are supposed to do! Put a bit of stick about! Get some answers out of Inspector Baynes and his lot! You were a St Crisps man, although I'm buggered if I can remember you from Adam! Doesn't that mean anything to you? This was an attack on our college! An attack on one is an attack on us all!"

"Us? Forgive me, but as I understand it, you don't even work there anymore!" Jammy snapped, his penchant for political point-scoring apparently prevailing over his instinct for self-preservation. McFadden started to lunge at Jammy, but fortunately a sweet voice distracted him before he could break anything important.

"Finlay!" My old friend, and one-time crush, Tanya Bullock stood in the doorway, flanked by Britta's husband, Neil. An English student, and now an academic of some renown, Tanya, like Britta, had ultimately returned to the Cambridge area after the statutory few years in London. She had, however, recently committed a shocking act of betrayal by accepting the offer of a much-coveted fellowship at another venerable university town that you may or may not have heard of.

It was Tanya who had spoken, and she had sounded genuinely delighted to see the old psychopath, which rather stopped him in his tracks. I was glad that Neil had turned up, though. He was the only one in our group who would have had a hope in hell of "containing" McFadden if things had really kicked off.

"Hmmm. This is quite a gathering you've got going on here, isn't it?" McFadden muttered.

"Yeah, and I was going to suggest we move next door to The Mitre," Ed cut in. "We're running out of space for all of us in here."

"Well, you have a lovely evening, ladies and gents." McFadden gave a sinister little bow.

"And you, Captain Shithead," he added, turning to Jammy, his belligerent index finger making another appearance. "Remember what I said!"

VI

"A veritable procession of shadows of the past!" I declared grandly as we were tucking into our second pints in The Mitre a few minutes later.

"I'm surprised Shippers hasn't made an appearance yet!" Steve grinned.

"Shippers," aka Professor Ronald Fairbanks, had been propping up the college bar for the better part of fifty years. An elderly man with a shabby wardrobe and a fluffy, tobacco-stained white beard, his resemblance to Harold Shipman, the fiendish mass murderer, and probable one-time Gerald Sinclair pen-pal, had earned him that unfortunate nickname even with some of his fellow Fellows, to the extent that most people tended to forget his real name. During his lengthy tenure, he had written a grand total of eleven articles, most of them unreadable even by the dry standards of legal literature, spent a bit of time playing cricket, and a lot more time bragging about it.

By the time we turned up as undergraduates, the rather more dynamic EU law expert David Williamson was running the show, and Shippers had been relegated to teaching first years. This was an effective arrangement, for first-year undergraduates' results don't count towards their degree. This usually means that they are almost as severely allergic to writing essays as Shippers was to marking them. I vividly remembered getting his first reading list through in my pigeon-hole towards the end of the very first week of my university career. This comprised a list of six texts with a note at the bottom saying "But you can read those next time. You're only young once, and I am rapidly running out of middle age. So this week, let's just chillax and drink port!"

Subsequent supervisions, a fortnightly opportunity to sit in on his burbling stream of consciousness, had left us little the wiser about the law of tort. If, however, a question had come up in the exam about the performance of the St Crispian College Cricket Club during Shippers' brief but (to him) memorable tenure as captain (1974-78), I might have ended up getting a better mark.

"Not yet, mate," Ed replied for me as he returned to his seat. "But the weekend is young...ooh, here comes another one!"

I had assumed that by this point our party was complete. It was with some surprise, therefore, that I beheld the uneasy sight of Sadie Simmons tottering towards us in heels so high that even from a seated position, I felt slightly unsteady on my feet just watching her.

Sadie was another fellow lawyer, so naturally had hung around with us as much as our mutual syllabus required back in the day, but she had never really been one of the crew. Like Jammy, she was desperate to be seen as a high-flier, although her ambitions lay in the field of the law rather than politics, and she was now a moderately successful but extremely publicity-hungry media barrister.

We had bumped into each other over the years at networking drinks and the like, and had had numerous perfectly civil conversations. But she had never been very good at disguising the fact that she was desperately scanning the room to find someone more influential to talk to.

As such, her presence here was somewhat perplexing. Yet here she was, doing the rounds, kissing and hugging everyone in a rather continental sort of way as she milked her entrance. I couldn't help noticing that my peck on the cheek was rather perfunctory compared to Steve's, but given the excess of cloying perfume she had doused herself in (possibly using a bucket), this did not come as too much of a disappointment to me. I got a distinct whiff of gin overlaying the perfume, though, and she was evidently already several sheets to the wind.

"Sorry I'm late, darling," she said to Ed, who winced. "I was having an early supper with Davie."

"David Williamson?" I asked but hadn't really needed to. Sadie had been disturbingly fixated with our esteemed supervisor from the moment she had arrived in Cambridge. Nobody else, needless to say, had ever called him "Davie," which was just one of many things about him to which Sadie was happily oblivious. A small man with thinning fair hair, Williamson was a few years younger than Sinclair, and probably even brighter. His dual missions in life had been to foster a more positive impression of the EU amongst his undergraduates, and to bring beige jumpers back into fashion. Neither mission had been an unadulterated success.

"He's written a new book about Brexit," Sadie announced in the tone of someone whose dog has learned to perform a new trick. She was one of those people who pronounced it "Breggsit," which has always baffled and irritated me in equal measure. I've never heard anyone talking about their "eggs" wife, after all, although perhaps that's just because I don't know any polygamous poultry farmers.

"Ooh, good," I exhaled wearily. "We've definitely not had enough people talking about THAT subject over the last few years."

She ignored me and proceeded to start flirting with Steve with bludgeon-like subtlety. Last I had heard, Sadie was married (although there was no wedding ring on her finger now), but why I expected that to have changed her behaviour, I am not sure. I had never much enjoyed Sadie's company, and Ed, the founder of this peculiar feast, had always been far more open than I had about his dislike for her. His guest list for the weekend was turning out to be as unexpected as it was motley.

I like to think that during the course of the evening, the solution of the "random guest list" would eventually have dawned on me. But as it happened, Steve, as ever one step ahead of me intellectually, got in there first.

"So tonight's the night then, Ed?" he surmised. Ed did his best "innocent face," which was, I have to say, staggeringly unconvincing.

"What are you on about, mate?"

"Well, I can't help noticing that the guest list for the weekend seems to align rather neatly with those of us who were in the room on Time Capsule Night."

"We're not doing that tonight, are we?" Dan interrupted. "I thought we were saving that for tomorrow?"

"We shall see, mate. We shall see." Ed grinned.

"Ridiculous charade," Sadie sniffed pompously, ostensibly to herself but definitely making sure that everyone heard.

"Funny you should say that," Ed said, his grin widening.

My heart sank. I only had hazy memories of "Time Capsule Night," an evening that had taken place in the second term of our third and (for most of us) final year in Cambridge. Finals had been looming large over our collective consciousnesses, and it had been one of the last major piss-ups we had indulged ourselves in before knuckling down to weeks of relentless revision.

But looming even larger in the background was the spectre of what would happen afterwards, after we pushed ourselves through that gruelling ordeal and, pass or fail, thrusted ourselves out beyond the cocoon-like confines of Cambridge into the wide world, whatever it might choose to make of us. The knowledge that, whatever glib promises we might make, we would not be seeing as much of each other as we were now.

Yes, my memories were hazy, but I did recall that we had all been feeling very keenly that the future was almost upon us. So when Ed had suggested that we all make a prediction about what we would be doing in fifteen years' time, put it in a time capsule and pledge to meet up on the anointed day to see how close our predictions had been, all of us had jumped at the idea.

Most of us had been in relationships at the time; that much I do remember. When one is the honourable exception to what had felt like a coordinated mass exercise of coupling up, one tends to notice these things.

My recollection was that I had written a rather self-pitying paragraph or two, predicting that I would still be alone in a soulless, dead-end job, with only my loving tabby cats to stave off the feelings of unbearable loneliness deep within my soul. Even more depressing was the fact that I had got it pretty much spot on, except that it was just the one cat, Clawed Rains, a rather elderly and degenerate little beast who I was rather fond of, and who was fortunately showing no signs of moving on to the great snuggle basket in the sky any time soon. My brother Sean had promised to look in on him on over the course of the weekend, and no doubt I would return to find that the fickle creature had unhesitatingly transferred his affections to my softie sibling, on the grounds that Sean always showered him with more cheesy catnip treats than I did.

I was therefore rather hoping that we would manage to get Ed drunk enough that he would spare our blushes and forget about the whole thing, especially as we had missed the allotted date by a couple of years due to that pandemic thingummy coming along and thoroughly embuggerating all our lives. The rather simian smile he flashed when saying "We shall see" led me to conclude that this was probably a forlorn hope, especially given how carefully he appeared to have picked the guest list.

Nevertheless, he did at least seem keen on the idea of getting extremely plastered. It was around a quarter to eleven when we began our weary and unsteady trek back up Castle Hill towards our accommodation, but Ed was anxious to make it clear that he had absolutely no intention of yielding to middle-aged social norms for a good while to come. He announced in no uncertain terms that he was not allowing anyone to go to bed yet, as he had bought in more booze for us to drink in his room.

Dan, who had started early and had somehow managed to sneak in a couple more drinks than the rest of us during the course of the evening, was lurching unevenly from one side of the pavement to the other. He had never been particularly good at knowing his limits, though, and he whooped when he heard that more drink would shortly be made available to him, picking up the pace of his staggering.

The street lighting is not particularly good when one gets to the top of Castle Hill. It was as cold as a penguin's chuff and as dark as a panther's nadgers. A striking contrast to the noisy frivolity of the pub. Cambridge suddenly felt rather empty and ever so slightly eerie. I had not had many opportunities for exercise lately, so I was wheezing slightly as we got to the flatter section of the walk. I decided to take a restorative slurp from my trusty hip flask, in which I had secreted a modest quantity of wonderfully warming 12-year-old Glengoyne. Truth be told, I was rather regretting having drunk so much, but I knew of old that it was far too late for me to avoid the next morning's hangover now, and that the difference that a swig or two of whisky would make was negligible.

"Alea bloody well jacta est," I muttered, taking another swig.

"Ah, you've brought the old hippers!" Ed grinned at me. Tanya, who had been walking just ahead of us with Jammy, turned and gave me a look.

"You haven't still got that thing, have you?" she asked, amused. I beamed at her, delighted to finally have a chance to chat. She had been deep in conversation with other people, mainly Ed, for most of the evening, so we had barely got two words in up to this point.

"Old habits die hard," I responded, far too plastered to come up with anything more original.

"So do worn-out livers!" Tanya retorted acerbically, although the warmth in her voice remained. Once upon a time, she had been very glad of that hip flask. It had helped me comfort her during her painful break-up with Neil, of all people, who had not let a huge amount of grass grow under his feet before taking up with Britta. A more unscrupulous man than I might have tried to take advantage of that situation. But then again, perhaps the warmth in her voice was a reflection of my not having done so. I proffered the flask, but Tanya wrinkled her nose and firmly declined. Britta, on the other hand...

"Oh, you legend, Rog," she beamed, snaffling it out of my hands and taking an unladylike glug, much to her far more sober husband's evident embarrassment. She passed the flask back to me, and I decided that a "swig or two" might as well turn into three. This turned out to be an error, for as the whisky was tumbling down my throat, I was startled into a choking fit by the sound of some incredibly sinister singing emanating from somewhere in the surrounding blackness.

VII

It was the tunnel song from *Willy Wonka & the Chocolate Factory*. I will not replicate the lyrics in full here, as I am too much of a tightwad to fork out for the copyright. But if as a child you thought that song was terrifying when sung by an avuncular twinkly man in a top hat, just imagine how potentially trouser ruining it was to hear it sung in pitch darkness by a psychotic Glaswegian with a penchant for extreme violence. As he finished the song, Mad Dog McFadden (for it was he) loomed out of the darkness with a terrifying rictus grin on his face. Saddam was nowhere to be found. Presumably, there comes a point at which even Iraqi dictators have to draw the line and make themselves scarce. The ex-Porter was greeted by a stunned silence.

"You kids have a good evening, now!" McFadden beamed at us with a terrifying bonhomie. And with that, he was off, giving us a sarcastic little wave and disappearing into the night, leaving us all thoroughly disconcerted.

By this time we had reached our destination, and the whole crowd of us trooped in gratefully through the Porter's Lodge. Gavin was no longer on duty. His replacement looked younger than we were. He gave us a disapproving look as we traipsed through, yammering away in unnaturally loud voices.

"I think I'll turn in," Neil announced.

"Don't let me stop you enjoying yourself, though," he added. This was presumably directed at Britta.

"I'll just stay for one more," she promised him without the remotest semblance of sincerity. Her taciturn husband nodded and sloped off gloomily to bed. As soon as he had disappeared, his wife turned to us and declared, "Right, let's fucking GET ON IT!"

"You haven't had many nights out lately, have you?" I surmised.

"Does it show?" Britta asked sweetly.

"Getting on it" turned out to primarily consist of lolling around in Ed's room drinking bottles of beer. Dan, who had been mumbling increasingly incoherently as the evening progressed, promptly fell asleep five minutes after bagging the comfiest chair.

The rest of us soon started chinwagging in smaller groups, with Britta, Ed, Tanya and myself reminiscing nostalgically, and Steve looking extremely uncomfortable next to Sadie. She had insisted on sitting him next to her on the floor and was speaking intently and intensely rather more closely into his ear than his sense of personal space demanded.

During our undergraduate years, Steve had, whilst not encouraging her advances, at least made the effort to rebuff them gently. So gently, in fact, that she had never quite got the hint. Now older, married (albeit not particularly happily) and several shades more callous, Steve was obviously no longer willing to extend her the same courtesies, for his body language was making it abundantly clear that he was paying no attention to her drunken ramblings and that he was vaguely repulsed by her proximity. After a few minutes, he even pulled out a small pad of paper from his trouser pocket and started doodling on it.

That left Jammy, who had spent virtually the entire evening not being the centre of attention, much to his chagrin. He disappeared briefly, only to return a couple of minutes later with, God help us, a guitar. The ghastly fellow proceeded to subject us to a Coldplay medley, glooming us into sombre silence, although Sadie continued to whisper at Steve.

When he had run out of Coldplay, he moved on to "Wonderwall," "Hotel California," an overlong version of "Everlong" by the Foo Fighters and numerous others. When he announced he was going to finish off with "The Sound of Silence," my hopes were temporarily raised, only to be dashed on the rocks when he started warbling the Paul Simon song of that name.

"How long have you been playing the guitar for, anyway?" Tanya asked as he finished that particular delightful ditty, in a not particularly subtle effort to distract him from offering us an encore.

"About ten years," said Jammy. Britta looked at the fruit-based device on her wrist.

"It's actually only been about half an hour," she muttered. "Bloody feels like ten years, though!"

"OK, let's move on!" Jammy snapped. This was clearly not the reaction he had been hoping for, and our pointed failure to applaud or join in had evidently not gone unnoticed. Presumably, on his Select Committee Away Days, his audience tended to be more polite. "Are we going to do the sodding time capsule or what? How about I hand them out at random, and everyone can read theirs out, and the rest of us can guess whose is whose?"

"That's not for tonight." Ed grinned, clearly savouring the

prospect of whatever it was he had planned. "We don't want to spoil the Easter treat, now do we?"

Jammy now looked like he was really struggling not to lose his rag. Sadie, looking pale, suddenly stopped clinging to Steve like a besotted limpet, tottered across the room and threw up noisily into the little bin by the door. I turned to Ed, assuming that, as the person who would be sleeping here tonight, he would be a tiny bit irritated by this development. But in fact, our host had a broad grin on his face, yelling out "Wahey!" before taking another slurp of beer.

"I'll get her to bed," Tanya offered in a rather disappointing display of adult behaviour. I felt pretty certain that Tanya would rather easily manage to resist the temptation to come back once she had taken care of the stricken Sadie, and that this was the last we would see of her that night. Meanwhile, Dan, awake again but still bleary, caught sight of Steve, who was still continuing with his artistic endeavours.

"Can I have a look, mate?" he demanded.

"No, mate," Steve replied curtly. "Sorry, I draw strictly for my own private amusement." Dan, who was an argumentative and aggressive drunkard at the best of times, indicated in no uncertain terms that he was underwhelmed by this excuse. After a few more attempts at persuasion, consisting principally of repeating "Go on!" over and over again and making a forlorn effort to turn it into a chant, he eventually took matters into his own hands. He stood up and snatched the pad out of Steve's hands, knocking over the budding doodler's drink in the process. Dan took one look at its contents and went bright crimson in the face.

"You bastard!" he snarled, violently hurling the pad of paper into a corner.

In my experience, such exclamations are usually a prelude to storming off in a huff. Dan did no such thing, but rather let his words hang there awkwardly while he and Steve stared at each other, eyes aflame, as they angrily circled each other like a pair of rutting stags.

"Come on, guys," Jammy pleaded with them half-heartedly, showing us a tantalising glimpse of the sophisticated diplomatic skills that would no doubt stand him in good stead if he ever made Foreign Secretary.

It was Steve who eventually capitulated under pressure, marching out of the room with a snarled "Twat!" There was a hinge-rattling bang as he slammed the door shut behind him.

I took this as a suitable cue to make my excuses and depart. The party was dwindling, the mood was souring, and I still had slender hopes of avoiding spending the whole day tomorrow feeling like a badger had defecated in my mouth. Britta followed my lead, as unlike the rest of the party, our rooms were in C Block in the next building (Ed and the others were all in D Block). We wandered into the courtyard for a couple of minutes to get a spot of fresh air before turning in.

"It'll all look ridiculously trivial in the morning," Britta commented. "I just hope Steve doesn't decide to skip the rest of the weekend. He and Dan were needling each other all evening, and he always did hold a grudge."

"What are you two up to during the day tomorrow?" I asked. Ed had outlined his plans for the evening—we were all due to meet up at 7:30pm tomorrow for dinner at The Ivy—but had assumed that we would prefer to make our own plans for the rest of the day and team up as appropriate.

"Neil's going to be working for most of the day," she said. "Do you want to grab breakfast somewhere and climb the Great St Mary's Tower? I've never done it, and apparently, you get the best views in Cambridge."

"How many stairs?" I asked dubiously. I had always admired GSM as a church, but as someone with a lifelong fear of both heights and strenuous exercise, this would not have been my first choice of activity to start off the day with. But Britta was a persuasive little dynamo, and I could already feel myself relenting as I asked the question.

"Hundreds of the buggers!" Britta replied cheerfully. "I'll wake you at seven. Ed told me earlier that he'd be up for it as well, so we'll drag him along if the others have let him get any sleep by then!"

"Seven? Steady on!" I spluttered.

"The early bird catches the worm, Rog!"

"He's bloody welcome to it!" I snorted. Sodding hell, I thought. Next she'll be suggesting that we get up at 5am for rowing practice. I had steered clear of the rowing during my undergraduate years precisely due to my allergy to early mornings. Britta had coxed for a bit but, unlike her husband, she had never been one of those rowers who you could never get off the subject of bloody rowing. It was one of the few subjects that could stir Neil into making conversation at all, but given the choice, most of us preferred his usual truculent silence.

I bade Britta goodnight and reeled off in the approximate direction of my bedchamber. When I got there, I took an enormous, gulpy drink of water in a rather depressingly middle-aged way before looking around and wondering whether I was going a bit potty. I was sure I had left my bag under the little table by my bed. Indeed, I remembered buggering about trying to squeeze it under the table in a forlorn attempt to make the rest of the room feel more spacious. And I had definitely left it zipped up. Now it was unzipped and leaning against a wall on the other side of the room.

I quickly rifled through it, trying to make a mental list of what I had packed so that I could work out if anything was missing. Spare clothes? Check. Pyjamas? Check. Toiletries? Check. Dog-eared copy of *Night Watch* by Terry Pratchett? Check. I had absolutely nothing remotely worth nicking, and if anyone had been in my room, and I wasn't going completely tonto, they had obviously drawn the same conclusion. As I drifted off into an overdue slumber, I made a vague mental note to remonstrate with whichever Porter was on duty about it in the morning.

VIII

I felt about as fresh and dynamic as a fossilised wheel of stilton when I was awoken—a little before 6am—by the sound of someone, who was clearly feeling a lot worse than me, frantically flushing the toilet. It sounded like it was coming from the next block where Ed and most of the others were sleeping (I had left my window open to get some fresh air). I groaned, stuck a pillow over my head and waited for it to stop. This it failed to do, for some considerable while. Clearly there was some sort of pitched battle going on: man vs latrine.

I must have nodded off again pretty quickly, as it only felt like a few minutes later when I heard Britta's firm and distinctive rap at my door. I groaned again, spent a couple of minutes blundering around the room whilst hastily dressing and deodorising, and opened the door to my depressingly bouncy-looking friend.

"Morning, matey!" she said. "The beds have improved a bit, haven't they? Less creaky, for one thing!"

Due to my horrendously inactive sex life, I had had less experience of the whole creaking phenomenon last time around, but I grunted some sort of vague platitude by way of response.

"Let's see how Ed's doing," I suggested. "Wouldn't be surprised if he ended up having fallen asleep on the couch!"

We turned the corner towards the door to his bedroom, and stopped in horror. The window to his room was sprayed with copious quantities of red fluid, spattered haphazardly across its entire surface.

"What the hell?" I breathed. Britta rapped at the door.

"Ed? Is everything OK?" She was met with an ominous silence. After a few seconds of terrified hesitation, I dared to look in through the window. Even without the blood (for I had already convinced myself it could be nothing else), it was extremely dirty, and I could barely make anything out. But there was definitely a human form in there, and it was lying by the side of the bed, not on it.

"This...this is one of Ed's pranks, right?" I stammered unconvincingly. Britta looked grim.

"We'd better get the Porter," she said.

Gavin was on duty again. I could only assume that he needed to work the extra overtime to pay for his ever-expanding porn collection. His reaction when we told him what we had just seen was typically surly and incredulous, but he grabbed the spare key from the wall and came out with us anyway.

Turning the key in the lock can only have taken Gavin a few seconds, but every millisecond seemed to drag on excruciatingly. When we got in, however, time seemed to stop altogether.

"Oh my giddy bitch of an aunt!" Gavin whispered.

To misquote old Brucie Willis in that film about the two sweary hitmen, Ed was dead, baby. Ed was dead. And he was not being subtle about it.

His shirt was ripped open, and his bare chest was exposed to us. Or at least what was left of it, for it had been slashed to ribbons by what had to be almost twenty stab wounds, several of them deep and gaping. The murder weapon had obviously been a large hunting knife, and we did not need Sherlock Holmes to tell us that much, as it had been left sticking out of Ed's neck. In fact, it had gone right through, with tremendous force, and appeared to now be pinning his body to the floor.

On his forehead was a scrap of paper, which had been fastened to his skull by a drawing pin. On the paper was drawn a small cartoon picture of a little devil, complete with horns, tail and pitchfork, with a malicious grin on his face. The expression on the face of my dead friend, however, was one of shock and utter terror.

Britta, who had quite a larynx on her, screamed. I feel absolutely no shame in admitting that I did too. Then I took a second look and immediately collapsed into a flood of tears.

CHAPTER 2

In which Gavin takes charge, the police arrive and relieve him of his command, much to his chagrin, I get a grilling but no breakfast, and I contribute to the hatching of a far-fetched but strangely plausible theory about the murder.

I

"Stay here," Gavin snapped. To give credit where credit's due, the Porter was displaying an air of command that I would not previously have associated with him. On a less creditable note, he was also barely bothering to disguise his evident glee at getting a bit of excitement.

"Where are you going?" I spluttered.

Gavin gave me an "I'm glad you asked" grin. "First, I'm calling the police. Second, I'm going to be guarding the lodge to make sure no bugger goes in or out of the complex till they get here. Which means you two need to guard the body. Chances are, whichever sod did this is still about. Only way in or out of here is through the lodge, unless you're a bloody good climber. CCTV will soon tell us all we need to know on that front." And with that, he was off, already punching the number into his phone in a singularly self-important manner.

"I need to get some air," Britta insisted as soon as he was gone. She looked nauseous. "Just because we've been assigned guard duty doesn't mean we have to actually stay in here and stare at...at THIS."

I could see tears spring into her eyes, and I nodded.

"Outdoors should do just fine," I agreed hoarsely. All the same, I could not quite bring myself to leave straight away without taking a further look around.

The attack had been vicious, vigorous and frenzied. There was blood everywhere. The rest of the room, on the other hand, was not as messy as I would have expected, with the exception of one rather lurid red keepsake box. It was the sort of box with a lock on it that could be used to store letters or jewellery. The box was lying on the floor, open, and the lock had evidently been smashed. It was, of course, empty, save for a scrap of paper that appeared to have been taped to the bottom of the lid.

I knew it was potential evidence, and that the police, not to mention the much more terrifying Gavin, were likely to take a dim view of my tampering with it. And yet, for some reason that I am still not entirely able to explain, I couldn't help myself. On the scrap of paper was another crude drawing, although it had clearly been drawn by a different and more childish doodler than the person responsible for the devil pinned to Ed's skull. It was a picture of what looked like two letter Cs, one inside the other, and next to it, a picture of a small, square bottle.

"What do you make of this?" I asked Britta, bringing it out to her. Shakily, she took it, looked at it and turned to me.

"Looks like one of Ed's drawings," she concluded. "Buggered if I know what it's supposed to be, though. Where did you find it?" She gave me a sharp look. I told her.

"You recognise the box, of course?" I asked.

Britta looked perplexed. "Should I? I'm not really able to think particularly straight right now, Rog!" I could tell that she was struggling to keep it together, so I gave her a big, fraternal bear hug. Truth be told, I needed it at least as much as she did.

"Look," I said at last. "If you wanted to go back and be with Neil, I can hold the fort here. He's probably rather better at the whole comforting thing than I am." I rummaged around in my pocket for my packet of polo mints and handed her one.

"Hardly," Britta said, looking like she had a bitter taste in her mouth. She swallowed the mint, which may have helped in a small way. "Anyway, he's not here. He left hours ago to go and do some work from home."

"On a Saturday? And Easter Saturday at that?"

"Welcome to my world." Britta sighed sarcastically. "He never really wanted to be doing this in the first place. Deep down, I knew this weekend would turn out to be a total sodding disaster. I mean, not 'this' disastrous, but…The most galling thing is that the morally high grounded bastard is probably completely justified at having had a few reservations about going on a weekend away with my ex, but…"

"Steve? He's not still sore about that, is he? That was years, decades ago. And I remain absolutely amazed that you put up with him for so long."

"Well, what can I say? Best sex I ever had," Britta muttered, a glimmer of mischief returning to her eyes for the first time.

My polo went down the wrong way.

When my spluttering had subsided, I found time to feel ever so slightly offended. It occurred to me that Britta might not actually remember it, given how utterly pixilated the pair of us had been on the evening in question. But there had been one glorious night, back in 2005 when… (although if I'm entirely honest, the third dot might be overegging the pudding somewhat, given the amount of college port we'd consumed beforehand). The following morning, she had told me, with her typical forthrightness and marked absence of tact, that it had been a horrible mistake and that I was never to speak of it again.

Which was fair enough, I had concluded, too much of a

coward to ask her to elaborate any further on why she had taken that view of things. This had probably been a wise choice, looking back on it. She might actually have given me an honest answer, and I had been rather prone to self-pity in those days. Reasonably attractive though she was, Britta had never been one of my hopeless crushes, and so our friendship had continued much the same as before.

"Until I met my husband, of course," she added, too late. Far too late. "And...ooh! Shit!"

"Indeed!" I agreed pointedly.

"You were probably in the top ten, Rog," she ventured in an attempt to mollify my wounded ego. As comfort went, this was definitely of the crumby variety. I had known her, and been in her confidence, for long enough to be reasonably sure that she had only ever had seven or eight partners.

"Jolly good," I replied benevolently. I wasn't sure how to follow this up, and I think both of us were out of chat, for understandable reasons. We contented ourselves to wait in companionable silence until DCI Baynes and DS Chen arrived some twenty minutes later, together with a number of constables and a tall, dapper-looking fellow in a well-cut suit who reminded me a bit of a black David Niven, complete with pencil moustache.

This, remarkably, turned out to be the pathologist. Decades of watching cosy crime dramas had given me a rather particular image of pathologists as ugly, bulbous little men, usually with a penchant for gallows humour. It is not a profession that I would ever have associated with the word 'suave,' but suave this chap undoubtedly was. He rolled up his sleeves, having first removed a rather stylish pair of cufflinks, which he secreted in his pocket, and got busy with examining the corpse straight away. If the corpse had not happened to have recently housed a close personal friend of mine, I would have been interested to stay and watch him in action, but as it was, I would not have had the opportunity in any event. DS Chen beckoned for us to come with her and led us into the Porter's Lodge.

II

Detective Sergeant Jacqueline Chen was one of those ladies who was small without being diminutive. If you looked at her and consciously thought about it, you would, at length, come to the unavoidable conclusion that she was a bit of a tiddler. But it was not something you would necessarily notice otherwise, perhaps because the force of her personality seemed to give her a few extra inches. She was a few years younger than me, but she gave off the air of someone who was already pretty seasoned in matters of this nature.

I am, as you may have gathered, a rather large, overweight fellow. My brother Sean and I, together with Desmond the dog, had grown up in a family of James Bond enthusiasts, but if Sean Connery had aged like a fine wine, Sean Whiteley had taken more of a Mackeson Stout approach to the ageing process. Slightly irritatingly from my perspective, however, big bro had gone on a health kick after people had started calling him "Sean Coronary" and was now in better shape than I was. Neither Whiteley brother, however, was a patch on Detective Chief Inspector Baynes in the girth department. A corpulent, jovial, red-faced man in his mid-forties, he was dressed in a rather scruffy old trench coat, the front of which was playing host to a number of greasy stains. Neither his scruffiness nor his weight made his presence any less commanding.

The chief inspector was still strolling around the crime scene barking out instructions when we left, but he followed us into the Porter's Lodge a few moments later. He sat down in Gavin's chair behind the desk, much to the latter's obvious irritation, and beckoned us over.

"Right," he began, in an overripe West Country accent that sounded rather like an audition tape for *The Archers* that had been rejected for being too over the top. "You folks have had a rough morning of it, I reckon, so Sergeant Chen and I will do what we can not to make this any more painful than it needs to be. As I understand it, you three found the body. So I'll need you to talk me through it. First of all, Gavin…"

Gavin grinned like a Cheshire Cat. If it had been socially acceptable, I think he would have started purring. He had clearly concluded that the fact that the inspector was addressing him first meant that his testimony was the most important.

"…fetch us a cup of coffee while I chat to these two, will you? I'm not used to being up this early on a Saturday!" Gavin's face fell. If looks could kill, the morning's body count would have instantly doubled.

"Milk but no sugar!" the inspector called out, chortling as Gavin stomped into the back room sulkily.

"So as I understand it," Baynes continued, leaning back in Gavin's chair and sticking his feet on the desk, "you lot were all up at uni here and are back for some sort of jolly, is that it?"

"Basically," Britta agreed.

"So you were having drinks with the deceased last night, then?" We nodded. "When and where?"

We went over the evening's events. Naturally, Baynes insisted on a full run-down of who had been there and when and where each of us had joined the group.

"So you two left Mr Dickinson's room about…what time?"

"One-thirty," Britta replied instantly, which was a relief as I hadn't had the faintest idea. "I was checking my watch pretty constantly while Jammy was playing that f…that fucking guitar! Time was definitely not passing quickly enough!"

I was not sure whether I was more amused by the fact that Britta, of all people, had been hesitant about the prospect of swearing in front of two police officers or by the fact that after her momentary hesitation, she had then decided to bloody well go for it anyway. I felt confident that even in the rarefied environs of this charming university town, they had probably heard worse.

"And when you left, who was still in 'the room where it happened'?" the inspector prompted.

"Well, Ed, obviously." Britta said. "Dan Finn. And I think Jammy was still there. They were the last ones standing I think."

"Standing might be putting it a bit strongly," I added. I felt that I had been letting Britta do most of the heavy lifting in the interview thus far and that it was probably time for me to chip in, even if it was only to throw in a bit of weak banter.

"So James Jeffers MP is a dirty old stop-up-late, is he?" Baynes chuckled. "Well, well, well. I shall enjoy catching up with him later."

"Now, let's talk a bit more about this barney you mentioned between Mr Finn and Mr Taylor," the detective went on. I am not sure I would have mentioned it myself, given how silly it had all been, but Britta had been erring on the side of full and frank disclosure. "Mr Dickinson didn't get involved at all in this?"

"No," Britta replied. "He just stayed out of it. That's the weird thing about all this. Ed was never particularly confrontational. He could be a bit of a shit-stirrer, and he sometimes got other people into trouble, but he usually managed to talk his way out of situations that looked like they might lead to a fight."

"Is that so?" Baynes raised an eyebrow. "Well, let's move on to the notebook that Mr Taylor was doodling in. What happened to it?"

"I have no idea," Britta said.

"It was thrown across the room," I piped up, happy at last to have something vaguely of substance to contribute.

"Someone must have picked it up, though," Baynes surmised. "Cos it ain't there now! Now that picture of the little devil we found pinned to his forrid—that wouldn't be the sort of thing Mr Taylor might have had in his repertoire, would it?"

Britta was silent for a moment.

"It might have been," she admitted quietly.

It was at that point that I remembered, with a sinking feeling in the pit of my stomach, that I still had the other picture I had found in my pocket: the one with the bottle and the weird-shaped Cs. Was I withholding vital evidence?

"Did anyone apart from Mr Finn see what was in the notebook?" Baynes asked after a ponderous pause.

"I don't think so," I said. Britta shook her head.

"Well, we'll be having words with both gentlemen in due course, I dare say," Baynes went on. The inspector was clearly preparing to move on to other matters, but Gavin interrupted him before he got the chance.

"You'll have to find 'em first," the Porter sneered.

"Oh, hello, my old cock!" Baynes turned to him in surprise, seemingly having forgotten about the Porter's existence, and cheerfully accepted the rather tardy cup of coffee that was being proffered to him extremely grudgingly.

"So they're not tucked up in bed sleeping it off then?" asked the inspector after taking a noisy slurp.

"Nah! Dan Finn was out of here at six this morning. Rushed through here like a bloody champagne cork out of a bottle! He had a face like a bulldog licking the piss off a nettle!"

"Is that right?" Baynes' tiny eyes narrowed, and he turned to Britta and myself. "Would either of you two have any ideas where Mr Finn might have sloped off to? Any favourite pubs?"

"It would probably be quicker to list the ones he doesn't like," I commented mildly.

"Ah," Baynes sighed. "Well, I dare say that me and my police posse are equipped with sufficient wiles and lowbrow cunning to be able to track him down sooner or later. What about Mr Taylor?" he went on, turning back to Gavin.

"Oh, he never slept here last night!" Gavin said, a sneer beginning to creep up the side of his face.

"He didn't?" I was surprised. "I thought he'd booked a room like the rest of us."

"No, well, he wouldn't, would he?" Gavin's sneer now stretched so far that I was expecting his facial muscles to buckle under the strain and go "twang" at any moment.

"And what exactly do you mean by that, sir?" Baynes turned to him, a sharp look of keen intelligence suddenly lighting up what had, up to that point, been a placid, stolid-looking face. This obviously put Gavin off his stride.

The Porter descended into a bout of incoherent spluttering. "Well…I…um…what I mean is, erm, well, I think he has a friend who lives locally."

"A friend who lives locally?" The inspector beamed. "Well, I'll be pressing you for further details on that score presently, given as how you seem to know more about Mr Taylor's goings-on than his friends here do! But first, you'd better tell me who else has been through here this morning. Were you on duty all night?"

"No, the lodge was locked up from 1am till my shift started at 4am."

"Well, what a coincidence!" Baynes boomed. "Our pathologist reckons that was right around the time he was killed! Between three-thirty and four-thirty, he said!"

I shuddered at the thought that when I had left Ed, he had only had a couple of hours left to live. Thankfully, he had seemed happily oblivious to his imminent fate, and the look on his face when we had discovered him had made it pretty clear that the poor chap hadn't had an inkling of what was to come.

"So, chances are that if our mally-factor came through here, you'd have seen him!" Baynes added, in case anyone had been in any doubt that this was what he had been getting at. "So, who else has bolted from the scene of the crime?"

"My husband will have been through at about five-thirty," Britta chipped in, clearly eager to get in with the innocent explanation before Gavin started casting aspersions with the tone of his voice. "He always intended to—he's gone home to get some work done. We have a house in Fulbourn."

"Usually an early riser, is he, your feller?"

"One of his many unsavoury habits, inspector!" Britta smiled wanly.

"And you saw him go through, did you, Gav?" Gav? Any doubts I had that Baynes was going out of his way to wind up the truculent Porter evaporated, and I found myself warming to the inspector considerably. Gavin deliberately pretended not to have heard him.

"Oh, GAVELAAR!" the inspector sang out. "Do pay attention, me old cocker. Otherwise, we'll have to take this down to the station where there's less distractions!"

I saw DS Chen mouthing "fewer" and immediately found myself warming to her as well. I'm always on the look-out for a fellow pedant.

"Yeah, I saw him," the Porter belatedly confirmed. "Tanya Bullock went through an' all, around 7am. Said she was off to get some sort of early morning spa treatment. Looked like she needed it, too. Highly strung, that one is. Them two and Finn were the only ones who came through before these two here turned up in a panic."

The derogatory tone he attached to the word "panic," as though we had been massively overreacting to the brutal murder of one of our oldest friends, made me seethe.

"I see," Inspector Baynes grunted before taking another slurp of coffee. "You haven't got any biscuits to go with these, have you? I never got my breakfast this morning."

"We're all out!" Gavin snapped a little too quickly, but not before Baynes had opened a drawer, his plump hand emerging triumphantly seconds later with a jammy dodger.

"Withholding vital evidence, Gav!" the inspector tutted, grinning from ear to ear. Gavin scowled.

"I'll need to commandeer your CCTV footage, of course," Baynes went on, talking with his mouth full and spreading so many crumbs in all directions that it felt like we were watching CSI Sesame Street. "But why don't you tell me who else is staying on campus, apart from Mr Dickinson and his group?"

"A couple of other alumni from the '67 intake. Nice old couple—I think they're reliving their teenage romance!"

"Married couple?" the inspector asked.

"Oh, they're married all right," Gavin sniggered. "But not to each other!"

Baynes raised an eyebrow but said nothing.

"Then there's a bunch of Korean teenagers here on a school trip. About twenty of 'em. They're in the Rosalind Franklin block though, down the lane. Doubt they'd have seen anything unless they'd gone for a walk in the middle of the night and been actively looking. Other than that, it's just this lot! And it won't have been an outsider," he added menacingly.

"Sure of that, are you?" Inspector Baynes seemed amused by the Porter's incorrigible pushiness.

"Course. Stands to reason. You'd have to be a bloody mountain goat to scale the walls round this complex. An' there's CCTV all round the walls anyway."

"Is there a camera that looks at the entrance to D Block?"

"Yeah, there is," Gavin confirmed. "None inside the staircase, though. None that are operational, anyway. But if your man went in, he'll have been caught on camera," he said with a grin. Britta and I looked at each other. I couldn't tell what she was feeling, but I was pretty relieved. I was in the clear unless the killer turned out to be a large blond doppelgänger of mine, and the same went for her and Neil.

However, as the only ones staying in the next-door block, we were the only ones to whom that applied. Gavin clearly sensed my relief, as he seemed to feel obliged to add a note of ambiguity to my apparent alibi.

"Unless he climbed in through the first-floor kitchen window at the back," he added. "That's a bit of a blind spot. There's a narrow path round the back between the outer walls of the complex and the walls of D Block. A half-decent climber could probably clamber up."

"We'll take a look," the inspector said, nodding meaningfully at Sergeant Chen in a manner that made it clear that he personally was going to delegate the aforementioned course of action. This probably also went for any other procedural steps that required him to leave the chair that he was currently doing such a good job of making himself at home in, I suspected.

"Meanwhile, Mr Whiteley, I wonder if you wouldn't mind doing me a quick favour," Baynes went on. "Could I ask you to give Mr Dickinson a quick call?"

"I'm sorry?" I spluttered, utterly perplexed. "Did you say Mr Dickinson?"

"Yes," Baynes said, nodding. "The dead feller!" he added helpfully.

"Um...I'm just not sure I'm going to be able to get through to him!" I pointed out. "Not with this bit of kit, anyway, although if anyone can rustle up a Ouija board or a cut-price necromancer at short notice, it's probably Gavin here!"

Baynes chortled at this, whilst the sheer venom of the look Gavin gave me suggested that my little joke might not have been too far off the mark.

"It's whether you get through to someone else I'm interested in," the inspector explained, giving me a sagacious look. "No phone was found with the body, see!"

I scrolled down my list of contacts with a bit of a lump in

my throat, my hands sweating slightly at the thought of who might be at the other end of the line. Dialling M for a murderer, I thought grimly. In the end, I got so nervous that I put the phone on speaker and dropped it onto the desk in front of Baynes as if it had been scaldingly hot. Somehow, it felt safer if others were listening in.

There was a ring on the other end of the line. Then another. Then another. Baynes, Britta, DS Chen and I exchanged glances. With the exception of the remarkably laid-back inspector, the rest of us were all looking a bit nervous.

Then a voice came on the line.

"You've reached the voicemail of Ed Dickinson. I can't take your call at the moment, but if you'd like to leave me a message after the tone, I'll get back to you as soon as I can."

"No need to leave a message, Mr Whiteley," Baynes said grimly, handing me back the phone. "Well, it was worth a try. Another line of enquiry we will be pursuing in due course."

"You'll want to check out the knife, an' all!" Gavin suggested.

"Oh really?" The inspector purred dangerously. "Thank goodness you mentioned that. It would have completely slipped my plodding mind otherwise!"

"All I'm saying," Gavin backtracked a little, realising he had overstepped the mark, "is that the killer made a mistake leaving it sticking out of his gullet like that. Even if he wiped the fingerprints off, someone might well recognise a lovely hunting knife like that! It's a beaut! If you do catch him, you should ask him where he got it from!"

"Perhaps you'd like to sit in on the interview?" Baynes suggested icily. "We can see if the murderer would be able to haggle a cheeky little discount for you with the seller?"

Now I could actually hear Gavin's teeth grinding as he struggled to suppress his fury.

"But before we get too engrossed in Gavin's Black Market

Bargain Hunt," Baynes continued, turning to Britta and myself, "is there any other information either of you two would like to volunteer?"

For once, Britta seemed content to leave the talking to me.

"Two things," I started hesitantly. "Firstly, I realise that there may not be anything inherently suspicious about flushing toilets, but..."

"Generally speaking, Mr Whiteley, I would share that opinion. We in the police are broadly in favour of the practice, in fact. So what is it about this particular instance of fiendish flushing that makes you feel the need to share it with us?"

"Well, the timing. Woke me up a little before six, it did. And Good God, the persistence! It seemed to go on for about ten minutes! I just wondered whether someone— the...the killer, I guess—might have been trying to flush away some evidence?"

"And do you have any theories as to what that evidence might have been, Mr Whiteley?"

"Well, I wouldn't want to tread on you chaps' toes," I continued nervously.

"You wouldn't?" The inspector snorted. "That's refreshing!"

He glared meaningfully at Gavin.

"But, well, it leads me onto the second point really. Which is this." I reached into my pocket and retrieved the scrap of paper that had been weighing me down like a lead anchor (if you'll excuse the mixed metaphors) ever since I had rather courageously taken it upon myself to tamper with the evidence.

"It was taped to the inside of the red box that had been smashed open," I explained. Sergeant Chen wordlessly took it out of my hands—it was not quite a snatch, but it was still forceful enough to convey a hint of reproach—and handed it to her reclining superior.

"Any idea what it's supposed to be?" Baynes asked after staring at it stolidly for a few moments.

"No, I hadn't quite got that far," I admitted.

"Well, it's told me one thing already," the inspector grunted. "We should probably be looking for our murderer outside of the artistic community!"

"Oh no, Ed drew this," I corrected him. "And I think I know what else was in that box."

"Go on," Baynes prompted.

"Predictions of the future, as jotted down circa 2006," I explained before launching into an explanation of Time Capsule Night. I had become increasingly convinced in my mind as the interview had progressed that the lurid red box had been the time capsule, although it still struck me as beyond extraordinary to think that it might be the reason Ed had been killed. I was pretty sure that I could remember him purloining the box from his then-girlfriend, Niamh the Gymnast, who had received it as an unwanted present from her parents.

Ed had clearly opened the box at least once in the last seventeen years, even if only to insert the mysterious drawing. Had he ever looked at our predictions? He had promised not to. He had said that it would spoil the magic. But of course he'd looked. And it turned out that he had been more right than he could possibly have known about the "spoiling the magic" thing as well.

"I think," Baynes ruminated after hearing me out, "that this would be an avenue worth exploring further, and I'd like to collect your further thoughts, and those of Mrs Norman here, separately. Not that I'm suggesting that you can't be trusted, but the truth is that your memories can't, not this far down the line. We've all passed a lot of water under the bridge since 2006, and I'll wager you were both pretty bladdered at the time. So I don't want to make it worse by having the two of you feeding ideas and false memories to each other. Mrs Norman, if you'll come into the back room, please. Gav, I'd be grateful if you could find an empty room for Detective Sergeant

Chen to grill Mr Whiteley in. Sounds like you'll be spoiled for choice, at this time of year!"

III

Baynes escorted Britta into the back room while Gavin grabbed a key from among the hundreds that hung on the back wall and beckoned Sergeant Chen and myself to follow him. True to form, the room he found for us was almost certainly the pokiest one available. Its choice of furniture was limited to a narrow, rickety bed, which Sergeant Chen invited me to sit on, and a hard, unsympathetic-looking armchair, which the sergeant took for herself.

"Do you need to use the bathroom?" Chen asked me before we started. She had one of those internationally schooled accents that always sound a bit American to me. "Now that we appear to be treating you as a witness rather than a suspect, pending the results of the CCTV footage, of course, a toilet break is permitted!"

She paused, looking a little embarrassed.

"Sorry, that was inappropriate," she admitted. "Working with Inspector Baynes for a few years means that his sense of humour has rubbed off on me a little."

"Don't worry," I reassured her. "I suppose you don't get many murders up here—must be a shock to the system for you as well!"

"Oh, you'd be surprised!" she replied a little archly, and I wondered whether my comment had come across as the tiniest bit patronising.

"Anyway, I think that the old waterworks can hold out," I replied, hoping that I wouldn't come to regret it. She smiled, presumably reassured that nothing she was likely to say was going to come off as too awkward in a conversation with a man who used terms like "waterworks" at the drop of a hat.

"You don't know what questions I'm going to ask yet," Chen pointed out. My conscious brain was aware that this was supposed to be a joke, but the relevant synapses had obviously failed to pass the message on to the panic muscles in my face. She went on to tell me to relax. Which, of course, is always the one thing that will absolutely ensure that I won't.

"I want to delve a little more into the evening you referred to as Time Capsule Night," she explained. "Obviously we are not drawing any conclusions that it is in any way linked to Mr Dickinson's death, or that that's what was in the box, but as the inspector said, it's an avenue we'd like to explore."

"He definitely had the contents of the capsule with him," I insisted. "So if you don't find them, someone's swiped them! He hinted at least twice last night that he was proposing to reveal our predictions over the course of the weekend. I'm sure of that, because I had been rather hoping he'd forget!"

"Well, it's the possibility that you weren't alone in that desire that we need to look into," the sergeant said. "Why were you so keen to avoid him opening the capsule?"

"Well, I wasn't at my best in my early twenties," I admitted. "I was single at the time... plus ça change! And extremely prone to feeling sorry for myself. Not a habit I've entirely managed to shake, but it was horrifically self-indulgent in retrospect, given that I was getting the best education in the world in a place like this.

"Anyway, I think I predicted that everything would all go tits up for me. And given what high-flyers some of the others are now, I couldn't help worrying that they might think there was a ring of truth to it when they read it. They may well think so anyway, but this would only have served to draw their attention to my inadequacies. Plus, I was extraordinarily pissed at the time, so my spelling was probably horrendously off!"

DS Chen broke off from scribbling in her pad and paused to look at me.

"You're a city lawyer, right?" she asked pointedly.

"Well, yes, but there are city lawyers, and there are city lawyers!" I replied.

"Yeah, I'm not sure that the public at large is fully aware of that distinction!" she pointed out, making me feel a little sheepish. She continued to write, but for some reason the only words of mine that she felt the need to say out loud as she wrote were "Horrifically self-indulgent!" I squirmed on the hard, uncomfortable bed as I waited for her to finish and move on to the next question.

"Ed was a lawyer too, right?" she asked at last.

"Sort of. He gave up the dog-eat-dog world of transactional work a couple of years ago to become a professional support lawyer in the thrillingly edge-of-your-seat field of corporate tax."

"Professional support lawyer?"

"Backroom boys!" I explained. "The people who tell the transactional lawyers what the law is. They keep abreast of legal developments, draft precedents and generally avoid shouty clients. Good ones are worth their weight in gold. I was a bit surprised that Ed went down that route, though, to be honest. He was always more of a people person than I am, and I'd have thought he would have done quite well with his firm's client base. But then again, he did always like to avoid unnecessary hassle. The change came too late to rescue his hairline, though."

"OK. Let's go through, in turn, everyone who was there on Time Capsule Night. Let's start with your friend Britta. She's here with her husband, right?"

"Yes. They're the only couple whose relationship has lasted since uni. Never saw that one lasting, but the fact that she was already Keith Cheggers when we took our finals may have had something to do with it."

"Keith Cheggers?"

"Oh, sorry. Rhyming slang, I'm afraid. 'Great with child' is probably the more appropriate term. Young Aaron turned up around Bonfire Night that year, so he must have been already en route when she was taking her exams."

"So what was Britta like at the time?" the sergeant asked.

"Much the same as she is now, only more so," I chortled. "Motherhood calmed her down a bit, but she's still a bit of a force of nature. Not massively focused, but she's got a huge appetite for life and everything it throws at her. She's also got a filthily inappropriate sense of humour. She and Steve even turned up to a Wild West-themed bop once dressed as Fred and Rosemary! She's highly affectionate to her mates but has never given much of a damn about what anyone else thought of her. Great fun to be around. Always hung out with the lads as much as the ladies!"

"Was that unconventional?" Chen asked, and once again, I was getting the impression of a silent reproach.

"Oh, everything Britta does is unconventional!" I joked, deftly skirting over the meat of the question and hiding out in the safety of the side salad. "But the thought of her as a real murderer is ludicrous."

"Why?"

"Well, look, I've known her for nearly twenty years," I blustered.

"Doesn't that apply to almost everyone in your group?" Chen asked, hammering home the likely reality that one of my oldest friends had just been murdered by another one, whichever of them it turned out to be. Could that really be the case? Surely there had to still be the possibility of an outside job, whatever Gavin said. And come to think of it, Gavin himself was hardly a paragon of trustworthiness, and he'd had as much opportunity as anyone to wield the knife.

"Well, I suppose so, but surely if I'm out, she's out. She was sleeping on C Block, same as me."

"What would you expect her to have written as a prediction in the time capsule?" Chen demanded, pointedly failing to acknowledge my point.

I paused to think about it.

"Something frivolous, I would imagine. Can't see it being anything she'd be massively worried about, though. She's not exactly the easily embarrassed type, our Britta. Presumably you're going to ask the same question about everyone?"

"That was the general idea," Sergeant Chen confirmed. "Shall we move on to her other half, then?"

"Neil? How would I describe him? Well, he's the strong and silent type, I suppose. Works for one of the Big Four accountancy firms, but for a bean counter, he's very keen on the outdoors and extreme sports."

"What do you think his time capsule prediction would have been?"

"Can't imagine it would have been anything too controversial. He's an amiable chap, Neil, but his sense of humour is not particularly well developed."

"And he was dating Britta throughout your time at uni?"

"No. There was a bit of musical chairs along the way. Mostly pretty amicable, though. Britta dated Steve Taylor in our first year, but that was always too volatile to turn into anything more durable. Steve could be pretty intense and moody. Neil dated Tanya that year and into the middle of our second year. Then they split up, and he and Britta started up a few weeks later."

"You said you never saw that relationship lasting. Why do you think they're so incompatible?"

"Well, truth be told, I've always found him a bit dull, although I suppose I ought to give him credit for a smidgen of dynamism, given that he used to be a bit of a daredevil. Think Bear Grylls meets Gonzo from The Muppets. Only less furry than either!" My stomach rumbled with an embarrassing degree of noisy gusto. Mentioning "Grylls" had served to remind me that I had not had any breakfast yet.

"Anyway, to fully answer your question, I always thought that Neil would end up with a fellow adventurer. Someone who he could exchange vows with whilst skydiving. He might have got Britta that far, until the accident at least, but a honeymoon spent rattling around the Mid-Atlantic in a lifeboat with a topless adrenalin nut and three days' supply of weevilly biscuits wouldn't have been her style at all."

"The accident?" Chen asked.

"Britta fell off a roof at one of Ed's parties at Chateau Dickinson, a couple of years after we left uni. She'd not taken to settling down as a young mother, so had left young Aaron in his father's care for the evening and had proceeded to get herself as pissed as the proverbial Gingrich. It was touch and go for a bit whether she'd ever walk again, as I recall. It single-handedly killed Neil's thrill-seeking urges, though, as you might imagine."

"Did either of them blame Ed for the accident?"

"I don't think so. I mean, his bashes were usually pretty debauched affairs, but it's not as if he forced those voddy and cokes down her gullet, is it?"

"Who else was there?" Sergeant Chen pressed me.

"Most of the others, I think. I couldn't make it myself; I only found out later."

"Where did this happen? You mentioned Chateau Dickinson, which I presume is another example of your weird Cantabrigian rhyming slang?"

"Just a nickname, in this instance," I said with a grin. "Daddy Dickinson was a property developer from Billericay who took his son's offer of a place at St Crisps as an opportunity to get on the Cambridge property ladder. He snapped up a small house just off Jesus Green and rented it out at a generous discount to Ed and three mates during our third year. Then, in subsequent years, younger students moved in. Although they didn't get the discount, naturally. It was often empty over the summer, so Ed sometimes borrowed the place for parties after we left, until his old man got fed up and decided to sell it. That was where Time Capsule Night happened, actually."

"Sadly, I wasn't living there as I wasn't one of the 'three musketeers' who made the cut. I was relegated to the Roy Kinnear role and shunted off up the hill to a ghastly concrete monstrosity on the way to Girton."

"A bit of a trek into town," Chen commented.

"You can say that again! By Cambridge standards, it's Outer Mongolia, only with slightly fewer yaks. I was licking my wounds for a while after missing out, I can tell you."

"So who were the lucky three, then?"

"Oh, well, Steve was obviously a shoo-in for one of the spots, as was Niamh."

"Niamh?"

"Ed's then girlfriend. Irish girl, who we always called 'The Gymnast.' I lost a coin-toss to Dan for the last room."

"Niamh didn't make the reunion? I haven't heard her name mentioned until now."

"No, well, there's a bit of a story behind that. She was a Natsci, you see, and…"

"A Nazi?"

"No, no, no, no, no," I backtracked hastily. "Well, not as far as I know, anyway. Natsci. Natural Sciences. Except that it turned out she was far from a natural scientist. Sometimes, the admissions people just really cock it up, you know. I've spent the last couple of decades wondering if I was the beneficiary of one of those cock ups, to be honest. But I managed to do OK in the exams in the end. Poor old Niamh, not so much. Poor girl failed her second year."

"But didn't Time Capsule Night happen in your third year?" Chen asked.

"Well, that's the thing. Everyone had made their accommodation arrangements for that final year well before the second-year exam results came out, and Niamh just didn't tell anyone she'd been kicked out of college. Not us, not her parents. I guess she felt humiliated, but she must have been terrified the entire time. I have no idea what her end game was, and I'm guessing she didn't either. Anyway, her parents found out first, at some point during the second term, and turned off the money taps. So Niamh wasn't able to pay Ed the rent. She managed to hang on in there for a few months with empty promises that the money was coming in any day now. But eventually, it must have been shortly after Time Capsule Night, she broke down and told Ed the whole story."

"And how did Ed react?"

"Badly. He felt pretty ashamed of himself in retrospect, but at the time, he felt used and betrayed. The "betrayed" part was a bit rich, to be honest, given his complete inability to keep his own trouser zip fastened whilst in a relationship. To my certain knowledge, he'd already cheated on her three times by that point. But all are not saints who go to church, as the saying goes. He, Steve and Dan behaved very heavy-handedly. We're talking packing her bags for her and throwing them out on the street. I only heard about it afterwards, and I don't think I ever saw her again. I think Britta and Tanya kept in touch with her, but the rest of us were pretty bloody useless."

"Do you know what happened to her?"

"No idea," I sighed. "I think she moved back to Dublin, although her parents had practically disowned her. I guess that if anyone had a good reason to want a dead Ed, it was her. But it's no good, of course. Ed would never have invited her, so how would she have known we were even here?"

"Unless someone told her," Chen pointed out. I was about to point out that that "someone" would also have had to tell her which room Ed had been staying in, but decided to hold my tongue. This was something she could quite easily have worked out for herself and, indeed, had undoubtedly already done so.

"Apart from Niamh," she went on, "was there anyone who contributed to the time capsule who didn't show up last night?"

"The only person I can think of is Random Chris—Chris Cleghorn, that is—who's gone off-grid..."

"Off-grid?"

"Well, we all just lost touch with him. I presume Ed couldn't get hold of a number for him."

"Did Ed say that?"

"No. Chris' name didn't come up last night, as far as I can remember." Chris had been a Northern lad, hailing from Bakewell. I only remember that much because he had invited a crowd of us up there to visit him once, and we had thoroughly disgraced ourselves by getting exceedingly drunk and wandering around the town centre in the dead of night demanding to know where the tarts were.

He had been known as "Random Chris" due to his tendency to turn up unannounced at parties hosted by people at best only slightly known to him, treat his hosts like lifelong buddies and make himself at home, usually at the very point that the bona fide guests were on the point of departure. We Brits are a reserved bunch, and generally too polite to point out to people when they have not, technically speaking, made the invite list. Chris had exploited this characteristic shamelessly to bag himself a hell of a lot of free beer in his three years. In a sense, the fact that we had all subsequently lost touch with him actually made it more surprising that he hadn't made it last night.

"OK," Chen said, turning a page in her notebook. "Tell me about Dan Finn."

"Dan is even less easily embarrassed than Britta," I said. "He'll have written something childish and stupid, but I just

72

don't think he would care. Although, actually, it might have been quite sad, come to think of it. He had a long-term girlfriend, Hannah, at the time. They'd been together since they were sixteen, and he was dead set on spending the rest of his life with her. Besotted, he was. She was at uni at Durham, and he was a completely different person whenever she was down, although he got seriously pissed off if anyone mentioned that. I think he was terrified that his status as one of the lads would have been put in jeopardy if we found out what an old softie he really was."

"What happened to her?" Chen asked softly.

"Killed in a skiing accident a couple of years after graduation. Dan was on the holiday with her, but he wasn't on the slopes at the time. He always preferred the après-ski to the actual skiing. Ed and Neil were there and did their best to help him keep it together, but he went into a long period of deep depression after that. He had been the one to book the holiday so he blamed himself. Really grim." I paused. "We're a pretty accident-prone bunch, it seems."

Chen did not respond, and I felt myself tearing up again, so hastily tried to move things along.

"Who's next? I'll bet you want to talk about Jammy Jeffers! Or were you saving that treat for last?"

"No, we can talk about him now." Chen smiled. "Anything in particular you would like to get off your chest about that titan of British politics?"

"Well, if we're focussing on Time Capsule Night, he was going out with Sadie Simmons at the time. Fortunately for Britain's sake, that relationship only lasted a couple of months. As a power couple those two would have made Lord and Lady Macbeth look like John and Norma Major. Jammy's politics have evolved a fair stretch since those days, of course. He had a pretty un-PC sense of humour back then, as well. Would he have been stupid enough to put anything inappropriate in writing? Undoubtedly!"

"Is Jammy currently in a relationship?"

"Well, he got married a couple of years ago to another semi-high flyer in the Labour Party, but I think they may be separated now. He made some slightly nauseating comment last night, about getting his knob away (his words, not mine) at the most recent party conference. Which must have been an enjoyable minibreak."

Sergeant Chen stifled a giggle.

"And Sadie?" she went on after a moment, poker face fully restored.

"Oh, God knows. She's doing OK as a barrister, but I suspect she had ambitions of taking silk, which clearly isn't going to happen now. She might have put something in the time capsule about that, but it's not much of a motive for murder, is it?"

"What about her love life?"

"Oh, there she was even more ambitious," I said with a chuckle. "Desperately trying to hook up with David Williamson, our EU law supervisor. When she wasn't trying to get her claws into Steve, that is!"

"Is that Steve Taylor?" I nodded. Sergeant Chen checked her notes. "He was one of Ed's closest friends, correct?"

"Indeed," I confirmed. "The fact that he managed to get Steve up here at all is testament to that. Steve's an aggressive workaholic. Trying to pin him down for a social activity over the last few years has been like wrestling an eel. I've always got the impression that his wife, Lydia, doesn't approve of most of us, which probably contributes to his general elusiveness."

"Did she approve of Ed?"

"Definitely not. She's quite a neurotic and disapproving character, although she was planning on gracing us with her presence this evening, apparently. Ed looked a bit disappointed when Steve told him last night. Probably concerned that

Lydia's presence was going to put a dampener on her husband's enthusiasm for juvenile hijinks. But Lydia only entered the picture after we graduated. Back at uni, Ed and Steve were inseparable most of the time, despite being a bit of an odd couple themselves, I guess. Ed was an optimistic sort, but Steve's very much on the opposite side when it comes to the glass half full versus glass half empty debate. Personally, I have always been more of a 'let me top that glass up for you' sort of a bloke, but that's by the by."

"I notice you said 'most of the time.' Did they ever fall out?"

"There was an incident," I admitted. "I never managed to get to the bottom of the source of their tension as they were both pretty tight-lipped about it, but Ed did something Steve found hard to forgive. Whatever it was left them barely on speaking terms for the better part of a term. It had all blown over long before Time Capsule Night, though."

"What would Steve have written in the time capsule, do you think?"

"Good question," I acknowledged, taking a moment to ruminate. "He's always had slightly morbid tendencies, has Steve. Hanging around with him tended to involve a bizarre mixture of long, drunken 3am conversations about the futility and worthlessness of human existence, and inappropriate practical jokes and prank calls. Maybe marriage has tamed his demons a bit. I don't really know. Sorry, I'm not being much help, am I?"

Sergeant Chen gave me a reassuring smile. "Utterly useless," she agreed.

"Well, look, I don't want to waste any more of your time on a wild goose chase…"

"It's true that the motives so far seem a bit paltry," she admitted. Her expression remained deadpan, but she had definitely pronounced it "poultry." Was that a deliberate pun, I wondered? I must admit I was rapidly developing a bit of a fancy for this petite policewoman with the irregular sense of humour.

"Still," she went on, turning the page on her notebook, "there's time to redeem yourself. Let's talk about Tanya Bullock. She was an English student, right? Now a fellow at St Matthew's College, Oxford?"

"Spot on, although I wouldn't have been able to remember the college. One doesn't pay too much attention when it's The Other Place. But Tanya's not your girl," I insisted forcefully. "She's a real sweetie. Barely a malicious bone in her body."

"What sort of comment do you think she would have put in the time capsule?"

"I don't know, although she was going through a bit of a rough time at that point, even leaving aside the looming existential threat of finals, so it might have been a tad on the gloomy side."

"Was this because of her break-up with Neil?"

"Oh no, that was ancient history by that point. They were another odd couple who obviously hadn't ever been likely to last the distance. Tanya is very much a creature of comfort, or at least she was back in those days. She liked dressing gowns, slippers, tea and musty library smells. Neil liked adventuring, rock-climbing, crossing the Atlantic in small yachts and trekking to see polar bears near the Arctic Circle. And then punching them in the face, probably."

"So what else was going on with her?"

"Well, if you must know, she'd run someone over during the Christmas hols that year. Tanya was never much of a drinker, so she tended to assume the role of designated driver more than her fair share of the time, and she hadn't had anything to drink that night. And that's on the record," I added defensively. "She'd been at a party hosted by one of the rich boatie wankers in the year below us, somewhere in Saffron Walden I think. Not being rich, or a boatie, I wasn't invited.

Not sure how Tanya made the cut, but I can only assume RBW had vague aspirations of getting inside her knickers."

"Anyway, Ed was there as well, and she was ferrying him home at the end of the evening. She hit an old gentleman on one of those nasty country roads with sharp corners. Nothing she could have done, but it completely broke her spirit. Turned out the poor bloke had been a philosophy lecturer at Wolfson College, so it wasn't as if getting back into Cambridge life even offered an escape route for her."

I broke off uncomfortably, feeling weirdly as though I had somehow committed a gross act of betrayal and pointed the finger of suspicion at Tanya by revealing all this, even though the evidently capable Chen was bound to have dredged the story up pretty quickly anyway. There ensued a short period of silence as the sergeant finished her prodigious note-taking. The sheer quantity of her efforts seemed to be vastly out of proportion to anything I had actually said, which made me feel just a little uneasy. Eventually, she finished up, turned to me and asked abruptly, "What are your plans for the rest of the day?"

"Now?" I paused. "Well, I have no idea. I had been expecting a jolly day out in Cambridge. Take in a few pubs, perhaps even get out on a punt if I could persuade someone else to take on the heavy lifting. We all had a dinner booked at The Ivy this evening. I don't think anyone's going to be in the mood for any of that now, though."

"You were scheduled to be in Cambridge the whole weekend?" Chen asked. I nodded.

"Good. It would be helpful if you don't leave Cambridge until further notice," she said in a tone that suggested I would be tap dancing on very thin ice indeed if I failed to follow this recommendation. "We'll be in touch if we have any more questions."

We shook hands. Her handshake was stronger than mine,

and significantly less sweaty.

"Nice meeting you," she added.

Nice meeting me? Were policewomen supposed to say that? I looked at her in surprise, and she did not seem quite able to look me in the eye. Was I imagining things, I wondered, or had I proved to be an unexpected hit with Detective Sergeant Jacqueline Chen?

CHAPTER 3

In which Gerald Sinclair takes me under his wing, feeds me up like a plump waffle-worm, brings me back to his nest and introduces me to his family, and I receive a spectral message.

I

Castle Hill, Cambridge, is an interesting spot in a number of respects.

Firstly, it is, and has been for many thousands of years, the highest landmark for miles around. Secondly, it is the site not only of the original Roman settlement of Duroliponte but also of Cambridge Castle, which was built by the Normans and massively expanded by King Edward I, aka Longshanks, the man famous for wanting to kill Mel Gibson long before such views became fashionable.

Sadly, the castle fell into disrepair in the fourteenth century, and Mad King Henry VI decided to exercise his royal prerogative to pilfer much of the remaining stonework to build King's College and Trinity Chapel, amongst other things. The upshot of which is that there's not much left there now for Indiana Jones or Tony Robinson to get their respective archaeological teeth into. The hill itself has hung about, though, as hills are wont to do, and it still boasts one of the best views of Cambridge you can get, assuming you don't have a helicopter handy.

You may have gathered by now that I am not one of life's

natural athletes. I am not the sort of fellow who will spring energetically into action when flopping flabbily off the couch and sauntering sedately in the direction of the nearest fridge remains an option. Castle Hill, however, is on a scale that even a chap like me can handle, and it always used to be my go-to spot for walking off a hangover. The nearby village of Grantchester is another option for that if you want a longer stretch of the legs. But then again, if you're hungover, you're probably wanting to avoid the Grantchester pubs, several of which are rather good, and there's not much else there except Jeffrey Archer and that rather smug crime-solving vicar.

At this point, the hangover was not affecting me too much, the trauma of my close friend's brutal murder having dropkicked it firmly off the top of the "matters affecting Roger Whiteley's delicate constitution" chart. But the hill was as good a place as any I could think of to try to clear my head and get my shit together, as the charming saying goes, and so that was where my legs took me after Sergeant Chen had finished with me.

Arriving at the lofty summit, a staggering twenty-five metres or so above sea level, I took a moment to take in the view. To my left, said view mostly consisted of trees stretching out into the distance, with the odd crane poking its head up through the foliage. Ahead of me, behind the stark, sloping slate roof of the Church of St Giles, stretched the turret-strewn City of Cambridge in all its pint-sized, picture-book majesty. To my right, the University Library—home to over eight million books and manuscripts and designed by the great gothic modernist Sir Giles Gilbert Scott (the same fellow who brought us the red telephone box)—loomed up in the distance like a rather sinister Jenga tower.

"Phallic monstrosity," I heard a familiar plummy voice muttering sardonically, directly behind me.

"Who are you calling a..." I thundered indignantly,

spinning around on the spot, only to break off, like a spluttering beached goldfish gasping for breath, when I saw who it was.

"Germaine Greer put it best, I think," Gerald Sinclair went on, beaming at me indulgently and gesturing back towards the "UL", as we Cantabrigians call it, with a flamboyant flourish of the pink umbrella he was brandishing. The umbrella had a flamingo handle with more than a passing resemblance to its owner. Its presence was a typical display of forward-thinking from Sinclair, and my lack of an equivalent probably said just as much about me. So far, I had been lucky. The clouds above us were threatening a spot of light drizzle, but at the moment, they were still at the "Do you feel lucky, punk?" stage of their threat, and just like Clint Eastwood, it was far from clear whether they were really proposing to make good on it.

"'To us', she once wrote, 'its undeniable ugliness is as irrelevant as the warts on the face of a beloved mother!'"

Well, it's damned difficult to come up with a witty retort when someone has just put the image of Germaine Greer's warty old mum into your head. As such, it was Sinclair who ended up providing the filling for the awkward pause that ensued.

"It's quite a view, though, isn't it? You can't see as far as usual today, of course. A bit too dreich for that, as we Scots are wont to put it. But on a good day, you can see a decent chunk of the city from here and even as far as Ely Cathedral.

"Cambridge has changed a fair bit over the last few years, of course, but mainly on the outskirts. Not much the City Council can do about the middle, what with the university spreading its tentacles everywhere like a languid octopus. So the city's spreading outwards instead! Soulless new developments encircling the town like an ever-expanding doughnut of despondency. But I'm rabbiting again! You're the returning hero, Whiteley; what do you think? Is Cambridge as you remember it?"

"More stabby," I replied darkly.

"Yes, well, that's academia for you!" Sinclair chuckled fondly. The smile drained from his face, however, when he noticed my failure to give this line the rich guffaw he doubtless felt it deserved.

"Are you all right, my dear chap? You look like death warmed up, if you don't mind my saying so!"

I told him what had happened. Sinclair remained inscrutable as I spoke, gazing fixedly at his flamingo, who stared stupidly back at him. Whilst he was clearly listening intently, the professor's hands could not stop fidgeting, and if he had been a cartoon character, I'm pretty sure his nose would have been twitching. That's not to imply that he was taking any ghoulish pleasure in the situation, however, and his expression when I finished speaking was grim.

"Poor Dickinson. I remember supervising him. A resolutely average student but pleasant enough company. Did the bare minimum to avoid looking stupid, but he got away with it in the end, as I recall. Not a literary man, of course. I once told him that I would have got a more coherent essay from Mr Dick, which was, of course, an allusion to David Copperfield. From the blankness of his reaction, I assume he thought I was making some sort of grotesque penis joke. Or possibly that Mr Dick was a Roger Hargreaves character!"

As he spoke, I felt a profound sense of relief that there was no realistic possibility of Sinclair being called upon to give a speech at Ed's funeral. Talk about damning with faint praise!

"Murder in college." Sinclair was muttering to himself now. "Emily will be most put out. This will need to be resolved quickly and discreetly. Do you remember the name of the inspector you spoke to?"

"Baynes," I said. "Couldn't quite get the measure of him. Felt like Hagrid doing an impression of Columbo."

"Oh that's very good!" Sinclair tittered. "I've known Torvill

Baynes for years. His nickname down at the station is 'Taters' because he talks a bit like Sam Gamgee, but don't let that fool you. He's the best of the bunch—sharp as a hedgehog's prickles. Still, he might need a hand with this one, given that it's 'gown' not 'town,' as 'twere!"

"He didn't seem to like Gavin the Porter very much," I commented.

"Yes, well, that's doubtless due to familiarity!" Sinclair grinned, then turned to look at me again. Seeing my evident discomfort, he adopted a more compassionate expression.

"My dear Whiteley, I can't imagine the shock you must have had. But loafing around up here won't help you, you know!"

Under normal circumstances, his incessant dynamism and energy would have been starting to grate on me by this point, but I was surprised to find myself actually feeling a little better for speaking to Sinclair. The morning's events had felt so shocking, so chaotic and so out of control, and here was a peculiar little man apparently trying to restore some semblance of order to my fractured universe. I could not help but feel grateful.

"What do you think I should be doing?" I asked, at this point perfectly willing to be "taken in hand" and given a direction of travel.

"We, my dear boy, we!" Sinclair corrected me. "I can't leave you to your own devices at a time like this! What sort of supervisor would I be?"

I was about to point out that he had ceased to be my supervisor some seventeen years ago. But then again, I reflected, perhaps that was when it had all started going wrong.

"Hang it all, man, let's go for a waffle!" Sinclair declared after a moment's reflection. "I know a good place in Lion's Yard. You can fill your belly and tell me everything!"

"In the dry," he added, opening his umbrella and heading

for the steps leading back down to civilisation, and waffles.

II

Given that (height-wise) I have a good few inches on Sinclair, I had not expected to be rushing to keep up with my former supervisor on the way down Castle Hill, but he turned out to be quite a bustler. In what felt like no time at all, we had made it down the hill, Castle Street had turned into Magdalene Street, then Bridge Street, then Sidney Street, and before we knew it, we were back in what I have always regarded as the town centre.

We headed to Lion's Yard, and a few minutes later we had made it to the front of the queue of Sinclair's recommended eatery. I looked at the menu and chuckled in spite of myself. Only in Cambridge would they name their waffles after well-known scientific geniuses. We ordered a "Turing" for me and a "Maxwell" for Sinclair (presumably named after James Clerk rather than Robert), and settled down to enjoy our fruit, chocolate and ice-cream bedecked snacks.

"Let's take them outside," Sinclair suggested, heading for one of the tables out front. After a few half-arsed specks of rain, the weather gods had, in the end, decided we weren't worth the effort of tormenting and had presumably breezed off to plague the citizens of Waterbeach or somewhere else in the neighbourhood.

"Why not?" I agreed, feeling vaguely contented for the first time that day. "The weather seems to be turning."

"Ah, well, that's because Aslan has returned to us!" Sinclair chortled, gesturing with his fork at a large, cheerful-looking, leonine Chow Chow who was reclining regally next to our table and admiring our waffles. He wagged his tail optimistically and beamed at us as we approached.

"You'd better resist his charm offensive," Sinclair warned.

"I'm told he's watching his waistline!"

"That makes two of us," I grimaced, giving the magnificent beast an "I feel your pain, buddy" look. I hope this went some way to compensate him for the fact that I was unrepentantly wolfing down what he had clearly regarded as his treat, right in front of his poor, hopeful eyes.

"You know, I seem to recall that 'waffle' was your adjective of choice when marking my essays!" I remarked whilst trying to avoid getting chocolate on my shirt. "Hadn't realised until now it was a compliment!"

Sinclair tittered.

"Well, you did have a tendency to go on a bit," he reminded me. I winced. Of the various essays I had submitted to him over the course of my three years, the one he had been most positive about was the one where I had inadvertently failed to hand in the first page. He had scrawled "A Powerful Start!" on the top of what had in fact been page 2. When I had realised my error and belatedly handed in page 1, he had ended up marking me down a grade.

"Pot, kettle!" I retorted amiably, thinking back to some of his rather dry, rambling seminars.

"Touché, my boy. Touché! And I will freely admit that I fell asleep during one of my own lectures once. But the expression 'don't do as I do, do as I tell you!' springs to mind! Anyway, enough of such tomfoolery—let's get down to business. I will of course take the case!"

"Well, I'm not sure anyone actually asked..."

"Don't try to talk me out of it, Whiteley," Sinclair replied grandly, holding a hand up. "I can't have people going around bumping off my ex-supervisees without permission! And Emily will want this dealt with promptly and efficiently. Heaven knows what a murder in college will do to our donor base. Although, for all I know, some of those appalling ghouls might actually increase their donations off the back of this. I have no idea; I don't really get involved in that side of things!"

I couldn't think why.

"And I do have a certain knack for winkling the truth out of even the most seemingly unprofitable lines of investigation," he went on modestly. "And it's just as well that somebody is able to do so around here! If you believe what you see on the television, of course, it's Oxford where all the dark and dastardly deeds are kicking off. I mean, I enjoy *Inspector Morse* as much as the next man. In moments of weakness, I even find myself occasionally tuning in to its various spin-offs, which spent twenty years flogging a dead Morse. But if you're really seeking out a truly wretched hive of scum and villainy, I present you with Cambridge City Centre!"

"Have you ever thought of applying for a job in the tourist information centre?" I asked innocently. Sinclair pursed his lips, fixed me with the sort of hard stare that one normally only receives from ursine Peruvians, and calmly navigated the conversation back onto more fertile terrain.

"You're no doubt wondering what I think of your pet theory about the time capsule?" He was, of course, completely right. If a chap as clever as Sinclair thought of it as a plausible prospect, it would give me the reassurance I needed that I wasn't going mad and wasting my time barking up a fruitless tree.

"Well," he ventured carefully, "I can think of no better way of answering your question than by looping back to Sherlock Holmes. "'If you eliminate the impossible, then whatever remains, however improbable, must be the truth!'"

"Unless there is another probable option also still on the table," I added pedantically. I could have added that when Sherlock Holmes had uttered that immortal phrase, he almost certainly wouldn't have had a small blob of strawberry ice cream on the end of his nose. But I refrained from pricking the old boy's balloon of vanity at this juncture.

"Given the time pressures Conan Doyle was under, I think we can forgive him a few logical leaps," Sinclair said sniffily. "The Sherlock Holmes stories are works of literary genius!"

"Could never get on with them myself," I responded. This was not entirely accurate, but I was in the mood for a bit of mischief, and I wanted to see his reaction. Sinclair peered coldly at me through his spectacles. There was a long, chilly silence, except for a low growl emanating from our friend Aslan.

"I have wasted my waffle money on a footling philistine," the good professor sighed at last.

"Well, I read them as a teenager, and my teenage sense of humour couldn't get past all the times Holmes is described as stopping in the street and suddenly ejaculating!" I explained.

"More repressed times, Whiteley. Things have to come out somehow! But anyway, as I was saying before you revealed yourself to be a complete and utter numpty, I actually think you might be onto something!"

"You do?"

"Indeed! To get to the bottom of this, we need to get to grips with why our killer made his decision, and to understand the decision, we need to break it down into its constituent parts. He, or she, did not just decide to kill your friend Mr Dickinson. He, or she, decided specifically to kill him last night rather than at some other time. Despite the fact that he was staying in a locked college. If the killer had wanted to narrow the pool of suspects, he, or she, could not have timed it more perfectly! But why on earth would he, or she, want that?"

"You don't have to keep saying 'he or she,' you know," I broke in. "All those pronouns are breaking your flow."

"Oh good." Sinclair looked relieved. "Well then, given that you're obviously a fellow unreconstructed troglodyte, let's call our killer 'Johnny Murderer'!

"Why would dear old Johnny not wait for a better

opportunity to strike? He may have thought there would not be another chance, but why? Mr Dickinson, I understand, worked in London. A bustling metropolis where a killer could easily strike at an opportune moment and then immediately vanish away into the sea of worker drones (no offence)!

"Unless it was a crime of passion, which seems unlikely, given that it does not explain why Johnny ransacked and vandalised the red box, the answer must be that, even at the cost of limiting the number of suspects, Mr Dickinson needed to be silenced immediately!"

Sinclair leaned forward with his eyebrows raised high.

"In other words, any delay would be even more fatal than, well, actually killing someone! And we know, or can be pretty sure, that your friend was proposing to open the time capsule tonight!"

"Which means that one of my friends is a killer," I said grimly.

"Oh, I wouldn't worry too much about that," Sinclair reassured me breezily. "In my line of work, I have to fraternise with all sorts of ne'er do wells! One gets used to it!"

"Yes, but you're a criminologist. Having to spend time with criminals sort of comes with the turf!"

"Oh yes, those ne'er do wells too. I was actually thinking about the students!" Sinclair chuckled. "But there remains an outside possibility that someone broke into college. It would have had to have been someone who knew the college grounds extremely well, though. Either that, or they must have done a hell of a lot of homework."

"Mad Dog McFadden!" I suddenly ejaculated (Conan Doyle's style is catching). "He was loitering outside college last night, very drunk, singing Willy Wonka songs."

"Really?" Sinclair put his hands together as if in prayer and pursed his lips. "Well, that is slightly suspicious behaviour even by his standards. McFadden would certainly have had the opportunity and the means. If he hasn't got knives stashed away in secret lockups all over Cambridge, I would be very surprised. Probably the motive, too, if being a complete maniac counts as motive. But I can't see why he would target Dickinson specifically. And I suppose I am right in assuming, am I not, that you and your comrades in drunkenness and debauchery did not invite Finlay McFadden to submit an entry for the time capsule?"

"God, no! None of us would have dared!"

"That's what I thought. And yet," he pondered, "it does not preclude his having been mentioned in someone else's prediction!"

"I really can't see any of us predicting a substantial role for a psychotic Porter in our future lives!" I scoffed. Sinclair looked at me a little testily.

"Well, look, if our theory is correct..." he began. *'Our' theory? Cheeky bugger*!

"If our theory is correct," he repeated, almost as if he had been interrupted by my reproving thoughts, "I think we can safely assume that at least one person in your crowd has written something a little more unconventional than the usual 'I'm going to move to St Albans and have two children and three cats and a motorbike and a mid-life crisis and an expanding waistline' drivel!"

He paused to finish the last remnants of his waffle. Aslan was now looking incredibly reproachful. A thought suddenly struck me.

"You saw this coming!" I exclaimed. "All that portentous Ides-of-March stuff you were coming out with on the train yesterday, insinuating that old Albert Ross had been bumped off!"

"Finlay McFadden saw it happen, and his suspicions dovetail with my own, as you may have gathered from his little outburst yesterday evening," Sinclair explained. "Not the first time the poor fellow has seen a man die, of course, but it must still have given a forceful jolt to his already unstable mental state. But that doesn't mean he was wrong."

"But you specifically asked about my intake. Do you think they're connected? What do you know that you're not telling me?"

"Steady on, Whiteley! I most certainly did not see it coming, and at this stage, I'm not sure I 'know' anything. I am merely starting to formulate the very inkiest of inklings. But rest assured that I will share my suspicions with you. At the apposite moment, of course!

"Listen, I don't know what you're planning to do with the rest of your day," he went on. "But I have a spare hour or so, which I had earmarked for tidying my study and clipping my toenails. I feel that I now know you well enough to involve you in at least one of these activities. I own a lot of heavy books, as you might imagine, and the assistance of a strapping young man like yourself would be invaluable. We can continue to explore this avenue of investigation, and any others that might occur to us, as we work!

"Come on," he added, his tone signifying that a negative response to his invitation would go down like a lead balloon tethered to a stink bomb, "wolf it down! The game's afoot!"

III

I was surprised to discover that Sinclair still had the same study that he had used for our supervisions all those years ago. For some reason, I had assumed that when he had received his free upgrade from Learned Don to Master's Husband, he would have moved his motley array of tomes and texts across to the Master's Lodge. When I put this to him, he laughed.

"No, I'm a creature of habit! This room suits my needs perfectly. They'd have to prise my fingernails from the paintwork of the doorway to get me out of here. And I'm reasonably confident that Emily wouldn't countenance such a brutal eviction," he added, chuckling a little nervously.

I had wondered whether he really needed the better part of an hour to clean his study. However, on taking one look at the messy piles of paper and precarious towers of books covering virtually every inch of his thickly carpeted floor, I started to worry about whether I was going to make it to dinner. It took us a couple of minutes even to notice the small boy sitting behind a particularly high stack of books, working on what looked ominously like a maths textbook whilst idly twiddling a Rubik's cube in his spare hand.

"Ah, you've stumbled upon my son Jasper," Sinclair beamed proudly. Jasper was a small, gangling little chap whose face consisted primarily of a large pair of eyes, possibly even sharper than his father's, and an even larger, and currently runnier, nose. "What are you doing in here, old chap?"

Jasper paused and looked pointedly at the exercise book that was open in front of him.

"Maths homework," he eventually piped up in a kindly tone that nevertheless gave the distinct impression that he considered his father, learned professor and celebrated criminologist though he was, to be a bit hard of thinking. "Mama has some donors in for lunch. She told me to skedaddle!"

Most small children his age would have attached a note of disdain to the words "maths homework." Jasper instead saved up the aforementioned disdainful note for the word "donors."

"Ah, well, I suspect that she thought that you'd find the grown-up chit-chat a bit boring!" his father explained reassuringly.

"It's not that. She didn't like my little joke!" Jasper sniffed.

"Ah," Sinclair grimaced. "You didn't say anything... scatological, did you?"

"What do you mean?" Jasper demanded, sounding a little affronted.

"Poos, wees and farts," I said, muscling my way into the conversation in the only way I knew how.

"I know what scatological means!" Jasper gave me a very grown-up look. "I'm just very disappointed in Daddy for suggesting that I would make such an appalling breach of etiquette! All I said was that they were all most welcome!"

"Well, that sounds all right," I declared, a little surprised and bemused.

"But not quite!"

Sinclair Senior threw back his head and whinnied with mirth, stepping over to his son and ruffling his hair affectionately. I chuckled too, in spite of myself, although naturally I was a split second slower on the uptake.

"I'm Roger," I introduced myself.

"Roger is one of my most...endearing ex-supervisees," Sinclair explained. "He's come to me with a little problem, and he's graciously agreed to help tidy up a bit around here whilst we tease it out!"

"Is it about the body?" Jasper asked excitedly.

"Oh good lord, has word spread already?" I groaned. I am not quite sure why this came as such grim news to me. After all, a murder in Cambridge—on a college campus, no less— was bound to be big news. But the fact that everyone knew, or would soon know, what had happened made it somehow feel as though the situation was slipping out of control, even though the objective, reasoned part of my brain knew full well that I, a mere witness, had at no point been in control of a single damn thing anyway.

"It's a small town, Whiteley," Sinclair reminded me. "Things will get about!"

"Are you sticking your oar in, Daddy?" Jasper persisted.

"The cheek of the boy!" Sinclair chuckled. "As it happens,

Mr Whiteley here has come to me with a potential line of enquiry. Given that he is a novice when it comes to this particular brand of skulduggery, I have concluded that the only responsible thing for me to do is to accompany him down his rabbit hole. That way, we can hopefully eliminate any risk of a Watership Down-style bloodbath!"

Jasper shuddered.

"Sorry, boy! Should have known better than to mention that film in your presence! Anyway, feel free to stick about while we tidy," Sinclair Senior went on, hoisting his first pile of books onto the table and sorting through them alphabetically.

"Will you still have time to read me some *To Kill a Mockingbird* later?" Jasper asked, in an outburst of literary enthusiasm that I found rather endearing.

"Of course!" Sinclair insisted. "I'm not letting some jumped-up murderer get in the way of introducing my son to the great works of modern literature!

"The trouble with having a wife who grew up in the States," he added, turning to me, "is that my attempts to affect an American accent when reading books of this nature are greeted with a rather unfair degree of ridicule. In an effort to avoid such mockery, I have had to resort to giving Atticus Finch a rather more colourful background than Harper Lee originally intended."

"Oh yes?" I replied, perplexed as ever by my ex-supervisor's meanderings.

"Yes. In my version, he's from Wolverhampton!" There was a knock at the door.

"Enter!" Sinclair thundered, and the Master of St Crispian's College entered the room. I had not seen Emily Morwyn for over a decade, and I was surprised and a tad resentful to see how little she had aged. Her black hair was still as dramatically wild as ever, with a single white lock now working its way through the left-hand side just above her ear like a jagged streak of lightning. Her expression was somewhat frazzled and harassed, but when her eyes lit on me, they softened sympathetically.

"Roger," she greeted me like a long-lost friend. "I'm so sorry about Ed."

And with that, she swept over to me, somehow navigating the myriad obstacles that her husband had left in between us without once having to look down, and enveloped me in the warm hug that I had so desperately needed all morning. Indeed, had I been alone with the Master, I would have dissolved into tears on the spot, which would have doubtless done wonders for getting my maelstrom of emotions out of the system.

As it was, however, the awkward looks that Messrs Sinclair and Sinclair were giving each other rather put me off. I got the impression that there was not much that made either Sinclair Senior or Sinclair Junior feel out of their depth, but interaction with normal human beings probably did the trick.

Eventually, and much too soon for my liking, Emily broke off the hug and whirled around to confront her husband.

"I might have known you would have got your claws into him already!" she huffed. As has already been alluded to, the Master had grown up in the States, with an American mother and an English father. Having now spent the majority of her existence back over here in the motherland, her voice only retained the faintest Transatlantic twang, which, to an untrained ear, almost sounded more Irish than American.

"I thought you'd be pleased, my dear," Sinclair said hesitantly, wringing his hands in a somewhat grovelling manner. "Duty to the college, and all that! We've got a scandal on our hands no matter what, but if we manage to knock it on the head, er, get it wrapped up as soon as possible, we can, ah, staunch the bleeding, as it were!"

"In spite of the hideously inappropriate analogy, given the

circumstances, I suppose you're right," Emily conceded. "But please try not to look like you're enjoying it. A man is dead, and that is no less of a tragedy just because he was a B-list supervisee! Gavin was bad enough. When he gleefully phoned me to report the news, he sounded like it was his birthday or something! I soon put paid to that attitude by coolly informing him that as the murderer must have either been let in by him or gained entry during his watch, I held him personally responsible until such time as the true culprit is found."

"Ah, well in that case, I might take the weekend off!" Sinclair chortled. "Let him sweat for a bit!"

"You seem to be discounting the possibility that the police will find the killer first," Emily pointed out.

"Stranger things have happened," Sinclair admitted, although there was a heavy note of scepticism in his voice. "You're quite right, though; we can't have that! And I've already made a start. Whiteley here has a theory that isn't completely cretinous!"

He briefly explained the bare bones of my theory.

"Can you draw the picture that you found?" Jasper piped up. I think all of us had almost forgotten he was still there. I duly obliged, producing the closest approximation that my limited artistic talents would allow.

"It's a charade!" Jasper declared immediately before I had even had the chance to put the lid back on the pen. His father looked disgruntled.

"I was about to say that!" he snapped peevishly. "Good grief, it's a proper little Wesley Crusher we've unleashed on the world, Emily! The weird curly shape on the left, that Whiteley here thought was a small letter 'c' inside a bigger one, is clearly an ear. So whatever we're looking for sounds like, um, bottle, apparently! Damn it, I don't know enough drunken ditties. Throw some rhymes at me! We'll see if anything sticks!"

"Throttle?" Emily suggested. "Mottle?"

"Glottal," was my contribution.

"Wattle?" Jasper suggested.

"Twaddle!" Sinclair grunted. "Oh my, what a conundrum. Perhaps 'bottle' isn't even the word we're looking for. Did Mr Dickinson ever strike you as a man with hidden depths, Whiteley?"

"Absolutely not!" I replied with complete confidence.

"Well, I'm just going to have to try to think the way he did," Sinclair sighed. "Although I may need a double dose of paracetamol if I spend too long down at that level, no offence, may his soul rest in eternal peace, etc! Have our esteemed donors naffed off yet, my dear? I think I'm going to need to spend some time with Lord Peter this afternoon!"

"Lord Peter?" I asked, befuddled by the thought of yet another peculiar unknown character being thrown into this unholy mix.

"That's what he calls his tuba," Jasper explained.

"Ah! I might have known it was a euphemism for something! You know Sherlock Holmes used to play the violin when he was trying to unravel a riddle," I pointed out.

"Yes. And I play the tuba!" Sinclair declared grandly.

"One might argue that one of those instruments is more, well, you know, 'great detective-y' than the other," I ventured provocatively. Sinclair's eyes bulged indignantly, and he drew himself up to his full height (for what that was worth).

"Only a moronic muttonhead who uses terms like 'great detective-y' would dare to impugn the reputation of my magnificent instrument!" he huffed. I saw Emily biting her lip.

"Well, whatever works for you," I said, picking up a pile of books, my tone now more conciliatory. I mustn't make fun, I told myself. Sinclair had gone out of his way to try to help me. Whilst he clearly had an ulterior motive for doing so, if he could work his way through this murky and tangled web of death and deceit, that only a few hours before had seemed like a harmless weekend jolly, it would come as an almighty relief.

"Will you stay for lunch, Roger?" Emily asked. "We put on a buffet for the donors, and there's plenty left over."

"That's not like those greedy gannets!" Sinclair muttered.

"And he wonders why I sent him for a walk before they arrived." Emily rolled her eyes.

"I'm OK for the moment, er, Master. Can I call you Emily now I've graduated?"

"Absolutely not!" she replied, but there was a look of amusement on her face.

"Anyway, I don't think I could eat anything just yet. I'm all full of waffle!"

"Plus ca change!" Sinclair murmured.

"I think after this, I might just potter around the Fitz for a bit," I went on, feeling as though I had already taken up enough of the Sinclair family's time. "Or maybe walk along the backs, then find a quiet pub and..."

I was interrupted by my phone buzzing. I took one look at it and almost dropped the infernal contraption in shock.

"Are you all right, Whiteley?" Sinclair asked. "It wasn't one of your clients, was it? At the risk of overusing a rather hackneyed cliché, you look like you've seen a ghost, my dear fellow!"

Not for the first or last time, my old supervisor had demonstrated an eerie prescience. Instead of responding, I merely laid down my phone on the table between us so that all of us could read the text I had just received. A text from a dead man.

"Rog, meet me in the University Arms as soon as you can. Come alone."

From: Ed Dickinson.

CHAPTER 4

In which I follow up a line of enquiry at the University Arms
Hotel and stumble into another one on Parker's Piece.

I

"Let me not burst in ignorance," Sinclair intoned, "but tell why thy canoniz'd bones, hears'd in death, have burst their cerements; why the sepulchre wherein we saw thee quietly inurn'd hath op'd its ponderous and marble jaws to cast thee up again!"

"What are you on about?" I spluttered.

"Daddy's quoting Hamlet again," Jasper explained wearily, following up his explanation with a pointed pause. The pause was presumably where the words "the pretentious old prick" would have slotted in neatly at the end of the sentence if the boy had been just a few years older. Even without any profane padding of this nature, Jasper's tone of voice was more than enough to demonstrate his disdain for his tedious old father's shameless Bard plundering.

"Was Ed's phone found on the body?" Emily asked, her sharp mind as ever slicing straight through the balderdash to the unexpectedly beating heart of the issue.

"No," I said, nervously recalling the rather tense few moments in the Porter's Lodge when Inspector Baynes had put me on the line to a killer. Who was now getting back to me!

"My G-God!" I stammered, so aghast that I was gulping down my "g"s like a middle-class Gollum. "My call obviously got the killer's attention. I can't believe Baynes put me in the firing line like this!"

"Yes, well, Torvill's approach is not always exactly what one might call protocoligorically correct," Sinclair said carefully, "but he gets results, you know! He was in Eswatini with Bob Macnab, and you know what that means!"

Jasper sniggered.

"That's all very well for you to say!" I snapped. "I'm being summoned to meet up with a murderer!"

"Let's not leap to conclusions, Whiteley," Sinclair cautioned me. "If the person who has purloined Mr Dickinson's mobile phone is the murderer, why is he making it so easy for us to identify him?"

"Or 'her'," Jasper added helpfully.

"If they aren't the killer, why would they have Ed's phone in the first place?" I asked.

"Well, that's what I suggest you toddle down to the University Arms to find out," Sinclair replied, taking my arm in a firm grasp and ushering me towards the door. "If you get into any trouble, hoot once like a barn owl and twice like a screech owl. I can guarantee that one of the motley crew of minions I've got scattered around the city will be on the scene within thirty to forty-five minutes. And do come straight back afterwards and report back. This is all starting to get rather lively!"

He steered me as far as the door. Then, as I made to go through it, he appeared to have a change of heart, refusing to let go of my now rather tender upper arm.

"You said that the plan was for all of you to go to dinner this evening?" he asked.

"Yes, that's right. We were all going to go to The Ivy. But I hardly think that now...well, no-one's going to be up for it, are they?"

"Not a bit of it!" Sinclair interrupted. "The show must go on. Dinner must be served! Dress it up as a celebration of the fact that the vast majority of the members of your social circle HAVEN'T been murdered yet! Glass half full, my laddo! If we're going to smoke this fiend out, we'll need to keep the blighter in Cambridge! If we don't crack this over the course of the weekend, there's every chance that our culprit will disappear off into the wide world and turn up in the jungles of Borneo with Lord Lucan and Shergar in a few years' time. Which might require me to start scurrying around further afield! And my brain doesn't work nearly as well when I get much beyond Trumpington!"

"Mill Road is pushing it," Jasper muttered loudly.

"Well, I'll do my best to persuade people," I replied dubiously, not feeling terribly confident about my chances. I had once participated in a Balloon Debate at school, and my efforts to convince my classmates not to throw God out of the balloon had been completely unsuccessful. Which would have been less embarrassing had the winner not been advocating for the survival of Russell Grant.

"Good man! In the meantime, I will work on solving your little charade so that we can go treasure hunting later!"

"Can I stay up till you've cracked it?" Jasper pleaded.

"Yes, yes," Sinclair reassured his son with a dismissive, absent-minded gesture, the great detective apparently oblivious to the warning looks his wife was giving him.

"You don't have to do this, Roger," Emily cautioned me. "You've had a horrible shock, and if you pass this message on to Torvill Baynes and let him deal with it, no-one will think any the less of you."

"I will!" Sinclair insisted, giving us both an unsympathetic sniff. "We can't give the police a head start, Emily! This murder was committed in your fiefdom!"

"It's not my fiefdom!" Emily sighed exasperatedly. "I'm the Master of the College, not a bloody Doge! Despite what you and the other overgrown children in the Porter's Lodge may think, the authority of the police doesn't end at the college gates! I've resigned myself to the fact that you will insist on endangering yourself with your little hobbies. Jasper and I would obviously miss you somewhat if you ever did end up on the receiving end of a brutal bludgeoning, but I am sure I could find another tuba player eventually, and it would spare Jasper from having to endure a Welsh Boo Radley. But you don't need to bring Roger into it!"

"He brought me into it!" Sinclair squeaked indignantly. "And he's only going to the University Arms! It's not exactly the Black Hole of Calcutta. Not since the refurb, anyway. It is staffed! You can't just bump people off willy-nilly in there! People would notice and make sniffy comments about it on Tripadvisor."

"It's fine, really," I reassured Emily, hastily edging out into the corridor. Whatever fate awaited me at the University Arms, it could hardly be worse than getting stuck in the middle of a protracted domestic, and I felt that both halves of this dynamic duo were just getting going with this one. Jasper meanwhile had retreated back into the comfort of his maths textbook, his Rubik's cube now fully solved and lying discarded on a nearby shelf.

"I'll keep you posted," I told them as I gracefully made my escape.

I crossed into the courtyard, my head in a spin. Whoever had texted me had called me "Rog." Assuming that Ed had not managed to find a phone signal in whichever afterlife he had been abruptly and prematurely shoved into, this immediately whittled down the field of suspects quite considerably. Gavin the Porter, for example, in the unlikely event of his choosing to confide in me of all people in the first place, would doubtless have begun his text with a less congenial "Oi, Twat!" So, with some degree of regret, it seemed that I could cross him off my suspect list. Damn it! The killer was someone I was close to. Had to be.

By the time I reached the University Arms, I had sufficiently overcome my head spin to at least be able to notice that the hotel had indeed been done up and thoroughly titivated since I had last visited Cambridge. I wondered whether I should book a room for the night. Going back up to C Block for another night after what I had seen this morning was unthinkable. Then I wondered whether I should spin on my heels and hot foot it back to Herne Hill, and safety. Sinclair would be terribly disappointed in me, of course. But judging by some of the more waspish comments he had scrawled on my essays over the years, that was unlikely to be anything new. However, in taking such a cowardly course of action, I would also be countermanding a polite but firm request from the rather fabulous Sergeant Chen, and that was another matter.

I decided to defer all consideration of my sleeping arrangements until later. I stalked straight through reception with what I hoped was a forbidding look on my face, but which probably veered more towards "constipated owl," and staked out a table in Parker's Tavern. I scoured the room for recognisable faces, to no avail. I felt a temporary sense of relief, which quickly gave way to a desire to get whatever was about to happen over and done with as quickly as possible.

A couple of minutes passed. I ordered a coffee. As I was doing so, a little old man scuttled in and bagged the table behind me. He looked rather like a beardless gnome, with a knobbly nose and a chin that jutted out in a manner reminiscent of a decrepit Mr Punch. There were several other people in the room, enjoying an early-ish lunch. But none of them looked familiar, certainly not familiar enough to call me "Rog."

"I'm here," I texted back after a few further tense minutes of waiting. The coffee arrived. I duly drank it, taking a punt that our murderer had not yet managed to infiltrate the hotel's kitchen staff. The first gulp was halfway down my throat when the door opened again, causing me to choke noisily when I saw who had come through it. Everyone turned around. The little old man took the liberty of getting up and giving me a vigorous thump on the back.

"Steady lad," he cautioned me in a thick Yorkshire accent. "Tha can't sup it like ale, not when it's that hot!"

I recovered myself sufficiently to thank him for his lifesaving efforts and for the invaluable lesson in coffee-drinking etiquette he had thrown in for good measure. Duly gratified, he shuffled back to his table, leaving me alone with Tanya Bullock, who had sat down opposite me.

II

"You?" I said, feeling as idiotic and clichéd as I undoubtedly sounded. She grimaced.

"You got my message, then! Rog, it's not what it looks like, OK. I'm not saying I've covered myself in glory here, but if you think this," she pulled out what presumably had to be Ed's phone and thrust it to the middle of the table, "means I killed Ed, you're dead wrong. I thought at least you'd know me well enough to appreciate that I'm not a murderer!" she ended bitterly.

I have already said one or two things about Tanya during the course of this narrative, but in view of her dramatic gazelle-like leap to the top of the suspect list, I suppose I ought to add a few more brushstrokes to your mental image. Tanya, in her younger days, had essentially been the embodiment of one of those geeky girls in a teen comedy from the 1990s who is already damned attractive before the makeover she gets during the course of the movie, despite everyone else in the film failing to notice this fact until she takes off her glasses.

Well, I had noticed, in Tanya's case, even before she switched to contact lenses. Almost two decades on, my childish crush on her was barely diminished. And much good it had done me. As is the case for most of the girls I fancy the pants off, Tanya was fond of me, I think, but it was in much the same way as she would have been fond of a loyal sheepdog (if she had happened to have one, and didn't happen to be a cat person).

I will give myself credit for having been a rock-solid yet thoroughly unthreatening shoulder for her to cry on at times during her tumultuous time at university, both when Neil dumped her in favour of her best friend Britta, and in the aftermath of the tragic accident that I had told Sergeant Chen about just a couple of hours ago. Since then, however, neither of us had been particularly good at keeping the friendship alive, and we had rather drifted apart over the years. The suggestion that I, of all people, had some special little window into her soul therefore surprised me a little.

"What makes you think I've formed any conclusions on that front," I protested weakly. I was pretty miffed that she had somehow found a way of making me feel guilty, given that she was the one who was, at the very least, withholding vital evidence from a police investigation.

"I bet you're a shit poker player, let's put it that way," she replied. I realised that my mouth was still hanging open slightly, and adjusted my expression accordingly.

"Look, I don't know what's going on here, but you'd better tell me why you've ended up with a dead man's phone and why you haven't handed it in to the police. Have you spoken to them yet?" She nodded.

"And you didn't mention it to them? Jesus, Tanya, there might be a text from the killer on there saying 'I'm coming for you, Ed, prepare to die, love Keith, smoking gun emoji'—or something."

"Believe it or not, I've looked, and there isn't," she replied, rolling her eyes.

"Oh well, looks like Keith's off the hook then," I blathered, which, given that I had just made the poor chap up, did not come as too much of a surprise.

"I didn't hand it in because I knew what it would look like," she hissed. "I'd immediately become their prime suspect, and even if I got cleared, my career and my life would still be totally screwed."

The order in which she listed those key considerations did not escape my attention. When had she become so career-focused? I knew that none of the relationships she had been in since university had lasted long, and I wondered whether she had thrown herself into her work to compensate. But she had made some oblique references the previous evening to her most recent boyfriend in a manner which had suggested, rather to my disappointment, that the flames of that relationship had not entirely gone out and that she still had some residual interest in making a return visit to the fireplace to stoke up whatever embers still remained.

A thought suddenly, and perhaps belatedly, struck me like a slow-motion mallet.

"You slept with Ed, didn't you!" I declared, pointing at her accusingly for emphasis. This was probably overdoing it, and much to my disappointment, my dramatic accusation came out as a histrionic squeak. I also further undermined the impact of my denunciation by hastily moving my chair back, in case I had got completely the wrong end of the stick and she decided to give me a well-deserved clip round the ear.

She made a move, but not the one I was expecting. She buried her face in her hands and started to sob. I remembered that her proneness to tears was one of the things about herself that Tanya had always hated the most. As such, I stayed silent and politely waited for her to get it out of her system.

"I knew it would happen, deep down," she began in between sobs. "However many times I swore to myself it wouldn't. He'd been sending me flirty texts for weeks. Even claimed that seeing me was the real reason he was organising all...all this. Bloody liar," she added bitterly, closing her eyes and grimacing.

"I don't get it! You never had a thing at uni, did you?" She looked away awkwardly, her face flushed.

"There were one or two occasions," she mumbled. "He obviously had fonder memories of those occasions than I did."

"You never told me!" I huffed petulantly. She gave a short laugh.

"Would you have approved?"

"Hell no! I hope the poor bugger rests in peace, but he was a shameless womaniser and got dangerously close to the line between touchy-feely and gropy every once in a while."

"Don't joke about it!" Tanya snapped. "Ed thought it was all a laugh too. He never had to suffer the consequences of his actions."

"Sorry. As I say, I didn't always approve of what he used to get up to, and looking back on it, the rest of us should absolutely have called him out on it more vigorously than we did. But that's not the point! You didn't approve when I drank a pint of Harvey's Best Bitter out of my bedder's shoe, and I still told you about it."

"It was sexier keeping it as our little secret," she admitted despondently. My efforts at lightening the tone had evidently foundered. "That's what he always said, anyway. Oh, I knew I couldn't trust him. Couldn't trust myself either, as it turned out. Jesus, Rog, I really wanted to give it another go with Rick. I spoke to him only last week. Told him I'd been a bloody idiot to call it off. I'd just been so wrapped up in trying to juggle all my work demands that I'd barely had time to think about him. Told myself it wasn't fair on him to keep stringing him along when I wasn't ready to commit.

"And now I am finally ready to commit, and it's too bloody late! Probably my last chance to start a family, and I've buggered it up! And the worst thing about it was that last night, I knew I had. Ed would have let something slip. He never could keep a secret, not if his life depended on it. But I didn't care, Rog. He'd been giving me signals all evening, and I fell for his shtick like a lovestruck teenager."

"I'm struggling with this a bit," I broke in, genuinely feeling bemused. "I liked Ed, but at the end of the day, he was a short, balding, average-looking man with notable personal hygiene issues. I never understood how he managed to cultivate this Casanova vibe!"

"He made me feel alive!" She sighed. "He made 'not giving a shit' seem so attractive. Sick, isn't it?"

She paused to look around to see if anyone was listening, then lowered her voice before continuing.

"The only guy who can make me feel that way is the one guy who was there when I literally ran over and killed a man. The scruffy unreliable sod made me actually want to throw it all away, everything I've worked for all these years, shutting out friends, family, working through Christmas three years on the trot! Exhausting myself so much that I didn't even have the energy to be interesting to, or interested in, the people I'm supposed to love!

She ran her hands through her hair in exasperation.

"He reminded me that I'd been wasting my bloody time, at work and at home, and it was time for all that to stop! And he made it seem so simple. Deep down, I knew he was nothing but a snake oil salesman, that he'd string me along for a few sex sessions and then drop me like a stone, but he still talked me into not caring. And now he's dead!"

She made that last statement sound as though it was just another entry in a long shopping list of things he had done deliberately to annoy her. I think she realised that she was coming across as just a tad callous and winced uncomfortably.

"It was as if Rick didn't exist," she said softly. "He'll find out now, won't he?" Her eyes, bloodshot with exhaustion and tears, were desperately begging me to find a way out for her.

"I really don't know," I sighed, letting her down as gently as I could. "The police will disclose what they feel they need to disclose to further their investigation, I guess. But surely he'll understand. You weren't properly back together, and I'm sure he hasn't kept his Shaft of Delight duct-taped to the side of his leg for a year, either!" Tanya gave me a look.

"That's supposed to cheer me up, is it?"

"Sorry! My head is in a slightly odd place too right now. When I've got this much to process, things like tact tend to take a bit of a back seat, I'm afraid."

"What if they charge me, Rog?"

"Well, then you're stuffed," I acknowledged. "But there's less chance of that if you 'fess up now. Hand over the phone, tell them everything. That Baynes fellow's not going to be interested in whether you had a one-off sheet shaking session; he has bigger fish to fry. He's not in the business of wrecking relationships for the sake of it."

"No, but I am, aren't I?" she asked, as if desperate for me to join her in a chorus of condemnation of her behaviour. I had enough common sense to dodge that bullet and clammed up like the cowardly mollusc I am.

"And it would have been twice if Dan hadn't been there," she added, her face reddening further.

III

You will already appreciate that I am not much cop when it comes to playing it cool, and my reaction to this statement was far from a calm and measured one. A number of questions jostled and elbowed each other around in my brain as they struggled for dominance, and surprisingly, it was the rather limp "What the hell?" that eventually won out and made its way to my lips.

"Oh God almighty, you really don't think much of me, do you?" She looked disgusted. "It wasn't a threesome, for Christ's sake. Wouldn't be surprised if Ed had been into that sort of thing, but that ratio would not have pleased him at all! You know what Dan's like. Practically narcoleptic when he's had a few. He fell asleep behind the sofa, probably just as everyone else was leaving, and I guess Ed just sort of forgot he was still in the room!"

"You'd left as well, though," I remembered suddenly. "You put Sadie to bed."

"Yes, that was me trying to be a good girl," she sighed. "And failing. If only Dan had woken up earlier, he might have saved me from myself, but he was so out of it he slept through the whole thing. It was only when he let out a huge snore a few minutes later that we realised he was there! Scared the hell out of me, and I was up and out of there like a scalded cat. That's why I grabbed the wrong phone."

"So you left Ed alone with Dan," I concluded succinctly.

"Unless there was someone else sleeping in the cupboard, yes!" Tanya replied.

"And this was what time?" I ventured.

"About 3am," said Tanya.

"Was Dan still out cold, or was he showing signs of waking up?"

"Dead to the world." She shuddered. "But come on, Rog, Dan didn't do this! He and Ed were friends, and Dan's always been ferociously loyal."

"You're probably right," I agreed. "And I don't like dropping him in it. Especially given the police are already wondering why he legged it out of the Porter's Lodge so early this morning.

109

I must admit I'm wondering about that too. But this is all information that the police need. You've got to come clean, Tanya. Sorry for the cliché, but you really should!"

"That isn't even everything," Tanya sighed. I was starting to wonder whether I should have brought a notebook.

"The phone. I did look at his messages. It didn't have the sort of smoking gun text you were talking about, but there were a couple that were pretty interesting." She reached into her coat pocket and thrust a pair of earphones at me. Intrigued, I stuck them in my ears whilst Tanya plugged them into Ed's phone. The volume was turned up to the maximum, but that wasn't the biggest shock.

It was Jammy's voice. Younger, higher, and altogether more natural than the politician's tone he affected these days, but unmistakable. He was telling jokes. The contents of the jokes I won't repeat. It is generally unwise to repeat politicians' jokes, firstly because it only encourages them, and secondly because they are usually the comedy equivalent of anti-matter, delivered with all the panache and dynamism of Kevin Costner on horse tranquilisers. But my censorship here is based on different considerations altogether, for these were not jokes any sane politician would have felt comfortable telling. Unprincipled weasel though I may be in many respects, I don't feel that dignifying racism and antisemitism of that nature by committing it to paper would be the decent thing to do.

I let it go on for a couple of minutes. Jammy had never been into the whole brevity thing, either. Eventually, I reached the end of my patience and removed the earphones in disgust.

"Well I'll be jiggered," I wheezed.

"That was a slightly more nineteenth-century version of what I was thinking," Tanya agreed.

"I remember him telling some dubious off-colour jokes in his time, but I never heard him come out with anything this bad, did you?"

"No," Tanya said, "but it's hardly surprising that he reserved his finest material for the times when we weren't around. He knew perfectly well that I'd have ripped him a second arsehole if he'd said it in front of me. And you would have given him that disapproving jowl-waggling look!"

"I didn't have jowls in those days!" I protested.

"No, but you had the air of someone who would grow into them, my dear!" Tanya informed me sweetly.

"Well, leaving my grotesque dewlaps to one side for a moment," I growled irritably, "I hate to say it, but we have a pretty damn powerful motive for murder here! The press gets a whiff of this, Jammy's career is over, even in these unenlightened times!"

The mind boggled. Could Jammy, who even as a friend I had always regarded as a bumptious but essentially harmless idiot, really have been a "wolf in twat's clothing" all these years?

"That recording must be more than fifteen years old," I mused. "Ed kept it all these years? Moved it from phone to phone?"

"And then texted it to Jammy just a few days ago with a 'looking forward to seeing you at the weekend' text," Tanya said, finishing my train of thought for me.

"Ed wouldn't have stooped to blackmail," I said, but it came out sounding more like a question than a vigorous defence of my late chum.

"Even if he was just messing with Jammy's head, how could Jammy be sure that Ed wouldn't try to use it against him down the line, if their friendship properly soured?" Tanya said, looking me in the eye for the first time since our conversation had begun, a contemplative expression on her face. "There's no way he could guarantee it."

She paused as we both processed the fact that it was bleeding obvious in light of recent events that her statement was fundamentally untrue. There was one way he could definitely have guaranteed it.

"There's something else." Tanya interrupted my troubled reverie by handing me the phone. She kept her hand on it as she let me read another text, sent only two days before. Clearly, she had still not made up her mind as to whether to hand the phone in to the police.

"I will be civil this weekend," it began. Always a promising start to any piece of correspondence. "For Britta's sake, as she still regards you as a friend. But one word out of line, and you will have cause to regret it. Neil."

IV

Tanya raised an eyebrow at me, clearly waiting for me to comment.

"Bloody hell!" I exhaled. "Is there anyone who didn't harbour a secret grudge against poor Ed? We seem to be one waspish John Gielgud cameo short of a full-on *Murder on the Orient Express*-type situation here!"

This cultural reference was clearly lost on her.

"Any idea what the backstory might be?" I asked.

"No. I did catch Neil looking daggers at Ed a couple of times yesterday evening when we were in The Mitre, but I thought it was just a general distaste for crude laddish banter."

"I missed that," I admitted.

"Well, Neil has always had a habit of sneaking under most people's radars," Tanya said gently.

"As threats go, it's a bit limp and lettuce-y though, isn't it?" I pointed out. "Especially the 'cause to regret it' line. Just leaving it as 'regret it' would have been much punchier. This is more Liam Neeson in *Love Actually* than Liam Neeson in *Taken*, if you know what I mean?"

Tanya got the cultural reference this time, although the

only reward I got from her was a slightly lopsided, rueful smile. I was not quite sure whether she was laughing with me, or gently mocking me for the fact that I felt the need to offer a literary critique of something that might well turn out to have been a death threat.

A nugget of an idea suddenly winkled its way to the surface of my brain.

"How far back into his message history did you delve?" I asked. "There wasn't anything from Albert Ross, was there?"

"Albert?" Tanya looked at me, astounded. "Why would there be?"

"Ed mentioned last night that he'd seen him recently. And you caught the tail end of all that stuff Mad Dog McFadden was spouting yesterday about the old boy's death. Don't you think it's possible that there's a connection?"

"No, Rog, I think that's insane! But just to humour you, the answer is that I haven't gone that far back, yet, given when Albert died. But given that he didn't even own a mobile phone…"

"Hang on, how do you know that?"

"Britta and I arranged to meet up with him a few weeks before he died—he was always so sweet about keeping in touch after we graduated. We had to call the Porter's Lodge to remind him."

"How was he?"

"Old and forgetful. He did seem a bit agitated about something. Like he was trying to put a brave face on things. But I don't think he was in fear of his life, if that's what you're asking—not from external factors, anyway. He was clearly not long for this world, and I wondered if he might be ill. But I only stayed for one drink. Britta has more stamina than I do these days, and it was a work night, so I left them to it. I left feeling utterly depressed, to be honest. Do we have to talk about this? I called you for advice, not to exchange internet-style conspiracy theories about real people who only just died."

"Well, I've given you my advice," I said firmly. "Hand in the damn phone!"

"How can I?" Tanya threw her arms in the air.

"How can you not?" I riposted incredulously. "You've already shown me two smoking guns. Who knows what else could be on there? There could be a veritable arsenal of the bloody things! You're covering up what could be vital evidence in a murder investigation!"

"A murder I'm not going down for, Rog, because I didn't bloody do it!" Tanya was vehement, and I could see that she was making a conscious effort not to shout. "I know what the police will think. They'll charge me, and the person who actually did this, the bastard who repeatedly and savagely slashed Ed's insides out with a knife, will get away with it and probably do it again!"

"So the police shouldn't bother their pretty little heads about this? Is that really what you're saying?"

"Ooh, I bet I can guess which officer interviewed you!" Tanya commented wryly, completely pulling the rug out from under me just as I was building up a healthy head of steam and moral outrage.

"Stop teasing me when I'm remonstrating with you!" I accused her grumpily. "If they find out you've kept this from them, you really will be prime suspect! They can trace phones, you know!"

"Not if I don't call anyone with it."

"Are you sure about that? If they trace it here, and find out that this is where you're staying..."

I thought letting that half-sentence hang malevolently in the air would pack more of a punch than finishing it off.

"I'm not staying here," Tanya hissed. "I'm only telling you because I know that you're the sort of person who'll let me make my own decisions."

Was I? Truth be told, she was putting me in a jolly awkward position. But for now, I thought that playing along was undoubtedly the wisest and safest course of action. Where had sweet, bookish Tanya's hitherto unsuspected ruthless streak come from? I am no Gerald Sinclair, but the silent "or else" at the end of her remark had not been lost on me.

"Shit!" Tanya exclaimed suddenly, before fixing me with a gloriously fake smile.

"See you this evening then, Rog," she continued in a louder voice, standing up and moving away.

"Hang on," I blustered, unnerved by the abrupt termination of the conversation just as I thought I might be getting somewhere in persuading her to see sense. I was soon able to glean the motivation behind her hasty departure, though, as I saw Sadie Simmons entering the room. She was accompanied by Steve, looking pale and uncomfortable, and hot on their heels was none other than our celebrated former lecturer and supervisor David Williamson, complete with what appeared to be the same beige jumper he had worn to every supervision I had attended all those years ago. It had a few extra crinkles now and was looking a bit dog-eared. So, too, was its owner.

Williamson had had a rather youthful, boyish look back in the day. Now, he looked tired and stressed. Either he had heard the grim news about Ed, or he had already had to endure up to several minutes of Sadie's company. Poor fellow. I knew from bitter experience how difficult she was to turn down when she had got it into her head that she wanted to take you out for lunch. Or a "lunch date," as she insisted on calling them, even when the lucky recipient of one of these illustrious invitations is someone like me, with whom she has less sexual chemistry than I do with my plumber (who, for what it's worth, is a seventy-year-old gentleman who suffers from halitosis and grows warts faster than he mends pipes).

I had to take my hat off to Tanya, annoyed with her though

I was, when I saw how skilfully she managed to glide straight past them without appearing to see them, despite Sadie gesticulating wildly to try to grab her attention. In her shoes, I would have panicked, which would have given the game away. Tanya, however, had obviously mastered—and was now a shameless practitioner of—the invaluable art of ignoring people without their realising.

The three unusual lunching companions were shown to their table, and I hastily ordered the bill before they spotted me. There was always a chance they might ask me to join them.

As I paid up, two troubling thoughts struck me. The first, I presume Tanya must have thought of already, given its more direct relevance to her, but it made her hesitancy about going to the police all the more maddening and perplexing. If she had taken Ed's phone by mistake, and no phone was found with the body, then the chances were that the murderer now had her phone. Unless Dan had taken it. And that was assuming that Dan and the killer were even two different people. I realised that, for all my protestations to Tanya, that was no longer something I could be absolutely sure of.

The second thought was that if Inspector Baynes and Sergeant Chen ever did lay their hands on Ed's phone, they would find on it a text addressed to one Roger Whiteley. Together with a response to that text sent by the aforementioned Mr Whiteley. In short, I would have a potential concealment of evidence charge to contend with. And that was before we even got into whether my conscience would enable me to sit tight and let her keep quiet about evidence that could, for all I knew as a layman, be vital for the apprehension of this repulsive killer. On the other hand, grassing up a mate was not something that came naturally to me.

I decided to speak to Sinclair about it. He had seen me get the text, so his fingerprints were all over this too, I reassured myself. He may be an eccentric and unorthodox fellow, I concluded, but this struck me as the sort of dilemma he would have a strong opinion about. I felt confident in his ability to talk me round most persuasively to whatever that opinion was. Then I could abdicate responsibility and hide behind his coattails.

I felt obliged to go and briefly pay my respects to Williamson before I left, although I did have to endure one of Sadie's hugs before she allowed me to get a word in edgeways with him. A hug from Sadie is an experience rather akin to using someone else's undeodorised armpit as a sauna. David Williamson looked up at me with the same sad little smile he had always graced me with when handing back one of my essays.

"Hello, Roger," said Williamson. "Good to see you again. I'm just sorry it has to be under these sad circumstances."

"Roger actually found the body," Sadie declared smugly. Williamson winced. In a marked contrast to his attitude to the minutiae of EU law, on this particular subject, he had clearly been hoping to avoid getting into gruesome points of detail. Sadie, by contrast, was clearly salivating at the prospect of getting my take on recent events. Williamson, never the most socially adept of fellows, was clearly struggling to think of anything to say that would steer the conversation back into safer waters, and Steve was nervously fiddling with his fork and struggling to meet my eye. It was left for me to fill in the awkward gap in the conversation.

"It's very hard to move on from seeing something like that," I said weakly. "I've been trying to distract myself by mooching around my old haunts. Not much else any of us can do, really. The police seem to be getting a good handle on things."

I may have thrown in a couple more equally mindless platitudes for good measure.

"Surely they must be close to making an arrest!" Sadie interrupted me. "Maybe they have already. It's not as if he's exactly inconspicuous!"

"Who?" I asked, struggling to keep up with her unexpected decisiveness.

"You know, that dreadful ex-Porter man. Mad Face McFeegle or whatever his name is!"

"Do you mean Finlay McFadden?" Williamson asked sharply.

"He was lurking outside the Porter's Lodge singing at us last night!" she explained as if that in and of itself proved his guilt beyond all reasonable doubt.

"I don't think we should be rushing to conclusions," Williamson said carefully. "I've known Finlay for a very long time. He is certainly a rather troubled man, but that's true of quite a lot of people in this town."

"Quite right," I agreed. I don't know why I found myself feeling so defensive of Finlay McFadden given the fact that even on a good day, the guy scared the willies out of me, but Sadie's sniffy, patronising assumption that it must be the troubled ex-member of staff rather riled me.

"Plenty of people round here with skeletons in their closets!" I added. Sadie just looked confused and a bit put out, but Steve's reaction was rather more unexpected. He shot out of his chair as if a rhinoceros had just emerged from under the seat, horn first.

"What the hell is that supposed to mean?" he roared, his eyes flashing with wild anger. Several of the other lunchers looked up from their plates.

"Noth...nothing," I stammered, wishing I had taken the impolite but safe option of blanking this extremely weird trio and getting out of here when I had the chance. The back of my collar was moistening rapidly. Williamson tugged at Steve's sleeve and gave him a kindly but firm warning look. This appeared to bring his volatile companion back to his senses. Steve sat back down, although the venomous look he shot me came very close to turning my already aggravated bowels to water.

I felt rather taken aback. There had definitely been something off about Steve the previous evening, but he had been perfectly affable with me. Admittedly, quite a lot had happened since then, but I couldn't see why he was taking it out on me.

"I was talking about Cambridge generally, not anyone in particular," I went on defensively. "There are a lot of hidden secrets in this town. That's what old Gerald Sinclair was telling me recently, anyway. You can't assume that just because Finlay McFadden isn't quite as good at hiding his rampant lunacy from the public eye as the rest of us, that means he's the only mad bugger in town."

Williamson smiled.

"I wouldn't have said this to you as an undergraduate, Roger," he said delicately, "but I would err on the side of taking Gerald Sinclair's comments with a pinch of salt. Yes, as I said, there are plenty of people in Cambridge with mental health issues, and you won't have to walk far before seeing ample evidence of that on our streets. But that isn't quite the same thing as saying that the town is a nest of mysterious vipers with deep, dark secrets. No more so than other places, anyway, give or take the odd instance of cheating and plagiarism by some of our sillier students.

"You're right that none of us should be jumping to conclusions, though," he added, giving Steve a steely, reproachful look. I turned to Sadie and was surprised to see that she had gone rather pale.

"Anyway, I'd better scoot," I said. "Will I see you both this evening? Given that the police seem to want us to stick around in Cambridge at least for the weekend, and we've got the table booked at The Ivy, I, for one, think it would be a devil of a shame if it went to waste.

"I know others feel the same way," I added, failing to add

the critical detail that "others" so far consisted of one interfering busybody who wasn't even on the guest list. Why Sinclair, in spite of his evident eccentricities and maverick nature, inspired such confidence in me that I felt I needed to follow his instructions to the letter, I was not quite sure. Doubtless David Williamson would have tried to talk me out of it had he known that pressing ahead with the dinner was one of the eminent professor's little wheezes. I would have to work on the rest of the crew later, but I might as well start somewhere. Steve glared at me, then shrugged and gave a stiff nod.

"Call for Eric Hitchmough," called out a hotel staff member. The little gnome-like fellow who had helped me out when I was having my choking fit earlier got up and scuttled out of the room in a hurry.

"What about you, Sadie?" I asked.

"Oh...um...yes, of course," she said distractedly before pulling herself together and feigning a bit more enthusiasm. "I'll be there with bells on!"

"Ah, the old leprosy still troubling you, is it?" I chuckled to a chorus of disapproving silence. Note to self, I thought—wisecracking about medieval ailments will rarely help to ameliorate an awkward situation. I decided to cut my losses, bade the unholy trinity the fondest farewell I could muster up in the circumstances, and retreated hastily out of the room.

V

Once out of the hotel, I wandered onto Parker's Piece, taking some deep breaths and attempting to gather my jumbled thoughts.

I did not manage to get more than a couple of seconds into this rather futile exercise before a further distraction arose. Out of the corner of my eye, I saw a familiar figure locked in a tight embrace with another figure who was altogether less familiar.

They were standing on Regent's Terrace, in front of where Pizza Hut used to be. I sauntered a little closer. I was still out of earshot but was close enough to see that whatever was going on here, emotions were running high. Which was odd, because Neil Norman, that Duke of Dreariness and Marquis of Monotony, had never struck me as being a particularly emotional person. I had clearly misjudged him, though, because after a few moments of seriously tight hugging, he upped the ante by dropping to his knees and clutching at his companion's hands. His back was turned to me, but from the way he was shaking, I could tell he was a man in severe distress. I'm perceptive like that.

I turned my attention to the lady he was pawing at. She was most definitely not Britta. She was about thirty, medium height, with short hair and a pleasant, roundish face. Right now, she looked awkward and anguished. I watched her pull Neil to his feet and envelop him in another tight hug, but this time, it was only a few seconds before she pulled herself away, giving him a "blink and you'd have missed it" peck on the cheek. Luckily, I have eyelids of steel and neither blinked nor missed it. Then she retreated up the road, fortunately in the opposite direction from where I was lurking.

Anxious not to be spotted, I darted behind a nearby tree. As I moved with leopard-like stealth, I spotted yet another familiar, scruffily dressed figure clutching a carrier bag and shuffling dismally out of the very hotel I had just vacated. Saddam had left the building.

Curiouser and curiouser. This dishevelled tramp was definitely not the sort of person I had envisaged being amongst the hotel's illustrious clientele. I pondered the idea of following him to see whether, after all these years, I could finally discover who this man really was and unpeel the layers of mystery surrounding this fragrant human onion. I decided against it.

Saddam was, at best, tangential to the mystery at hand, with no obvious connection to Ed Dickinson. The same might equally be true of whatever Neil had been getting up to, but even if it had nothing to do with Ed's death, as Britta's friend, I felt it incumbent on me to do something.

The obvious "something" in this instance would have been to confront Neil, but when I turned around again, he had disappeared. I squinted into the windows of a couple of the restaurants on the street in case he had decided to console himself with a bit of nosh following what had evidently been some sort of rejection. I had been on the receiving end of enough of them to know the signs. It was to no avail. Buggering hell. I had let a trail of enquiry peter out right in front of my nose. I was starting to worry that I was not cut out for this detective malarkey.

When I returned to the main road, however, I was handed an unexpected and undeserved lifeline, for I saw the mysterious femme fatale waiting by a bus stop. Thirty seconds later, I would have been too late, for a bus pulled up at that very moment. FF was clearly distracted, as she shamelessly queue-jumped before stepping onto the bus. I charitably put this down to emotional distress arising from her recent encounter with Baron McBoring. Impulsively, I followed her on board, although in my case, naturally, I joined the back of the queue like a good little boy. By the time I boarded, there was only space several rows behind her.

The bus pulled away. I had not had the chance to find out where it was going, having ordered a single to the end of the line in a rather cavalier manner. I still had several hours before dinner time, though, so I decided to follow wherever this line of investigation might take me.

VI

Settling back in my seat, I fired off a volley of text messages to the rest of my chums to see whether people were still planning on meeting for dinner. Despite the fact that these were all people I had been friends with for half my life, I was alarmed to discover I was already starting to think of them collectively as "the suspects."

It soon became apparent that the bus was bound for Addenbrooke's, and sure enough, it was there that FF alighted. Right. Crunch time was now upon me. What the hell was I going to do now?

Now, I may be a blundering blockhead at times, but I am not completely insensitive. I knew I was stepping into a delicate situation here, and not only was I unfamiliar with the latest etiquette for confronting adulterers, but I was not entirely sure she even was an adulterer. She had not done anything to give me the impression that she was encouraging Neil's advances in any way.

Plus, of course, even if she had been stringing him along like a marionette, technically, she was not the adulterer. Not unless she too was partnered up. I am a lawyer. These distinctions matter. And even if she was herself happily married, and even if she and Neil were rogering (no relation) like rabbits at every available opportunity, the real story would doubtless still be far from simple. Marriages are complicated beasts.

Still, nothing ventured, nothing gained, and in the end, I opted for a direct approach. I followed her off the bus and called out to her with a rather strangulated "Excuse me!"

She turned, looking somewhat unnerved, as well she might on being confronted by a gesticulating oaf.

"Look, you don't know me," I began, instantly giving myself a mental kick up the backside. Why did I say that? Of course she didn't know me. And she knew she didn't know me. Was I somehow seeking to reassure her that I wasn't secretly her spinster aunt Mildred in a wig and a fat suit?

"I'm Roger," I continued, on firmer ground this time. She did not respond in kind, but the name tag over her top pocket was more forthcoming. I was addressing one "Daisy Seaman," and from the uniform she was wearing under her coat, and the fact that she was on her way into a hospital, I deduced that she had to be some sort of nurse. There are no flies on Whiteley PI.

"Look," I went on. She already was. Staring, in fact. "I couldn't help witnessing your recent encounter with Mr Norman on Parker's Piece. Well, actually, I could have helped it, but I decided to hide behind a tree and gawp instead. And then I followed you here on the bus, which I definitely could have avoided doing had I been minded to. So, if you were feeling uncharitable, you might think I'm maybe butting in a little bit. But the fact is that Britta's an old pal of mine, and I'd hate to see her get hurt, and..."

And that was all I had. I stammered to a halt and waited for her to rescue me. Surprisingly, she did.

"Look, OK, this is weird," she began, pretty reasonably. Her accent was soft Brummie. "I know you have no reason to believe me, but I am honestly not having an affair with Neil Norman, and he's never tried to instigate one. He really is a lovely man, and Britta's lucky to have him."

"So what was he doing getting down on his knees, then?" I demanded, feeling rather like a dog who realises that the bone it has had its eye on all afternoon is at risk of being misappropriated by its killjoy owner.

"He's been a really good friend," she said, her eyes softening. Her complete absence of wariness or defensiveness had rather disarmed me. "He got brought in here last year with a broken leg. I got to know him pretty well when he was on the mend. We kept in touch. He's been going through a tough time. I've been trying to give him some support. I can't go into the details because it would be betraying his trust. But you should know that he's a good guy with a strong moral code, and he hasn't deserved some of the stuff he's had to deal with recently. I know he's reserved, but he feels things very deeply. He really does."

She broke off helplessly. It seemed she wanted to say more, to bolster her case, as it were, but couldn't.

"And how does he feel about you?" I asked sharply. A look of pain crossed her face, and I knew my arrow had, perhaps through sheer random luck, hit its mark. Whether or not Neil had actually been having his wicked way with her, one thing was clear: his thoughts had certainly strayed, even if his John-Thomas had yet to defy the strictures of his trouser zip.

"Look, I've said my piece," she replied, "and I really have to go. I'm late as it is."

She turned away from me and disappeared through the automatic doors before I had time to rally and lob in another humdinger of a question.

I was left standing on the street, feeling like a bit of a lemon, and a rather confused one at that. Objectively, Daisy Seaman had given the impression of being a kind, lovely, loyal young lady, a credit to the fine institution for which she worked, and altogether not the sort of person who would be naturally prone to a spot of marriage-wrecking of a Saturday afternoon.

So why, in spite of her gentle demeanour and her outwardly plausible protestations of innocence, did I come away feeling instinctively mistrustful of Ms Seaman? For I was left with the unmistakable feeling that my new acquaintance was thoroughly tangled up in this mystery, like a fish in a net. The only question in my mind was whether she was a red herring, or a shark.

CHAPTER 5

In which I am instrumental in cracking Ed's little charade,
patronised and plied with booze by two of my former supervisors,
and afforded the opportunity to get reacquainted with The Keeper
of The Keys. In short, a veritable blitz of dynamic activity, whilst
the man nominally in charge of the investigation spends at least
half of the chapter stuffing his face at The Van of Life.
You're welcome.

I

I decided to hoof it back to Central Cambridge rather than hopping onto another bus. This would give me a chance to think.

As usual, this was a mistake. I won't trouble you with the various outlandish theories my over-fertile imagination cooked up as I trundled on my merry way. Suffice it to say that in the fullness of time, they all turned out to be dead wrong. And, of course, I was well outside the bubble I used to spend all my time in whilst a student (the edges of which had coincided neatly with my favourite pubs), so I proceeded to get myself ever so slightly lost. The upshot of this was that by the time I managed to navigate my way back into the centre of town, it was already late afternoon, and I only had a couple of hours before our scheduled dinner at The Ivy.

I was conscious that Sinclair had asked me to report straight back to him after my rendez vous at the University Arms. We

126

had swapped WhatsApp details earlier. Whilst the marked lack of concerned messages I had received had not gone unnoticed, I still felt it incumbent upon me to stroll back over to St Crisps to reassure the old boy that I had made it through the mysterious encounter in one piece.

As I arrived at St Crisps' Porter's Lodge, I was pleasantly surprised to be greeted with the sight of a Porter that I not only recognised but remembered actually quite liking. His real name was something like Derek, but we had nicknamed him "Harry Porter" because he was small and wore very thick spectacles. He had aged a good thirty years in the last fifteen and now looked more like Ian Holm as Bilbo Baggins after a couple of weeks on the "Gollum Diet." He beamed at me as I wandered in.

"Ah, Mr Whiteley, we've been expecting you!" he declared, sounding like a particularly underwhelming Bond villain, probably from the Brosnan era. "You're bang on schedule."

"Am I?"

"Professor Sinclair phoned not two minutes ago, sir. Said you would be here any minute. He told me to let you into the Master's Lodge and to tell you that you should make yourself at home while he finishes off the trial of some Robinson feller! He's always getting himself mixed up in shenanigans of that sort."

"Do come in, my dear Whiteley," the Great Man's emollient voice called to me from upstairs as Harry let me in. "We're bumping off the Mockingbird a little early today because Jasper's attending a digital sleepover hosted by the Fitz this evening. Make yourself at home—I'll be down in just a tick. There's a cheeky little German refrigerating in the kitchen!"

"Some sort of exchange student, is he?" I asked, bemused.

"My sides are heaving with mirth, Whiteley," came his acidic retort. "Pour yourself a glass, there's a good chap. At least if you're sipping, you're not quipping!"

I found my way to the Sinclairs' exceedingly well-stocked fridge and emerged a minute or so later with a generously brimming glass of Riesling. I then strolled back into the main lounge, sat down on the comfiest-looking sofa, and twiddled my thumbs for a bit. I had been entertained in that room a few times before over the years, of course, for the pre-dinner "chit chat and canapés" section of the various social shindigs that had been organised by the college in a largely tokenistic effort to ensure that we undergrads were kept out of mischief for at least some of the time.

That had been during the illustrious reign of the old master, of course, one Dr Donald Ffiske, who had been a celebrated geologist and part-time taxidermist. Dear old Ffonald Ffuck, as he had inevitably been rechristened by my cruel intake before we had even ffinished Ffresher's week, had insisted on decorating the place with a mixture of interesting rocks and meteorites—which Emily had chosen to keep—and various overstuffed and misshapen forest mammals with curiously strained expressions, none of which had survived the reshuffle.

Given Sinclair's peculiar little hobbies, I had been wondering whether I was going to find that the poor deformed creatures had been replaced by even more grim mementoes from the crimes he had been involved in solving or writing about; perhaps even a brain in a jar labelled "Abnormal" pickling quietly above the mantelpiece. However, if Sinclair had ever put any aesthetic suggestions along those lines to his formidable wife, they had clearly been vetoed, probably on grounds of taste, rather than as a result of any heightened risk of being burgled by a cackling hunchbacked henchman.

Instead, the walls were decorated with copies (I assumed) of various Canalettos, as well as a number of frames containing beautifully calligraphed Latin verses from Emily's favourite ancient Roman poets. I turned around and peered at the one behind my sofa. My Latin was decidedly rusty, but what I was able to translate was pretty raunchy material. Probably by that scamp Catullus.

"Smutty bunch, those Romans!" Sinclair declared as he swept regally into the room. "If you took out all the filth, there'd be nothing left! Marvellous stuff! Ah good, you've helped yourself! I'll join you."

He scuttled into the kitchen. I could hear the faint sound of young feet stomping around upstairs, with a small voice muttering something about an "egregious miscarriage of justice."

"He's really getting into To Kill a Mockingbird, isn't he?" I asked Sinclair as he returned, glass in hand.

"My storytelling efforts and whatever delights the Fitzwilliam Museum is cooking up will serve as a temporary distraction only, I fear," Sinclair said with a chuckle. "My guess is that we've got two minutes before the boy slopes off to his den with his little black book, pulling out all the stops to solve the crime before I do! Trying to eclipse his old dad. I'm hoping to hold him off until he's at least eleven, but I'm already feeling like a bit of a Cnut, if you excuse the expression. Trying to hold back the waves of progress," he added helpfully.

"Although actually," I interjected, "the whole point of that story was that Canute was trying to prove a point to his overly obsequious courtiers that he COULDN'T actually control the waves."

Sinclair smiled warmly (after a slightly icy pause) and gave me a gentle, paternal pat on the arm.

"A word of advice, Whiteley. If you happen to have a piece of obscure historical knowledge like that stored up in that marvellous noggin of yours, best just to assume that I probably already know it too. There's a good fellow!"

As he sat down heavily in his preferred armchair with a leathery thump, he added, "But irrespective of whether or not Jasper is getting anywhere, we now need to crack on as a matter of urgency. The journos have got wind of the college's little dead body problem and will be making enough hay with it to fill a hungry carthorse unless we present them with our killer pretty damn sharpish. If we can do that, then they still get a splashy story but, to continue the aquatic theme, it's a mermaid! No legs. A bit about the victim, a bit about the killer, not too much by way of collateral claptrap about what a scandal-ridden college we are. It'll be "sorted," as they say in that rather predictable soap opera. You know, the one about potato-headed cockneys overreacting to things!"

"Is that an *EastEnders* reference?" I asked, flabbergasted.

"Yes, that's the chap!" Sinclair replied absent-mindedly. "Is that show still on?"

I shrugged. "I think so—although I stopped watching when Larry Lamb got chopped! I do feel we're digressing, though."

"Quite right!" Sinclair acknowledged, taking a delicate sip of wine. "Emily keeps telling me I have to get better at 'small talk.' I thought I would take the opportunity to try it out. I have to say, likeable fellow though you are, I'm finding it a bit of a strain. Do you like football?"

"Not in the slightest," I replied breezily.

"Thank God for that! Right, now that ghastly experiment's over, let's get back to the relative comfort of investigating your friend's barbaric murder. What have you learned?"

I gave him a potted rundown of the day's events. Sinclair listened intently, taking occasional cautious sips of wine, whilst the rest of the time, he rested his head on his hands, which were steepled as if in prayer.

"Well, well," he declared as I tailed off. "A very, ah, spirited effort on your part, Whiteley! Really, I must commend you. When it comes to determining motive, I'm rather spoiled for choice with you lot!"

"Hang on," I interjected. "I hope you're not lumping me in

with the rest of them!"

"No, no," Sinclair made a dismissive motion. "Don't worry, my dear fellow, I ruled you out as a serious suspect some hours ago. Not solely because of your good looks and charm, I'm afraid. It was more that the image of you clambering up the back wall of D Block like a paunchy middle-aged Spider-Man struck me as a distinctly implausible one. Certainly not without having done a lot more damage to the masonry, anyway!"

"You'll be relieved to hear that the professionals have come to the same conclusion, Mr Whiteley," came a rumbling voice from the doorway. Inspector Baynes trundled through it, grinning at Sinclair.

"Ah, Taters," Sinclair welcomed him warmly. "I thought you'd be busy Sweeneying around all over town, knocking heads together and so forth!"

"Nope. I'm delegating!" Baynes' grin widened as he heaved his ample carcass onto the sofa opposite me. "Still on duty though, more's the pity, but I thought I'd pop by to give you a rundown of where we've got to. Seeing as how you're an interested party, or at least your wife is, as Master of the College an' all! Around, is she?"

"No, she's finishing off a paper and then wining and dining this evening, so I've been left to my own devices!"

"That's trusting of her, what with all this mischief afoot," Baynes chuckled. "Anyways, Mr Whiteley here'll be interested to know that one of the two tip-offs he gave me earlier might have something to it. I think we can discount the clue of the flushing lavatory, I'm afraid. My lads have had a good old rummage down them there sewers. Going through the motions, you might say!"

"Did you delegate that congenial task as well?" I asked.

"It would have been a shockin' dereliction of my supervisory role not to," Baynes said breezily. "In this game, there's no substitute for hands-on experience. Anyway, they didn't find much down there, except the usual, of course. So if your little hunch was that our killer did Mr Dickinson in so that he could nick the evidence from the time capsule and destroy it, we can safely say that flushing it down the bog wasn't how they went about doing it."

The inspector leaned forward and lifted a porky finger emphatically.

"Our working theory is that the murderer might well have been after whatever it was that one of your mates wrote down all them years ago that's caused all this trouble, just like you suggested. But we don't think the time capsule entries were ever in that box to begin with. The state of the room would suggest that our killer went a bit off the deep end after they did the deed, see. Proper berserk, in fact. Meaning there's every chance that they're still looking for whatever was in there!"

"Which means that Johnny Murderer might not be particularly well endowed in the cerebral matter department," Sinclair jumped in. "Much as I would prefer to be crossing swords with a bona fide criminal mastermind, we have to face up to the fact that we may be dealing with a bit of a thickie!"

"There might be something to that," Baynes acknowledged. "Still, the fact that no-one's likely to drown in his gene pool don't make him any less dangerous. Dumb luck can get you a long way in this world. We ain't caught him yet, which means so far, he's winning! And the game only gets trickier from here."

"It hasn't been twenty-four hours yet!" I protested. "Isn't it supposed to be forty-eight hours before your chances of solving a crime are cut in half?"

"That would explain why that Ripper chap is proving such a tough nut for me to crack," Sinclair murmured. As was so often the case, I was not entirely sure whether he was joking.

"Ninety-three per cent of those sorts of statistics are a pile of bollocks," Baynes grunted. "But it's true that a cold trail is harder to follow, even for a bloodhound with a nose as keen as my old schnozzle! Which probably means that I ought to grab a cheesy chips from the Van of Life and get back to the old torture chamber before it dissipates any further. Just wanted to check in to let you know the latest and see if you'd had any bright ideas? About that picture Mr Whiteley here found in the box?"

Needless to say, despite the fact that it was I who had known the victim for fully half of his unfortunately curtailed existence, it was Sinclair who Baynes was looking at.

"I was going to ask you about that myself," I said. "I've been racking my brains, going over all of the conversations I ever had with Ed that I have the faintest recollection of, to see if any memories spring out at me, but I've come up with the square root of sweet Fanny Adams!"

Sinclair grimaced, looking a little irritated.

"I have had a similar lack of success, I'm afraid," he declared gloomily. "And I just can't understand it. Damn it all, I'm nothing but an old dunderhead!"

He paused to allow us time to set him straight on that point, but I glanced at Baynes, who had a mischievous look in his eyes, and we took the mutual decision to stay ominously silent.

"Your friend was a prankster, Whiteley," Sinclair went on rather sniffily. "He was obviously planning on presenting you all with an empty box and a clue as to where he had actually stashed the contents of the capsule. A treasure hunt, just as Torvill said. But it wasn't set for a wily old fox like me!"

So much for the false modesty.

"Nor indeed," he went on, "was it set for some fiendish, diabolically clever criminal mastermind. No, it was something that his mates should have been able to crack after a few minutes following a heavy evening on the sauce. You lot would have got bored and given up if it had taken any longer than that! In short, this is not something that should require a Bletchley Park-level intellect to solve!"

"Ah well," Baynes sighed, heaving himself to his feet. "Keep me in the loop if anything occurs to you! Enjoy your plonk, and spare a thought for those of us who have to work on a miserable Saturday evening. Cheery-bye, folks!"

With a resigned grin, he shuffled out of the room, the prospect of a pile of chips on a polystyrene bed blanketed in a cheesy duvet luring him away from us like some sort of invisible magnetic force.

II

Sinclair reached into his pocket and pulled out a very old-fashioned pocket watch. He glanced at it, tutting nervously.

"The evening is ebbing away from us, Whiteley," he sighed. "What are you looking at me like that for?"

"Have you got a snuff box in there as well, perchance?" I asked him sarcastically.

"I'll have you know I was given this timepiece by the best horologist in all of Hoxton," Sinclair declared defensively. "I got him off a small murder charge by proving his alibi. Ironically, if he had kept track of the time on the night in question, my involvement would never have proved necessary, but there we are.

"Anyway, young Whiteley, you're one to talk, with that pretentious hip flask you used to whip out at every opportunity when you were an undergraduate! You may have thought that your doddery old supervisors weren't paying attention, and in most cases, you'd have been right, but this one was! And we academics have positively elephantine memories. Doubtless, you have grown out of such childish affectations."

"That's entirely different!" I protested. "I was young and foolish!"

"Left it up the hill, did you?" Sinclair's eyes were infuriatingly twinkly.

"Well, as it happens..." I confessed. "I've left all my stuff up there, even the old hippers! Went for a walk to clear my head after being grilled by the police, then met you, and I've been scurrying around Cambridge ever since. I haven't had a chance to work out where I'm supposed to hit the hay tonight or, indeed, to contemplate the prospect of going back up the hill to retrieve my worldly goods. I don't relish a trip back up to the scene of the crime, but needs must, I suppose!"

I sighed. Normally when one is regaling a companion with details of such unfortunate circumstances, one expects one's listener to make a few commiserating noises or pull a few sympathetic expressions. Perhaps a light moan, maybe even a grimace. Never one to leave a trend knowingly unbucked, Sinclair was grinning from ear to ear.

"Whiteley, think no more about it! I will get one of the Porters to bring your belongings to this very spot quicker than you can say Eureka! You can bunk in our spare room for the night. You'll have the place to yourself! Snug little space—no-one's slept in that bed since my mother-in-law died in it, so the springs should be suitably, er, springy. Which is more than she was for the last few years of her life," he added jovially. "But that is an entirely different story."

"Well," I stammered gratefully, in truth very happy to take him up on the offer and not particularly perturbed by the prospect of being bunkies with the ghost of the Master's late mother. "That would be great, actually. Thanks ever so much."

"No, Whiteley. Thank *you*! For you have just done me a great service, my friend. You, sir, are the apple dropping onto Newton's cranium! You are Archimedes' mucky bath water! You are the ribald joke that Mr Da Vinci told Ms Lisa just before he put paintbrush to canvas! You're Benjamin Franklin's rod! You're a walking, talking genius trigger, Mein Herr!"

"What did I trigger?" I called after Sinclair, baffled, as he suddenly bustled out of the room without warning, only to return after a few seconds with his tweed jacket in hand. "And how did I trigger it? And is there any way I can stop doing it? Being *anyone*'s rod sounds like a worrying amount of responsibility to me!"

"Not at all," Sinclair chortled, heading for the front door and beckoning for me to follow. "Just carry on with your wastrel ways, and our relationship could yet prove incredibly fruitful. You said 'hippers,' don't you see?"

"I do see," (said Roger Whiteley, who didn't), "but just for the sake of argument: assuming that I am still a couple of microseconds behind you...where are we going, exactly?"

"We are off, my dear old thing, to visit the lair of Dr Harold Shipman! Let us hope that he's entertaining this evening."

III

I suddenly felt like quite the dimwit and slapped myself on the forehead. Of course! How could I have missed it?

"Hippers! Sounds like Shippers!" I yelled after him as he headed out into the chilly quadrangle.

"By George, he's got it," Sinclair said distractedly. "Knew we'd get there eventually."

"But why on earth would Ed have given the time capsule to old Ron Fairbanks, of all people?"

"Well, let's not get ahead of ourselves," Sinclair cautioned. "If your friend had gone to the trouble of organising an elaborate treasure hunt, one clue is hardly likely to get us all the way to our destination, I fear. I would hypothesise that dear old Ronnie is no more than a link in the chain. One of the rustier ones, at that!"

"How did you know we used to call him 'Shippers,' anyway?" I asked. My query was met with a hearty guffaw from my companion.

"Young people really have no idea how their voices carry. Yours in particular was a great loss to the theatrical world. It was not particularly difficult to elucidate who you might have been referring to when using that rather disrespectful nickname!"

"Shouldn't we let Inspector Baynes know?" I panted as I tried to keep in step with him. A look of distaste passed over Sinclair's face. He pulled out his phone and punched in Baynes' number. Holding the phone to his ear, he allowed it to ring a grand total of once before hanging up.

"I'll text him in a minute," he declared. "I wouldn't want to deprive him of a chance to enjoy his chips."

We were now in one of the more obscure little nooks that St Crisps is teeming with. This one was playing host to the college recycling skip, from which a rather full-bodied smell wafted towards us.

"I'll bet you wish I were the proud possessor of a snuff box now, eh, Whiteley?" Sinclair chuckled as he strode purposefully towards a door a little way past the skip.

"Is this where his office is now?" I asked. "You've moved him!"

"Such matters are above my humble station," Sinclair replied with modesty that could not have been more "faux" if it had worn a fake moustache and dark glasses. "But my understanding is that there is a sense amongst the upper echelons of the college that dear old Ronnie is rather outstaying his welcome. He is reacting in a rather Nelsonian fashion to the beckoning hand of retirement. He hasn't been responding to the subtler hints that they've been dropping his way with a resounding clang. They've tried everything. Not letting him loose on any more students. Presenting him with a carriage clock and various books about fishing. Holding retirement parties for him. That unfortunate accident during the Fellows' clay pigeon shooting expedition. All to no avail. So it was felt that inching him out by offering him less congenial accommodation, pointedly close to the fire escape, might have the desired effect. The results thus far have been disappointing, I fear!"

At least they had allowed the poor old sod to stay on the ground floor, I was relieved to discover. Sinclair rapped smartly on the door to his office. We heard movement from within, followed by a fit of productively phlegmatic-sounding coughing and some protracted fumbling with the latch. It was a full minute and a half before the door opened and a bleary birds' nest of a face peeked out at us.

Ronald Fairbanks had to be in his early seventies by now, but he looked a decade older. A devotee of shabby brown suits, Fairbanks had not been the most dapper of men even two decades ago, and even then, the tobacco stains on his fingers had been matched by the ones spreading down his dishevelled beard like brown fungus. Both sets of stains had since darkened to an unhealthy mahogany colour.

The old boy grinned, revealing an incomplete collection of copper-coloured teeth, which had visibly dwindled since I had last seen him. If I was being unkind, I might have suggested that Santa had been down a few too many chimneys. He had certainly sampled far too many glasses of brandy at the bottom of them. But for a man who was obviously falling apart faster than a suspension bridge made entirely of bran flakes, he seemed remarkably cheerful.

"Jerry Sinclair, you frisky old fornicator," he chirped at us in a reedy voice. "How's it hanging?"

Sinclair winced. Needless to say, he refrained from answering the question directly. I got the sense that, bizarrely inapt though the description of my supercilious companion as a "frisky old fornicator" might be, he was in fact more offended by being referred to as "Jerry."

"Hello, Ronnie. How's the article going?" he responded instead. "Something about Rylands v Fletcher, wasn't it?"

"Don't talk to me about that prize pair of 'See You Next Wednesdays!'" Fairbanks exclaimed. "I sincerely wish they had never crossed paths. Can't think of one original thing to write about either of the smug bastards. My Muse was always a tempestuous harlot at the best of times, but now it seems she has shacked up permanently with that twat from Downing who churns out three articles a month, damn his eyes!"

Stifling a belch, not particularly successfully, Fairbanks waved us into the room, gesturing vaguely in the direction of two armchairs that had perfected that much sought-after "just hauled out of a skip" vibe. The one item of furniture in the room that bore even the faintest veneer of respectability was a wooden globe in front of his bookshelf. Thither Fairbanks tottered unsteadily, turning and giving us a gleeful grin as he reached it.

"Sharpener?" he asked, raising the lid of the globe to reveal an impressive array of whiskies. I was not particularly surprised. The drinks globe was a recent (post-2006) innovation, but not an uncharacteristic one. When I had been an undergraduate, I had known for a fact that the cover of Craig and De Burca's *EU Law: Texts, Cases and Materials* on his bookshelf had played host to a rather delightful bottle of Bunnahabhain, which he had allowed his supervisees to sample one rainy afternoon. To this day it remains the only time I have ever derived any pleasure from opening that book.

"I don't believe I am in need of sharpening right now, thank you," Sinclair declined gracefully as we got ourselves as comfortable as was realistically achievable in his sagging armchairs. "Although I am sure Whiteley here will join you!"

I was not quite sure I cared for the insinuation, but my pride quickly gave way to my thirst, and I had no hesitation in accepting a wee dram of 18-year-old Glenfiddich.

"So, what brings you and Mr, er, Whately, is it?"

"Whiteley," Sinclair corrected him before I got the chance. "This is Roger Whiteley. He studied here a few years ago. You taught him tort. Which is not as tautological as it sounds!"

"Tort in the first year, land law in the second year, equity in the third year," I added helpfully. It was no coincidence, I suspect, that my three weakest marks had been in those very subjects. I vividly remember the revision seminar just before my equity exam in my final year. We were supposed to come in with any questions we had from rereading the texts that he had set us during the year. My first question was met with an incredibly reassuring "FUCK! FUCK! Right, don't panic! We've still got a week till the exam; let's see what flotsam and jetsam we can salvage...." In the end, most of us had scraped through.

"Not ringing any bells at the moment, I'm afraid," the old boy warbled apologetically. "There's so many of you buggering students, you see. Can't possibly be expected to remember them all. What years were you up?"

"2003 to 2006," I told him, and the old man's face suddenly lit up.

"Oh, you were in Sadie Simmons' year!" He trilled adoringly. "A fine vintage, Mr Wattling! Tell me, are you still in touch with dear Sadie?"

"Well, as it happens, I spent yesterday evening in her company, and I'm seeing her again for dinner in an hour or so."

"Oh, she's in town, is she? Do let her know that there is a fond old man who would be sorely grateful for a visit, if she has the time. Got the best mark in her equity paper of anyone I ever supervised," Fairbanks recalled wistfully.

I had forgotten, but he was right. It had come as something of a surprise to the rest of us, given the mediocre results she had obtained in the first two years, and even more of a surprise that she had achieved such a stunning mark in a subject taught by Fairbanks, a man she had spent most of her time as an undergraduate trying to avoid being supervised by. I had little hope of persuading her to grace the old boy with a visit. She only had eyes for David Williamson. But I refrained from vocalising this brutal assessment, taking a tactful sip of whisky instead.

"Oh, you take it neat, do you?" Fairbanks asked.

"Well, yes," I replied, a little surprised that this was even in question. Fairbanks was now rummaging around in a mini-fridge on the other side of the room.

"I like my whisky the way I like my women," Fairbanks chortled. "Eighteen years old and full of coke!"

I almost retched into my glass, and Sinclair and I exchanged a look.

"Believe it or not, he's given you the toned-down version of that joke," Sinclair whispered dryly. Fairbanks was indeed topping up his dram with a can of ice-cold Coca-Cola. This would explain why he was losing all his teeth, anyway, I thought to myself.

"Have you had any encounters with anyone else from Whiteley's year lately, Ronnie?" Sinclair asked at a slightly more elevated volume than usual. Presumably, Fairbanks was going deaf as well.

"Shouldn't think so," Fairbanks said, shaking his head. "People visit me so rarely these days, you see."

"What about a fellow by the name of Dickinson? Edward Dickinson?" Sinclair persisted.

"Dickinson? Oh, was he the smug balding chap with the body odour that came to visit me a few weeks ago? Couldn't remember him from Adam, to be honest, but he was terribly gracious about my supervisions. Nice enough lad, if a bit scruffy."

Sinclair gave me a beady look, cautioning me not to giggle at the old duffer's chronic lack of self-awareness.

"Did he say why he was visiting you?" Sinclair went on intently. "Did he give you anything?"

"Ah yes, as it happens, he did!" Fairbanks replied excitedly. "Good God, it would be this evening, wouldn't it? I'd completely lost track! Not sure I should be spilling the beans to you, old boy, but as it seems you know all about it...he had organised some sort of treasure hunt for his old chums over the Easter period, and he asked if I minded holding onto one of the clues for him. I expect we'll have seven or eight of them traipsing in here later this evening, trying to relive their youth! Well, good luck to 'em, I say!"

He raised his fizzing glass in a silent toast. Sinclair and I exchanged awkward glances.

"I don't think there will be anyone else coming, Ronnie," Sinclair told him gently. Fairbanks sighed.

"Everyone got too busy, did they? Ah well, 'tis the way of the modern world. Would have been nice if he'd let me know, though, even if it was just a note in the old pigeon-hole."

"The thing is, Dickinson's dead," I butted in. A little brutal, perhaps, but I knew of old that once Fairbanks started rambling, there was no knowing where the conversation might meander off to.

"Oh, well, fair enough then," Fairbanks said, shrugging graciously.

"You don't sound too shocked," Sinclair commented.

"No, well, most people are, these days. Dead, that is. Most people I know, anyway. One mustn't judge!"

There was a long, stagnant pause.

"So, about that clue?" Sinclair ventured, desperate to move things along before the stagnation became intolerable.

"Oh yes, what was I thinking? It's over here." He lurched to his feet, coming precariously close to toppling over altogether, then wended his way unsteadily back to the bookcase, retrieving a large wooden egg.

"Easter egg hunt, you see!" he explained, perhaps a trifle unnecessarily. He handed it to Sinclair, who examined it, gleaned immediately that it separated at the middle rather like a Matryoshka doll, and proceeded to open it up.

"Ha!" Sinclair exclaimed, extracting the contents of the egg. This turned out to be a small reusable bottle containing what appeared to be approximately 25ml of red wine, wrapped in a scrap of lined paper that looked as though it had been torn out of one of those little notebooks one can buy at WH Smith or Rymans.

He took a sip, grimacing as he did so.

"Ah yes, the all too sadly familiar tang of college plonk," he declared grandly in conclusion. "I think he let a bit of air get in, but frankly, the difference it has made is pretty negligible!"

"I gave that stuff up for Lent once," I remarked.

"Red wine?" Fairbanks asked, his jaw dropping so dramatically it felt almost like an impression of Marley's Ghost.

"Oh Christ no. I'm not Gandhi, you know," I clarified helpfully. "I only swore off the college-branded stuff. Used to give me the most throbbing hangovers anyway!"

Sinclair was looking at me and shaking his head, a smile playing on his lips.

"What?" I asked, rather suspecting that I was having fun poked at me.

"Just contemplating the enormity of your vaultingly ambitious sacrifice, Whiteley!"

"The damn cheek of the fellow!" Fairbanks lamented. "Bought me booze and didn't even tell me it was there!"

I suspected that this had been a bit of deliberate mischief on Ed's part, to see whether Fairbanks (a) was nosy enough to open the egg in the first place and (b) had the degree of self-restraint required to leave the bottle untouched. It was fortunate that the doddery old man had passed the first test, for there was little doubt in my mind that he would have failed the second. It had been rather mean-spirited of Ed to leave temptation in the path of such an obvious temptation fan.

Meanwhile, Sinclair was unwrapping the notepaper with all the feverish anticipation of a small child opening his first birthday present.

"Plenty more where that came from," he read out. The line fell flat, and Sinclair looked deeply disappointed, like a small child who had opened his first birthday present and discovered that mummy and daddy had accidentally wrapped up one of their utility bills.

"Call that a fucking clue?" Fairbanks scoffed.

"Your late friend was not exactly a latter-day Sphinx, was he?" Sinclair commented acerbically.

"That is probably a fair comment," I conceded, "although he did have very hairy legs. So where to next, then? College bar?"

"I think not," Sinclair replied. "Can you imagine for one moment Wilma the bar lady entertaining this sort of hijinks?"

I couldn't. Wilma had been there in my day, and she had been as terrifying as she was legendary. The only reason she has never been the subject of a biopic is that Lee Marvin is no longer available.

"No," Sinclair went on. "She'd have told Dickinson to sling his hook, and he doesn't strike me as a man who would have been courageous or foolhardy enough to venture into that lion's den! Which leaves only one possibility. You see, Whiteley, the Sherlockian dictum in action. Mr Dickinson got into our cellars, or I'm a Dutchman! To the Porter's Lodge, laddie! At the double!"

I gulped down the last of my whisky, giving myself acute throat burn in the process, and scuttled obediently after him.

"Have fun storming the castle!" Fairbanks called after us cheerfully as we made our hasty exit.

IV

"Do you have a key to the college cellars?" I asked Sinclair as we once again wended our way swiftly across the college grounds.

"Good heavens, no! I may still be arguably the biggest swinging dick in the Cambridge Criminology Department, but round here, I'm just FLOTUS. I don't have that sort of power. No, we'll have to procure them from The Keeper of The Keys!" He spoke the name reverentially.

"And who is...The Keeper of The Keys?" I inquired, upping the reverential ante further by prefacing the words with a suitably ominous pause.

"Eric the Porter!" said Sinclair, pulling out his pocket watch once again. In fact, he had been consulting it with such neurotic regularity over the course of the evening that he was starting to remind me of the White Rabbit, with me as a slightly tiddly Alice following him down a very deep hole.

"I always thought he was called Derek!" I said, but Sinclair was distracted by his phone buzzing.

"I think it's the 1930s calling to report one of their detectives missing," I muttered to myself.

"It's the Fuzz!" Sinclair declared. He returned his pocket watch to one pocket and retrieved his iPhone from the other. I peered over his shoulder. It was a text from someone who appeared in his contact list as "Taters Plod."

"Nice work, me old cock. That there's a fine bit of deducting. Just finishin' off me chips. Be right over. Don't do nothing without me."

"He actually texts in a West Country accent!" I said incredulously.

"Inspector Baynes is what one would call a Prime Dorset Ham, Whiteley. He plays up his Piddletrenthide roots because it lulls everyone into the false sense that they're dealing with a bit of a bumpkin. Plus, I think he rather enjoys it."

Sinclair was clearly in a state of heightened excitement. The spring in his step as we made our way around the quadrangle to the Porter's Lodge was now approaching bunny hop territory and he nearly bumped his head on a low hanging archway as we navigated our way to Front Court.

Baynes was obviously rather swifter of foot than I had expected, for his huge frame was already cluttering up the Porter's Lodge when we got there. He was leaning over the front desk chinwagging with Eric/Derek/Harry Porter/ Illustrious Keeper of the Keys. As Sinclair quickly gave him a rundown of recent events, my eyes wandered over to the alcove containing several hundred pigeon-holes, each of which was labelled with the name of a current undergrad, grad student, Fellow, or member of staff. By a remarkable coincidence, one of the first names that caught my eye was one I recognised.

"Daisy Seaman?" I exclaimed. "Is she...?"

"Our college nurse!" Eric piped up. "Very popular girl, she is! Always getting her pigeon-hole clogged up!"

Sinclair looked slightly pained.

"Can we borrow the keys to the wine cellar, Eric?" he asked.

"Certainly," the diminutive Porter assented, his expression brightening. "Would you like me to make some recommendations from our new arrivals, sir?"

"I don't think we shall have need of your services this evening, my friend! We are not going down there for the wine!"

"Well, there's not much else down there unless you've developed a taste for rodents," Eric cautioned us, "but you gentlemen must please yourselves, of course!"

"You won't mind if I accompany you," he added as he reached into a drawer and brought out an impressive ring of keys that looked as though it belonged on the belt of a Victorian jailer. The Porter's tone was as obsequious as ever, but there was an edge to his voice that indicated he had no intention of letting us interpret his statement as a question. "Only our spare set went missing for a few days recently, so I'm keeping a firm watch on these now. Not that I don't trust you, but...."

The silence where the end of his sentence should have been spoke volumes.

"The spare set went missing?" Baynes asked sharply.

"Well, we think it did. It was in poor old Albert's final days, and he wasn't really with it at that point. They turned up again just before he had his accident. Nothing taken, in the end. I reckon whoever took them knew that they'd still have to get past us if they wanted to lift anything valuable. And there's no wine in the world sweet enough to justify that sort of a risk!" he concluded grimly.

This statement should have been hilarious coming from such a Lilliputian specimen, but somehow it wasn't. I had never thought about the possibility that Eric, like most of his fellow Porters, might have had military experience, but whatever his training, looking at the set of his jaw, it occurred to me that he was a scrappy little chappie who probably fought extremely dirty.

He scuttled out of the Lodge and led us across the lawn (oh, the privilege!) to a small door leading into the oldest building in college, a lumpy walled red brick building that dated back to the 1590s and was festooned with creeping ivy.

The door looked barely wide enough to entertain Inspector Baynes' shoulder blades, but the burly policeman managed to manoeuvre himself through. From thence, the four of us commenced a winding descent down a very archaic, cobwebby flight of damp smelling stairs that seemed to lead us into the very bowels of the earth. I must confess that a tingle of excitement passed down my spine as I descended. For very wise policy reasons, they had never let us down here as undergraduates, and visits were reserved for Fellows (the senior ones) and donors (the real cash splashers). I did not begrudge our visit to old Fairbanks, who had obviously been in need of the company, but it was only now that this was starting to feel like a real treasure hunt.

"I don't suppose Ed Dickinson ever asked you to give him access to these here cellars?" Baynes asked Eric as we continued our descent.

"Not me, sir. And if he had, I am afraid that I would have had to politely decline the request." He turned to me in the darkness. "Don't get me wrong, Mr Whiteley. I liked your friend, but he never struck me as a bloke who was used to weathering the weight of great responsibility on his shoulders!"

He flicked a switch, which failed to have the usual effect.

"Bulb gone," he squeaked, producing a chunky torch that looked like it weighed almost as much as he did, and switching it on. I had assumed from all this rigmarole that we had "touched bottom," but the stairs continued downwards for the equivalent of another couple of flights. Eventually, we reached a grand old wooden door that had to be a couple of hundred years old. Someone had rather ruined the effect by nailing a disappointingly modern and corporate sign to the door, which read "College Wine Cellar." I wasn't sure what else anyone could have thought it might be, although I supposed that they might eventually shift Ron Fairbanks' office down there if he still failed to take the hint.

Eric drew out the heavy keychain, selected a particularly toothy, rusty specimen, and inserted it into the keyhole. His first attempt at opening the weighty door failed to shift it more than a few inches, but it turned out that the little fellow's scrawny physique belied his wiry strength. With a mild grunt of effort, he succeeded in opening the weighty door on his fourth or fifth attempt. Its contents, though, were worth the effort. Albeit I appreciate that that is always easier to say when one is not the one making the effort but merely looking on appreciatively with one's hands safely in pockets.

The cellar was every bit as old and atmospheric as a good wine cellar should be. None of these new-fangled glass cabinets or funny implements designed to achieve the perfect temperature for a particular vintage. Such contraptions might sound like a very fine thing indeed in a more modern setting where tradition comes at less of a premium. But not here. No, this was back to basics stuff, and for a moment I felt like I had been transported into a novel by Umberto Eco or Carlos Ruiz Zafon.

Cavernous space, lots of bricks missing from the walls, an uneven stone floor, plenty of dust, a reassuring musty smell, and, of course, row upon row of bottles. These ranged from recent deliveries (it was with some amusement that I saw a stack labelled "Cheeky Little Germans") to ancient-looking specimens that seemed as though they had settled in several decades ago. The latter were the ones I was particularly tempted by. It was with no little regret that I reminded myself that the wine was not the objective here and that we were not going to be able to pause our investigations for a few hours to get stuck in. On the other hand...

"Gerald," I began, "it strikes me that we're doing pretty well here!" I spoke quietly so that Baynes wouldn't overhear. As far as I could tell, Baynes and Sinclair had thus far adopted a thoroughly genial and collegiate approach when engaging in their respective investigative efforts, but there was definitely a touch of unspoken rivalry lurking beneath the surface. Whilst I rather liked the inspector, when the chips were down, in this cock fight, I was backing the other one. No-one reads a Conan Doyle story and roots for Lestrade, not when Holmes is available, or even a short, balding, middle-aged, myopic, bombastic, tell-me fantastic, tuba-playing Scottish variant of the basic Sherlockian model.

"Beware of complacency, Whiteley!" Sinclair warned.

"Shine the torch over there, Eric."

The Porter duly obliged, and we ventured further into the belly of the college.

"But whatever we find here, we must be one step ahead of Johnny Murderer," I pointed out. "He never even got to Fairbanks. I mean, the old boy would have mentioned it, wouldn't he?"

"Indubitably! But you forget that Johnny may not be playing by the same rulebook as we are," Sinclair replied. "We followed the clue that Mr Dickinson left us because it was the only one available by the time you discovered the body. There may have been others that our dastardly antagonist lifted from the scene, which may enable him to take a shortcut to wherever that time capsule is located. No, Whiteley, we must proceed on the basis that time is of the absolute essence. So no tasters!"

"Oh well," I grumbled ruefully. "I didn't bring any Camembert with me anyway."

"Hello, hello," Baynes rumbled softly, causing me to jump slightly. Was he addressing some precious-hoarding cavern lurker who had been hiding in the shadows the whole time and was about to slope out of the gloomy darkness?

As it turned out, no. He borrowed the torch from Eric and shone it down onto the floor.

"Someone's been here, recently," he commented. We saw that the dust on the floor had been recently disturbed by a set of footprints. To my untrained eye, they looked as though they could be as little as a few hours old. Were these the footsteps of a murderer, I wondered?

"Looks like I was right about someone purloining the spare set of keys," Eric snarled balefully, the thought of some ne'er do well violating the sanctity of a critical section of his beat clearly having triggered a raising of his hackles.

"Where are they now?" Sinclair asked.

"Safely under lock and key," the Porter replied.

"But are the lock and key safely under lock and key?" I pestered him.

"I think we can safely say that it's not the original copies we need to worry about at this point," Sinclair butted in. "It's pretty clear to me that someone took advantage of poor old Albert's deteriorating mental state, got themselves a five-finger discount on those keys and made themselves a copy."

"Well then," I exclaimed, "can't we blitz all the locksmiths in Cambridge and find out if any of them have taken a copy of a key like this in the last few weeks? There can't be that many locksmiths in town, and surely they'd remember an assignment like this. Those keys are not exactly nondescript!"

"You raise what is almost a very good point, Whiteley," Sinclair responded. "If it were not for the small matter of the invention of the automobile and the railway locomotive, I think that might have proven to be an illuminating line of enquiry. Although, even if they were copied in Cambridge, we would not be able to follow it up until Tuesday. In any event, I am reasonably confident that I know already whose name would be on the ledger."

"Careful, fellers," Baynes called out from up ahead before I could interrogate the good professor any further. "There's some broken glass over here!"

"Hardly surprising," Sinclair said, catching sight of my deflated expression. "The next clue, whatever it was, must have been inside an empty wine bottle. The smashed remnants of which are now scattered before us. If Johnny Murderer has been here before us, as I think we must infer from those footprints, he was hardly going to leave the next clue intact for us to retrieve, was he? No, I think we can safely say that we've been leapfrogged, my friend!"

"I don't much care for being leapfrogged," I commented grumpily.

"No? Don't be disheartened, my lad. This is where it gets

really interesting! Did Long John Silver get disheartened when the quest for Captain Flint's treasure looked hopeless? No, he just rolled his eyes, shot another sailor and got on with the job! A broken bottle is no more than a jigsaw puzzle. So let's go and get a dustpan and brush and see what we can piece together, shall we? Our antagonist has left a trail of chaos in his wake. And we will follow it like a pack of sniffer dogs!"

And with that, he scuttled off back in the direction we had come, in search of a dustpan, a brush and, I hoped, a solution.

"We'll have our doggie biscuits yet, Mr Whiteley," Inspector Baynes chortled as we stared after him. "You wait and see!"

CHAPTER 6

*In which the suspects gather for an awkward dinner, I order the
pork cutlets, and wild accusations are thrown around willy and
indeed nilly, including by your narrator, who decides to test his
powers of deductive reasoning, with mixed results. Oh, and some
people are arrested.*

I

Within minutes of our leaving the cellar, Inspector Baynes
had his forensics boys crawling all over the area, leaving
Sinclair's dustpan and brush and Roger Whiteley Esquire in
the same boat, i.e. somewhat surplus to requirements. It was
almost time for my dinner rendezvous anyway, so I bade
farewell to Sinclair. The good professor, evidently disappointed
that he was not going to have unfettered access to the evidence
for the purposes of pursuing his own investigations, greeted
my departure with a vague absent-minded wave. He had
clearly decided to hang around and "make himself useful," as
he put it, by keeping an eye on what the forensics team were up
to. They looked less than thrilled at this prospect.

I was a little early, so upon arrival at The Ivy, I decided to
grab a drink at the bar. I had a look around to see if any of my
comrades in arms had arrived yet and was confronted by the
sight of a large, graceful green hat.

I looked to see what was underneath it and was surprised to
see that it was currently housing none other than Detective

Sergeant Jacqueline Chen. As you may have gathered, I had taken rather a shine to this pint-sized policewoman even when she had been on duty. Now, although I had my suspicions as to whether she was genuinely off duty, she was dressed up so elegantly that I could not help praising her with a faint "damn" under my breath.

If there was a momentary flicker of discomposure in her eyes on catching sight of me, presumably arriving rather earlier than she had expected, she concealed it very quickly and looked up at me with a warm, sympathetic smile.

"We meet again, Mr Whiteley," she said cheerfully.

"In far more congenial circumstances, Sergeant," I agreed, trying in vain to attract the barman's attention in a very English sort of way. "Am I allowed to ask how the investigation is going?"

"Of course you are. The slight fly in the ointment is that I am not allowed to give you a meaningful answer to the question!" She evidently played it by the book a little more than her boss did, I thought, but decided not to push it nonetheless.

"And it's Jacqui, by the way," she added. She didn't pronounce it with a "q", obviously, because that would have been damn weird; I found out how she spelt it later on. The similarity that her name bore to a certain Hong Kongese martial artist star of the silver screen had of course not escaped me, and it is a testament to just how enamoured I was of her that I neglected to make a side-splittingly hilarious joke on the subject.

"Are you off duty, then?"

"I am," she said with a smile, sounding almost convincing. "But in case you're worried that we're not devoting our full resources towards investigating your friend's death, rest assured that this evening is the full extent of my Easter break."

"Crikey," I exclaimed sympathetically. "Won't they even

give you Monday off if you catch the bastard tomorrow?"

"It depends how quickly I get through the paperwork," she said, her tone humorous but at the same time not filling me with optimism that the scenario I had outlined was at all likely.

"Daaarling," a drawling voice interjected from behind her, and I was surprised to see the dapper pathologist from this morning looming up behind Jacqui with a hint of a smug smirk on his lips. He seemed to be wearing an identical suit to the one he'd had on this morning and was still carrying it off with a sickening degree of aplomb. I presumed that he must have changed, though, as the suit did not seem to be stained with any bits of Ed.

I had not imagined that Jacqui would be dining here alone, but still I found the emergence of a debonair gentleman companion distinctly unwelcome, especially one as suave as Mr Cut and Slice. Nevertheless, I was scrupulously—if grudgingly—polite, extending my arm for a handshake. He looked at me with amusement for an instant before taking my hand and doing his level best to crush it to powder.

"Hi," he said with a grin. "Simon Silkington, good to see you!" He then moved swiftly on before I had even had a chance to blurt my name out, saying, "Look, Jax, love—the waiter chappie just told me our table was ready, so we'd better toddle."

As he laid a proprietary arm around Jacqui's waist, he repeated, "Good to see you," his voice dripping with insincerity like poison from the tongue of a serpent. If I'm being brutally honest, I was really struggling to warm to the fellow.

"Bye, Roger." Jacqui shrugged apologetically as she was firmly escorted to her table by her "hot date." It may have been wishful thinking, but I thought I saw a slight grimace pass over her face. Blood boiling, I had another crack at hailing the barman, this time successfully. Perhaps the sight of my thunderous expression was enough to signal that I was not a customer it was safe to ignore.

II

As it transpired, they had our table ready before the barman had even had a chance to pour me my beer.

There followed twenty minutes or so of awkward solitary pint sipping. As a confirmed bachelor, I normally don't mind dining solo. But doing it at so large a table felt decidedly awkward, and I couldn't help feeling that I was being watched by the other diners. And not just Jacqui and her egotistical escort, either, although the fact that they had bagged themselves a table that allowed them to watch us without their being in our line of vision themselves eliminated any doubt in my mind that the charming Detective Sergeant was here in an official capacity. No, it was everyone else giving me funny looks. I felt like a goldfish on display. Surely no-one knew who I was? Was Ed's murder the talk of Cambridge?

Britta and Neil were the next to arrive. Neil was behaving in a revoltingly ordinary manner, given the filthy secrets he was keeping, but I could hardly have expected anything else. Still, he and I would be exchanging words as soon as I got the opportunity. Britta was putting a brave face on things, but even with her, normally the bubbliest of individuals, the conversation felt somewhat mechanical.

For once, I found myself actually pleased to see Lydia, Steve's wife, who came in followed by her husband a couple of minutes later. I had forgotten that she had been planning to make an appearance this evening and was surprised that she was willing to make the effort, given her obvious disdain for all of her husband's mates, your humble servant included, and that was leaving aside the whole murder thing. But at least conversation around her was always awkward, which might mean that the evening would feel more normal after all.

Only, of course, it wasn't the slightest bit normal. It

occurred to me that this would probably be the last time all of us would be gathered in one place. Of course, we would continue to meet up in twos and threes here and there, but given the events of the last twenty-four hours, the next twenty-four would have to be pretty bloody spectacular for anyone to be up for a repeat of the experience in another twenty years. At this point, any further reunion of any kind would feel like the most pointless sequel since *The Coward Robert Ford Strikes Again*. Looking at my deflated chums, I was pretty confident that none of us had it in us to turn the weekend around at this point.

Steve grabbed my arm as he sat down.

"Sorry about earlier. I was out of order," he said quietly.

"Don't worry," I replied magnanimously. "We're all a bit on edge at the moment. What have you been up to since lunch?" Steve shrugged.

"Just wandering around on my own. Revisiting old haunts, and trying to lay some ghosts to rest." He was prevented from going further by an inappropriately proprietorial hand being placed on his shoulder.

Naturally, the hand belonged to Sadie, who had evidently not got the memo that Lydia would be joining us. She was wearing more make-up than The Joker and was looking at least as deranged, which could only mean one thing. She had come here to flirt. She was horrified to see Steve sitting between me and his wife, meaning that she had no easy route of access to him. Left with no alternative but to sit next to Neil, which was in truth no alternative at all, she nabbed the seat next to Lydia and proceeded to spread her elbows as wide as possible to maximise her personal space at the expense of her neighbour's. Remarkably, she remained completely oblivious to the sharp glares she was receiving.

Jammy arrived fashionably late, as was presumably his prerogative as an MP, and so did Tanya. The latter studiously avoided meeting my eye. Dan, however, was nowhere in sight, which troubled me somewhat. We gave him twenty minutes, then ordered. None of us seemed particularly keen to drag this out.

Conversation was stilted. None of us, to the best of my knowledge, had been caught up in a situation like this before. In my experience, normally when someone dies, the conversation revolves around what a lovely person they were (even if they weren't), how much they had loved their family (as if this was some sort of novelty), with everyone exchanging funny stories and anecdotes about them (even if objectively they weren't all that funny).

"Lovely" might have been stretching it, but all of us did have plenty of genuinely amusing stories about Ed. He had been a laugh. But it didn't seem appropriate to go into any of that now, given how he had died, and given how the elephantine spectre of suspicion was looming over us so heavily that it might as well have spared itself the effort, parked itself in one of the spare seats, and ordered itself a G&T.

Talking about the murder itself was obviously somewhat problematic. Of course, our minds were buzzing with little else, and I was sure that every one of my companions was as keen as I was to find out everyone else's take on "whodunnit." But where did one start? Who was going to be the first to put their head above the parapet?

Strangely enough, all this awkwardness set me to thinking about the rules regarding not walking on the college lawns back in our undergraduate days. That had been one of the few college rules we had all strictly adhered to, principally due to the "hilarious" anecdote that Mad Dog McFadden had regaled us with during Fresher's Week, about the time he had held a transgressor upside down from a fourth-floor window and shaken them up and down like a bottle of Paul Newman salad dressing until they had begged forgiveness for their despicable misdeed. He had probably been exaggerating (slightly), but he had definitely achieved his aim of making it clear that we could expect rigorous and vigorous enforcement of this particular college decree.

Right now, when it came to the murder, we were all "tiptoeing around the verge"—just as we had back then, this time through fear of opening that macabre can of worms and where that might lead us, rather than the iron fist of the tyrannical ex-Porter. Sadie, with her typical lack of tact, ended up being the first to sink her stiletto into the sacred grass.

"I just hope the police don't expect us to come back up here if they have any more questions," she broke in plaintively, interrupting Neil, who had been saying something safely anodyne about how funny it was that the shops might change but the feel of the place never did. "I thought they were being so heavy-handed. We all have lives to get on with. They just need to clear this up as quickly as possible. Obviously, none of us could have had anything to do with...with what happened, so why treat us all as if we're under suspicion?"

"Cos we are all under suspicion, bitches!" came a slurred voice from behind her. Sadie jumped out of her skin as Dan Finn, very drunk indeed, practically slid into her, giving her a taste of her own medicine with an excessively intrusive shoulder hug from behind, and visibly recoiling when he caught a whiff of her cloying perfume. He stumbled into one of the spare chairs, stuck his hand in the air, and clicked his fingers.

"Can we have some service over here, please?" he shouted aggressively. "What's everyone having?"

I gently pointed out that we had already ordered drinks and they were on their way but added that he should feel free to get himself one (a cowardly error).

"Or not," Tanya added sharply. Dan gave her such a glare that I wondered for a second whether he had in fact been quite as fast asleep as she had assumed when she and Ed had been dancing the Paphian jig the night before. The same thought had obviously occurred to Tanya, because she quietened down quite quickly after that.

"So who's the favourite then?" Dan demanded boisterously, looking around accusingly at all of us.

"Favourite for what?" Sadie asked idiotically, wrinkling her nose. Dan rolled his eyes and made an aggressive stabbing motion.

"Come on, hasn't anyone opened a book on it yet? It's what Ed would have done if one of you cocksuckers had got yourself skewered!"

I could see Lydia cringing. She leaned over in Steve's ear and whispered something. She needn't have bothered lowering her voice; it was quite clear that she was pushing for a hasty exit before Dan really started making a scene. But she was too late. I knew of old that once he had slipped a "cocksucker" into the conversation, other "c" words would be hot on its heels.

"Well, you might as well come out with it?" Dan barked aggressively. "I s'pose you all think it was me cos I passed out in his room. Reasonable assumption, I guess. In fact, I reckon that was what the police were supposed to think. Except it's bollocks, and that's why they let me go. Kept me in there for hours, but they couldn't pin a single thing on me!"

His tone was now triumphant.

"Cos I loved that guy, and whichever of you did this had better pray that the police get to you before I do! Cos if I find you first, I'll fillet you!" He banged his fist on the table, knocking over a glass in the process and getting a lapful of icy water for his pains.

The one positive that came from that little speech was that I now knew I had been paranoid earlier when I had believed that everyone else in the restaurant was surreptitiously sneaking glances at our table. They hadn't been then. But they sure as hell were now. Only minus the surreptitious bit.

"OK, that'll do!" Steve rose to his feet, clearly itching to deck the bellicose dipsomaniac. I looked at Tanya, who looked terrified that someone was about to get seriously hurt. She was not the only one. Jammy Jeffers looked like he was examining the space under the table to assess whether he could get away with hiding under there, curled up in the foetal position, until the staff managed to kick Dan out. Sure enough, a waiter was coming over, his face thunderous. I decided it was time to engage in a spot of de-escalation.

"Can I have a quiet word?" I whispered in Dan's ear, laying a hand on his shoulder and steering him, gently but firmly, in the direction of the gents. I made a gesture for Neil to help me out. Neil looked perplexed and gave me a "Why me?" look. It was understandable that he would normally expect me to have volunteered Steve instead, but I was damned if I was going to pass up this opportunity to corner the wannabe adulterer. Britta nudged him, and he reluctantly inched out of his spot and laid his hand on Dan's other shoulder.

III

Together, Neil and I successfully managed to navigate him all the way to the latrines without knocking over any of the other tables or any stray diners, although Jacqui's magnificent hat nearly came a cropper as we passed her table. I noted with some small degree of pleasure that they had skipped the starter and moved straight to the main course, although Simon Silkington's smirk was still very much present and correct.

As we moved off, I heard Sadie say, "I can't believe he thinks it was one of us!" and Britta bluntly telling her to shut up. With Sadie, one could only remain tactful for so long before the urge to be rude bubbled up inexorably to the surface.

Once we had reached the safety of the lavatories, we stood Dan over the sink and splashed some cold water over his face.

His reaction was a tad uncouth, but it seemed to bring him back closer to what one might loosely term "his senses."

"How much have you had to drink?" Neil asked.

"I dunno, man," Dan slurred, apparently considering the question to be of limited relevance. "A few."

He turned to me and breathed beery fumes into my face.

"I was in the room, Rog! Slept right through my best mate being murdered when he needed my help. Woke up to find him just lying there..." This recollection was clearly too much for him, and he lurched away from me and vomited noisily into the nearest loo. I inched towards him, despite the fact that both of my nostrils were clamouring for me to run for the hills.

"Why didn't you alert someone? When you found him?" I demanded as he raised his head. He gave me an uncomprehending, bloodshot stare.

"Well, I panicked, didn't I? Didn't want it pinned on me. Stupid really. Didn't get me anything except a shitload of extra suspicion. That fat copper dragged it out of me without too much difficulty in the end." He leaned back against the cubicle wall and slowly started descending onto the floor. I hoiked him back up, not out of sympathy or any particular desire to rescue my old pal from getting a damp bottom, but because a disturbing thought had just occurred to me, triggered no doubt by his use of the word "pinned."

"If you found the body, then you know what was found on his forehead," I said fiercely. "Pinned there, in fact. Was that you? You had a bit of a run-in with Steve last night. Maybe it occurred to you to use his artistic tendencies against him. Throw him to the wolves to save your own skin, was that it? I should have let him wallop you out there!"

I surprised myself with my aggression, but the more I thought about it, the more it made sense. Dan could be a childish son of a bitch when he wanted to be, and he held grudges.

"What? I don't know what you're on about, mate. I saw there was something on his face, but to be honest I was more concerned about what was sticking out of his chest!"

Neil was sidling towards the door, looking awkward and guilty in equal measure.

"Oh, no you don't!" I pointed a finger at him. "I want a word with you!"

Neil sighed and rolled his eyes.

"What is it?" he asked stiffly. I glanced back at Dan, who now looked as though he was rallying a bit, albeit from a very low base.

"If I send you back out there, are you going to knock anything over, assault anyone, or accuse anyone of murder?" I demanded bluntly.

"No, man!" He waved his arm in what he presumably believed was a reassuring manner. "I've got it all out of my system. I'll be a fucking choirboy for the rest of the evening, scout's honour!"

The image of Dan standing up on a table and subjecting his unfortunate co-diners to a rousing chorus of "panis angelicus" briefly fluttered through my mind like a whimsical butterfly. In the end, though, I decided to trust him. My common sense was in this instance overridden by the thought that, just perhaps, my accusation had been unfair. After all, it had in no way been supported by any evidence other than almost twenty years of watching him generally behave like a petulant prick whenever somebody rubbed him up the wrong way. Dan managed to work out how the door worked on the third attempt and made a typically graceful exit, leaving me alone with a seething Neil.

"Well?" he asked, folding his arms in a rather I'm not angry, I'm just disappointed primary school teacher sort of way.

"Saw you on Parker's Piece earlier, old boy," I commented. "With the delightful Daisy! Care to explain the nature of your relationship with that young lady and why it seems to involve quite so much hand wringing and knee bending? Was there a bit of 'give me your answer do' going on?"

"Fucking hell!" Neil snarled with such ferocity that I instinctively took a step backwards. I was expecting hostility, but I had at least expected it to be tempered with a bit of defensiveness and some half-hearted attempt to explain himself.

"You bastards really are a pack of vultures, aren't you?"

"I think the collective noun for vultures is 'committee,' I bleated feebly, baffled by the way the conversation had tumbled so quickly into the field of ornithology. "Or 'kettle,' when they're in flight formation!"

"Piss off!" Neil spat. "I don't know what you think you saw, but you're not getting a penny out of me! And for what it's worth, not that it's any of your business, Daisy and I are friends, and that's it. If you know her name, I guess you must have spoken to her. Did she tell you any different? Well, did she?"

I had to confess, he'd got me bang to rights there. I was still reasonably convinced that the two of them had, despite their protestations to the contrary, been at it like rabbits, but so far, I was no closer to snaring this pair of deceitful coneys than I had been when I had first caught sight of them on Parker's Piece.

But his instinctive reaction had, I thought, been rather interesting. Why had he immediately assumed that I was intending to blackmail him rather than sticking up for a pal? His reference to "vultures" suggested that I had not been the first of our pack, flock, parliament, puddle or flange, depending on whereabouts in the bestiary you think we slot in best, to broach this sore subject with him.

My mind was suddenly wrenched back to the threatening text message Tanya had shown me earlier that day, in which he had indicated that Ed would have cause to regret it if there was one word out of line, and to Tanya's comment about his looking daggers at Ed in The Mitre. Would Ed, that most congenial of companions, for whom "laissez-faire" had been close to a religion, really have stooped to blackmailing Neil over a spot of illicit trouser-dropping, something that he himself had been not entirely averse to on occasion? Well, perhaps. It was becoming increasingly clear to me that I had not known my old friend quite as well as I had always supposed.

"Now, if you've quite finished, I'd appreciate it if you'd stop meddling and keep out of my business!"

"Britta is my friend," I retaliated coldly. "If you hurt her..."

"My wife is quite capable of taking care of herself. Something you'd know if you were really as close to her as you like to think you are. You'd also know that I'm not the one with fidelity issues!"

"I beg your pardon?" I spluttered, rather knocked for six by this latest salvo. Neil's bland face curled up into a bitter sneer.

"Didn't tell you that, did she?"

"Who was it...I mean...?"

"You met my cousin Alan, I expect? He always was 'social.'" He spat. "You'll probably remember him from our wedding, ironically!"

A memory half stirred in the back of my mind. There had been a cousin on the stag do, I recalled. A dominant character, bit of an attention hog, but entertaining. Practically identical to Neil physically, only more fun. I had never really understood what Britta had seen in Neil, whose admittedly good looks had never struck me as being anything like sufficient compensation for his cavernous charisma deficit. Yet, for all that, it had never occurred to me that Britta wasn't satisfied in her marriage. This sort of made sense when I thought about it, though. Alan, the roguish black sheep of the Norman clan, offered all of the upside, with none of the downside.

"They were doing 'rock-climbing classes' together, or something like that," he snarled. "That was her story. And I swallowed it hook, line and sinker. Even thought it was nice that she was getting to know my family better."

"One can certainly have too much of a good thing," I muttered under my breath. Fortunately, he didn't hear me.

"Oh, it's all over now, of course. Persuaded me that it was a mistake. Just a bit of fun that got out of hand. That it didn't mean anything. Christ! For someone with such an anarchic spirit, she doesn't half talk in clichés sometimes."

"When was this?" I ventured.

"Last year," Neil replied curtly. "It was what it was, and now we've moved on. I've invested very heavily in this marriage." A wooden, stolid, stubborn look had appeared on his face. It was a troublingly transactional turn of phrase, I thought.

"If I wasn't married, would Daisy and I have had some sort of future together? Maybe. But it's not something I'm prepared to even contemplate. And that's what I told her this afternoon. I was on my knees because I wanted to keep her friendship, on the basis that both of us had to understand that it couldn't ever be anything more. That wasn't something she was prepared to accommodate," he added stiffly. "So that's that."

Was it? I couldn't help wondering.

"Well, that will leave you more time to focus on your marriage," I suggested acerbically. Perhaps unnecessarily so. The poor chap was, after all, opening up to me far more than I had expected him to. I could see him clenching and unclenching his fists and his teeth, and the squeaking noise from his shoes suggested that even his toes were probably at it.

"Look," I mumbled awkwardly, slightly worried that my agitated companion was about to burst. "I do remember Alan, and it is my considered opinion that he's a bit of a twat, and deep down, Britta will know that too. Her twat-radar was always uncannily accurate. And at the end of the day, she chose you. She loves you. I have no idea how hard marriages are because I've never been a principal participant in one, but I can assure you that I wasn't bringing this all up to blackmail you or anything. That is very much not how I roll."

"You?" He laughed hysterically.

"Sorry to break it to you, 'mate,'" he went on. The word "mate" was definitely in speech marks, and it had definitely been deliberate. "But you're the least of my worries."

He yanked open the door with such force that the handle almost came off, and stalked out.

I scurried after him, but much to my horror, rather than sitting back down at our table and going for the standard British approach of putting on a brave face, the fuming cuckold simply kept walking, not even looking at his startled wife as he stormed past.

"Neil?" Britta called after him, shooting me a confused, accusing glance as she got up, then pushing past me as she tried to catch up with him. Feeling like I rather owned this mess, even if I was not the ultimate instigator, I followed in their wake. By the time Britta and I made it outside, Neil had already disappeared from view. Tears in her eyes, she rounded on me furiously.

"What did you say to him?" she demanded, her eyes blazing.

"Well...I...er..." my sentence spluttered to an abrupt halt. I waited, hoping that she would fill the void of painful silence, even if it was to give me an earful. She was obviously not feeling that merciful, though. She let the silence linger, raising a barbed eyebrow and waiting for me to explain myself properly. Oh well, in for a penny and all that...

"I got it into my head that your husband was boffing one of the nurses at Addenbrooke's," I explained. "They both strenuously deny the charge. And then he spilled the beans about your little dalliance with Adultery Alan."

"He told you about that!" she exclaimed furiously.

"Well, I think he was a tad upset," I explained delicately.

"Jesus Christ, he's never going to let it go, is he?" She was shaking now, and close to tears. "God, I'm so bloody ashamed. It was a mistake. A stupid, childish, immature mistake. It meant nothing. Believe it or not, Roger, I really, really love my husband. You have no idea what I've had to do to make things right between us. And I really thought it had worked. He hadn't mentioned it for months until you stuck your oar in. He finally had me believing that he'd moved on, that it was ancient history. But no, he just loves to cling on, wallow in his inflated sense of victimhood, and now he's airing our dirty laundry all over Cambridge. Sodding brilliant! And what the hell's all this about a nurse?"

"Well, I think that's better coming from him, all things considered."

"Oh no you don't!" she hissed, grabbing my arm vigorously. "You've missed your chance to stay in the trenches, Rog! You're in no-man's land now, so you'd better start spilling the beans before the machine gun fire starts up!"

"We've got to that stage of the evening already, have we?" came an amused, lilting voice from behind me. A very familiar voice, but one I had not heard for seventeen years.

IV

"Niamh!" In spite of the gaping hole I had rather awkwardly just torn in the fabric of her marriage, Britta's flushed face lit up at the sight of her old friend. She shoved me out of the way to give her erstwhile bosom buddy a warm embrace.

I have already alluded to the fact that Niamh the Gymnast had not had an altogether idyllic time in Cambridge last time round, what with the singularly brutal way that the University, her tyrannical parents, and Ed had lined up and taken it in turns to give her the boot after she had failed to come up with the goods in her second-year exams.

I had known her as a moderately attractive blonde girl, slightly chaotic, perennially stressed out, with hair that was rarely properly brushed. The sort of girl who was always dropping her bags on the floor and spilling them everywhere. She had been a shocking lightweight when it came to drinking, but she hadn't let that little detail affect her rate of consumption.

And when she got pissed, she got weepy. It had soon become "tears before 9pm" most nights of the week, and it hadn't been long before her reputation as a bit of a handful had got so widespread that even the College Welfare Officer had started avoiding her.

Given that, of all of us, it had been Britta who had been Niamh's rock, always the most tolerant of her histrionics, and at times almost like an older sister to her erratic friend, it was a trifle odd to see their situations now reversed. Now it was Britta whose personal life was falling apart before her, whose tears were falling before 9pm. In contrast, the impression I was getting from Niamh was that at some point over the last seventeen years, she had taken the active and wise decision to get her shit together. Here she was, returning to the scene of her ignominious downfall, with immaculate hair, a small compact handbag that looked very secure indeed, and a wry smile playing on her lips.

"Hello, Roger," she greeted me after Britta had released her from her warm clutches. "Bet you never thought you'd see me again!"

"And how delighted I am to be proved wrong, Niamh," I responded smoothly, oozing so much charm that I may well have left a puddle of the stuff glistening in my wake. "But I must say I am amazed to see you. Is this..."

I stumbled, wondering how to broach the delicate question of just what the hell she was doing here. Her presence here surely couldn't be coincidence, yet I could not for a moment imagine Ed having invited her to join the merry party.

"All part of the grand plan? Oh yes. I'm sure dear Ed will fill you in when we go inside." My mouth dropped open. Clearly, news didn't travel quite as fast as I would have expected.

"I would query that," I began gently, but Niamh had already lost interest in me and turned back to Britta, clearly having sensed from the intensity of the hug she had received that something was amiss.

"You are coming back in, right? You're not going to leave me to the tender mercies of these judgemental imperialist English bastards on my own, are you?" Her tone was jocular, but I could see the pleading look in her eyes. Niamh had come a long way from the tremulous wreck I had once known, but I could still sense that she was expecting this meeting to be far from an easy one. Why on earth had she thought it worth the hassle of coming all this way, after having made such an apparently decent fist of moving on with her life? If it was all about closure, and laying ghosts to rest, then I feared she was in for a bit of a shock.

I looked at Britta, feeling that she would have a better sense than I did about how best to broach the sticky subject of Ed's gruesome stabbing without undoing seventeen years of getting over the selfish bastard's emotional manipulation in one fell swoop. But Britta did not meet my eyes. Clearly, I was still in the doghouse.

"It's OK," Britta said while grinning, almost succeeding in masking her pain. "Neil's gone off in a huff, that's all. Bollocks to it! I'm going to let him stew in his own juices for an hour or two."

She linked arms with Niamh and they both ventured back inside, leaving me once again lagging behind, looking and feeling just a tad stupid.

"There is something I need to tell you, though, " Britta said as we wandered over to the table.

But her attempts to soften the inevitable emotional gut punch Niamh was about to receive were thwarted by a hearty and not particularly welcoming "Fuck me!" from Dan as the two ladies approached.

"Good to see you again too, Daniel," Niamh riposted. "That gift of the gab of yours hasn't diminished with age, I see."

Dan gave her a surly look, as he usually did whenever anyone drew attention to the fact that he wasn't exactly the same age as he had been when he was twenty. Tanya got up and embraced Niamh warmly, and others followed suit, in most cases noticeably more half-heartedly. Sadie was unable to muster up more than a dismissive wave.

"You look amazing!" Tanya gushed. "I've been meaning to text you for ages. How are Eoin and Lee?"

Niamh grimaced.

"Eoin's dead," she said, sounding awkwardly apologetic at inviting death into the conversation. "Heart attack got him last year."

I vaguely recalled Britta mentioning in conversation a few years ago that Niamh had landed herself a much older husband. I believe that "coffin dodger" was the phrase she had actually used. Clearly, the poor fellow had finally forgotten to duck. Lee was presumably the son.

"Lee's doing well, though, considering," Niamh went on, rolling her eyes. "Typical moody teen, though. I left him in our hotel room playing games on his phone. I think spending an evening with a bunch of weird middle-aged strangers was pretty much his idea of hell."

"He's here in Cambridge?" Britta asked.

"Yeah, I thought I told you I was bringing him?" So Britta at least had known that Niamh would be making an appearance. I wondered how many others that applied to.

"In spite of my horror stories, he still wants to apply to Cambridge, believe it or not," Niamh went on. "No doubt he wants to prove he can outdo his old mam. We flew in last night, and we've been doing the rounds of colleges all day. He likes the look of Tit Hall, of all places."

"Typical teenager then," I jibed. This comment elicited a few tepid chuckles, which was probably more than it deserved. Niamh sat down, much to my relief. My pork cutlet had arrived, and I was having a mild panic about the prospect of it getting cold before I had a chance to sink my carnivorous teeth into it.

"So Ed invited you, then?" Steve asked, sounding a little disbelieving and more hostile than I felt was really warranted, given the way he had treated her back in the day. I had fully expected Dan, who had behaved with similar boorishness, to remain truculently hostile, but I would have banked on Steve having a bit more tact. "Or did you just happen to be visiting at the same time as the rest of us?"

"Steve!" Lydia tutted, slapping him on the arm, not particularly gently.

"If it was the second of those, are you planning on kicking me out again, Steve?" Niamh responded caustically. Steve frowned and looked down at his plate, apparently wrestling with whether to respond with something aggressively defensive or to back down and admit that he had indeed behaved like a prize cock when he had joined forces with Ed and Dan to eject her from Chateau Dickinson. Fortunately for him, Niamh had no interest in further salty wound rubbing.

"I'm sure dear old Ed will explain all when he gets back, anyway," Niamh continued. "I'd hate to steal his thunder. Where is he, by the way?"

There followed a short, awkward silence.

"Ed's dead, Niamh," Tanya said, bravely taking the plunge. Niamh's instinctive reaction was—oddly enough—to laugh, her nose wrinkling in disbelief.

"What? Is this some sort of wind-up? Some sort of practical joke, is it?" She was getting pretty worked up now.

"After the way you all treated me, I'm still the butt of the joke? You bastards haven't moved on at all, have you? He texted me yesterday, and the point of my being here this evening is to introduce him to his son if either of them actually deign to show up at some point. So really, Tanya, not that funny! I'd have expected something like this from the rest of this merry band of jokers, but not from you!" Behind her, our waiter cleared his throat.

"Can I take your order?"

"FUCK OFF!" Niamh yelled. He fucked off, briskly.

Tanya looked crestfallen as she glanced around at the rest of us imploringly for back up. I'm sorry to say, chivalrous chap though I usually am, that I was still too busy digesting this latest bombshell from Niamh (not to mention what had turned out to be a rather juicy cutlet) to be of much assistance. Unfortunately, it was Dan who filled in the silence.

"He really is dead. Someone stabbed him," he declared, helpfully reinforcing his point with an illustrative movement with his steak knife, just in case she was in any doubt as to what the word "stabbed" meant. Niamh went pale and clutched her hands to the side of her face as if trying to tear off a mask, her previous poise and composure now thrown to the winds. She looked around at all of us once more, moving from face to face as if imploring one of us, any of us, to deny it. No denial came. At length, Britta put a steadying hand on her arm and proffered her own glass of wine. Niamh took a sizeable glug.

"Oh, put that thing down, you alpha prick," Britta snapped at Dan, who was still holding his steak knife in a rather perilous position. "It's true, I'm afraid, Niamh. We're not sure what happened. The police are investigating."

"My God," Niamh gasped after she finally got her breath

back following the shock. Or possibly the huge gulp of wine. "He finally pushed someone too far, then."

"Lee was his son?" Tanya asked, looking stunned. Niamh gave her a withering look.

"Oh, come on, Tanya, you must have done the maths!" Tanya, like Britta, had stuck by Niamh in her difficult days, but while Niamh absolutely revered Britta and indeed, now I recalled, had made her Lee's godmother, I had never detected much by way of similar warm feelings towards Tanya. It was clear from the glances around the table that there was a general feeling that Niamh had been unnecessarily rude. But then again, she did have the unenviable task ahead of her of having to go back and tell her son that he was not going to get a chance to forge a relationship with the father he had never known, because the aforementioned father had just been brutally murdered.

"Look," I broke in when it was clear that no-one else was going to, "I know that this is a bit weird...."

"You think?" Lydia scoffed.

"But," I interjected, waving a finger in the air, "as we're all here, we might as well make the best of it. Niamh, order something to eat, for goodness sake. We've got nearly twenty years of catching up to do. I don't even know what you're doing for a living!"

Niamh shook her head and pushed back her chair.

"Counselling," she replied, "which is why I know that sitting here and making small talk with you guys when I should be with Lee is a seriously bad idea and one that he won't forgive me for."

Suddenly, there was a loud buzz from someone's phone. Several of us around the table jumped nervously, and then everyone went through the time-honoured ritual of checking their pockets simultaneously. The buzzing continued.

"Whose is that?" Jammy eventually demanded, rather

irritably. He had been very subdued for the entire evening and had doubtless been dwelling gloomily on his dwindling re-election chances if (when) his involvement in these turbulent events became public knowledge.

"I think it's coming from under the table," Sadie said, naturally making no move to be the one to retrieve it.

"Oh, for crying out loud," Britta sighed, rolling her eyes and diving under. She emerged a few seconds later with a phone. By this time, the buzzing had stopped. Tanya had gone pale.

"Is that..." I began, drying up as it occurred to me that there was a non-negligible chance of Tanya making an impromptu pair of earrings with my testicles if I continued the sentence. Her horrified expression had told me the answer anyway, and she had evidently seen the writing on the wall as she reached over and grabbed it from Britta.

"It's my phone," she stated flatly, glaring around the table belligerently. "I left it in Ed's room last night."

She was clearly done with "meek and mild."

"Oh my GOD!" she yelped as she saw that the phone was spattered all over with dark stains. "I don't know which of you did this, but you could at least have wiped off the bloodstains, you sick bastard!"

There was a chorus of horrified gasps, which were swiftly silenced by Tanya's scream as she suddenly sensed the presence of someone immediately behind her. It was a female waiter this time. The first guy was presumably still recovering from his abrupt dismissal earlier.

"Is everything OK with your meal?" she asked.

There was an awkward and oh so very British mumbling of assent, but I don't think any of us were entirely devoting our minds to the question. No, we were well and truly distracted by the unwelcome unravelling of the "it must have been a complete stranger, probably some sort of lunatic" comfort blanket that so many of us had been clinging to all day.

"Screw this—I'm out of here," Tanya hissed, throwing a couple of notes on the table and rising to her feet.

"I hope you're not taking that phone with you, Miss Bullock," came a rumbling, familiar voice from a few paces away.

V

Inspector Baynes strode cheerfully towards us, flanked by a couple of junior police officers who, unlike their boss, looked as though they were no strangers to the gymnasium.

"I hope you've all supped well, ladies and gentlemen," Baynes continued jovially as he approached. "I see you've already had your main course. I'm glad of that; I don't much care for arresting people when they haven't had a proper meal down 'em. Tends to make 'em cranky."

"Now, let's move on to the 'just desserts,' shall we?" he went on, throwing out that terrible line with such lip-smacking relish that even the late Robert Newton might have encouraged him to tone it down a bit. I couldn't help glancing over at Jacqui, who shook her head imperceptibly and mouthed something at me that, inexpert lip reader though I am, I had no difficulty interpreting as "He does this all the time!"

"A little update, to begin with," the inspector continued. "We've done a pretty thorough examination of that there CCTV footage of the entrance to D Block to see whether some mysterious stranger came stalking in there with a great big knife at the dead of night, and do you know what we found? The square root of bugger all."

"Nobody ever goes in, and nobody ever goes out!" I murmured.

"Could everyone please pack it in with all the Willy bloody Wonka quotes!" Britta said, glowering at me.

"I prob'ly don't need to tell you what that means, do I?" Baynes continued inexorably. "Means he was done in by someone sleeping in the same corridor. Or else some expert climber who somehow snuck in through the back. But either way, our pool of suspects has shrunk quite considerably.

"Now, we're not quite ready to make an arrest just yet, but we are going to have to take a couple of you down to the station to answer some questions about some new information we've recently received. Willingly would be good, but kicking and screaming can also be accommodated, you'll understand. The end result will be just the same either way. Both of my goons here are trained in jujitsu, taekwondo, karate, kickboxing and naked mud wrestling, so I'd recommend coming quietly, if I was you!"

Both of the aforementioned goons remained impressively impassive and expressionless.

"All clear? Right, well then, in no particular order, let's start with you, Miss Bullock. We'll need you to come with us. We'll let you have your phone back sooner or later; it'll be sooner if you let us know where we can lay our hands on Mr Dickinson's phone. Might also help your chances as we decide whether or not to charge you for holding onto it in the first place!" Tanya had gone puce. She slowly turned her head to look at me.

"You bastard, Roger!" she hissed. I spread my hands wide, not wanting to say anything for fear of getting added to the inspector's little list. However he had come to find out about Tanya's little peccadillo, it had naff all to do with me. It was going to be an uphill struggle to persuade her of that, though. Quiet, bookish Tanya had always had a bit of a volcanic temper bubbling up under the surface, but it had become apparent from the events of the last twenty-four hours that she had more of a tendency to erupt than she used to.

I am ashamed to say that at this point, the uncharitable part of me was hoping that she would end up spending the night in the cells. At least that would give me a bit of a head start before she started hunting me down like a dog. I found myself wondering when the next flight to Paraguay was due to leave.

"And who's the other feller I was after?" Baynes mumbled, checking his list. "Can't read my own handwriting, but there was someone else I wanted to talk to. Something about a video of a racist, anti-Semitic rant that Mr Dickinson had got wind of and the perpetrator wouldn't have wanted disseminated. Oh yes, I remember now, it's our local MP. James Thaddeus Jeffers, Hesquire. We've had you down to the station before, as I recall, sir. Gave you a nice exclusive tour when you first got elected! This time it might be a rather more intimate experience!"

Baynes allowed himself a gruesome chuckle.

"This is outrageous," Jammy snarled, flouncing to his feet. "I'm happy to assist with enquiries, Inspector Baynes, but you'll regret trying to humiliate me in public!"

"Oh, I sincerely doubt that, sir! I'm a singularly petty-minded individual. It's stuff like this that allows me to sleep easy in my bed at night. Now, shall we be on our way? Mind how you go, ladies and gents. Do enjoy the rest of your evening. I think Happy Hour is still going on at Las Iguanas if you're interested! Cheery-bye!"

The inspector and his posse trooped out, Tanya and Jammy accompanying them. Both looked shell-shocked, catatonic even. Those of us who remained weren't much livelier. Only Baynes seemed to be in good spirits. He started whistling "A Policeman's Lot is Not a Happy One" on his way out, but he was fooling no-one. He was having the time of his life; the proverbial pig in shit, and that surely meant that he must be confident of getting a result. One way or another, this dreadful uncertainty would soon be at an end. The truth would emerge, and the cloud of suspicion would lift from everyone else, meaning that I would be able to rest easy in the knowledge that I still had at least a few friends who I could pretty conclusively state weren't homicidal arseholes.

"Shall we get the bill?" I suggested.

CHAPTER 7

In which my quiet pint with Steve Taylor ends in a spot of mild bloodshedding, a missing cast member finally makes an appearance, along with a prodigal son, Saddam Hussein shows his true colours, we almost discover the time capsule, and almost get ourselves killed in the process.

I

My suggestion of skipping dessert, just or otherwise, had not met with much resistance. Britta had disappeared immediately anyway to seek out her seething spouse, while Niamh had gone back to her hotel to break the tragic news to young Lee, so our numbers were by this point getting pretty thin. I noted that Jacqui and old Smoothie-chops Silkington had already made a discreet exit as well, and I wondered whether all this hoo-ha had prompted a change in her evening plans.

The waiter was, unsurprisingly, prompt with the bill, given the disruption we had caused. Having been the first one in, I ended up being the last one out. In spite of my eagerness to meet up with Sinclair again to update him on what had transpired, all the excitement had necessitated another nature call before I departed. I had therefore bid a cursory farewell to the other stragglers, and by the time I returned, they had all left.

As I strode down Trinity Street, however, I could not help passing Steve and Lydia, who were arguing noisily in the street. There was nowhere obvious for me to stop and skulk undetected in order to catch the finer points of detail, but even if I hadn't been an incorrigibly nosy old sod, I could not have helped but catch a bit of it. They were really going at it hammer and tongs.

"Have you any idea what I've sacrificed for you?" Steve was roaring as I slunk past them on the other side of the road. Sadly, I could hardly stick my hand up and say, "I don't." But whatever it may have been, Lydia's response to her apparently self-sacrificing husband was neither grateful nor gracious, and involved accusations of selfishness and illegitimacy, following which she stormed off in a terrifying fury. I attempted to move on discreetly but flubbed it entirely by walking into a bollard.

"Rog," Steve called after me, his voice cracking.

"Are you all right?" I asked.

"Yeah, yeah," he creased his face into an unconvincing smile. "Just a bit of a domestic. Come for a drink with me, will you? Haven't seen enough of you over the last ten years, and you're a good mate, Rog, a really good mate. Let's check out The Pickerel, see if their offering's changed since we were last in there. Come on, one last pint?"

I hesitated, keen to get back to Sinclair to pursue whatever new line of investigation he might have plucked out of thin air since we parted. But I felt it incumbent on me to make the most of Steve's overtures, given that he usually played his cards so close to his chest. He had been behaving oddly all weekend, but in truth, I had also been rather missing him, so if he didn't turn out to be harbouring murderous secrets, it would be a useful opportunity for a catch-up. And I was also very keen to get to the bottom of what had prompted the very noisy and vitriolic ding-dong I had just witnessed.

"Ah, go on then, you've twisted my arm," I acquiesced cheerfully.

The Pickerel has a reasonable claim to be the oldest boozer

in Cambridge. Nestled on Magdalene Street just over the bridge, it had once held the honour of being CS Lewis' favourite haunt when he was in town and fancying a night on the tiles. Dating back to the 16th century, it had variously been a gin palace, a hotel, a brothel, a brewery and a funeral parlour (presumably an unusually lively one). We were just ambling over the bridge when I heard a loud "Eh up!"

Normally, when I am accosted in that part of the world, it is by some obnoxiously youthful tout in a straw hat aggressively trying to entice me to go punting. It was a bit late in the day for that, but my instincts kicked in, and I immediately started looking at my shoes to avoid any possibility of eye contact.

"ST! Roger the Dodger!" the voice came again, in an unmistakable northern accent. We turned to see Random Chris Cleghorn bearing down on us with an expression of almost deranged delight on his round face.

"Well, well, well, if it isn't the invisible chump," I muttered to myself. The completist in me had been wondering whether he was going to be making an appearance at some point. The cast list from Time Capsule Night had now been fully reassembled.

"How are you diddling, lads?" he demanded as he enveloped each of us in a rather awkward hug. I immediately detected that his approach to deodorising remained defiantly minimalist.

"Um..."

We told him about Ed, sticking to the salient points and omitting the grisly details.

"Chuffing Nora!" Chris exhaled. "Well, that explains why he hasn't been picking up his phone."

"Did you try calling him a few minutes ago?" I asked, wondering whether I had uncovered the source of the mysterious phone call that had scared the bejesus out of us all. Then I remembered that that had been Tanya's phone. Bugger, I thought. I'm going to have to write all this down at some point. Rookie errors and all.

"I've been trying him on and off all day," Chris replied non-committally. "Wanted to tell him I could make it along to the thing he'd organised for tonight after all. You went ahead without him, then? Honouring his memory and the like, I suppose."

"Something like that," Steve muttered.

"Are you lads off home, then?"

"No we're…" I caught sight of Steve's savage expression and piped down, but I had already been gesturing in the direction of the pub and failed to lower my arm quickly enough. Whilst Chris was a chap who was on occasion slow to take the hint, this was not one of those occasions.

"Quick bevvy in The Pickerel, eh? I'll join you. You can give me the full lowdown on whatever the hell's been going on! I'm buying." Blimey! This wasn't the Chris I remembered. If he was dusting the cobwebs off his wallet, he had to be pretty damn curious.

II

The Pickerel had always been pretty popular in my student days. Judging from the crowds through which we had to navigate our entry, business was still booming. Steve and I managed to secure a table covered in empty glasses near the back of the room, while Chris disappeared into the throng to get the drinks in.

"The police suspect me, you know," Steve whispered as soon as Chris was safely out of earshot. His expression was grim, without even a flicker of frivolity in his eyes.

"Oh, what bollocks!" I protested, conscious that this was getting pretty heavy, pretty quickly, and that I didn't even have the reassuring presence of a drink in my hand. "You're not one of the ones they took in for a second round of enhanced interrogation. That's got to be a good thing, right?"

"Lulling me into a false sense of security," Steve growled.

"Rather ineffectively, by the look of it!" I replied. "Look, you had no particular beef with Ed. Not recently, anyway! Why would they pick on you as being any more of a suspicious character than the rest of us disreputable rogues?"

"Let's just say I didn't make a particularly favourable impression when they interviewed me earlier," Steve said and sneered bitterly. "I was sweating like a pig through the whole thing!"

"Well, we're thirtysomethings who had just come out of an evening trying to party like tweenagers! We were all hung over to buggery; they'll have taken that into account!" Steve laughed, and again, if you'll pardon the melodramatic flourish, it sounded to my untrained ear like the hollow laughter of despair.

"If only that was all it was," he snorted at last.

"Oh, for the love of Michael Flatley, whatever deep dark secret you're harbouring, will you just spit it out?" I exclaimed. "Isn't that why you dragged me over here? A friendly listening ear?" Steve burst out laughing.

"You want the truth?" he demanded. The statutory Jack Nicholson impression never came. Instead, he simply smiled wearily and continued speaking at a normal volume.

"Lydia's pregnant. Baby's due in September. So in light of the new parental responsibilities that will be coming my way, I've spent the last few weeks trying to finally kick the cocaine addiction that I've been wrestling with for the last twenty years. And it's turning me into a sweaty, suspicious, paranoid wreck!"

"Ah," I exhaled. Cocaine made a lot of sense now that I thought about it. Steve was a hell of a networker when he bothered to put in the legwork. He had managed to get himself invited to a fair few parties with the more rarefied students back in the day, whilst the rest of us had been far too unfashionable to get a look in. It was entirely unsurprising to me that such substances might have been passed around at gatherings of that nature. And he had been looking distinctly peaky all weekend.

"Well, congratulations on the sprog," I began hesitantly. I thought it was best to start with the easy bit. Even I know the proper etiquette for reacting to baby news. Warm congratulations and don't focus on how gruesomely awful all those sleepless nights will be. I knew they had been trying for a baby for a number of years, so it was rather depressing to see Steve now looking so daunted and overwhelmed by the prospect.

"As for the other bit," I added, "well, that's good too, I guess. It'll save you plenty of money for cuddly toys and jumperoos, anyway!"

He laughed, but the moment of levity was short-lived.

"Look, I'm sorry," I went on, striking a more serious note. "I'm an unobservant oafish cretin at the best of times, but I really had no idea. Have you really been on the stuff since university? I thought that was the preserve of the corporate lawyers. And bankers, of course. Must have cost you a sodding fortune!"

"I've had to dip into Lydia's reserves on more than one occasion," he admitted. "I've been a complete shit to her. It's not surprising that she's been having second thoughts about our marriage. Looking at what else is out there!"

He was gripping his now empty glass so tightly at this point that I was afraid it might shatter.

"But this was an opportunity to turn the corner on that," he went on. "If I was strong enough."

"You will be," I declared reassuringly. "You'll have to be! Fatherhood changes a man; it's a well-known phenomenon!"

Steve snorted (just air, before you ask).

"Redemption isn't that easy. There's no magic button!"

"Oh, come on, no feeling sorry for yourself. You've got it made! Good career that you've managed to excel at in spite of all your powdery peccadillos! Kid on the way. A loving wife." I tried to avoid hesitating before the last entry on the list but did not completely succeed.

"She does know about this, doesn't she?" Steve shook his head slowly.

"We don't have that sort of marriage," he sighed. "She can't know. She mustn't know! Ever! I've blotted my copybook too many times already."

I'm no marriage counsellor, but that sounded distinctly unhealthy and unsustainable to me.

"Who else does know?" I asked.

"Britta, of course. She even did it with me a few times, when we were together. Ed knew too. Even threw away my stash once, back at uni. Flushed it down the bog, the bastard. Refused to speak to him for weeks after that. I knew deep down that he was trying to help, but I was still furious. Whatever shit he might have pulled on other people, Ed was a better friend to me than I gave him credit for. In spite of everything."

"What has Britta said?" I asked. Britta was quite good at handling this sort of crisis, and I was wondering whether she might have provided some advice I could potentially piggy-back off.

"I talked to her about it this afternoon. She wants me to come clean," Steve scoffed. "To Lydia, to the police, to everyone. It's all very well for her to preach 'honesty is the best policy' when it's someone else's life on the line, but in my position, there's no way she'd fess up. She can keep secrets with the best of them, that one!"

"Yes, she told me about that fling with Neil's cousin," I commented. "There are plenty of secrets in our group. You'll have worked out already what Tanya was getting up to with Ed last night. At least that's something you don't need to worry about in your marriage. Not with Lydia. Anyone who's devoted enough to you to spend the evening in the company of a group of prize twats who she obviously despises isn't going to dump you at the drop of a hat, you know! Not permanently, and especially not if you do manage to clean yourself up."

If I had thought that my words would reassure and placate my worked-up companion, I had miscalculated cataclysmically. The pint glass finally buckled beneath the redoubled pressure coming from his furiously clenched fingers and smashed, gashing his hand open. He immediately started bleeding all over the table.

"Golly!" I exclaimed in a disturbingly Joyce Grenfell-esque manner as Steve plucked a shard of glass out of his bloodied hand. "I didn't think that was physically possible. Must have been some sort of flaw in the glass, I suppose."

We were getting some extremely dubious looks from the other patrons.

"Why can women make you do the stupidest shit?" he demanded, apropos of nothing, as I handed him a hanky I happened to have in my pocket to staunch the bleeding.

"I don't think that womankind played any part in you going all Greek on me!" I retorted, surprised to hear such misogynistic bile coming out of the mouth of a man who had prided himself on being a feminist even in the Neanderthal days of the early Noughties. "Or is it just plates they like to smash up? Anyway, isn't it time you took some responsibility for your own actions? Your wife may be a bit standoffish at times, but from everything you've just told me, I don't see how you can possibly say she's been the one in the wrong! And whilst I applaud your efforts to kick the habit, you need to rein things in. I know you're suffering, but there's no call to start behaving like a Poundshop Incredible Hulk!"

"That's just it, though," Steve cried out. I was unsure whether the beads of moisture lining his cheeks were tears or sweat, but his eyes were bloodshot to hell, and he was really getting himself into a right old state. "I'm out of control! I don't know what to do!"

"Did you kill Ed?" I asked him suddenly, leaning forward, my voice sharpening as I cut to the chase. A bit direct, I'll admit, but there had been quite enough pussyfooting about for one evening, and exhaustion was starting to gnaw away at my patience.

Unfortunately, my interrogation was interrupted by a sudden commotion at the bar. I looked up to see Niamh brusquely elbowing her way through the crowd towards where a hairy but noticeably youthful-looking lad was trying to catch the barman's eye.

She reached him and walloped the poor lad around the face. This was greeted by a lot of staring and a few cheers. No-one, alas, stepped in to defend the mortified youth.

"You selfish little bastard," she spat. "I've been looking for you all over town! Do you have any idea how worried I've been?"

"Jesus, mam," Lee muttered. "I thought you were out for the evening!"

"So you thought that while that cat was away, the mouse would go out and get pissed, is that it?"

"I was just trying to get a pint, mam!" a red-faced Lee protested. "I wasn't injecting heroin into me eyeballs!"

"Don't you take that tone with me, Lee, not after the evening I've had!" Niamh shouted.

"I wanted to get a feel for the place," Lee said sulkily, "without being smothered. Sod all chance of that with you around!"

"Smothering you? Is that what I'm doing? Do you think I don't know that you were out of your room last night? I'm supposed to be relaxed about the fact that you're creeping off into a town you don't even know at the dead of night? Have you got a girl here, Lee? Is that it? Met her over the internet, did you? You're just like..." she broke off, slamming the nearest chair in frustration and causing its occupant, who I was strangely unsurprised to be able to identify as one Mr S Hussein, to almost jump out of his skin. Talk about a bad penny, I thought. At this point, the man was practically auditioning to be my new shadow.

"You may as well say it," Lee said quietly, his tone cold and sullen. "You think I don't know why you really brought me here?"

Niamh's eyes widened, and a look of pain passed over her face.

"Why do you think I brought you here?" she asked at last.

"You wanted to introduce me to my father," Lee said derisively. "I could have told you you were wasting your time. Eoin was my dad. I'm not on the market for a replacement, and I have absolutely no interest in meeting him!"

"Yeah, well, that won't be happening now anyway," Niamh said quietly. At this, she looked up and finally caught sight of me. Her mouth tightened, and her eyes sharpened. I waved at her awkwardly, then turned to Steve to assess his reaction, only to discover that he had disappeared.

III

I scanned the entire pub, but Steve was nowhere to be seen.

Was it something I'd said?

"We'll talk about it on the way back to the hotel," Niamh said shortly, placing a fist in the small of her unfortunate son's back and escorting him firmly off the premises. Lee looked thoroughly relieved that his mother had finally realised what a spectacle she was making of both of them, but he still kept his head down as he made for the exit, clearly unable to bear the prospect of meeting the eyes of any of the mocking punters.

Chris, meanwhile, was finally making his way over with our drinks. Placing the beers on the table, he gestured back over his shoulder.

"Did you hear all the kerfuffle back there? I think that was whatshername. You know…"

"It was," I agreed. "And that was her son. They'd never have served him anyway. I know for a fact he's only sixteen. She had him bang to rights, though. The mens rea was there."

"They're nowt *but* mens rea at that age!" Chris agreed sagely.

"Where's Steve gone, anyway?" He looked around.

"I sort of accused him of murder, and he went off in a snit!"

"Oh aye?" Chris's relentless cheeriness was unabated. "Well, you're drinking his pint then, and while you're at it, you can fill me in on what's been going on!"

So I did.

"Flippin' heck," he exhaled as I finished my tale. "So if I'd come along last night, I'd probably have ended up spending most of today in a police interrogation room like the rest of you! And Niamh turning up like a spectre at the feast? She were trouble, that one! And she'd been up the duff when Ed kicked her out all them years ago? Bloody hell, I've heard it all now!"

Not quite, I thought wryly. I had omitted all mention of my time capsule theory. Nor had I mentioned Sinclair, or the fact that he was, with my assistance (such as it was), investigating the murder. Chris had always struck me as a fairly trusting chap, but I didn't want to say anything that would put him on his guard and cause him to clam up. His involvement in all this was probably entirely tangential, and he certainly had the whiff of a red herring about him. Or perhaps that was just sweaty armpit. But at this point, I wasn't prepared to rule anything out.

"So why were you planning on giving our little shindig a miss, then?" I asked. "You were missed!"

"Oh, I doubt that," Chris snorted, "though it's decent of you to pretend! Truth is, I'd kind of had the hump with the lot of you over the last ten years or so. Don't get me wrong, deep down I always knew I never fit in with your crew, no matter how hard I tried to play along. It just took me a while to admit it to myself. Though the fact that you all gave me the cold shoulder after we graduated helped me along a bit, I have to say!"

I started to protest; a lot of noise came out of my mouth, but very little of it was intelligible even to me.

"It's all right, mate." He cuffed my shoulder with a grin. "You were better than most of the rest of them, and anyway, I'm a big boy now. No point in feeling sorry for meself. I did kind of resent it, mind, which was why I ignored old Ed's texts and emails for so long when he tried to set this all up. Too little, too late, mate, was my first reaction. But I got up this morning regretting not having showed up last night, if I'm honest. We're all older now, I thought. Perhaps things'll be different. And if they're not, well, what's one evening out of a lifetime?

"But then I couldn't get hold of Ed, and when I showed up at The Ivy, Gary the waiter said you'd all gone. Very cagey, he was. I can see why now! I was on my way home when I spotted you lads on t' bridge."

There was a sudden fit of coughing from behind us, and I turned to see old Saddam shuffling about, still trying to find somewhere to park his pint of Guinness. I pointed him out to Chris, who looked baffled.

"The Iraqi guy?" he asked, as though I might possibly have been talking about the other Saddam Hussein who ran a fish and chip shop in Llandudno. "Can't see the resemblance, if I'm honest."

Evidently, this was an in-joke that Chris had not managed to get in on back in the day. Distracting though the constant presence of my scruffy stalker was, I tried to redirect the conversation back to more pressing matters.

"So if you were on your way home, you must still live locally then?" I surmised shrewdly.

"Yup, we've got a place off Histon Road, and our shop's on Mill Road, so a nice easy commute."

"The shop? Sorry, I obviously have a lot to catch up on!" Frankly, the "we" was news to me as well, but I thought it best not to sound too incredulous about that development.

"Yeah, we've set up a fancy wine and cheese shop. We're aiming to be Cambridge's answer to Valvona and Crolla. Early days yet, but we've made a good start, and we're cautiously optimistic. It's fun, actually. Exhausting but fun."

"Kids yet?" I asked. Chris' eyes lit up with delight and pride as he grinned broadly.

"Yep, three of the little scamps! Lucy's working on the fourth as we speak. Not like that!" he added, seeing my amused expression. "She's just coming into her third trimester. Look, I've got some photos if you want to see them."

Few parents accept "no" as a legitimate answer to this question, so I acquiesced gracefully. He had, of course, already brought out his phone and started scrolling through his photos. I made all the right noises (I think) as I was treated to several hundred photographs of the various mini-Chrisses getting up to all the things that small children normally get up to.

Back in his university days, Chris had dreamt of becoming a prominent film director. Whilst I can't imagine Guillermo Del Toro's backup plan would have involved selling Stilton, it struck me now that Random Chris had almost certainly ended up being the happiest and most balanced of all of us. Weird, smelly, and overly intense, my cheese-hawking companion had nevertheless found his groove in life and settled into it with cheerful gusto.

Chris kept scrolling through his photos, but suddenly, one came up that was rather at odds with the "cute children frolicking" theme of the rest of the album. Unless one of his children had had one hell of a growth spurt and suddenly developed a pair of horns.

"What's that?" I asked.

"Ah, nothing!" Chris said evasively, immediately pocketing his phone, but not before I had got a close enough glimpse to determine that the figure in the photo was unmistakably Chris himself, caked in red make-up and dressed up as Beelzebub. And Halloween was six months away.

"Do you think that the police'll want to talk to me?" he asked.

"I don't know," I replied, wondering whether I should press him on the photo.

"Well, I hope they catch the bastard soon! This is starting to give me the willies. Fancy another?" he added, seeing that I had finally got to the bottom of my glass.

"No, I'd better get back," I declared, rising to my feet and extending my hand. "Good to see you, Chris. We really should keep in touch this time!"

He expressed his agreement with this proposition, but I could see from his face that he thought I was being insincere. I wasn't, actually. Chris meant well, even if he was harbouring a resentment against the rest of us for our decade or more of shameful snubbery. I did, however, wonder whether that resentment might have gone far deeper than his breezy demeanour would have us believe. Was there truth in that old saying, "Never fuck with a cheesemonger"?

We parted ways on the corner of Bridge Street and St Johns Street. I yawned as I mooched back to St Crisps to update Sinclair on what had transpired. I was fervently hoping that the good professor would decide to call it a night and that I wouldn't have to do any more detecting that evening. It wasn't so much the clear and present danger of getting horribly killed that was putting me off; put simply, I was cream-crackered.

The door to the Master's Lodge had been left unlatched so I let myself in. I wandered around the ground floor, but Sinclair was nowhere in sight. I didn't want to call out because I presumed that young Jasper would be asleep by now, so I settled back onto the sofa, grabbing a book from one of the available bookshelves to read while I waited. I said to myself that I would give him fifteen minutes before I hit the hay. I devoted my attention to Chapter 1 of *The Strange Case of Dr Jekyll and Mr Hyde*: "The Story of the Door".

It transpired that I would not have long to wait, for I had barely got past Mr Utterson's rugged countenance when the door opened and someone walked through it. I looked up and immediately felt as though I had been thrust into a 3D virtual reality version of one of those children's flap books that match up the top half of one animal with the bottom half of another, to create a "Tigerdillo" or what have you.

The bottom half of Sinclair's face was present and correct. That chin was unmistakable. What was more surprising was the fact that he was also holding onto someone else's chin, dangling loose in his hand, complete with a scraggly beard trailing below it in tangled wisps.

The top half of his face was unrecognisable. Or unrecognisable as Sinclair, at any rate. He was in the process of removing the end of his own nose when he spotted me lurking on the sofa. Figuratively speaking, I think it is safe to say that he jumped out of the skin that he had already been in the process of pulling off. A number of pieces in the jumbled jigsaw puzzle I had spent the last twenty-four hours living through suddenly slotted into place in my confused brain. I clicked my fingers triumphantly.

"Hello, Saddam!" I said.

IV

"Saddam?" Sinclair squeaked indignantly as he casually pulled off a bushy eyebrow and deposited it in a convenient waste-paper basket. "I don't look anything like Saddam!"

"Think 'post-invasion hole-dwelling Saddam'," I said. The transforming criminologist grunted noncommittally as he peeled off his other eyebrow and started wiping what appeared to be a thick layer of make-up off his face with a tissue.

"That was not at all what I was going for when I created Neville Brotchenbeerdigen," he grumbled peevishly.

"Neville who?" I spluttered incredulously.

"Please don't splutter incredulously like that, Whiteley. You're getting saliva all over our brand-new coffee table. Dear old Neville has served me very well over the years, as it happens, and his backstory is far too complicated for me to explain at this juncture. But I'm damned if I'll stand by and listen to him being compared to a subterranean despot!"

Completing the transformation back into his familiar old self, Sinclair pulled off his wig and threw it onto a bust of Churchill that was sitting on the mantelpiece, where it nestled incongruously.

"Whilst your enthusiasm for updating me on the fruits of your evening's labours is commendable, I hadn't realised you would be coming back here quite so quickly!" he sniffed. "Emily is slowly inching her way towards vegetarianism, I'm afraid, and had reminded me we were all out of mung beans. I felt sure I could get a quick Sainsbury's run in before you resurfaced. It's always the little things that catch you out in the end!"

"So this is a hobby of yours, is it?" I asked as neutrally and non-judgementally as I could, determined not to allow him an inch of space to shift the conversation onto the subject of legumes.

"No, no, no! You're making it sound frivolous! As you know, I have developed a certain degree of deductive dexterity over the years, which I have used to my advantage in carrying out extensive investigations into Cambridge's fetid and festering criminal underbelly! Well, I can scarcely inveigle my way into the confidences of such rapscallions and ragamuffins when I'm Gerald Sinclair, can I? In their eyes, I am just another pompous, port-supping, tweed-jacketed tit from the university! Relish this rare moment of self-deprecation, Whiteley, without sniggering, if at all possible. I'm not going to be making a habit of it.

"Anyway, in order to circumvent such shortcomings, I have gradually developed a number of grubby and unsavoury alter egos. These characters have become familiar figures around town over the years. So frequently are these fragrant rascals seen, patronising their regular haunts and generally bringing down the tone of the neighbourhood, that no-one would take seriously for a moment the possibility that every single one of them is in fact married to the Master of St Crispian's College!"

"Next you're going to tell me you're the guy who hangs around town playing the guitar in the bin to terrify the tourists!" I commented sarcastically.

"No, no. The musician in me wouldn't be able to tolerate the acoustics. But Cambridge's plethora of eccentrics does provide me with the perfect cover. It's an unorthodox approach, I'll admit, but the police tolerate me, as my persistence has paid dividends. In the last two years alone, I have managed to unmask five sex pests, three knife attackers, two gangs who specialise in the swift removal of catalytic converters from the quieter Cambridge car parks, and…"

"A partridge in a pear tree?" I ventured.

"Very witty! But as it happens, I've got my eye on a much

bigger bird now, unrelated to the matter at hand, but if I used the phrase 'Napoleon of Bike-Napping' it might give you a sense of the stakes at play here!"

"I saw you coming out of The University Arms earlier today," I suddenly remembered. "Were you keeping an eye on me?"

"Well, naturally!" Sinclair declared unrepentantly. "You didn't really think I would let you out on the motorway without stabilisers on day one, did you?"

"Any vehicle that needs stabilisers shouldn't be on the motorway anyway," I pointed out pedantically.

"Hah! Your tendency towards overcautious defeatism was another of my concerns!"

"But where were you? Saddam, sorry, Neville Brobdinag or whatever his name is, was nowhere to be seen when I was talking to Tanya!"

"Well, no, I didn't want to overexpose poor Neville; I knew you had seen him last night. Quite plausible to have him lurking around The Baron of Beef and indeed quietly pickling himself in The Pickerel, but The University Arms is not really his arena. I had to make an abrupt costume change when I was summoned to investigate another little problem on the other side of town, where Neville was more likely to be the man for the moment. I was rather put out with myself when I saw that you had spotted me."

"So you were..." I felt as though I was thinking my way through a bowl of thick soup, but the brothy mists suddenly cleared, and I realised that I knew who "Eric Hitchmough" was, "...the gnome with the thick Yorkshire accent who got me through that coughing fit in one piece."

"Aye, 'tis true, that! I probably saved thy life, lad," Sinclair ventured modestly.

"But what I still don't understand is what you were up to last night, hanging around with Mad Dog McFadden in The

Baron of Beef? Even you can't possibly have been investigating a murder that hadn't been committed yet!"

"Ah," Sinclair exhaled, steepling his hands together and staring into the distance before replying. "Well, you see, I think perhaps I was, although I didn't realise it at the time."

"Can we notch this down a couple of reading levels?" I pleaded. "You've completely lost me!"

"Don't you remember what Finlay McFadden was laying into our esteemed MP about?" Sinclair helped me out, teasing the thoughts out of my brain like wool being pulled off the backside of a stubborn old ram.

"Oh, we're back to Albert Ross, are we?" A thought suddenly struck me, and I grinned ruefully. "You reminded me earlier about Mad Dog laying out his suspicions last night, but I'd never mentioned it. You could only possibly have known about that if you'd been there. I can't believe you've had me fooled all these years."

"Yes, well, it was quite the battle of wits," Sinclair murmured dryly. "Finlay McFadden and Gerald Sinclair have always had a respectful and business-like but distant relationship. I am Edinburgh to his Glasgow, essentially. Besides, although I had nothing to do with the decision, I am part of the 'establishment' that booted him out of college. The same establishment that in his eyes is behind Albert's demise. Apparently, we've moved on from Princess Diana to slightly less glamorous targets. No, if he knew more than he was letting on about that so-called accident, he was never going to confide in Gerald. It was clear to me that I needed to get Neville Brotchenbeerdigen on the case!"

"So did McFadden give you anything?"

"Well, no. To tell you the truth, it was all rather disappointing. He can't complain about crimes going unsolved if he isn't going to go to the trouble of procuring me some half-decent clues! But there's nothing to spice up an investigation like a second murder."

"But where's the connection?" I demanded.

"Well, let's take a step back, shall we? Let me rustle up a couple of glasses of port, and I'll explain where I think we've got to!"

V

A few minutes later, when our glasses were suitably replenished, Sinclair smiled at me indulgently and said, "Do feel free to interject at any point if you disagree with me. I'm always happy to set people straight when they've got the wrong end of the stick!"

"This feature of your personality had not gone unnoticed," I commented quietly. Sinclair, as was his custom, prattled on undeterred, pretending that I had not spoken.

"So, in short, I think that what has transpired is this. Ed Dickinson, laddish trickster that he was, decided that gathering all his old cronies together for a few drinks and a slap-up meal in the usual way one does was far too dull a prospect. Remembering that he was still in possession of the now infamous time capsule, he decided that instead of just handing them out at the end of the evening, he would ramp up the nostalgia factor by setting a treasure hunt around college.

"Clue One was easy. All he had to do was pop over and see dear old Ronnie and persuade him to hold onto the Easter egg. Starved of company and grateful for the attention, the old fellow was putty in his manipulative hands. Clue Two was more ambitious. We know that both sets of keys to the wine cellar are now in the custodianship of our reliable friend Eric. Now, Eric is a fastidious stickler when it comes to college rules. He was always going to be a tough nut to crack, so Mr Dickinson had to look elsewhere for a weak chink in the college armour.

"He found it in the late Albert Ross, who used to be left in charge of the spare set before his recent demise. Don't you remember that Dickinson intimated to you last night that he had seen the dear old fellow shortly before his death? Albert was always one for keeping in touch with his old students, heaven help us, and taking them out for drinks whenever they were in town. It is also worth noting that in the last few years of his life, his bladder control was tenuous at best. Perhaps Dickinson pilfered the keys while Albert was off pointing Percy at the porcelain, as it were. Alternatively, he may have lifted them from the old man's belt as he helped him home after a few too many. In any event, the opportunity arose. Indeed, it may have been that opportunity that triggered Dickinson's entire plan in the first place."

Sinclair took a moment to swirl the port in his glass. He took a sip, smacking his lips with relish as I waited impatiently for the infuriating fellow to crank up the narrative.

"So, he went on at last. "He finds himself unexpectedly in possession of the treasured wine cellar keys. He doesn't keep them long, simply taking a copy and sneaking them back into the Porter's Lodge. They're gone long enough for even dozy old Albert to notice they're missing, it's true. But when they turn up again, our late lamented Porter presumably concludes that no harm has been done. The fact that nothing is taken from the wine cellar provides added reassurance."

"Could that have been what was worrying Albert?" I wondered.

"Well now, there's a question," he mused. "As I said, Emily couldn't get much sense out of him when he rang her up before he died, but he did say he'd messed up three times, and that it was a particular weakness for your intake that led him astray. Hence my warning to you on the train, which you must admit proved remarkably prescient even by my standards. Unfortunately, Albert provided no further detail, but I think we have now got to the bottom of one of his little peccadillos.

"You will also now see why I poured such cold scorn on your suggestion that we interrogate the cream of Cambridge's crop of locksmiths. We might well have discovered, eventually, who had them copied, but I am almost certain that the name on the ledger would have been Dickinson. He needed a copy of the keys if the treasure hunt was going to work. Our murderer must have only got his hands on them last night, after discovering that the time capsule itself was nowhere to be found. He clearly realised, as we did, that Dickinson had formulated this treasure hunt idea. Unfortunately, he worked out what the keys were for. They are unmistakable, after all. Which meant that he was able to gambol gamely straight across to Clue Two while we were still fornicating about with Clue One."

"So what about the next clues?" I asked. "Given that Johnny Murderer has beaten us to Clue Two, where do we even start?"

"My suspicion, Whiteley, is that the third clue is the next and final one. Which means that we really don't have very much time at all, alas."

"What makes you say that?"

"Human impatience, my dear boy. This was supposed to be a frothy bit of light fun to cap off an entertaining evening catching up with old comrades in arms! Not the basis for a twisty-turny Robert Langdon novel! Ed was trying to keep you all entertained. He would have correctly calculated that if he had made the treasure hunt too laborious, you would have all started peeling off to the pub. So let's work on the assumption that if we can work out where Clue Three is before our homicidal opponent does, we will find our time capsule. Now, unfortunately, the police have taken possession of the shards of the bottle that originally housed the final clue…"

"Well, I can't imagine that those would have helped us much!" I grunted.

"Fortunately, I was able to make enough of a nuisance of myself earlier that Torvill's lackeys let me take a couple of snaps in the interests of making me go away!" Sinclair laid his phone on the table, and we peered together at the photographs he had taken of the glass shards.

"You'll see that we've been rather lucky," Sinclair pointed out. "Dickinson obviously rolled up the clue face up inside the bottle and failed to properly drain the bottle of wine before he inserted it! Look, the ink has run!"

He pointed, and I saw that he was quite right. The larger shards of the bottle were marked with faint inky lines.

"But we're never going to be able to read it," I complained whingily.

"If I had wanted spoonfeeding, I would never have left the crèche!" Sinclair snorted. "You forget that you are speaking to a keen graphologist. The study of handwriting is my toast and marmalade, dear boy! I even came top of the class in those forgery-themed evening classes I took a few years ago!"

"Really?"

"Well, no. Actually, I was somewhere in the middle, but I did well enough to produce a damn convincing certificate that says I came top of the class! Which suggests that I got my money's worth."

"So you're saying you can read the message that was in there, just from the imprint on these tiny shards of glass?"

"Oh goodness me no; that would be far too much to expect! But I have a rough idea of what was in there, all the same."

"What? And how?"

"Dealing with your second question first, like the contrarian I am, I would draw your attention to the length of the line on the biggest shard."

He scrolled back to the relevant photo.

"This isn't writing at all. Our clue is undoubtedly pictorial in nature. So we know we are looking at a drawing. We also know that Mr Dickinson used to work for the well-known London and Reading based law firm of Forsyte Markby. In other words, the very firm which prepared the building contract for the recent structural alteration works that were carried out in college. It would have been fairly easy for Dickinson to lay his hands on the contract drawings and print out a copy of the schematic he was looking for. I am going to take a small but calculated logical leap and surmise that this is exactly what he did. Fortunately for us, the ink cartridge in his printer was evidently full to the brim when he did so!"

"So Clue Three is in college, just like Clues One and Two," I declared. "Well, that's all well and good, but we don't know where, and Johnny Murderer does! And we don't know when he found Clue Two. It could have been at any time after he killed Ed. He's had all day!"

"Well, what a pair of plucky little underdogs that makes us!" Sinclair said jovially. "Still, let's see if we can at least bite at the other fellow's ankles, shall we? Were there any places in college that Ed regarded as particularly special?"

And then it suddenly hit me, before he had even finished his sentence. The answer was obvious!

VI

"It's up the bell tower!" I proclaimed excitedly. "It has to be!"

Sinclair raised an eyebrow.

"We used to go up there sometimes, after a skinful! Or at least Ed, Dan, Steve, Neil and Britta did. Sometimes Jammy too."

"But it's inaccessible!" Sinclair protested.

"Not if you know what you're doing," I replied smugly, milking for all it was worth the novel pleasure of knowing something Sinclair didn't. "There's a hatchway near the toilet next to the college bar. If you stand on someone's shoulders, you can clamber up into the void area directly above. There's a lot of pipes and a couple of boilers in the way. But with a bit of luck and a following wind, you can scramble through to the ladder leading up to the tower."

"Dear Lord," Sinclair exhaled, looking horrified. "And you say that your crowd were scurrying around up there, like a bunch of tipsy overgrown rodents, on a regular basis!"

"Don't look at me in that tone of voice!" I moaned. "I only went up there twice after being subjected to dangerous doses of peer pressure, and I can't say that I cared for it much. The view's not bad, of course, but I happen to suffer from a combination of vertigo and claustrophobia, which was pretty lethal in that context. I'm not all that wild about asbestos poisoning either. Ed and the others couldn't get enough of it, though. On several occasions, the mad buggers actually stripped naked and went out onto the rooftop. Somewhere, there's a very unpleasant photo of them all sitting astride the gable in a line with their knackers hanging out. It was like some sort of pornographic re-enactment of the boat race!"

"If only Clare Balding had been available for the commentary," Sinclair said sardonically, rolling his eyes heavenward. "Well, your account of all that tomfoolery has led me to an important deduction, Whiteley."

"What's that?"

"That you and your friends are a bunch of trouser dropping nincompoops! Ah well, there's nothing else for it but to head on up there, I suppose. It does sound like exactly the sort of spot that Mr Dickinson would choose to end the treasure hunt. I'd better give Taters a call; he'll get all crabby with me if I cut the police out of the loop on this one." He bustled out of the room, his phone already to his ear, absent-mindedly gesturing for me to follow.

We only had a few minutes to wait for the cavalry to arrive, and it was no surprise that Inspector Baynes had decided to delegate the task of joining us in our perilous ascent to Jacqui. Naturally, she had changed into something more sensible. She gave me a quick wry smile, but her attitude now was brisk and businesslike. Simon Silkington was thankfully nowhere in sight. This was no surprise either. Whilst our forthcoming adventure might have afforded the smug corpse botherer the opportunity to impress his date, he would never have been prepared to take on the risk of doing irreparable damage to his nice shiny suit. I had completely ruined a hired tux making that ascent once. I've only just managed to get myself off TM Lewin's shit list.

Jacqui, small and sylphlike, was as ideal for this particular exercise as I was completely unsuitable for it. Last time I had been up the bell tower, I had been twenty and comparatively svelte. I was now a long way, and several trouser sizes, from either state of affairs. It would take a hardy man indeed to bear my weight on his shoulders without risk of injury. Fortunately, Jacqui had brought along one of her more megalithic colleagues, a lumbering constable by the name of Larry, to serve as our man on the ground.

"Good to see you, professor," she greeted Sinclair with a suitable degree of deference, which promptly got switched off when she turned to me. "Hello again, Roger. You guys have been having quite a lot of fun, haven't you? OK, well, let's see what's on the other end of the lead you've been following!"

Just as long as it's not a rottweiler, I thought grimly. She went up first, followed by Sinclair, who was not entirely paunch-free but the possessor of a much slighter frame than yours truly. He clambered onto Larry's shoulders without that indomitable fellow feeling the need to emit so much as a grunt of exertion. The renowned criminologist somehow managed to haul himself through the trapdoor, grimacing and muttering under his breath all the while, and then it was my turn.

By this time, I was definitely coming to the conclusion that nostalgia had been better in the old days. But rather to my surprise—in spite of my intense anxiety at the thought of having to scramble around in that hot, dark, stuffy, uncomfortable environment—curiosity, together with the desire not to embarrass myself in front of the delectable DS Chen, pricked me on. I just about managed to get through the hole before it pricked me off again and I realised what a terrible, terrible idea it was not to leave this silly stuntery to the professionals. By that point, of course, it was too late.

"Are you up, Roger?" Jacqui called out from the darkness. "Have you got the torch?"

I turned it on and shone it around. The glare glinted off Sinclair's spectacles as I located him.

"Ah, good!" the professor muttered sarcastically. "A bit of light on a dark subject. I'm rather curious to discover which variety of animal droppings I have just inadvertently dipped my hand into!"

"Is it that way?" Jacqui asked from a little way ahead. I shone the light in her direction and saw that she was gesturing at a small space beyond the end of the large boiler, which was eating up most of the available space in the confined room like a great overheating beached whale. There seemed to be a strange, faint, flickering light coming from up ahead.

"That sounds right," I replied hesitantly. My efforts to block out the unpleasant memory of my earlier forays into this dark and sinister environment had been rather too successful for our present purposes. I blundered towards the others, pranging my leg on a low-flying pipe in the process. Slowly, uncomfortably, awkwardly, the three of us worked our way towards the gap, the torch in my shaky hand unsteadily guiding our way.

Jacqui ducked through the gap into another chamber. This one was boiler-free but with a lower ceiling, so we had to crouch. Ahead of me, Gerald Sinclair, esteemed criminologist, was shuffling along like the world's most erudite gorilla.

The second chamber looked as though it ended in a dead end, but in fact, there was an alcove on the right-hand side that was just wide enough for a corpulent man to squeeze through (as it transpired) before opening out into a wider, loft-like space, in the middle of which stood the ladder leading us to our precarious destination. I say "middle," but in truth it was difficult to tell exactly how far beyond the ladder the loft space stretched. It certainly felt as though there was a lot of murky darkness back there, though.

"You go on ahead, Whiteley," Sinclair insisted, wheezing slightly. He looked even more uncomfortable than I felt. "In his efforts to aid me to our destination, I am afraid our new friend Larry jostled bits of me that are unused to such jostling!"

As we got closer to the ladder, it became clear that the flickering light was emanating from the tower itself, and it seemed to be growing more intense. Jacqui was at the foot of the ladder now, and without waiting for me to catch up, she started clambering upwards, demonstrating gazelle-like surefootedness. My own ascent was more elephantine than anything else, but I did at least manage to avoid any embarrassing pratfalls.

The air seemed to be thickening as I ascended, and I had to stop to clear my throat when I was about three-quarters of the way up. Was that smoke? I suddenly heard a loud thump from behind me.

"Gerald?" I called out, looking downwards and thus almost missing Jacqui's heel descending rapidly towards me, gravitating perilously close to my unprotected fizzog.

"Back down, Roger!" the sergeant ordered calmly. "I don't want to rush you, but the top of the ladder is about to catch fire!"

"Jesus Christ!" I exhaled, in my panic committing the shameful sin of taking the names of two of Cambridge's lesser colleges in vain.

"Yes indeed," Jacqui agreed, the calmness in her voice now wavering slightly. "And if the ladder catches fire, the top of my head will be the next thing to go, and that would be a really crappy way to end what was supposed to be my evening off! So, quickly please?"

As I doubled back on myself as quickly as I could, I saw a dark hooded shadow pass underneath the ladder, giving it a little nudge in the process. Which, unfortunately, all it took to send the ladder, and its occupants, flying. Jacqui got the better end of the deal, as it transpired, in that she at least had something soft to land on. As the "something soft" in question, I was rather less fortunate. There was a sickening crunch as floorboard made contact with buttock and got the better of the exchange. The torch went flying, and went out.

VII

I roared out in pain, my bellow stifled only when Jacqui landed on top of me, winding me and sending me into paroxysms of agony. The doughty policewoman was not down for long, though. She launched herself back to her feet, using my long-suffering groin as an impromptu springboard, and scurried after the figure retreating in the darkness.

There was a brief silence.

"Are you alive, Whiteley?" I heard Sinclair whisper through gritted teeth from a few metres away.

"Just about," I wheezed, scrabbling to turn on the light on my phone. "Although when Jacqui comes back, I might ask her to put me out of my misery and beat me to death with that shoe that nearly took my eye out a minute ago!"

"Now is not the time to feel sorry for yourself, my laddie!" Sinclair reproached me, rising to his feet with the faintest of groans and limping over to give me a hand-up. He was clearly suffering, and as soon as he had hauled me to my feet, he bent over again, clutching his head and putting his hands on the floor as if to steady himself. As he rose again, I saw a slip of paper clutched in his hand. I squinted at it and could just about make out the letters "ST" at the bottom of the page, but Sinclair surreptitiously secreted it in his pocket before I could read any more.

"What was that?" I asked.

"Oh, just…." Sinclair paused mid-sentence, suddenly looking confused and rather frail.

"Are you alright? Did you get clobbered?"

"Just a glancing blow, but enough to temporarily discombobulate me!" he grunted. "But let's hold fire on the post-match analysis until after we've eliminated any possibility of being incinerated, shall we?"

It was a good point, well made. The flames had indeed started lapping at the top of the ladder, which had landed back in its original spot after much wobbling about. Given that the aforementioned ladder was made of wood, even a lesser intellect like me was able to deduce that sitting around on my bruised posterior feeling sorry for myself might not be a sustainable long-term option. I could see Jacqui running back towards us, her expression grimly frustrated. Evidently, Johnny Murderer had given her the slip, but frankly, I was just relieved to see that she hadn't ended up on the wrong end of a knife in the dark.

"You OK?" I asked breathlessly. She nodded briefly.

"Let's go!" she said curtly.

Jacqui, Sinclair and I walked, hobbled and tottered respectively back the way we had come. It had not escaped my attention that our would-be murderer had gone in the other direction, which suggested that there must be another way out of this infernal rabbit warren that none of us had discovered. But there was no chance of us catching up with him or her now. Time to cut our losses and clamber back to safety and whatever was left of that port.

Larry was still at his post, patiently waiting for us. The doughty PC did his best to avoid pressing on any sore spots as he helped to haul the wounded warriors back down to terra firma. Needless to say, he had not seen hide nor hair of anyone else since we had last seen him, and he made reassuringly sympathetic indignant noises on our behalf when we told him that someone had done their level best to treat us to a permanent, seafood accompanied nap, as Mario Puzo might have put it.

Before we got a chance to venture out into the quadrangle, however, the lights went out.

"Oh, not a bloody power cut!" I moaned. I heard a derisive snort from the darkness.

"A bit too much of a coincidence for that, wouldn't you say?" Sinclair hissed. "No, our old friend Johnny Murderer's tripped the switches! He may be more quick-witted than we've given him credit for! To the Porter's Lodge, lady and gentlemen, at the double!"

We scrabbled through the darkness to the door and found ourselves in the quadrangle. The power was out all over college. Luckily, the moon was unobscured by cloud, so we were able to see where we were going well enough to stumble across the lawn, spurning the diktat of the neat little "Keep off the Grass" signs in our desperate haste.

We arrived at the Lodge to the sound of rummaging in the back room. The back room had always been regarded by us students as a mysterious other realm which was, if anything, an even more dauntingly forbidding prospect than Dante's Inferno, in that it was territory into which we mere mortals would not have dared follow even if Virgil, or some alternative licensed tour guide, had been available to hold our hands.

"Lights are out!" Eric called out helpfully from within. "Someone must have been fiddling around in the substation, damn their britches! I'd better get over there; see if there's anything I can do. Might have to get a man out."

I could hear the distaste in his voice as he spoke. Clearly to Eric, having to "get a man out" to do anything was the beginning of a descent down the slippery slope leading inexorably down to whatever the Porter equivalent of a knacker's yard was.

"Has anyone been through here in the last few minutes?" Sinclair demanded.

"Don't think so!"

"Double drat!" Sinclair snarled. "He's pulled a fast one on us and no mistake. The scoundrel will be well away by now!"

"But how did he get out of college, if not through here?" I asked. Sinclair beckoned me over to him.

"There's one thing you have to remember," he said, summoning me still closer and whispering in my ear. "Eric over there is as blind as a bat! I wouldn't bet against someone managing to sneak past him even in broad daylight!"

"I can hear a duck fart at thirty paces, though," Eric commented icily.

"Was there anything up in the bell tower?" I asked Jacqui. "He must have set fire to something. Could it have been the papers from the time capsule?"

"Looked more like old newspapers," Jacqui said. "But I didn't want to get too close, given the whole fire thing. I quite like having eyebrows."

I chuckled.

"You've had quite an evening, haven't you?" she said with a smile. "But can I suggest that both of you go to bed now? Inspector Baynes and I can take it from here!"

"Quite right!" Sinclair agreed warmly, much to my surprise. "Do let me know when you've caught the bounder, won't you?"

Jacqui looked at him sceptically, then gestured to her colleague.

"Come on, Larry. Paperwork time!" As they filed out, I turned to Sinclair, only to find that he was already bustling towards the Master's Lodge. I staggered after him.

"I've had a thought," I said.

"Oh, frabjous day!" the good professor muttered sarcastically.

"Tanya and Britta went for a drink with Albert a few weeks before he died. I tried talking to Tanya about it earlier, but she didn't have much to tell me, but maybe Britta remembers something Tanya didn't? Maybe I should give her a ring?"

I waited until we were comfortably ensconced back in the Master's Lodge with a fully replenished drink. Sinclair had spent several minutes fumbling around in the cupboard under the stairs attempting to find candles, only for the lights to come back on again just as he had located the right dust-covered box.

I took a long drink before pressing the call button. I was aware that it was a bit soon for her to have completely forgiven me for clumsily removing the stitches from the festering wound at the heart of her marriage just a couple of hours before. Truth be told, I had known that I ought to be calling her anyway, but without the ulterior motive, I doubt that I would have bucked up the courage to do so. I made sure that my phone was on speaker so that Sinclair could listen in, although in truth, he seemed to be lost in his own thoughts.

Unsurprisingly, Britta took a pointedly long time to pick up, and when she answered, it was with a brusque, "What?"

"Um…hi…" I faltered. "I just wanted to check in to see that everything's OK after…you know. With Neil?"

"No, Roger, it isn't. When Neil goes off in a huff like that, it's not just a case of him spending half an hour letting off steam and getting it out of his system. He could be gone for days. He has before. But I suppose I ought to be thanking you for opening my eyes to the delusional false belief I was labouring under, that he'd actually forgiven me for screwing everything up!"

"Look, I'm sure he'll come round," I said in what I hoped was a soothing tone. "You've been together, what, almost twenty years? He's not going to want to throw all that away." I could hear her exhaling noisily in frustration.

"Roger, I'm bloody exhausted, and right now, I don't need a therapy session. I just want to go to bed."

"OK, understood. I'll leave you in peace. It's just, well, there was something else, actually." I could almost hear her eyes rolling on the other end of the line.

"Go on," she said, an edge of frosty ferocity in her voice.

"You and Tanya went for a drink with Albert Ross. Right before he died," I began.

"Mmm-hmmm."

"Well, what Mad Dog McFadden said yesterday has been going round and round in my brain. What if Albert's death was no accident? What if all this is connected?"

"Oh, for Christ's sake. Pack it in, and call it a night, Roger!" Britta sighed. "For what it's worth, we saw Albert for a grand total of half an hour, twenty minutes of which were spent waiting for him to get to the punchline of his Japanese golfer joke, which, as I could have predicted from halfway through minute one, was 'What do you mean, wrong hole?' But he never mentioned the fact that he and Ed were about to be murdered, so I'm afraid I can't help you. Are we done now? Good!"

She hung up.

"Well, that was a fat lot of help!" I grunted. There was a long silence followed by a loud snore from my companion.

"Oh, sorry, Whiteley, are you still talking?" he asked, having been jerked awake by the sound of his own snore. "I'm afraid I was drifting slightly. I fear we may have to pick up the trail afresh in the cold light of morning!"

"Well, that suits me fine," I agreed, yawning a contented

yawn. "I've barely had a moment's peace since I got here. Even last night, I didn't feel altogether comfortable in my room, knowing that someone had been mucking about with my kit and caboodle."

"I beg your pardon?" Sinclair looked up sharply, his eyes narrowing accusingly.

"Last night, when I tumbled into my room half-cut, I discovered my stuff had been moved around a bit, and I got the distinct impression that someone had been rifling through it," I explained.

"And you never thought to mention this?" Sinclair asked, his voice dripping with subliminal menace.

"Funnily enough, there have been one or two supervening events since then, which rather drove it out of my mind until just now!" I pointed out, raising my voice defensively.

"That's no excuse," Sinclair snapped. He was wide awake now and was pacing frantically up and down the room, bristling with irritation. "The wheel is still spinning, but the hamster's long dead, isn't it? Honestly, it's like trying to solve a mystery with Goofy! Do you know that your lackadaisical approach to the dissemination of vital information may have just put another human being in mortal danger?"

"Who?" I asked, a feeling of creeping terror gathering in my bowels.

VIII

"Gavin, the Porter!" Sinclair replied. There was a long pause, as he glared at me reprovingly. "But even so..."

"Gavin? Are you saying that he was the one who went through my things?"

"Well, of course it was," Sinclair huffed. "The man's a ghastly creep of the first water! We've suspected that he's been mucking about with the belongings of our esteemed college guests for a while, but we've never had any hard evidence. He never takes anything, as far as we can tell."

"Just nosy, eh?"

"I fear that there's a little more harm in it than that. I am sure there was nothing in your own travel kit that the grubby little opportunist could exploit to his advantage. But he may have had more luck elsewhere. You told me this morning that he seemed to be rather harping on about the knife that was used to dispatch Mr Dickinson, when you were being interrogated by Inspector Baynes?"

"Well, yes, but that could just be because he's a weaponry nut," I said. "I bet he's got hundreds of similar trophies adorning every room in his house!"

"That is what we shall shortly find out, Whiteley, if you will forgive my harsh words and grace me with your extremely genial companionship on the next leg of our exciting jaunt. A jaunt which is even now drawing to its inexorable conclusion! I know it's your first day, but a few unfortunate cockups aside, I genuinely do think you're sidekicking splendidly so far!"

"We're going to Gavin's house?" I asked, bemused.

"That is indeed the nub of my proposal!"

"Not to bed, then?"

"While I am reliably informed that Gavin sleeps with anything that moves, Whiteley, I fear that he would make an exception in your case. Come, my friend, we have no time to lose!"

"At least two of the suspects are still being interrogated by the police, though," I pointed out. "If the murderer is one of the ones still at large, he'd be a fool to try anything now."

"Hogwash, Whiteley! Torvill messaged me a few minutes ago, and it transpires that your friend Tanya was released hours ago. Our overambitious arse of an MP took a little longer, but he's out too. It's a free-for-all out there, my friend. There's no knowing who's killing whom as we speak!" Sinclair was pacing up and down now, and gesticulating so vehemently that the remaining port almost flew out of his glass.

The professor continued, "We only know that Gavin is almost certainly putting himself in the frame as the overwhelmingly likely next victim. The man couldn't be acting more recklessly if he stripped naked, drenched himself in honey and threw himself into a pit of ravenous bears!"

"How can you possibly know that for sure? Do you think he knows who did it?" I asked.

"As to your first question, I'll explain later, but as to your second, frankly, I'm certain of it! The tricky part will be persuading him to share that information with us. The damn fool no doubt thinks he's sitting on a gold mine!"

"Blackmail?"

"Well, it would hardly be radically out of character, would it? It will not even have occurred to him that someone who has already killed once, if not twice, would be more likely to make a point of adding Gavin's severed testicles to his trophy board than to meekly 'cough up the dough,' as the town scallywags are wont to put it!"

Sinclair's theory struck me as depressingly credible. On the rare occasions when we had managed to get Gavin off the endlessly fascinating subject of how many fit Romanians he had bedded over the years, his second favourite topic of discussion had been how handy he was in a scrap, and how easy it would be for him to kill any of us in a matter of seconds. He would be completely confident of his ability to handle any threat from our murderer. Our efforts at a speedy exit were, however, unfortunately thwarted when we heard a faint wailing noise coming from upstairs.

"Ah!" Sinclair paused. "Young Jasper is having another of his nightmares. I have no idea what the underlying cause of the poor lad's anxiety is, but I had better see to it."

"You don't think it might be the regular references to

severed testicles and trophy boards that his father keeps spouting?" I suggested helpfully.

"I sincerely doubt it, although you never know with youngsters. Jasper is quite the enigma. He has already presented me with five different theories as to the identity of the Zodiac Killer. Three of which were faintly plausible, as it happens. But plop him in front of *Bambi*, the massacre scene from *Finding Nemo*, or Tim Curry trying to out ham Miss Piggy in *Muppet Treasure Island*, and the boy's a nervous wreck for weeks!" He patted me on the shoulder and headed rapidly upstairs to offer a bit of paternal comfort to the troubled bairn.

I picked up my book and got about half a paragraph further into the grisly tale of Dr Jekyll and his dodgy mate, before the Master herself burst through the door. Her tired and harassed expression suggested to me that, if anything, she had had an even more frantic evening than we had. Such, I presume, are the sacrifices that have to be made when wooing the donor classes.

"Oh, hello, Roger," she greeted me distractedly, looking around the room. "Oh, for heaven's sake, he's left bits of Neville Brotchenbeerdigen all over the room! Why can't you Y-chromosome-wielding idiots ever clean up after yourselves? Is there any more wine?"

I shook my head sorrowfully. She shrugged and went into the kitchen, coming out with something that looked rather stronger.

"You know all about Neville, then," I commented, feeling somewhat relieved by this revelation. This sort of hobby was really not the sort of thing one half of a married couple should be concealing from the other.

"It was Neville I first got together with," she said, a mocking twinkle in her eye.

"And I always had you down as more of an Eric Hitchmough girl!" Either I was getting carried away by all this excitement or it was the booze talking; normally I would never have dared speak to the Master of a Cambridge college like that.

"He must really have rated your efforts at assisting him if he let you in on the secret!"

"Well, as it happens, I busted him!" I revealed proudly. She bit her lip in a vain attempt to stifle a giggle.

"So the pupil has become the teacher! Well done, Roger. It's good when someone punctures his vanity bubble once in a while. I do try to keep him grounded, really I do, but it's like trying to lasso a jumbo jet." She smiled dryly. "Honestly, if he'd never met me, I worry that he might have ended up going a bit eccentric!"

I think I have already intimated that my poker face does not always cut the mustard, but I did my best to keep my expression impassive.

"Have you had an interesting evening?" she asked, taking a sip of brandy and visibly relaxing. "Any near-death experiences?"

"Just the one," I admitted. The Master looked neither overwhelmed nor underwhelmed by this revelation; she was "whelmed," if you will, raising a quizzical eyebrow but refraining from grilling me for grisly details.

"I hope you've been having more fun than I have, anyway," she went on. "Dinner was utterly interminable, and the duck was distinctly sub-par."

"Sounds absolutely fowl!" There followed a deafening silence where the gales of uproarious laughter should have been. I put this down to fatigue.

"And then I had to spend two hours cheering up poor David."

"What, David Williamson?" She nodded. "I saw him at lunch. He seemed all right then!"

'Although he was not very complimentary about your husband,' I might have added, but I obviously didn't. It struck me as odd that Williamson seemed simultaneously to be so

218

close to one half of this power couple, and so scathing in his assessment of the other. I wondered whether he too could at one point have been competing with Sinclair and his various bewhiskered alter egos for the good lady's affections.

"That's because he will always insist on bottling things up and putting on a brave face for the world. Makes it much more difficult to pick up the pieces when it does all come bubbling up." She sighed. "Where is Gerald, anyway?"

"Up looking after Jasper. Poor young chap had a bit of a nightmare."

"Oh hell," Emily sighed. "I'd better go and check in on them. Gerald does his best, bless him. But if I've told him once that poring over cold cases in the middle of the night is not what an impressionable little boy needs to help him conquer his night terrors. I've told him a thousand times."

"No need, my love!" Sinclair announced from the stairs. "The lad has returned to the warm embrace of blissful slumberland! When all else fails, the old snake charmer's flute works a treat, I find. And I even had time to look up our surly chum Gavin's address. He's holed up in Fen Ditton, it transpires! The dodgy end, naturally! But even so, I can only assume he must have clobbered an elderly relative to get his foot on the property ladder there!"

"Gavin? Why on earth would you be visiting that..." she checked herself, aware that she was referring to a valued member of the College staff, "...that fine, hard-working individual at this time of night?"

"I would be delighted to explain in the fullness of time, my sweet pumpkin, but alas, our taxi will be arriving imminently! Whiteley, are you in?"

I took ten seconds to rally my remaining reserves of energy, and then we headed back out into the night.

CHAPTER 8

In which we take a little excursion to visit one of Fen Ditton's less salubrious inhabitants, meet an old friend en route, and I almost get a damn good thrashing from another one on my return, while Sinclair pulls some strings and arrives at a solution. Which he doesn't let me in on. The bastard.

I

The driver of the taxi Sinclair had booked for us (a Panther, naturally) was whistling an irritatingly jaunty tune as I got into the back seat next to the good professor, much to the latter's evident irritation. My companion soon perked up when we got underway, however.

"So," he began cheerfully, his own energy reserves clearly fully restored, "you never did explain to me where that sudden urge to accuse Steve Taylor of murder sprang from! My flabber was well and truly gasted when I heard that, I don't mind admitting!"

"Was I way off piste?" I asked, feeling just a tad embarrassed about the whole thing now I was looking back on it.

"That remains to be seen! You can't win a game of Cluedo just by loudly roaring "COLONEL MUSTARD!" into the other players' faces, you know. *Why* do you think he did it?"

"Well..." I paused. In truth I hadn't really got that far. And I felt that if I led with "he was behaving really weirdly," Sinclair's deconstruction of my analysis would be merciless. I rallied eventually with, "Ed knew about his addiction, and he seemed pretty determined that Lydia mustn't know about it. Perhaps Ed was threatening to tell her the truth, and Steve decided to shut him up with the sharp end of a knife?"

Sinclair's expression suggested that I might have been better off going with the "behaving weirdly" line.

"There are one or two little snagging holes in that theory, I fear," he said. "Firstly, did Mr Dickinson ever strike you as the sort of chap to go tattling to the missus whenever one of his chums strayed from the path of virtue? No, Dickinson was a rascal, a roisterer, a rogerer (no offence). He would have deplored such appallingly snitchy behaviour. Secondly, if you had just killed somebody in order to keep a secret, would your next step be to tell that very same secret to someone else?"

"So you think Steve's off the hook, then?"

"Well, I don't know about you, but I'm not quite ready to put away my fishing tackle—no sniggering at the back there! I think Mr Taylor told you the truth earlier. It may even have been nothing but the truth. But the whole truth, it certainly wasn't. Perhaps he would have been ready to come clean about the really deep, dark secrets he's been keeping if your conversation had not been interrupted by Niamh Redmond throwing that rather marvellous wobbly! But he was certainly holding something back. And from his uncharacteristic outburst at the end of your conversation, you can bet your bottom dollar there's a woman at the bottom of it! The only question is, which woman?"

"Well, Lydia, surely?" I theorised. "Hey, you don't think she and Ed were, well, 'at it,' do you? That would explain why his comment about Ed being such a good mate sounded so heavily caveated. The only problem is that Lydia seemed to detest Ed even more than she detests the rest of us."

"Well, that could have been acting, dear boy. Still, we have no evidence, any more than we have any evidence of exam rigging!"

"Exam rigging? What are you on about now?"

"Missed that one, did you? Well, all will become clear in the fullness of time, my dear Whiteley." Sinclair chuckled smugly. I was starting to feel distinctly grumpy about his caginess. It struck me that he was revelling in this secretiveness for the sake of it. This perhaps explains, but does not excuse, the rather spiteful remark I made next.

"I didn't know your wife and David Williamson were so close," I commented. If I had been expecting a burst of volcanic, Othelloesque rage, I would have been disappointed.

"Yes, well, she has been a great support to him," he clucked. "It's a relief that he's willing to confide in someone. David has always been a very private man. Everyone thinks it's easy for a fellow of our age to come out in this day and age, and perhaps for many it is, but you have to remember that the law prohibited him from getting married until he was over forty."

"He's gay? I had no idea!"

"You thought he had his eye on my wife, eh?" he chortled.

"Well, I never thought she would entertain his overtures, but, you know, she's a bit of a catch, your Emily!"

"It's certainly reassuring to know that you think so," Sinclair replied a little sniffily. "Although I do feel that we could safely get away with retiring the fishing imagery for the rest of the journey!"

"Not the time or the plaice?" I asked.

"Driver, could you please pull over and deposit this man on the darkest patch of roadside you can find?" Sinclair called to the driver. The driver looked slightly panicked for a moment. I knew how he felt.

"It's all right, I was being facetious," Sinclair explained patiently. "I'll let him off with a yellow card. I believe that is a footballing expression. I'm not entirely sure what it means, but it sounds vaguely appropriate!"

"So do you know what Williamson was upset about?" I asked him, eager to get back to the meat of the conversation and away from the deluge of sauce. "Is he officially 'out'?"

"Oh, I think so; he has sort of inched his way uncomfortably out of the old closet over the course of the last ten years or so. I think anyone who is paying attention is probably aware of his proclivities at this point. His parents are still alive, and have been rather difficult about it, I'm afraid. Ah, I do believe we've arrived. Pull up just here, please!"

II

I was familiar with Fen Ditton of old, of course, since it was home to The Plough, which is quite a good pub to base oneself in if you're interested in watching The Bumps. I wasn't, particularly, but I had nevertheless been dragged along one year by a couple of my old school chums who had ended up at other colleges. I had tried my best to at least give off the impression of being moderately engaged in what was going on, even if I was not prepared to go as far as joining in with the nonsensical chanting of lines like "SALT IN THE WOUNDS, LADY MARGARET!" I fully admit to being worthy of a Level 2 or 3 in the public school-educated Oxbridge twatbag championship myself, but these guys had been in a whole different league.

"Could I possibly ask you to wait here, ready to live up to your name and spring into action when we give you the signal?" Sinclair asked the Panther driver.

"I'll have to leave the meter on," the driver cautioned him, looking surly. From the paraphernalia on his dashboard, it looked as though the name he was being asked to live up to was actually "Bob."

"Oh, will you indeed?" Sinclair snorted derisively. "Text 'Eulalia' to Balachandra Panther and see what he has to say about that!"

"What was that all about?" I asked as we got out of the car and traipsed down the dark road in the direction of Gavin's humble abode.

"Let's just call it a personal discount code and leave it at that," Sinclair said cryptically, giving me a sly grin. "Oh look, there's a familiar face coming out of Gavin's place! I wonder what act we're catching him in. Let's go and accost him, shall we?"

I followed his gaze and saw a furtive-looking figure sloping out of a house several doors down and looking around anxiously. As he turned in our direction, I saw who it was. The moonlight rendered his face even paler than usual.

"Hello, Neil!" I called out in a loud, hearty voice. "Fancy seeing you here! A bit off your patch, isn't it?"

Neil's face froze, seamlessly melding panic and hostility into a single expression.

"Gerald Sinclair!" My companion introduced himself, marching towards the terrified accountant with his hand outstretched. "You must be Neil Norman. I've heard ever so much about you from Whiteley here."

He reached Neil, who pointedly failed to accept the handshake. Instead, he simply stood there stupidly with his mouth agape.

"Now, forgive my directness, but what brings you to the back end of Fen Ditton on a dark and gloomy night like this one, eh? A visit to dear old Gavin, is it? I'll wager he's never been this popular!"

"I had some personal business to discuss with him," Neil said stiffly after what felt like an aeon of awkwardness, even by our stilted British standards.

"Oh yes?" Sinclair beamed at him with an owlishly expectant expression.

"It was a personal matter," Neil repeated woodenly. "Now,

if you don't mind, it's late..."

"I really would advise you to confide in us, Mr Norman. I am the soul of discretion, and as for Whiteley here, well, I am working on him. If our oleaginous friend indoors is blackmailing you, it would be better in the long run if you lance the boil now. There are larger considerations at play here! Without wishing to over-egg the melodramatic pudding— there's nothing worse than a melodramatic pudding—lives may be at stake!"

"Exactly!" I added sternly, nodding my head emphatically in an attempt to pretend that I had the faintest idea what my eccentric companion was wittering on about.

"Don't pretend you have any concern for me or my situation," Neil said hoarsely. "You and him in there, you're welcome to each other!"

He pushed past us and stalked off down the street, his body hunched like a vulture. Neil had never been at risk of rivalling Crocodile Dundee or The Dude Lebowski in the "laid-back" stakes, but right now, he was a man with more stress on his shoulders than Atlas.

"They'll manage to trace the knife, sooner or later," Sinclair called after him sharply. Neil turned, and now he had a look of incredulity on his face.

"Murder? Is that what you think? Why would I...Jesus, you've got completely the wrong idea! Tell him, Roger!" And with that, he was off, rounding the corner as though the hounds of hell were after him rather than Cambridge's answer to Snoopy and Woodstock. I did not voice these thoughts to Sinclair, as I did not feel he would appreciate the analogy. Besides, I was trying to work out what it was that I was supposed to be telling Sinclair. For in truth, I was flummoxed, not for the first time. Sinclair saw my expression and patted me paternally on the shoulder.

"Don't worry, Whiteley, he understands even less of this

than you do, poor fellow! Let's see if Gavin is still entertaining, shall we?"

"Still? It would be a first in my experience," I snorted, following my companion down the garden path towards Gavin's door. Sinclair rang the bell, and we waited for what seemed like an eternity. Sinclair bit his lip, looking anxious.

"Well, we know he's at home," I commented irritably. "We don't know what state he's in, admittedly, but if he's gone to meet his maker, dear old Dr Frankenstein, we'll know Neil did it. But he's probably just having a quiet wank."

It was of course at that precise moment that the door opened. Gavin, leaning against the doorway, looked me up and down in that disdainful way of his, his lip curled into that trademark sneer as he noisily chewed gum at me.

"Well, well. Look what the cat's dragged in now!" the Porter tutted.

III

Gavin was still kitted out in the rather anodyne "short-sleeved white shirt, grey trousers and bucket loads of cheap deodorant" combo that he always wore when he was on duty. There were a couple more undone buttons than usual, though, meaning that the top of his matted profusion of chest hair was on full display. When he noticed Sinclair, he at least had the courtesy to straighten up slightly.

"Oh, evening, Mr Sinclair. Didn't see you there. Is this college business?"

"That is certainly how I see it, Gavin," Sinclair replied severely.

"What's bollockface doing here then?" he asked, clearly deciding, after a moment's hesitation, that the presence of the First Gentleman of St Crispian's College was insufficient reason for him to mask his disdain.

"I was hoping that some of your witty repartee might rub off on me!" I responded icily. "And it's 'esteemed alumnus bollockface' to you!"

"Didn't know you two were all matey!" Gavin taunted us. The insinuation was unmistakable. I recollected Gavin being very vocal on the subject of "woofters" and "shirtlifters" when I had been an undergraduate, and age did not appear to have mellowed his antediluvian views on the subject. Clearly, the idea of my being Sinclair's "glass of tea" was faintly ludicrous, but I was tempted to start holding my esteemed professor's hand at that point just to watch the ghastly homophobe squirm.

"Yes, yes, he's my sidekick of the month! Now, may we come in?" Sinclair asked impatiently.

Gavin rolled his eyes and sighed but nevertheless vacated the doorway and let us through, baring his teeth at me like a rabid hound as I passed him. The copious amounts of chewing gum he had sloshing around the inside of his mouth had done nothing to ameliorate the rancidity of his breath.

Gavin's living room was very much a testament to his character. The one tiny bookshelf, which looked like it was about to come tumbling off the walls at any moment, was a cluttered shrine to the twin deities of Andy McNab and Polish pornography. The walls themselves were the scene of a battle for dominance between some impressively depraved posters on the one hand and an equally impressive arsenal of knives, swords, nunchucks and various highly illegal firearms on the other. I could have been teleported into the room from the other side of the world and still have been able to guess whose room it was in seconds.

"Beer?" he offered. I declined. I wasn't particularly worried about him surreptitiously poisoning my drink, but the prospect of him gobbing in it was far from implausible. Sinclair, to my surprise, did not share my reluctance and accepted a can of

Carling, of all things. He took a satisfied slurp of the stuff before launching straight in.

"I'll come straight to the point, Gavin, because it's been a long night, and I wouldn't want to miss seeing the Easter Chicken laying my son's Easter eggs in the morning! I think you know who killed Ed Dickinson, and I'd like you to tell me.

"You may not like the cut of my jib all that much," he went on. "Which is perfectly understandable. I have a notoriously badly cut jib! But I am part of the St Crisps' family. And if that doesn't cause those dusty old heartstrings of yours to stir faintly with collegiate pride, I would also point out that I have one even more important thing going for me. Namely, that I am not Inspector Torvill Baynes. Now, I know for a fact that he rubbed you up the wrong way this morning. I heard he had even his fingers in your biscuit tin, the infernal cad. Now's your chance to give the portly plodder a poke in the eye, by helping me to solve the thing first. That will really get the fellow's goat, believe me! What do you say?"

"I say I'd very much like to help you, Mr Sinclair," he said, with all the sincerity of Uriah Heep at his most unctuous, his face a picture of sorrowful virtue. "It's just that I haven't the faintest idea why you'd think I know anything!"

"Dear me," Sinclair grimaced. "I should never have accepted that beer! Once again, my eyes were bigger than my bladder. Which way is your powder room, Gavin?"

"If it's the pisser you want, it's out that way," Gavin said and gestured grumpily.

"I say potato, you say pisspot, eh? Jolly good. Well, I'll leave you to the tender mercies of Knuckles Whiteley here! Whiteley, I expect you to prise a full and grovelling confession out of him by the time I return! Try not to get too much mess on the carpet!"

Sinclair stepped jauntily out of the room, leaving me alone

with my nemesis in his fragrant, pornographic lair. Well, unlikely bad cop though I was, two very English thoughts passed through my mind at this point. Firstly, that I should do my duty, and secondly, that anything was better than more awkward silence. All things considered, I thought I might as well take a punt at it.

"So, Mr, er, Gavin," I began, seamlessly covering up the fact that his surname was still evading me. "When I got back to my room last night, someone had been rummaging through my bags! And the only people who had a key to that room, are now standing in this room. Now I'm prepared to let that drop..."

"Just as well," Gavin growled threateningly. He took a step closer to me, just in case I needed reminding that whilst I might have a height advantage if things got ugly, that was pretty much my only advantage. He was well known as a hand-to-hand combat enthusiast, whilst I was even more of a civilian than most civilians. Nevertheless, in this instance, I soldiered on.

"I'm prepared to let that drop," I repeated. "But if you went through my stuff, I'm willing to bet that I wasn't getting special treatment. You know where that knife came from, don't you? Because you've seen it before, haven't you? Whose is it? Is that what Neil Norman was doing here just now?"

"I get all sorts of unlikely people visiting me!" Gavin commented smugly.

"Now, I don't happen to think Neil's our man," I went on. "He seemed genuinely puzzled when we suggested that his presence here had something to do with the murder. I think you've got something else on him."

"Is that so?" Gavin looked amused. "Maybe he just came to old Gavin here for a bit of attention after being made to feel left out by your little clique. I'd have had some sympathy with him, if he had. Always used to be poor Niamh Redmond, back in the day. Always so tight, you lot, weren't you? Woe betide anyone who didn't make the cut, eh? Now, it never bothered me that Ed Dickinson was always finding himself knee-deep in pussy, even though he looked like he'd been turned down for a PG Tips ad for being too scruffy. I knew all about his dirty secrets, but I never let on to any of his girlfriends. Not my place. But you lot cast Niamh adrift when she was up the duff! You left her with nothing, and now you have the temerity to stand there judging me!"

"You can't lay that at my door!" I spluttered. "As it happens, I thought Ed behaved very badly. And I didn't know she was pregnant! Didn't know that until tonight, as it happens. What could I have done?"

"You could have been there for her, comforted her! Like I did!" He grinned lasciviously. "And you really think Ed was the father of that kid? Well, I know better!"

Could he be insinuating what I thought he was insinuating? Surely even Niamh, at the height of her wobbly immaturity, would have had more sense than to fall into Gavin's lecherous lap. Having seen Lee, I couldn't see much of a resemblance to Gavin, but, frankly, he hadn't looked much like Ed either. I felt a bit of pork chop flavoured sick bubbling up in my throat as he leered disgustingly at me.

"You're trying to wind me up," I growled hotly.

He was succeeding.

"Now I know you know whose knife it was, and you know that I know that you know, so let's stop beating around the bush!" I tried to ignore his widening smirk. "I'm going to name some names. Tell me if I'm getting warm."

I watched his smug, slappable face intently as I ran through my list.

"Jammy Jeffers. Dan Finn." Damn, the poker-faced bastard was good at this. No tell-tale twitch, that self-satisfied expression just sat there on his unsavoury swinish face, motionless and unyielding to my brilliant line of questioning.

"Sadie Simmons. Steve Taylor."

"House!" Sinclair suddenly yelled out as he strode cheerfully back into the room. "Still no joy, eh, Whiteley? Well, I dare say Torquemada himself couldn't have done any better! Gavin, I am going to waste no more time on this unseemly back and forth. You are shielding someone who has already killed once, almost certainly twice. If someone else is killed as a result of your pig-headed greed, then that will prey for the rest of your life on that miserable husk of a thing that passes for your conscience! I hope whatever you get out of the villain is going to be enough to make up for the fact that I will personally see to it that you never work in this town again! And I probably won't even leave Oxford open to you! I know people there too, you know. Strings will be pulled."

"I have nothing more to say to you..." Gavin bore down on him angrily, getting right in Sinclair's face, "...except 'do your worst!'"

"I very much doubt I shall have to," Sinclair retorted crisply, impressively unintimidated. "Who do you think is odds-on favourite to be the next victim right now? You're playing a dangerous game, Gavin."

Suddenly, Sinclair looked straight past the Porter to an empty bracket just above our host's smutty bookshelf.

"I say, you seem to have an empty spot over there! Something gone missing, has it? I'd take care if I were you. You can't afford to lose too many more of those if you're only relying on yourself for protection. And if you want *my* protection, you have ten more seconds to spill the beans. I'm not going to beg, because ultimately it isn't my popo on the line!"

Gavin folded his arms and blanked us, staring pointedly into the middle distance. Nonetheless, I could have sworn there had been a flicker of panic on his face when Sinclair had mentioned the empty spot on the wall where a vicious looking armament should have been. Sinclair pulled out his pocket watch, counted to ten in a barely audible mutter, then returned it to his pocket with a flamboyant flourish.

"Your funeral, Gavin," he declared once the "final countdown" was concluded. "And all I can say is that I hope that it is sparsely attended! Good night to you, sir!"

With that, he stalked out of the room. I assumed that his intention was for me to follow, so follow I did, giving Gavin a final glare, just in case he was wondering whether I too was deeply disgusted by his avaricious intransigence. He responded in kind and threw a rude gesture in for good measure.

IV

Once we were safely out of "The Pratcave," Sinclair's mood seemed immediately to improve. The severe expression on his face relaxed out into a twinkly beam, and he even started humming.

"An excellent few minutes' work, I feel, Whiteley!"

"What are you talking about?" I asked incredulously. "The stroppy bastard completely stonewalled us!"

"Well of course he did! The grasping little pettifogger thinks he's found the goldmine at the end of the rainbow! He believes that because he can handle himself in a scrap and he's armed to the teeth besides, he's more than capable of seeing off any vengeful leprechauns if they turn violent. He is one hundred per cent wrong about that, of course, and in fact if we hadn't turned up when we did, he wouldn't be alive now! But I doubt he'll be easily persuaded of that fact."

"What?" I protested.

"You did a very good job distracting him while I was rooting around upstairs, Whiteley. I'm proud of you!"

"You..."

"I am not as weak of bladder as I sometimes like to pretend. That's why I accepted that revolting can of tepid drain-pour, to add verisimilitude to my conveniently timed toilet break. If I'd been just a little quicker to answer nature's call, I would have caught the blighter red-handed. As it is, they'd made their exit through the window by the time I got upstairs. But I'll wager I only missed them by a minute or so! Sorry I couldn't let you in on the chase, but I wanted to keep it discreet. Besides, there were things in his bedroom that, frankly, I'm not sure you're old enough to cope with. Still, our timely arrival almost certainly bought Gavin a few hours' reprieve."

"You mean the murderer was actually there?" I exclaimed as we got back into the taxi. "We got there just as he was about to kill Gavin?"

"Succinctly summarised, Whiteley. Yes, that's precisely what I mean."

"But how did he get in without Gavin knowing? He's a Porter. Surely someone as security conscious as him would have a decent alarm system fitted?"

"Oh, I am sure that Gavin was perfectly aware that he was playing host to a viper. Although I think the fact that our unknown murderer managed to pilfer that missing firearm without him noticing rather knocked him for six!"

"He let someone into his house knowing they had murdered Ed and probably Albert Ross as well?" I whistled. "He's even more stupid than I thought."

"Oh, absolutely," Sinclair agreed. "If he were any slower, he'd have moss growing on him! But they had business to attend to, remember? Gavin was inviting an offer in order to buy his silence. Now, I am fairly sure that the only genuine offer our killer was prepared to make was a bullet in the brain. But our elusive nemesis, Johnny Murderer, was undoubtedly seeking to lull our deluded chum into a false sense of security. My hunch is that the false offer Gavin was being tempted with was not wholly pecuniary in nature."

"What?" I exclaimed.

"If I know Gavin," Sinclair hypothesised, "he only lets his wallet do the thinking for him when his trouser-pilchard is unavailable!"

"The murderer was going to sleep with him, then kill him? Sounds to me like adding an unnecessarily distasteful step into what would otherwise be a pretty sound plan!"

"Oh, I doubt things would have been allowed to get to that stage," said Sinclair. "All that Johnny needed to do was get him upstairs, away from any handy cleavers and cutlasses. Then our murderer could strike while the mind of Victim Number Three was sufficiently distracted by thoughts of his forthcoming treat!"

"Shouldn't we be calling Johnny 'Jenny' now then?"

"Maybe. But don't you think there's a touch of 'the lady doth protest too much, methinks' about his incessant digs at our homosexual brethren?"

"You think he's overcompensating?" I asked.

"It's possible. Anyway, I think I've scared them off for tonight, but Gavin is still a marked man, so I need to make a phone call." He punched some numbers into his phone.

"Finlay? Gerald Sinclair here. Didn't wake you, did I? Of course I didn't. Right, there's a little job I need you to do for me, and it has to be tonight. There'll be Easter eggs all round if your mission is successful, naturally. Can you get a couple of the boys together? Is Piss-and-Vinegar Pepe available? Oh, you're quite right, I had forgotten about the Pilates incident. Oh well, you'll just have to round up the usual suspects, then. Denby, Chase and Doyle should do the trick. The mission? It's Gavin Shufflebottom. Yes, I want you to run him out of Dodge. As smoothly as possible. No rough stuff, but you can put the frighteners on him to the extent necessary! Try not to enjoy yourself too much, though. Excellent, I knew I could rely on your delicate negotiating skills. And you have a good evening too, sir! Cheerio."

"Was that Mad Dog McFadden?" I asked in astonishment.

"I told you we had a business-like relationship," Sinclair pointed out. "I am not one to call in the muscle at the drop of a hat. I prefer to rely more on brains than brawn as a habit, as you're aware. But just occasionally, dear Finlay is a very useful person to know. Gavin's only chance of survival now is if he makes himself scarce. And if he doesn't disappear of his own volition, then someone else needs to do it for him. You have to admit that we did try asking nicely, Whiteley!"

Truth be told, although my general attitude to hired thugs is cautious opposition, I could not really fault his logic. It had become pretty clear that even if we had devoted half the night to the attempt, we would not have been able to say anything that would have changed Gavin's mind. And dislike him though I did, I didn't really want to see the disagreeable dickhead go the same way as poor old Ed.

Sinclair had now lapsed into inscrutable silence, steepling his fingers and staring into space.

"What are you thinking?" I asked eventually.

"Are you familiar with that eccentric-looking actor from Mousehunt? Christopher Walken?" Sinclair answered my question with another question. Needless to say, it was not the one I had been expecting.

"Yes, of course," I said, wondering whether to dare an impression of that seasoned thespian. I decided against it on the grounds that my companion might think I was having a mild seizure.

"I was just wondering whether he is able to resist the urge to launch into the chorus of 'These Boots Were Made for Walken' every time he puts on his shoes."

"Oh!" I said, struggling to keep the irritation out of my voice. "So you weren't deep in thought trying to figure out who bumped off one of my oldest friends, then?"

"Oh dear me no! I got to the bottom of that one ages ago!"

"You did?" I exclaimed. He nodded and gave me an infuriating little wink.

"Well, would you care to share?" I demanded.

"Oh look, here we are!" Sinclair deflected deftly, alighting from the vehicle and fumbling for his wallet to pay the driver. The taxi departed, and the two of us strolled towards the Porter's Lodge. I was not planning on letting the smug secretive so-and-so get away that easily and was on the point of pressing him for the gory details. Alas, however, I was prevented from doing so, for I suddenly found myself being assaulted by an angry assailant who had stepped out of a conveniently placed alcove.

I say "assaulted," but we were not in the realms of GBH here. I don't doubt that the desire was there, but the technique left much to be desired—it was more Ronnie Corbett than Ronnie Kray. Nevertheless, I was rather caught off guard by a rough collar grab, and my attacker and I stumbled together into the opposite wall, tussling vigorously.

Jammy Jeffers, for it was he, was clearly a wee bit steamed up about something. His face was as red as a beetroot, and his expression was every bit as gruesome and vengeful as that of the gargoyle protruding from the wall immediately above the spot he'd been lurking in. I could not detect the heavy reek of booze, though, meaning that he did not even have the excuse that most of the other people who had been behaving like maniacs that evening were able to fall back on. He started clawing at my face like a demented feline trying to grab hold of a laser beam, screaming "Judas" and showering my unprotected face with copious quantities of spittle.

"What the hell are you doing?" I demanded hotly when I was finally given enough space to formulate a sentence. My attacker had seized me by a low-hanging jowl during our skirmish, so I was frantically trying to catch my breath.

"Tanya told me what you did, you treacherous serpent!"

"Dear me, this is turning into quite the roll call of Biblical villains!" Sinclair chimed in. He was leaning on his umbrella and watching us with amusement. He did not seem particularly inclined to join the fray to try and save my bacon. "Make sure you don't leave out Nebuchadnezzar or Potiphar's wife! From what I remember of the Book of Genesis, she was supposedly a dead ringer for Whiteley here!"

"I didn't tell the police anything," I insisted in the gaps between my gulps for air, as I tried to get my breath back.

"He's telling the truth, you know," Sinclair confirmed. "I am the one you should be scrimmaging with, if anyone! Although I would strongly advise against doing so, if you don't want to spend the rest of the night writhing in pain, while Addenbrookes' finest delicately attempt to debrollify your rectum!"

He waved his umbrella in the air in a gruesomely illustrative motion.

"What's this got to do with you, anyway?" Jammy spat balefully.

"Given my status as Cambridge's most indefatigable busybody, the question hardly seems relevant! But if you must know, I wanted to spare Whiteley the difficulty of having to choose between 'dobbing in his mates,' as they put it in the common parlance, or concealing vital evidence from a live police investigation. I happened to overhear what Ms Bullock was saying to him earlier, and I was the one that peached to the rozzers! Now, if you're determined to engage in an unseemly fracas, now would be the time to do it, young sir!"

Jammy glared at him but stayed put. He was already puffing and panting heavily.

"No?" Sinclair beamed. "Well, if I were a more committed vulgarian, there's a well-known expression involving procreation and travel that I'd be hurling in your general direction right about now!"

"My career's in ruins!" Jammy howled, his face now almost apoplectic. "I was arrested in front of a whole restaurant this evening! Think of how that'll look in the papers, even if the police never release that recording! Local MP arrested in connection with brutal stabbing. Even if they convict the real killer, I'll be tarred for life; fed to the bloody jackals! Guilty until proven innocent, that's how the press see it if you're a politician! Christ alive, what's my wife going to say?"

"I thought she was out of the picture?" I remarked. "Weren't you bragging to us last night about a comradely snuggle you'd had with some girl at the party conference?"

The adulterous little weasel did at least have the decency to look embarrassed.

"That wasn't intended for wider dissemination," he mumbled.

"Well, you'll have to do better at covering your tracks if you want to make it into the Cabinet," I scoffed. "Look, you're in for a rough few weeks, and you'll get some bad taste jokes made about you on *Have I Got News For You* for a while. But once they've got the real killer in custody, nobody except a few people on the fringes of Twitter will seriously believe that you had anything to do with it! Anyway, Gerald here says he knows who did it!"

Jammy turned to Sinclair, his eyes all agog.

"You do? Who was it?"

"All will be revealed in the fullness of time! Tomorrow morning, to be exact! Where shall I host the big reveal?" He pondered for a moment. "How about Fitzbillies? There's no beating the old favourites sometimes, and I have a sudden hankering for their shakshuka! You'll be there for the denouement, won't you, Mr Jeffers? Say 11:30?"

Jammy paused, then nodded stiffly.

"Sorry, Rog," he said awkwardly, laying a hand on my shoulder. Feeling that I was entitled to a moment of mild petulance after the way he had behaved, I shook it off angrily.

"Go home! And try to remember next time that nothing kills a political career as fast as behaving like a total thrombosis!" I counselled him.

"A what?"

"A bloody clot!"

Jammy shuffled off down the road, looking pretty broken, not quite willing or able to make eye contact with either of us.

"That's what too long at the Cambridge Union does to you!" Sinclair snorted. "Master Jeffers is not the first fellow who achieved the status of Big Fish in that small pond, only to swim out into the big wide ocean of life and find himself hopelessly lost!"

"He did get into Parliament," I pointed out. Sinclair greeted this remark with a dismissive scoff and muttered something about "political plankton."

"How did he know I would be here, with you, anyway?" I wondered aloud as we made our way back into college, heading over to the Master's Lodge and a much delayed, and much needed, night's sleep.

"Ah, well, perhaps he called in a favour with Mr Starmer, who I'm fairly sure has been having me watched ever since his DPP days!" Sinclair yawned. "Anyway, that's another story. Your last task for tonight, Whiteley, is to text everyone you have a number for who has been involved in the events of the last twenty-four hours. Tell them to convene at Fitzbillies tomorrow at 11:30. That should give anyone who has already bunked off down to London enough time to get back up here. That's assuming they're willing and able to fork out the extortionate price of another train ticket!"

"We're actually doing this are we?" I asked a little sceptically.

"The whole 'gathering the suspects' thing?"

"Yes, we are 'actually doing it'!" Sinclair insisted irritably. "You know a little of my penchant for amateur dramatics. You didn't honestly think I would pass up an opportunity like this, did you? It will be my greatest triumph since I last had a crack at Sir Despard Murgatroyd!"

And with that, he went merrily skipping up the stairs, like a redeemed Scrooge buoyed up by three doses of heavy Spirits. As for me, if my repose was haunted by the ghost of Emily's late mother, I remained blissfully unaware of it, for I zonked out before my head hit the pillow.

CHAPTER 9

In which, given that we are nearing the moment of truth, the reader is cordially invited to read the whole damn chapter for herself (or himself) without the aid of a rather archaic spoiler-heavy summary! You're nearly there now, honest!

I

"The year is 2006 of the Common Era, or Anno Domini, if you are so inclined!" Sinclair began, with a suitable injection of bombast. "Elizabeth II is sitting on the throne, Tony Blair is Prime Minister, Beyoncé is storming the charts, and Jeremy Beadle is dead."

Emily rolled her eyes. I looked at her quizzically.

"Gerald got done up like a kipper on *Beadle's About* when he was a very young man," she murmured to me. "Processing that trauma is probably what turned him into the master of observation he is today."

Meanwhile, Sinclair was continuing full throttle with his introduction.

"Pluto has just been downgraded to a dwarf planet (disgracefully in my view). And a bunch of students are gathering in Ed Dickinson's room for a rambunctious piss-up!"

The time was ten minutes to twelve. The place: Fitzbillies. Founded in 1921 by Frederick Farquharson Fitzbilly (the similarity in name to the nearby Fitzwilliam Museum is purely coincidental), Fitzbillies has been a sticky-cake-exporting Cambridge institution for over a century. I am told they even ship them to Antarctica. The bakery cum cafe-restaurant has survived some torrid and turbulent trials over the years, from fires to financial disasters to pandemics, but it has always returned to delight the hordes of hungry tourists who come tramping down Trumpington Street in search of nourishment throughout the year. I was willing to bet that it would survive Gerald Sinclair "putting on a show" as well.

Easter morning was rapidly ebbing away from us, but Sinclair was now finally getting into his stride after an initial complication involving a regrettable shortfall of murder suspects. I have to confess that the logistical difficulties associated with arranging the "suspect gathering" that has been the hallmark of various ITV mystery dramas for many a decade is something that had simply never occurred to me whilst tuning in on a Sunday evening. Presumably, all that organisational faff takes place during the ad breaks, and DCI Barnaby from *Midsomer Murders* presumably never needs to worry about the curse of the "rail replacement bus service" that had delayed the arrival of several of our suspects, returning from London or whichever suburb thereof they had skedaddled back to the previous night after all the fun and games.

Even now our ranks were incomplete, although Tanya, Chris, Dan (extremely hungover but strangely animated), and Niamh (with Lee in tow) were all present and correct, and Jammy had broken the habit of a lifetime and kept his promise by gracing us with his presence. Even Sadie had shown up, albeit unapologetically tardy and looking decidedly sniffy about the whole affair. Her disdain for the whole business had evidently yielded to her natural curiosity.

"Shouldn't we wait for the Taylors and the Normans?" I interjected.

"Don't worry, I know where they are. I've granted them a

special dispensation," Sinclair said, smiling cryptically.

"I must have missed your husband being elected Pope," Inspector Baynes muttered to Emily, who had turned up with an uncharacteristically quiet and baggy-eyed Jasper to provide moral support to the Sinclair paterfamilias in his moment of triumph. Baynes was looking increasingly anxious and uncomfortable, although his frown had temporarily been "turned upside down" a couple of minutes earlier by the arrival of his full English breakfast. Clearly, Sinclair's methods were a little too far outside the box even for this most unorthodox of policemen.

"If the matinee is sold out, my husband is generally happy to throw in an evening performance for those who miss out," Emily replied.

"Sold out?" Baynes snorted in between sausage-y mouthfuls. "I thought until a few minutes ago, we weren't going to have any suspects turning up at all! What would he have done if we'd had a complete no-show?"

"I must admit I was afraid for a moment that he was going to bring out the puppets!" Emily murmured back, a wry smile playing on her lips. Sinclair was now looking distinctly miffed.

"You're interrupting my flow, my dearest! Where was I?"

"2006, rambunctious piss up, darling," Emily reminded him sweetly.

"Ah, yes indeed! Present and correct at this boozy gathering are Dickinson himself, his then ladyfriend Niamh Redmond, and his other housemates Dan Finn and Steven Taylor. Also present was the future MP for Cambridge James Thaddeus Jeffers, who was then coupled up with Sadie Simmons, also in attendance. Rounding off the guest list were Neil Norman, Britta Prendergast (as she then was), Tanya Bullock, Chris Cleghorn, and Roger Whiteley.

"These giddy youths all had one thing in common. The end of their time in Cambridge, at least as undergraduates, was drawing nigh. They had gathered in the knowledge that The Real World was about to extend an inviting arm to gather them up and scatter them in all sorts of interesting directions. They might have still had one eye on the next drink or the next opportunity for a spot of copulation. But the other eye was staring fixedly into the future! I am still uncertain as to whether it was Dickinson or one of the others who came up with the idea of everyone in the room making a prediction about what they would be doing in fifteen years' time and sticking it in a time capsule to be opened in the future. But it was certainly Dickinson who was responsible for organising the belated sequel to what I hope was an entertaining evening, given all the trouble that has since flowed from it!

"Now let us fast forward, to the here and now. If you will compare and contrast with the 'there and then,' you will find that Cambridge has changed, just a little bit, but the dramatis personae remains extraordinarily constant. I find it remarkable that every single person who was in attendance at the evening in 2006 that I have just described has made an appearance in Cambridge over the course of this weekend. Orchestrating such a gathering was a singularly impressive organisational feat on Dickinson's part, if you're prepared to skate over the unfortunate side effect of his own death.

"Indeed, in addition to the attendees of Dickinson's 2006 boozy bacchanal, we have on hand several of the Porters, or ex-Porters, who were already on the Cambridge scene at the time. Two of these, Finlay McFadden and Gavin Shufflebottom, I shall return to shortly! We also have David Williamson, an estimable colleague of mine who is nevertheless worthy of mention on the basis that he taught several of those attendees and has remained in touch with at least a couple of them. And finally, we have young Lee, who was in a sense present at the occasion as well, albeit in embryonic form." Sinclair beamed at Lee, who was sitting in a corner, pointedly playing on his phone and trying to put as much space between himself and his irritable-looking mother as possible.

"Lee!" Niamh snapped at him. "Listen, would you? He says he knows who killed your father, for God's sake!"

"He wasn't my father!" Lee retorted. "Just some selfish twat I never even met."

He looked up, belatedly cottoning on to the fact that Sinclair was looking at him expectantly. "Go on, man," the teenager sighed.

"Why thank you, kind sir. Completing the roll call, then, the only outsiders who I feel we need to bring into the conversation are as follows. One, Lydia Taylor, who could conceivably have been working in cahoots with her husband, in spite of the apparently turbulent nature of their relationship. And two, Daisy Seaman, who is connected to this mysterious affair both by virtue of being the college nurse and as the possible cause of the strange behaviour we have been witnessing from the elusive Neil Norman this weekend!

"Now, our killer must either be (a) someone who was on the same staircase as Dickinson on Friday night, (b) someone who was holed up in a neighbouring staircase and prepared to take the scenic route of entry into D Block via the first-floor kitchen window, or (c) someone who was sufficiently familiar with the college layout to be able to gain entry both to college and to D Block specifically. Given those parameters, I think we can safely confine our list of suspects to those people I have already mentioned!

"Finlay McFadden, I eliminated quite quickly, and believe it or not, it was his psychology that got him off the list! Really, the only count we have against him is the entirely circumstantial point that he was in the vicinity at the time, highly intoxicated and behaving in a manner that some might have perceived as threatening! And if we were to condemn everyone who occasionally popped up in a dark passageway to terrorise passers-by by reciting sinister ditties from beloved childhood classics, who amongst us would 'scape whipping?

"Finlay may indeed be a Scotch egg short of a picnic, and I have no doubt that he could be quite easily provoked into a bout of brutal bloodletting in the right circumstances. But I was with him myself for at least part of that evening. And I can attest to the fact that there was only one thing on his mind: he wanted to get to the bottom of what had happened to his late friend and colleague, Albert Ross. It briefly occurred to me that he might somehow have got it into his head that Dickinson had arranged Albert's little accident and taken the opportunity to wreak his bloody revenge. But he would never have done so in a manner that would risk bringing the college into disrepute. We may have effectively fired him, but his devotion to St Crispian's nevertheless remained absolute, and unconditional. No, he'd have followed him to London and 'done him in' down some dark alleyway.

"Whilst we're looking at the more outwardly volatile amongst our cast of characters, we should perhaps next turn to Steven Taylor, who showed a similar degree of volatility on Friday evening when Mr Finn took issue with some of his artistic endeavours. I think it is fair to say that the argument between Finn and Taylor was met with bemusement by the others in the room. And then there was the question of the drawings. Firstly, the missing one that Mr Finn had such a fierce objection to, and secondly, the one later pinned to Mr Dickinson's forehead.

"As to the former, I doubt that we shall ever be able to lay our hands on the original, but a rather bleary Mr Taylor did do me the courtesy of whipping me up an impromptu copy when I raised the subject with him earlier this morning. You see, I've already been busy and bustling today. He drew me a larger version this time."

He reached into his pocket and brought out a sheet of paper.

This he unfolded slowly to reveal a drawing of two people standing next to each other.

The first figure, standing on the left, was Dan Finn aged eighteen or nineteen, a fresh-faced fresher. Almost fresh-faced, anyway. In spite of his hairiness, I had forgotten what a good-looking lad he had been in those days. He had been quite the smoulderer.

The second figure, on the right, was also Dan Finn, but this time in his present state—prematurely aged by the ravages of beer—all beard, paunch, nose hair and sandals. The contradistinction between Dan Finn Alpha and Dan Finn Beta had been exaggerated, but only slightly. Nevertheless, the effect of the contrast on the sad middle-aged figure on the right was a cruel one. Samson next to Silenus. Now I understood. Steve had done the one thing that Dan would never be able to accept, much less forgive. He had drawn the truth.

I looked at Dan, who was scowling. His general enthusiasm for the Gerald Sinclair experience appeared now to be rapidly ebbing away. It was a testament to his affection for the good professor that he didn't storm out then and there.

"And the doodle?" I asked. "The little dancing devil on the corpse? Was it Steve's handiwork, or Dan trying to frame Steve, or someone else trying to frame Dan by making it look like Dan was framing Steve?" I looked at Dan nervously, wondering if he was going to lose it, but he just gave me the thumbs up.

"Yeah, I'd be interested to know the answer to that too," he said. There was a dangerous edge to his voice.

"Steve certainly thought it was Mr Finn trying to pin the blame on him," Sinclair commented. "You will understand now, Whiteley, why you drove him into such a rage in the University Arms yesterday? With your suggestion that it would be a 'devil of a shame' if he missed dinner at The Ivy? What with that and your reference to 'skeletons in the closet,' which was a turn of phrase he was particularly sensitive to for reasons which will soon become apparent, he must have thought you were a thoroughly despicable wind-up merchant!

"But are you guilty, Mr Finn? It is hardly surprising that you look rather different to the young lad you were twenty years ago. The last decade or two cannot have been short of life experiences for you. One of these was a particularly painful one. Your college girlfriend, Hannah, died in a skiing accident in 2008, didn't she? She had never skied before, and she would never do so again. That must have been a grievous blow. You've been blaming yourself for what happened all these years, haven't you? Because it was you who organised the trip?

"I would like you all to imagine the fury of Mr Finn if he discovered, after over a decade of self-flagellation over a tragic accident, that his good friend Edward Dickinson had been goading poor Hannah into trying the Black Run, or whatever the trickiest slopes are calling themselves these days. Dickinson could, after all, be as persistent as he was persuasive—he was usually able to wheedle his way to what he wanted. Could Finn have woken up to find his friend maudlin, addled with drink, perhaps starting to feel the vaguest stirrings of a guilty conscience, and ready at last to admit the truth to his old friend?"

Dan was now rallying. His visible distress at the mention of Hannah had now been superseded by an insincere grin, and he started applauding.

"This is great, lads," he declared cheerfully. "These guys, they never go for the real killer this early in the speech! He knows everything he just said was bullshit. I'm off the hook! Oh, I've missed you, Prof!"

"Or," Sinclair went on, resuming the narrative as if Dan had not spoken, "if Ed was feeling guilty about past misdeeds and wishing to atone, his obvious starting point would have been you, Niamh Redmond. The girl he turfed out onto the street, broke and pregnant, knowing full well that her parents had abandoned her, Cambridge had abandoned her, fully cognisant of the fact that he was all she had left, yet caring not a jot for her hopeless misery!

"Few would blame you for harbouring vengeful thoughts in your head all these years. Whilst you may not have been staying on campus on Friday night, it would hardly have been beyond the capabilities of a gymnast of your calibre to scale a couple of walls and get yourself into college and then into the first-floor kitchen of D Block. Perhaps you didn't even need to scale the first wall at all. Not when you were fortunate enough to have Gavin on duty. Your unlikely knight errant who had harboured such a soft spot for you all those years ago. Not a hard man to manipulate, our friend Gavin. From the kitchen, it would have been a straightforward saunter downstairs to the victim who had been waiting to feel the sharp end of your wrath for so long!

"Mam, what's he on about?" Lee snapped, looking up from his phone for the first time. Niamh shot a cold glare in Sinclair's direction, but the professor chuntered on before she could interject.

"Or is all that tumbling and trapezing in your genes, perhaps? We know that young Lee was out and about on Friday night. We know that for all intents and purposes, he had grown up regarding that other chap as his father, the one with the surplus vowels in his name. And anything Niamh told him about his biological father is likely to have engendered exactly the wrong kind of warm feelings in the young man. We know also that Lee was here to do a bit of research into Cambridge as a possible university choice. Perhaps he had already done rather more research than we thought, of an altogether less wholesome variety!"

"Ah, piss off, man!" Lee grunted, resuming his phone

scrolling.

"You're not live tweeting this, are you, Lee?" Niamh demanded, suddenly looking rather panicked.

"No, because I'm not forty!"

"Shall we move on to Chris Cleghorn?" Sinclair suggested rhetorically. "A late entrant into this whole affair, or so it would seem, but as a Cambridge inhabitant, he was, after all, not so very far from the scene of the crime. Whiteley here described him to me as having gone off-grid in the years since you were all up here as mostly happy and entirely un-murdered undergraduates. That expression, 'off-grid', makes it sound a little more Jack Reacher than the reality of opening an upmarket artisanal cheese shop really justifies. But the fact is that you all shunned him, forgot he existed, dropped him like the proverbial hot potato. And his efforts to mask his resentment at such shabby treatment were superficial at best! Perhaps given that Dickinson was the unofficial social secretary of your little group, the brunt of Cleghorn's ire was directed at him? Perhaps he was never invited to your little gathering at all, and only found out about it by accident? Perhaps that was the spark that caused his long-smouldering grudge to burst out into a conflagration of vicious retribution?

"He may not have been at The Ivy last night, but I note from his conversation with Whiteley that he is on first-name terms with at least one of the waiters. How easy it would have been for him to slip in there early, secrete Tanya Bullock's phone under the table, having discovered by that point that he had picked up the wrong one. Then, he would have the perfect opportunity to put the wind up everyone and create a bit of havoc by calling her number at an opportune moment. To make everyone think that it must have been someone at the table who planted it!"

"Now look," Chris grimaced, "I were a bit pissed off, but doing all that? Would have been a bit of an overreaction, don't you think?"

"For someone mentally balanced, perhaps. But mentally balanced people don't tend to have pictures of themselves dressed as Satan on their mobile phones! Everyone has been assuming that that little devil picture was Mr Taylor's handiwork, but perhaps we've been wrong. Is that your calling card, Mr Cleghorn?"

"I've no idea what you're blathering on about," Chris snapped, "but if you're talking about the photo Rog got a peep at last night, there's no bloody mystery about that. That's me playing Mephistopheles in the Bottisham Players production of Faust!"

"YOU got that part...?" Sinclair seemed to have been knocked off his stride for the first time, but he quickly pulled himself together.

"The director was clearly an imbecile," he sniffed. "Which leads us neatly on to Sadie Simmons. Never underestimate the lengths to which a social climber will go, to keep their grasping fingers on the ladder. Did Ed Dickinson know something about you that might hinder your career, Sadie? Perhaps something about that equity exam in your third year, when you not only exceeded expectations but soared over them with all the grace of a seagull carefully preparing to defecate on a tourist?

"Yes, you went very quiet in the University Arms yesterday, when your beloved and bejumpered mentor David Williamson made a chance reference to cheating and plagiarism scandals in Cambridge. I am sure that it was entirely unwitting on his part, and he doubtless failed to notice the colour draining from your face. But I noticed, Sadie! I noticed!"

Sadie jumped out of her seat, about to protest.

"Before you ask, yes you do have to stay here to be insulted, Ms Simmons!" Baynes informed her with a satisfied grin. If the inspector bore any resentment towards Sinclair for stealing his thunder, it had been more than compensated for by his ample breakfast. He was now leaning back in his chair, a picture of avuncular contentment, several of his shirt buttons having apparently given up and moved on to pastures new.

"It's all right," Sinclair said with a smile. "I think we can move on. For now. Let's sidestep into the political arena, shall we? Always a dangerous, cut-throat world, and one that James Thaddeus Jeffers, recently voted the fifteenth most likely MP to engage in obnoxious bouts of unnecessary roaring during PMQs, took to like a fish to water! Perhaps Ed Dickinson is merely the latest in a long line of victims of the Cambridge Union mafia.

"Given the toe-curling quality of some of the witticisms that our front-line politicians feel the need to come out with in the modern political era, producing a truly career-ending joke nowadays takes some doing. But you, Mr Jeffers, not only pulled it off but had it committed to celluloid, or its twenty-first-century equivalent. Dickinson had the video, and therefore he had control over your political career. He could have ended it at a stroke. It actually put him in an extremely powerful position. But I doubt that using that power for the social good ever occurred to our responsibility-shirking protagonist.

"Was Dickinson blackmailing you? Even if he wasn't, teasing the occasional threat would have been entirely in character for a man with such a penchant for the wind-up. You must have been living in constant terror, Mr Jeffers. And you were very keen to encourage Mr Dickinson to open the time capsule on Friday night."

"Surely that shows I have nothing to hide!" Jammy pointed out furiously, his face a picture of outrage.

"But of course, how foolish of me!" Sinclair hooted. "No doubt when you offered to take the capsule and hand the predictions out yourself, you were only trying to be helpful!

You had absolutely no intention of sneaking your own entry up the sleeve in which you keep the knife you're normally backstabbing your esteemed colleagues with? With the greatest respect to my right honourable friend, I would direct him to pull the other one; he might find that it jingles!

"What about you, Tanya Bullock?" Sinclair now moved back around the table. "Without wishing to sound unduly sordid, you were the last person to share carnal relations with the deceased. Your relationship with...Rick, is it, was already on the rocks, and you freely admitted that Dickinson was not exactly up there with J Edgar Hoover when it came to keeping secrets! He had always been a master manipulator, and it wasn't the first time he had put you in a terrible position, was it? Christmas 2005. Was it really you driving that night, when poor Professor Welch got hit by your car?" He stopped right in front of her and looked into her eyes. Tanya refused to meet them.

"I think that's enough. We're getting off-topic here!" I broke in.

"I was driving," Tanya said in a low, almost catatonic voice.

"But...?" Sinclair pressed her. "He tried to make a pass at you, didn't he? But he was too drunk, being too silly. You weren't interested, not then."

"That'd be a first," Niamh muttered nastily.

"It was my fault," Tanya insisted.

"What was it you said, Whiteley? Mr Dickinson got dangerously close to the line between touchy-feely and gropy every once in a while? Small wonder you were distracted, Miss Bullock. The more I've discovered about Dickinson over the last twenty-four hours, the more obvious it's become to me that there was a thoroughly nasty piece of work hiding behind that superficial veneer of chilled-out charm. He didn't deserve your silence, you know! About his part in the accident. And what's more, you knew, on Friday night, that he wouldn't return the favour. The only way you could guarantee that he would keep his mouth shut was if you stopped him breathing through it there and then. He'd mucked up your life once too often. As you said to Whiteley, he'd never suffered the consequences of his own actions. Perhaps you'd decided it was time for that to change? Putting an end to him would also have the beneficial side effect of removing the temptation for further relationship-damaging shenanigans!"

"No," Tanya whispered. She was trembling now, and her eyes were brimming. "You're wrong."

"Am I? Well, perhaps it might not have been such a simple fix. If Steven and Lydia Taylor had been able to join us this morning, I am sure they would have been able to attest to that. Relationships are complicated beasts. I think we can eliminate the possibility of Lydia having committed the actual crime, on the basis that climbing through a first-floor window in her delicate condition would be a tad unwise. But then again, Lady Macbeth managed to make all sorts of mischief without actually wielding the dagger in her own right.

"Why did she bother to show up yesterday evening anyway? As I understand it, she never made the slightest effort to veil her disgust for her husband's social circle. Was her decision to join in the festivities on Saturday evening a demonstration that she simply couldn't bear to be away from her husband for a whole weekend, even if it meant having to spend time with that pack of bibulous hyenas he calls friends—no offence to anyone present? Or was she keeping an eye on her husband? Or yet, was there an altogether darker motivation in play?

"The relationship between Taylor and Dickinson is one that I have found particularly fascinating. Closer than Charles Ryder and Sebastian Flyte most of the time, their usually warm relationship was punctuated by occasional bursts of sub-Antarctic frostiness. Why such turbulence? Yes, Dickinson put himself in the firing line with one of his rare acts of altruism, when he flushed away Taylor's stash of special powder back in the day. But was that really all Taylor had in mind when he told Whiteley last night that Dickinson had been a better friend to him than he had ever given him credit for, 'in spite of everything'?

"In spite of what? We know that Dickinson had a roving eye, a buccaneering cock, and hands with a tendency to delve into inappropriate places! We also know that Lydia reserved a particularly intense level of contempt for our late lecher. Could she have been another unwilling recipient of those roaming fingers?

"We have no way of knowing the truth, given that the real Taylors are a no-show, but I suspect that he might well have tried his luck at one point. However, I now believe that it was something else that was uppermost in Steve's mind last night. It was Gavin, of all people, who hinted at the truth. What was it he said, Whiteley?"

I had no idea what he was babbling on about, for I couldn't recall Gavin having mentioned the Taylors once. Luckily, however, our showboating host had absolutely no intention of letting me make even a cameo appearance in his seemingly interminable monologue, for he interrupted me before I had a chance to get it wrong.

"He said, and I quote, 'You really think Ed was the father of that kid? Well, I know better!' You thought that our philandering Porter was putting himself forward as an alternative candidate, didn't you, Whiteley? It would be consistent with his tendency to brag about what is a genuinely remarkable litany of conquests, given his general repulsiveness."

"But what if that wasn't what he meant at all? It strikes me that if Niamh Redmond were to stray, she would have been altogether more discerning in her choice of 'straying partner.' And who had a better opportunity to fulfil that role than their broodingly handsome fellow resident of Chateau Dickinson,

Steven Taylor?"

I opened my mouth to protest, but the words stuck in my throat when my brain caught up and realised that Sinclair's theory was actually eminently plausible. Ed had been a neglectful boyfriend at times, and whilst I am pretty sure that Niamh was unaware of the full extent of his moonlighting in other people's bedrooms, she was bright enough to know that their relationship had some defective elements to it. And Steve was increasingly demonstrating that whatever other talents he might be possessed of, resistance to temptation was not among them.

Eminently plausible, but wrong, as it turned out. Dan suddenly stood up, an unusually mature expression on his face.

"I wasn't going to do this here," he said.

"Shut up, Dan!" Niamh hissed.

"And I hate that this is the way you've had to find out the truth, son," Dan continued, ignoring her. "But 'son' is right, I'm afraid. If it's true that you're not Ed's kid, you must be mine."

Lee had put his phone down and was looking at Dan, his expression a particularly teenage mixture of bemusement, disgust, and acute embarrassment.

"This guy? Seriously?" he said, scowling. Niamh looked as though she was about to crumble.

"I don't know," she said shakily. "I was going to ask them both if they'd be prepared to do a DNA test. It's right that you should know. Even if neither of them were fit to lick Eoin's boots," she added fiercely.

"But then I found out that Ed was dead, and Dan's still the self-obsessed drunken dickhead he always was. Don't you dare call him 'son,' Dan. You don't get to do that. Not now."

"Definitely not now," Sinclair agreed irritably, ushering Dan gently but firmly back to his seat. "I'm not here to drum up interest in a reboot of *The Jerry Springer Show*! I'm in the middle of unmasking a killer, for heaven's sake! Although Mr Finn's intervention may answer certain questions, it raises others. Like Mr Taylor's reaction to your comment that fatherhood changes a man, when you were giving him your pep talk last night, Whiteley? Your sentiments were greeted with scorn and derision. It was immediately obvious to me that you were talking to a man who had already been a father for some considerable period, and sniffing and snorting away to his heart's content the whole time!"

"But if he's not Lee's father..." I stammered.

"Then there's another mystery wandering around out there somewhere," Sinclair said while smiling.

"But how can that have anything to do with the murder?"

"A good question, Whiteley! No need to drag me, handcuffed, back to the topic at hand. I will come quietly, guvnor! You may also have spotted that whilst I have identified a vast spectrum of possible motives for murder from virtually all of you, none of them directly relate to the time capsule with which we began our narrative! The secrets that Ed Dickinson had hoarded for seventeen years like Smaug sitting on his treasure trove, that were about to be revealed at long last.

"There has been a lot of speculation about Dickinson as a potential blackmailer, but blackmailers rely for their livelihood on their ability to keep secrets. If they don't, the money dries up! Tanya Bullock hit the nail on the head when she highlighted Dickinson's chronic inability to keep a secret. He might well have used the threat of that video he had kept on his phone to lure Mr Jeffers back up for the reunion. He was fortunate enough to be in possession of a video of a future political star, or a political brown dwarf at the very least, carrying out an act of character assassination on himself. Can any of us honestly say that if we were in possession of a similar political landmine, we would delete it rather than saving it for a rainy day? But we have no evidence that he did anything more about it or had any intention of doing so. For Ed Dickinson, it was 'wind-up fodder,' nothing more.

"Neil Norman, on the other hand, definitely was being blackmailed by someone, and I know, Whiteley, that you suspected Dickinson of being the culprit. But we now know that, unfortunately for Mr Norman, the true culprit is still very much alive and kicking!"

Kicking and screaming, once Mad Dog McFadden has finished with him, I thought.

"The more interesting question in the Neil Norman saga, though, is not so much the who as the what," Sinclair continued cryptically. "We know Gavin was blackmailing him, but what was he blackmailing him about? That, my friends, is where we find ourselves entering a rather black comedy of errors."

II

"When Whiteley and I confronted Mr Norman last night," Sinclair went on, "our furtive financial advisor seemed genuinely astonished, and not a little put out, by my suggestion that Gavin had been blackmailing him because he had known that Norman was in possession of the murder weapon.

"What, then, was it that he was trying to cover up instead? Why, it surely then had to be his clandestine relationship with our exceptionally efficient college nurse, Daisy Seaman? That is why he thought you might be able to get me off his back, Whiteley! He knew you had all the grubby details of that business and would be able to persuade me that he had nothing to do with the murder at all!

"After all, Eric the Porter mentioned to us that her pigeon-hole is rarely free of correspondence. Much of this, I suspect, is likely to consist of passionate and highly melodramatic missives from Mr Norman. He may not have physically strayed from the marital road. But in spirit, there seems little doubt that he has at least veered onto the hard shoulder! And we know that Gavin has a penchant for rummaging through the suitcases and handbags of college guests. Can we be certain that he has not been similarly guilty of violating the sacred privacy of the college pigeon-holes?

"And yet...and yet, this is Gavin Shufflebottom we're talking about! He made one thing quite clear when chatting to Whiteley yesterday evening, when he thought I was out of earshot. He clarified that Dickinson's playing away when in a relationship with Niamh had not been something that he found particularly morally troubling, although he used an altogether grubbier, feline analogy to express such sentiments. In short, we have to factor in the fact that we are dealing with someone whose moral code is twistier than a corkscrew!

"Imagine yourself in Gavin's head for an instant. Imagine that you discover that Neil Norman wants to sow his wild oats over a rather larger area than his marital vows would strictly allow? Would your reaction not be, 'Wahey, good luck to him! That miserable stuffed shirt must be one of the lads after all!'? When you, Whiteley, told him that you didn't believe he was blackmailing Norman about the murder, he seemed rather tickled. A petty, vindictive man taking petty, vindictive pleasure in watching you get the wrong end of the stick by eliminating a suspect prematurely!"

"Now I'm confused," I said, starting to worry that I might be developing a catchphrase. "Was he blackmailing Norman about the murder, or wasn't he?"

"He was, but Norman didn't realise he was. That's where the comedy of errors comes in. I can't claim to have ever personally visited a blackmailer to hand over an envelope crammed full of dosh. I will leave you to decide whether that is due to my irreproachable character or an excess of lowbrow sneakiness in concealing my deficiencies. But were I to do so, I suspect that I would be disinclined to spend too much time on expository chit-chat!

"Norman got a message from Gavin threatening to expose his little secret if he didn't 'bung him some bangers.' Or is it 'bang him some bungers'? It is possible that neither expression was used. But it is the lack of specificity that is the key. Norman probably assumed that it was all about what he'd been putting in Ms Seaman's pigeon-hole. It was an understandable assumption, given Gavin's role as college Porter, with plenty of opportunity to rifle through any illicit correspondence. But in truth, whilst he has form when it comes to rifling, in this case, he may not even have known about Norman's feelings for Ms Seaman. Even if he did, he wouldn't have given a tinker's cuss! No, it was the knife he was interested in!"

"But...but then..." I stammered.

"He was hedging his bets, you see! When he found the knife in their room, then later saw the same knife inserted into Mr Dickinson, he had no way of knowing whether it was Mr Norman or Mrs Norman who had done the dirty deed, or whether they were in it together. So he just took a punt. For the eavesdropping tourists, I should explain that that is just a turn of phrase, and no flat-bottomed boats were involved. He decided to blackmail the both of them! His insufferable smugness levels must have rocketed all the way up to 'Piers Morgan' when they both turned up separately to pay him a visit yesterday evening!

"Neil came bearing a stuffed envelope, but Britta, I have no doubt, was altogether more creative. Gavin had lusted after her for a long, long while, and she knew it. Besides, for a keen military historian like Gavin, the prospect of following in the footsteps of King William I with a Norman Conquest of his own was clearly too enticing to pass up. The fact that her husband turned up before he got a chance to get started doubtless added to the thrill of it for him. But he would never have got a chance to really enjoy himself, even if Whiteley and

I had not turned up like a pair of gooseberries in the middle of it all!"

"You're not saying that Britta had anything to do with this, are you?" I blurted out, aghast.

"Brace yourself, Whiteley. I know that this won't be pleasant for you to hear. But yes, it was she. Of course it was!"

Unpleasant was, of course, a ridiculous understatement; I had, of course, already been girding my loins, knowing full well that the revelation that one of my close (or at least close-ish) friends had perpetrated this foul crime was now pretty much inevitable. But Britta? Others were looking similarly incredulous and disbelieving.

"Oh, for God's sake!" Niamh scoffed.

"Hear me out, please." Sinclair's tone was gentler now, more wistful. "Who was it who met up with Albert Ross just before he died? She was initially accompanied by Tanya Bullock when she went to meet him. But although Britta claimed last night that both of them stayed for only half an hour, Tanya had earlier made it clear that she and she alone left early, meaning that Britta had the doddery old doofus all to herself.

"What were they talking about, and why did Ross appear so agitated to Tanya? He should have been like a pig in the proverbial, being wined and dined and flirted with by a pair of attractive females young enough to be his granddaughters! But if he already knew that Britta's ulterior motive for summoning him there was to winkle college secrets out of him, then one can understand his disquiet. I'm sure that the motive she presented to him was an entirely innocent one. Doubtless something to do with the reunion, which he already knew about from Dickinson. But Albert had always been a stickler for the rules, and bean-spilling would not have come naturally to him.

"Nevertheless, he was a weak and silly old fellow, much

though we all loved him, and Britta Norman had always been his favourite. The questions she was asking him might have seemed odd, and she was sweetly enticing him well outside his comfort zone, it's true. But if she wanted to know a bit about the layout of the new accommodation, what could possibly be the harm, he would have said to himself, even if she was venturing into some odd security-related questions?

"As it happens, she didn't give him long to ponder the matter. Shortly afterwards, he was killed, and any inconvenient details about what he and Britta really talked about that evening died with him. Snipping the old boy's brakes was the easiest thing in the world! But then Albert's assassination was a relatively simple prelude to the main affair. A starter, as it were, with Dickinson's murder the sumptuous main course!"

"This is complete conjecture," I bristled.

"You think so? Very well, then. Let's move on to yesterday morning, when Torvill had the two of you in the Porter's Lodge for interrogation, and Gavin was lurking like a bad smell, waiting to lob his grenade into the conversation about the knife. What was it he said?"

Baynes cleared his throat.

"I quote," the inspector rumbled, "'The killer made a mistake leaving it sticking out of his gullet like that. Even if he wiped the fingerprints off, someone might well recognise a lovely hunting knife like that!'"

"Why would he say that then and there?" Sinclair demanded. "There's no point dropping hints like that unless the person you're blackmailing is in the room with you! No doubt, he sent her something more explicit later on, and she pretended that she was prepared to do whatever he wanted to buy his silence. And in Gavin's case, it was not hard to imagine what that might be!"

"But if she killed Ross to make it easier for her to kill Ed, why the hell did she kill Ed?" I demanded.

"Because of the time capsule, Whiteley! You had it right all along! Back then, young Britta Prendergast was a carefree young thing, living for the here and now! She didn't give a damn about much, and certainly not about what she'd be doing nearly twenty years in the future! So she went into explicit detail about exactly what she had got up to as a wild undergraduate. Only fast forward seventeen years, and it turns out this sedentary, boring middle-aged family life thing is rather pleasant after all, and now she's in it, she doesn't want to give it up. Whether she is aware that her husband is half crazy all for the love of Ms Seaman or not, she can sense that her grip on his affections is loosening. If he were to find out what she'd written in the capsule, she knew that they could slip out of her grasp altogether!

"Neil has already caught her playing away once, with dastardly cousin Alan. Doubtless this roguish offshoot of the Norman dynasty had his uses! Taught her rock climbing, for one thing! Must have come in pretty useful for her when she was scaling the wall behind D Block, knowing, thanks to Albert, that in doing so, she'd be able to avoid those pesky cameras. Neil thought that the whole rock-climbing thing was an excuse, but my suspicion is that it was the sex that was purely incidental! No, no, Cousin Alan was just a bit player, a red herring. Britta had bigger fish to fry!"

"What? She was seeing someone else? Who?"

"The same fellow who smashed a glass last night when you mentioned Britta's little tryst to him. I believe that that little act of hooliganism was his reaction to the discovery that the love triangle he had been cheerfully participating in for years had suddenly got a bit quadrilateral! Or possibly pentagonal, but I'll get to that in a bit."

"Steve?"

"Why not? They had history!"

"Ancient history," I pointed out. "They split up at the end of the first year."

"Ah, but the bonds between them were not so easily severed. Two such dynamic, selfish, self-destructive individuals could never have settled down to an easy, comfortable relationship. But a secret, torrid, at times frenzied love affair that spanned two decades and outlasted several more conventional relationships that both of them were involved in during that period? Well, that's quite another matter.

"That's what she put in the time capsule. She freely 'fessed up to the fact that she had been cheating on poor Mr Norman throughout their relationship, that she had thoroughly enjoyed the whole experience, and that if she had her time all over, she'd do it again! Who cared if it all got read out in seventeen years? What were the chances that anyone would even remember that the time capsule existed by then? Oh yes, a live wire like Britta would have had absolutely no qualms about taking a chance on something like that! It would have been 'a laugh.'

"And imagine how Neil Norman would have reacted, hearing something like that. Discovering that far from having made an unfortunate mistake once or twice, there had never been a time in their relationship when she had not been cheating on him! He had given up even seeing Daisy Seaman, for whom he was developing feelings of a very deep and passionate nature, because he had wanted to make his marriage work, and for what? No, Britta could not allow that to happen. She needed Dickinson out of the way, but not just Dickinson. Torvill, I think it's time we checked in on Mr Taylor, don't you?"

"This is pure suppository!" I exclaimed, storming to my feet furiously, almost upsetting my cup of tea, such was the extent of my indignant rage.

"I think you mean 'supposition,' Whiteley," Sinclair replied carefully.

"No, I bloody well don't! And you know where you can stick it!" I was fully intending to flounce out at this point, but being British, I did have to pause to shell out a couple of notes from my wallet to cover my share of brunch plus a tip. Meanwhile, Inspector Baynes had opened a large bag by his chair and drawn out a laptop. He opened it up and turned the screen around so that we were all able to see what appeared to be live video footage of a dimly lit hotel room with a slumped figure lying in the bed. Which rather stopped me in my tracks.

"Doesn't look like we've missed the show!" Sinclair smiled.

"No, you've timed it perfectly, thanks to the unexpected bit of extra family drama!" Baynes chortled, turning up the volume on the footage. "She's on her way up. What you are witnessing, ladies and gents, is live footage of a room at the Hilton, just down the road!"

We heard the sound of a door unlocking, and then Britta Norman stepped into shot.

III

I barely realised it was her at first. She was wearing a hat, dark glasses, a large overcoat and one of those COVID-era face masks. As she started disrobing, the figure lying on the bed stirred.

"What's the time?" the figure asked. It was clearly Steve, although his voice was so hoarse it was barely audible.

"Half twelve," Britta told him.

"You shouldn't be here!"

"Relax! Lydia left town in a huff, remember. We're quite safe. Fancy some lunch?"

She waved a small packet of something in his face.

"No. I've told you," Steve snarled. "I can't do that anymore. Or this."

He gestured between the pair of them.

"It was you who got nostalgic on me yesterday," Britta pointed out.

"I get confused," Steve moaned. "What happened to Ed really messed me up, you know? I wasn't thinking straight. But I need to straighten myself out for the baby. I know I couldn't be there for Aaron. Neil was the right father figure for him, and I get that. I was willing to make that sacrifice, not just for the sake of my marriage to Lydia but for you too, and for Aaron. Because having me in his life would only have messed him up. But now it's my turn. If I can just kick all this shit, once and for all, I can finally be a decent husband to Lydia and a good dad to this kid, and maybe more, who knows?"

"Oh yes, I'm sure you'll have a nice, big, happy family," Britta snapped.

"Oh, here we go!" Steve buried his head in his pillow. "I am so sick of you bringing this up! I didn't force you up onto that roof all those years ago, and neither did Ed!"

"Don't you walk away from your responsibility, you utter bastard!" Britta was shaking with anger now. "You'd been plying me with drinks all night, both of you! You because you were trying to get me into bed; Ed because he thought it was funny.

"And what was your response, Steve? Did you come and visit me in hospital, tell me how sorry you were, beg forgiveness? Or did you and Ed buy me a funny get-well card from fucking moonpig.com—one card between the two of you, mind; you couldn't even stretch to one each!"

"I didn't want to get in the way. I've always wanted what's best for you, you know that!"

Britta snorted. "What's best for me? Do you even remember that night? 'Down it, down it!'" she mimicked. "And don't tell me you and Ed didn't spike my drink with something! Thought it would be funny, did you? Get the new mum off her face on who knows what? One slip, and that was it. Insides ruptured to buggery, and no more chance at having kids. Which means all Neil gets is his cuckoo in the nest. He's got one hell of a temper, you know! Do you know what he'd do to you if I ever told him?"

A look of concern and confusion passed over Steve's face.

"Jesus, Britta, it wasn't him, was it?"

Britta's face fixed into a hateful sneer, and she laughed.

"Ha! It's always the quiet ones you have to watch, isn't it? But not this time. Even though Neil and Ed did hate each other. They were thrown together on a business deal a few years ago when Ed was still doing fee-earning work. Some sort of tax restructuring thing. Neil was doing the accounting side, and Ed and his team were doing the legal work. Neil reckoned that Ed was overcharging the client, sneaking through tens of thousands of pounds of unjustified fees and expenses, and got him bumped off the deal."

"Ed was desperate," Steve muttered. "He had gambling debts. I ended up bailing him out with money I'd been putting aside for Lydia's fertility treatments. She found out about it and never forgave him, or me."

"Oh, I remember," Britta's lip curled. "You came seeking solace in my arms a lot more often that year than I'd been accustomed to. Such stamina! But your noble sacrifice was just a sticking plaster, Steve. Ed made the shift away from transactional work shortly afterwards, and it wasn't coincidental. The partners at his firm had obviously lost faith in him. Ed must have known that Neil had tipped the client the wink. He behaved like a complete dick every time we met up with him after that—always winding Neil up. He always knew how to press his buttons, and there were a couple of times it almost ended up in a punch-up. Neil didn't want to come this weekend. Not at first. Jesus, if he hadn't changed his mind, this weekend might have turned out quite differently." She reached into her pocket.

"But you said it wasn't him?" Steve pressed her. She turned around, and his eyes widened as he saw what was in her hand. I am not a gun nerd, so I was not able to identify her oversized firearm, but it certainly looked like it would have fitted neatly into that spot on Gavin's wall that had been so conspicuously empty last night. I later established that this monstrosity was a Smith & Wesson Number 29, the same shooter wielded by Clint Eastwood when he played Filthy Harold all those years ago.

"Britta, what the hell?" Steve spluttered, scrambling away from her on the bed.

"You'll stay right where you are and take your medicine!" Britta glared at him balefully, glancing in the direction of the packet of powder she had left by the bedside table.

"What have you done to it?" Steve was shaking uncontrollably now. Britta's face was still in shot, just about. I leaned towards the screen and gazed at a face I had known for over fifteen years, and saw a stranger's eyes staring back at me. I hoped against hope for them to soften into a familiar expression. To see a hint of that warm, mischievous smile I had always been so fond of. But it retained a hatchet-like implacability.

"Added a sprinkling of rat poison to give it a special 'kick.' Don't look at me like that. Unlike you, I'm honest enough to tell you exactly what your refreshments are lined with! And it's not impossible that you'd survive it. After all, I've never actually poisoned anyone before. I've never shot anyone either, of course, which is your other option, but I think you'll agree the margin of error at this range is much smaller." She gestured again with the gun.

"Jesus, Britta!" Steve was whimpering. "It was you? You killed Ed. Just because of the accident? Christ, it was fifteen years ago!"

"That and the time capsule," Britta said. "Either one

probably wouldn't have been enough on its own. The funny thing is, I'd pretty much forgiven you both. It's not as if it had stopped me shagging you every time Neil's back was turned. OK, so I obviously still had some resentment festering deep down, but if it hadn't been for what he was planning this week, I could probably have let it die.

"Ed was a pathetically inadequate man-child and a walking HR complaints file, so it's not as though he'll be a great loss to humanity. But I didn't want to have to end him. I tried to talk him out of the whole time capsule reveal extravaganza so many bloody times, but nothing I could say seemed to dampen his childish enthusiasm for the idea. So yes, I guess my residual grudge did get stirred up a bit by the fact that the stupid shit-stirring bastard was happy to let something I wrote down more than fifteen years ago, in a fit of spiteful nihilism, while pissed out of my skull, fuck up my marriage!"

"But was it really that bad, what was in there? We were practically kids."

"Well, you've read it!" Britta snorted. "Where is it, by the way? I will find it; you won't have had the chance to stash it anywhere safe, so you might as well tell me."

"What are you talking about?" Steve's eyes were wide and his whole body was trembling now.

"You always were a shit liar, Steve! I don't know why you left the note saying you had it, or how in God's name you managed to track it down before I did. Perhaps you can talk me through it while the rat poison kicks in…your time's up on that, by the way. You've got ten seconds to snort the lot, or I'll shoot you in the nuts. One…"

There was a click, and the door opened. A slight figure appeared in the doorway.

"ST?" David Williamson's voice called out querulously.

"Get out, David!" Steve yelled.

"He's in here," Britta said matter-of-factly. "Come and join the party."

Williamson was halfway across the room before he saw the gun. He swallowed sharply and raised his hand. "What the…"

"Get on the bed," Britta insisted. "Why the hell did you have to wander into this?"

There was a pause.

"Oh, I see." She laughed as the answer dawned on her. "No wonder you were so anxious to be rid of me, Steve. Two-timing the charming Lydia wasn't quite edgy enough for you on its own, eh? You just had to add an extra dimension, is that it? You've been seeing this shabby sack of a man, and *I* was the one you decided to give up for Lent. You utter prick! To think I was actually feeling guilty about having to shoot you."

"I was about to end it with him, too," Steve wailed desperately. "Sorry, David. I've messed everything up. But you don't have to shoot him. Please, Britta. He's not part of this."

"What the hell have you got me into, Steven?" David demanded. His voice was more wistful than accusatory, and it sounded to me like the tone of a man who had known he was reaching the end of the line, at least on the relationship front. Being confronted by an unhinged gunwoman had evidently come as more of a surprise.

"Sorry, no time to explain," Britta interrupted before Steve could speak. "Not sure there's enough of the white stuff for both of you, so we'll have to do this the old-fashioned way."

She raised her weapon and was immediately caught off guard as Detective Sergeant Jacqueline Chen launched herself out of the cupboard, five foot one and a half inches of determined dynamism bearing down relentlessly on the would-be assassin. She was wielding nothing but a taser and several barrel loads of pure unadulterated gumption, and apparently giving fewer fucks than you'd find in a nunnery about the fact that an iconically deadly weapon was now being trained on her. She moved quickly, but Britta's reactions were faster. She pulled the trigger.

EPILOGUE

In which loose ends are tied up, resolutions are resolved, and I make some life-changing decisions, almost accidentally assaulting a random tourist in the process because, as the Bishop of Southwark once famously said, "It's what I do!"

"Well, of course I knew the gun wasn't loaded," Sinclair declared, accompanying his assertion with a suitably derisive guffaw.

It was the following day, the last day of the longest Easter weekend I could remember. Sinclair and Emily had decided to take me out for a lunchtime pie and a pint at The Anchor. This was presumably an act of atonement for the fact that the whole college accommodation experience had been rather more fraught and generally sanguinary than their website had promised. The word "tranquil" had featured heavily in the alumni accommodation section.

We were sitting outside, as it was starting to feel for the first time as though summer might be stirring. One of Cambridge's best-known pubs, The Anchor is nestled in an enviable location on Silver Street overlooking the Cam and, on a pleasant day like this one, dozens of punting tourists of variable skills trying their luck on the river.

Believe me, my young friend, a very wise rodent once said, there is nothing—absolutely nothing—half so much worth doing as simply messing about in boats. There were plenty of people out there that lunchtime eager to sign up to that philosophy. But as for me, after a rather unusually active weekend, I was more than happy settling into the role of spectator, with my feet on the ground and a pint glass in my hand.

Young Jasper was conspicuous by his absence. Perhaps the precocious little chap was out and about following a lead pertaining to some other nefarious activities afoot elsewhere in the city.

"How did you know it wasn't loaded?" I demanded suspiciously, not quite ready to let the subject drop just yet.

"Because she pinched it from Gavin on a whim, and once she had it, she didn't know what to do with it! Finlay McFadden did not have too much difficulty ascertaining from our friend Gavin which of his firearms had been pilfered. When he relayed that discovery to me, I was immediately able to breathe a huge sigh of relief. My dear Whiteley, have you ever tried purchasing ammunition for a .44 Magnum in Cambridge town centre on Easter morning?"

I paused for a moment.

"I have not," I admitted grudgingly.

"I suspected as much!" Sinclair smiled triumphantly. "It is far from straightforward, believe me!"

"But what if the Magnum had just been insurance?" I persisted. "What if she'd had another gun?"

There was another long pause.

"I asked him that question earlier," Emily said and smiled at me. Sinclair's shirt collar seemed to be causing him some measure of discomfort, which, I must admit, made me feel a little better. Emily had obviously given him the mother of all bollockings, next to which the traumatic experiences that had befallen DS Chen in that hotel room undoubtedly paled by comparison. "We had quite a frank exchange of views about it, in fact, didn't we Gerald?"

Sinclair cleared his throat nervously.

"As I said to Emily, I had every confidence that DS Chen would think of something. She's a very resourceful young lady. Did you want another bread roll, by the way?"

I had sworn to myself that I would stay in a huff with the smug so-and-so for at least a week for putting Jacqui in such a tight spot, even if it had been essentially part of her job. But the crafty old devil was making it very difficult for me by continually offering me such excellent food. I accepted his offer but made a point of sniffing disdainfully as I did so.

"And here's another question," I continued as crumbs cascaded down my cleanish shirt. "We thought she had the time capsule, so why did she think Steve had it?"

"Ah yes, that's a knotty one, isn't it?" Sinclair said with the smug air of a man watching *Game of Thrones* having read the books first in the company of someone who hasn't. "But it was the logical thing for her to think after what she saw up in the bell tower. Fortunately, I spotted it too."

He handed me a slip of paper. I unravelled it.

"To whom it may concern," the note began. "If you want the contents of the box you left up here back, please contact me. ST."

"It fluttered down from the tower in the nick of time whilst the scraps of old newspaper she stuffed up there in her attempt to roast us were catching on fire. I managed to retrieve it from the floor before we beat our hasty retreat!"

"I forgot about that in all the excitement," I admitted. "I can't believe you squirreled away a clue that important without telling me!"

"And what would you have made of it if I had shown it to you?" Sinclair grinned at me impenitently.

"Well," I blustered, "I suppose I probably would have reached the same conclusion Britta did, that Steve had somehow managed to beat us both to the time capsule."

"Precisely. And how on earth would he have managed to

squeeze that little feat of detective work into his busy schedule of police interrogations, cocaine binges and valiant attempts at breaking things off with his slew of sexual partners? As soon as I picked up the paper, I immediately realised two things. Firstly, that our murderer would instantly jump to the conclusion that ST stood for Steve Taylor, thus placing that rather overburdened fellow in an incredibly dangerous predicament, and secondly, that our murderer was dead wrong!"

"So who is ST?"

"That's Senior Tutor to you," a heavily accented voice boomed down at us. I looked up and saw, approaching us, a large, beefy-looking fellow with a completely bald scalp that looked as though it was regularly doused in fragrant and soothing massage oils. In one hand, he was carrying a Boots bag. He extended his other tough, sinewy hand and introduced himself.

"Dr Richard Du Toit, Senior Tutor at St Crispian's," he declared. "ST to the students. I thought using an acronym sounded jauntier, more fun. Thought it might help me ingratiate myself with the youngsters so they'd feel less aggrieved when I took a few necessary steps to curb their drinking habits! So far, the jury's out on that one!"

"Roger, allow me to introduce you to the one man in Cambridge who's even less 'down with the kids' than my husband," Emily interjected mischievously.

Dr Du Toit wasted no time in inviting himself to sit down at our table, emptying the contents of the Boots bag onto it. Said contents consisted solely of a small Tupperware container, which he proceeded to open.

"I hear everyone's been looking for this!" He grinned. "I found it a few weeks ago and added it to my confiscated items drawer! It's getting like the inside of Mary Poppins' handbag in there these days. If she was peddling narcotics on her

Tuesdays off, anyway. I could have saved people a lot of hassle, but what are you gonna do? I was out of town, enjoying a heavily brass rubbing oriented weekend away. Only just got back and heard about what's going on! I'm about to cycle over to the police station to hand this in, but Gerald here prevailed on me to swing by here first. Told me you'd earned it by lending him invaluable assistance! From a glance at today's papers, I'd say he was right. You guys made page eleven of the Daily Star!"

He gave me a hearty pat on the back, and his grin widened even further. I stared down at the contents of the Tupperware Time Capsule. There, folded, crumpled and a little dusty but essentially undamaged and completely unsinged, were ten scraps of paper containing the future hopes and dreams of a bunch of inebriated youngsters, still just on the cusp of adulthood, most of whom would barely recognise their future selves if they had been able to see us now. All of a sudden, I felt rather moved and was almost overcome by an overwhelming sense of reluctance about disturbing this remarkable pile of papers.

"Should we be looking at this?" I asked nervously. "Isn't it vital police evidence or something?"

"Don't worry your pretty little head about that, Whiteley!" Sinclair said. "I've cleared it with the powers that be! As long as you don't swallow any of them, I think we'll be fine! Browse to your heart's content."

Overcoming my initial hesitation, I picked up the one on the top and then started reading through them in turn. I won't set them all out in detail here, dear reader. You know who killed Ed (and Albert) now, so you've got what you came for, and no doubt you are now itching for me to wrap things up.

A few highlights: I was quite startled to see that Chris Cleghorn, as well as being surprisingly realistic about his chances as the next Stanley Kubrick, had predicted both the 2008 stock market crash and the results of the 2007 Belgian

Federal Elections with an uncanny degree of accuracy. Rather less presciently, Sadie Simmons had predicted that she would be eleven years into her marriage with David Williamson by this point, to which I can only say "bless." And Dan Finn had concluded that the world would have ended by now, which begs the question of why he had bothered to write anything down at all.

I will, however, provide you with the full text of Britta's entry, and my own. Britta's read as follows:

"Fifteen years' time? Fuck knows; I'll be halfway to death by then! I'll probably still be snuggling up with Neil by day and getting my extra fix of horizontal refreshment from that horny beast Steve Taylor by night. Ha, Neil, bet you didn't see that one coming! Screw it; if I'm not tired of you by then, this revelation might butt-kick me into reminding myself that you truly are a very, very boring man. Hope you've climbed K2, though! God knows if I've had to listen to all your tedious chat about how exciting you find that prospect, even during sex, all for nothing, I swear I'm going to set the fucking Terminator on you. He's around by the 2020s, right?"

I can only assume that she and Neil had had a row earlier in the day. The dreadful thing was that it had probably been quite a trivial one, for I don't recall any surface frostiness from either of them that evening. Not since the Homeric era has a domestic bust-up led to quite as much collateral damage. Mine, of course, was far less revelatory, albeit it was every bit as self-indulgently maudlin as I remembered:

"As one of the only singletons in the room, and seemingly perennially so, I hope that I will have found a cure for my chronic gaucheness by then and settled down with a female of some description, rather than ending up as a dried-out old bachelor with seventeen tabby cats who are sucking up to me principally because

they are waiting for me to die so that they can eat me as an accompaniment to their fish snacks before the undertaker arrives. It is, of course, possible that I am selling myself short and that I will be a beatific billionaire with a sideline in swashbuckling crime fighting. But it'll probably be the tabby cats."

There was one more slip underneath my own, but before I could reach out, the Senior Tutor briskly reapplied the lid.

"Seen enough, my friend? The future is perhaps not quite what it used to be, eh?"

"There was one he missed," Sinclair pointed out.

"Must have been Tanya's," I said, having done the working out in my head.

"Ah, well, now just a second..." Dr Richard Du Toit, Senior Tutor, was a man who effortlessly dominated a room, or indeed a courtyard, just by walking into it, even when it contained such larger-than-life characters as the Sinclairs. So I was surprised to see that he was now looking rather uncomfortable.

"Oh good grief, I hadn't put two and two together," Emily exclaimed. "Is that your Tanya? The one you keep telling us about?"

"His Tanya?" I interjected sharply. "Oh my God! You're the Rick she was talking about yesterday!"

"Yeah!" Dr Du Toit grinned. "I gave up on trying to make the ST thing stick as far as she was concerned—she said she'd only agree to call me that if I changed my middle name to 'hi'!"

"So you're back on, then?" said Emily.

"As of yesterday evening, yes, I'm pleased to say we've officially decided to give it another go," Du Toit announced proudly.

"Don't look so worried, my friend!" he said with a chuckle, seeing my now somewhat long-faced expression. "She told me all about her little romp romp in the stomp stomp with the dead guy!"

"And it doesn't bother you?" I asked, surprised. Du Toit made a dismissive noise in his throat.

"We're grown-ups. Dickinson, on the other hand, was an overgrown child. I'm sorry he was killed before he had a chance to mature, but let's not try to lionise a mangy hyena. The working arrangements are the more serious complication. The time it takes to get from Oxford to Cambridge in this day and age is utterly ridiculous. But we'll work something out!"

"So the good end happily, and the bad, unhappily!" Sinclair said, chuckling.

"I wouldn't go that far," I said gloomily. "What about poor old Neil? And Britta's boy, Aaron? Finding out his mum's a murderess, his dad isn't really his dad, and his real dad is a coke-addled love rat!"

I was also wondering what the aforementioned verminous creature was doing, and how he was feeling. It turned out that Steve had not been quite as out of it as he had appeared on the video, having already had a visit from Sinclair earlier that morning. Sinclair had tipped him off about the fact that the police would be using him as sacrificial mutton, or bait to catch the murderous fly, and installed the secret camera in the hotel room. The good professor had obviously been more open with Inspector Baynes about his suspicions than he had been with me but had not gone so far as to reveal the killer's identity to Steve. Nevertheless, given that the cheating coke fiend had coaxed Britta into a confession, it had to be conceded that he had played his part well, notwithstanding his ignorance and hungover state.

Nevertheless, when one looked at the wider picture, I was finding it hard to feel much sympathy for Steve. He had really, really screwed up, I concluded. His role as the catalyst behind Britta's descent into madness had not yet made the press, but it was only a matter of time, and then doubtless there would be another child growing up in a family pulled apart by these tragic events.

As one of his oldest friends, I did wonder whether I should make contact, but then again, I was also starting to wonder whether I had ever really known him at all, any more than I had truly known Britta. After all, it had transpired that I had known nothing about either of his two principal hobbies. I should have twigged that he was holding something back from the fact that he'd said in front of Lydia that he'd been wandering around on his own yesterday afternoon, but just a couple of hours later had told me he'd seen Britta.

Well, his web of lies was well and truly untangled now. We lawyers are notorious for our propensity for sexual infidelity, but I was still trying to wrap my head around the fact that Steve had somehow managed to conduct affairs with both Britta and David Williamson (the latter presumably being the skeleton in the closet he had been so sensitive about, as well as the source of Gavin's snide innuendoes) whilst still finding time to impregnate his wife, indulge a chronic cocaine habit and hold down an incredibly taxing day job. Where had he managed to find the energy?

The image of Steve furiously smashing the glass at The Pickerel popped back unbidden into my brain. Even though he had just dumped her, it must have been my mention of Britta having played away with someone other than himself that had got him riled up. Yes, one of my friends had turned out to be a double murderer, but this selfish control freak had not come out of it smelling much sweeter.

Sinclair took off his glasses and wiped them with his handkerchief.

"It's going to be incredibly difficult for them," he admitted sombrely. "But the young often display inner strengths when tested by such trials that we older folk cannot begin to fathom. And at least Miss Seaman is on hand to give poor Neil the support he needs."

Naturally, despite all of us suffering from various degrees of shell shock, after the dramatic revelations of yesterday morning, we had all piled out of Fitzbillies to see if we could catch sight of Britta being bundled into a police car after attempting to shoot Jacqui. We had only got there in time to see the car pull off. But in the distance, I had seen Neil looking on helplessly. His eyes had been crimson, and he had been more hunched over than ever, as though he had just been punched in the gut. Then the mysterious Miss Seaman had arrived, her face a picture of horror and concern. He had turned, seen her, and collapsed into her arms like a folding deckchair, his shoulders heaving with silent sobs. We had tactfully left them to it at that point.

"I suppose it was you who tipped her off that she might be needed in the vicinity of the hotel as well?" I surmised. "Because you knew that Neil would need her."

"I insisted on that," Emily interjected. "I know that it's not as simple as substituting one wife and mother figure for another, but she's a fine young lady who cares very deeply for him and will do what it takes to make sure he comes through this intact."

"It's odd," I said. "I was so convinced that she was somehow up to her neck in all this! I have no idea why I suspected her at all now. She seems like a perfectly nice woman!"

"The name 'Seaman' doubtless brought to mind 'The Rime of the Ancient Mariner' by Samuel Taylor Coleridge," Sinclair surmised, "in which the aforementioned nautical gent whips out a crossbow and kills an albatross—'Albert Ross'—and then proceeds to spend an inordinate amount of time wanging on about it!"

"Could be that," I conceded dubiously. On further reflection, it struck me that Daisy bore a slight resemblance to a rather disagreeable lady who had rear-ended me on the Elephant and

Castle roundabout a couple of weeks previously, but Sinclair seemed so delighted by his more literary explanation for my irrational suspicions that I decided not to mention this.

"What about the clue of the flushed khazi?" I piped up suddenly. "We never got to the bottom of that one, did we?"

"I am reasonably confident that Dan Finn was guilty of perpetrating that heinous crime against the college's archaic plumbing system," Sinclair declared. "Upon discovering that he had been merrily snoozing away whilst his friend was being messily butchered just a sofaspace away from him, his digestive system would understandably have been somewhat unsettled even if he hadn't consumed enough alcohol to floor a small rhinoceros the evening before!"

"And what about the 'in spite of everything' phrase that you were drawing so much attention to in your big speech?" I asked. "Presumably that was the gambling debt thing?"

Sinclair nodded.

"Because you intimated that that was because Steve was secretly Lee's father, when in fact…"

"I only said that to coax your emotionally stunted friend Mr Finn into admitting the truth," Sinclair snorted. "I noticed the family resemblance even if you didn't. They're both so damned hairy! It's just as well that the room numbers in the new accommodation are clearly marked, Emily, given the amount of bedroom hopping that seems to go on amongst our students!"

"What I want to know is how Niamh never saw it!" I said. "She was swearing blind in The Ivy that Lee was Ed's son!"

Sinclair grimaced. "Emily, I think this is one for you, given that we're now delving into the realm of human emotions!"

"She saw what she wanted to see." Emily smiled sadly. "From what I heard, Dan's behaviour in The Ivy on Saturday night was hardly a convincing audition for the role of paterfamilias. But more importantly, she was in love with Ed, even though deep down she knew what sort of man he was. You get subjected to far more detail about this sort of thing than is entirely healthy when you're the College Dean, I'm afraid."

I had called Dan earlier that morning, having last seen him escorting a very shaken and surprisingly acquiescent Niamh and Lee to The Eagle after the big reveal. In spite of everything, he had been positively buzzing, infused by a sense of purpose that I hadn't seen in him for many a year. Sometimes, you need to give people that second audition.

"So was Britta trying to frame Dan or Steve when she pinned that devil to Ed's forehead?" I wondered aloud.

"Both, I imagine," Sinclair grimaced. "She had obviously noticed where Finn had thrown the pad earlier and seized the opportunity to rip out the most sinister picture she could find and pin it to the corpse. Smoke and mirrors, dear boy. It was also Britta who told Ed about Lee, of course. She coaxed poor Dickinson into reaching out to his scorned ex, for the sake of their son. She had no idea about Niamh's dalliance with Mr Finn either, but it wouldn't have mattered. All that mattered was expanding the field of suspects and drawing more unwitting strands into the tangle."

"I can understand her feeling desperate enough to kill Ed. And Steve for that matter," I mused. "The boundary between lust and hate is notoriously porous, I'm told. But cutting Albert's brakes? That was cold."

"She probably justified it to herself on the basis that he was an old man, almost at the end of his innings, and that she was sparing him the pain of a longer, more drawn-out demise," Emily said. "Or perhaps I'm giving her too much credit. She clearly isn't in her right mind. I just wish I'd managed to speak to him properly before it happened. He felt things so deeply; maybe getting things off his chest would have given him a bit of peace."

We supped in solemn silence for a few moments.

"Sadie's made herself very scarce since you accused her of cheating," I commented at last. "Which suggests you might have been onto something."

"Well of course I was!" Sinclair snorted. "I suspect that that was the third (or chronologically speaking, the first) of Albert's little favours to your rather infamous intake. You may recall that he mentioned three errors of judgment when he spoke to Emily before he died. The best porters have a wide-ranging network of contacts, and whatever Albert's other flaws, he always got on with everybody. It would certainly not have been beyond him to put her in touch with someone who could have procured her an exam paper or two ahead of schedule. Alas, she left the poor weak-willed old blighter with yet another guilty secret gnawing away at him."

"And young Lee?" I asked, determined to tie up any remaining loose threads. "Where did he disappear off to on Friday night?"

"Oh, good grief, I really have no idea!" Sinclair shrugged dismissively. "Wherever youngsters go!"

So there were limits to the learned professor's omniscience after all. Apparently, there were still some areas where even Saddam Hussein was unlikely to be of much help to him. I was also pleased that Inspector Baynes had managed to find a chink in Sinclair's armour. He had collared the good professor after "the big reveal" and cheerfully pointed out that Jeremy Beadle had not actually died until 2008.

"A deliberate mistake, my dear Taters," Sinclair had retorted when confronted with this egregious error. "I have to throw one in every so often—if my explanations were completely infallible, people might accuse me of being smug!"

The Senior Tutor rose to his feet.

"Anyway, I'd better be on my way," he declared. "Good to meet you, Roger! Enjoy your pie!"

He jogged off energetically in search of his velocipede, leaving the three of us in companionable silence.

"I note he didn't encourage me to enjoy my pint," I commented. "He really is taking the whole deboozification of college thing seriously, isn't he?"

"We're trying to curb some of his more excessively Cromwellian tactics," Emily reassured me, "but he does have a point!"

"You know what?" I replied. "I do believe you're right. And not just about the booze, either. He called Ed an overgrown child, but I think most of us forgot to grow up somewhere along the way, myself included!"

A symbolic gesture was called for, I felt, to accompany this rare moment of self-reflection. Retrieving my hipflask from the confines of a warm trouser pocket, I toddled over to the wall overlooking the river and hurled it in. As I returned to my seat, I heard someone behind me yelling, "You bloody idiot! You almost knocked me off my punt!"

I took another sip from my pint (there were, after all, limits to my newfound abstemiousness). As I lifted my glass, I saw that a slip of paper had been slipped under it. I looked at Sinclair, who graced me with a jovial wink. Old nimble-fingers had struck again. I opened it up.

"In fifteen years, I would like to think that I will have settled down with a couple of kids and will be bringing them up somewhere rural, with lots of green space, within easy commuting distance of whichever university town I happen to be working in. Challenging, with an academic's salary, but hopefully that daft apeth Roger will eventually buck up the courage to confess that he rather likes me and will have conquered those niggling self-doubts of his so that he can go out and make a fortune in the city. Although not if he has to work the hours my dad used to work. Also, I would like to have finally got the hang of knitting. Tanya."

I drew a long, deep breath.

"Well...bugger!" I said at last.

"Quite so," Sinclair agreed sympathetically. Emily put a consoling hand on my arm.

"Still, I guess it stands to reason that some of those blasted 'ships that pass in the night' eventually veer off in a South African direction!" I grunted. "I suppose I should be happy that hers appears to be headed for the Cape of Good Hope! Experiences like this are there to be learned from, after all."

"Not to miss the boat next time, you mean?" Sinclair interjected. His wife gave him a withering look, but he was, not for the first time, absolutely spot on. Tanya was at least speaking to me again, now that she knew that I hadn't been the one to drop her in it over the phone mix-up. But in truth, whatever it was that had once bonded us together had been severed by the ravages of time, and for that, both of us bore a share of the blame.

"I'd better head over to the police station and hand this in, hadn't I?" I smiled. "I mean, it's pretty tangential to the case they'll be building against Britta, but it's still evidence. And it might give me a chance to properly check in with the marvellous Sergeant Chen. She did save Steve's life, and he is my friend, even if he did turn out to be a bit of a shit. Williamson's too. Given that neither of them is likely to be in a fit psychological state to properly thank her, I think that someone ought to take her out to a nice slap-up dinner somewhere fancy and pathologist-free!"

"Here endeth the lesson!" Sinclair said in that rather grand way of his.

"Perhaps not!" I riposted, relishing the chance to be the cryptic one for a change. Sinclair raised a quizzical eyebrow.

"What do you mean, Roger?" Emily asked when her husband failed to give me the satisfaction of doing so.

"Well, I feel I've been treading water for a while at the office, and my prospects of promotion are currently bleaker than the outtakes at the end of *Sophie's Choice*. It's not even as if I can sleep my way to the top. Let's be honest, I'm no Chris Grayling! But one of the benefits of being perennially single, as my rather self-pitying younger incarnation might have put it, is that it does make it a lot easier to squirrel away a few bob for a rainy day. I've been thinking a lot lately about treating myself to a little career break, and I thought that taking a year out to have a crack at a Master's degree in Criminology might be just the ticket, if Cambridge will have me!"

"That's wonderful!" Emily gushed. "It'll be good to have you back, Roger. Gerald hasn't seemed this satisfied with one of his sidekicks since Wilberforce Marchini disappeared."

"I keep telling you he'll turn up sooner or later!" Sinclair said testily. "But I am indeed delighted to hear that you will be returning to our hallowed halls, Whiteley!"

"And in the meantime," I went on, "I thought I might try to supplement my income by writing down my account of recent events, as they seem to have caught the public attention. A kiss and tell without the kissing, if you will! I'll try to keep it vaguely accurate. I mean, it's hardly as if the story needs much sensationalising, is it? But I'll run it by you before sending it off to any publishers, of course!"

My remark had been directed at Emily, motivated by a desire to reassure her that I would not be spicing up my narrative with anything that might risk sullying the fine reputation of St Crispian's College. However, it was, of course, her attention-hogging husband who butted in first.

"Dear Lord, I have quite enough marking to do as it is, Whiteley! It's your story as much as anyone's. Tell it in any way you see fit!

"I will, however, take the liberty of offering you two small pieces of advice," the canny criminologist went on grandiloquently. "First of all, always leave the reader wanting more!"

Printed in Dunstable, United Kingdom

66354610R00167